The Immortal Continent

by Virlyce

© 2019, Virlyce

All rights reserved. No portion of this book may be reproduced in any form without permission from the publisher, except as permitted by U.S. copyright law. For permissions contact:

virlyce@gmail.com
Visit the author's website at www.virlyce.com.

This book is dedicated to Mare Trevathan, the wonderful narrator who brings Lucia to life.

Chapter 1

Today's the day! The day is finally today! Durandal's entering the legendary realm! I've waited months for this. Months! Let's see.

Food available in the fridge for a romantic dinner? Check.

Alcohol? Check.

Scented candles? Check.

Firestarter for the candles? Check.

Clean bedsheet and blankets? Check.

Spirit-restraining ropes? Check.

Enchanted cuffs and whips? Check.

Pole-stiffening medicinal pills? …Pole-stiffening medicinal pills? Where'd they go? "Ilya! Where'd you put my pole-stiffening pills!?"

The room to my door opened as Ilya walked in, wearing her pajamas and pink fuzzy slippers. Why did she look so annoyed? Oh, she was probably sleeping. The sun hasn't risen yet. Ilya rubbed her eyes and sighed. "Your what pills?"

"My pole-stiffening pills. You know, the ones in the little green bottle I keep in my interspacial ring."

"You don't let me touch your interspacial ring, Lucia. And why would I even need pole-stiffening … pills? Pole-stiffening pills!?" Ilya's purple face turned red as her eyes widened.

What? There's no need to be so surprised. The first time can't be disappointing! "So you don't know where they are?"

"No!" Ilya slammed the door on her way out. Jeez, what was her problem? If she wasn't the one who stole my pills, then it definitely had to be…

tombstone. "Isn't life great, Snow? You know, if you weren't an idiot who tried to poison me, you could've been living like an empress like me. But you had to do something stupid and get yourself possessed by a plant. Of all things to be possessed by, why a plant? Do you know how wimpy that sounds? The mighty Snow poisoned the legendary Lucia and forced her into dire straits. Then he was murdered by a plant. C'mon, do you know how dumb that makes me look? You stupid dummy."

Puppers crouched down in front of me. He was a bit blurry. It must've been the steam coming off my mug of chocolate. "Are you crying, Lucia?"

I'm not crying! Legend's never cry! "I'm going to stab you."

"I didn't see anything," Puppers said. It seems like I didn't train him well enough. The leaves on the trees rustled despite the fact there was no breeze. How odd. Puppers raised his snout into the air, his nose twitching. "Who's there!?"

Hmm? I stopped mid-sip and raised my head. Someone was approaching the sleeping Mrs. Bushytail! I grabbed mini-DalDal from my waist and swung as I stood up. "Unrelenting Path of Slaughter: Breaking Blade!"

"Huh!?" a deep voice shouted as a figure and a bunch of branches fell to the ground. A second later, Mrs. Bushytail landed on top of the figure, causing it to cry out again. "My leg!"

Puppers appeared by the figure's side before I could react. A large sock that had been filled with starch and twisted until it was as sharp as a spear was pointed at the figure's face. Puppers bared his teeth and snarled. "Who are you?"

The figure grunted as Mrs. Bushytail woke up, stiffening and running up a nearby tree. A sad-sounding voice came out of the figure's mouth, "It's only been a single day since the pocket realm opened, and I ran into two saint-realm experts?

Your Excellencies, please, show mercy to this lowly mortal-realm junior!"

…What's with his weird way of speaking? "Puppers. Translate."

Puppers looks confused. So it wasn't just me—I don't feel like an idiot anymore. …Not that I ever did, okay? I'm smart! Puppers lowered his sock-spear and frowned at the man…. Child? Teenager? I've never seen a human with a physique like his. He's too slim, and his skin is so white that I can see it in the dark like a beacon of light. Was he a man or not?

"Seniors?" the weird person asked as he looked back and forth between me and Puppers.

"What do you mean by pocket realm?" Puppers asked.

"This…." The weird person scratched his head. "You can call me Junior Chu. I'm from the Shadow Devil Sect. I traveled with my sect members to partake in the exploring of a pocket realm, which is your realm, the sky and earth plane. Have you two heard of the Immortal Continent?"

Nope. But it sounds really cool. Immortality? Wouldn't I be a legend for forever if I became immortal?

The weird person lowered his head, bowing until his torso was parallel to the ground. Wow. He sure knows how to brown nose. I love it when people kiss up to me—it makes my stomach feel fuzzy and nice. "I understand. You two seniors must be the strongest people within this realm, am I correct?"

"That's right!" I'm the strongest person here! I bet I could take on Durandal, Puppers, and the man in the sky at the same time. "How'd you know?"

"Only mortal-realm cultivators can enter this secret realm. If saint-realm experts came in, the world would be thrown off balance and possibly be destroyed. According to my sect elder, there are no more than five saint-realm experts residing here."

"So you're here to temper yourself," Puppers said.

Huh? What did he mean by that? Where did tempering come in when this man was clearly praising me?

"Senior is correct," the man who called himself Junior Chu said. Was his first name Junior? Or was that just an honorific of sorts? I've met a noble from the fae who was called Junior Junior the Second, so this isn't a stupid question!

"What's a mortal-realm cultivator and what's a saint-realm expert?" Puppers asked. He still hadn't put away his sock-spear even though he should've. It's not very intimidating. What happened to that metal dwarven heirloom spear I gave him back at the Godking's Brawl?

"I am a mortal-realm cultivator," Junior Chu said. "You are a saint-realm expert. Perhaps they're called different things in your plane?"

Puppers' eyes lit up. "Are there people stronger than saint-realm experts?"

"Yes," Junior Chu said. His eyes were glued to the ground. Was there something interesting down there? ...Nope. Maybe he's scared of eye contact. What a weirdo. "Earth-realm and sky-realm experts are above saint-realm experts. And above them, there are immortals."

I feel like I've been transported to some kind of weird fantasy novel. Maybe this person was delusional. Yes, that must be it. I should pry open his skull and see if his brain's abnormal or not. Alright, up you go, mini-DalDal. Two hundred pounds should be enough to crack it open but not turn it into a bloody paste.

"Stop!"

...Why'd Puppers stop me? I definitely went wrong with his training somewhere. I blame Ilya. I'm not sure why it's her fault, but I just feel like it is. She and Puppers have been awfully chummy lately, creating an anti-Durandal fan club. I don't understand why Ilya doesn't like Durandal. He's so perfect.

"Lucia," Puppers said, smiling at me like a wolf. "Aren't you interested at all in this Immortal Continent? Powerhouses stronger than the legendary realm! Think of how far you'll go."

"Nope. Not interested." Why the heck would I go to a place where there are people stronger than me? Isn't that just stupid? I'm an empress here. I can do whatever the hell I want with no consequences. I have servants farming acorns and cocoa beans. I have servants cleaning my mansion and preparing my hot baths. Why would I ever give up this cozy life?

Puppers drew his head back in confusion. "But…. The opportunities to grow stronger. Haven't you stagnated for the past year?"

"So? Didn't you hear what this weirdo said? People as strong as me can't enter this plane. I'm the strongest person here. There's nothing at all to threaten my happy life as a tyrant." I remember what it was like being a weak beastkin in the army. It wasn't fun, not fun at all. Nope. Nuh-uh. Never going back to that state of weakness again.

"Since I answered your questions, will you two excuse me?" the weirdo asked. "I'm being pursued by a few rival sect members."

"What? You break into my backyard and think you can get away scot-free?" I wouldn't be doing my job properly as a tyrant if I didn't extort people! Ahem, I mean empress. I'm an empress, not a tyrant.

"W-what would you like me to do?" the weirdo asked, his face paling.

I held out my hand and rubbed my thumb against my index and middle fingers. The weirdo's eyes lit up as he pulled out a bulging sack and placed it into my palm. It looks like the sign for bribery is universal! And this sack feels pretty heavy—heavier than gold would be. I wonder what's inside. Ooh. Are these spirit stones? These are really rare! "Alright, you can go."

"Many thanks, Senior," the weirdo said and bowed. As he turned around and took a step, he stiffened and froze.

"Where do you think you're going, Sly Devil Chu!?" a thundering voice asked. Mrs. Bushytail jumped out of her tree in fright and ran behind me. My tail wasn't stiffening, so I wasn't sure why she was scared. Five figures dressed in odd, white, robe-like clothes flew out of the trees and landed in front of the weirdo. "It's time we rid ourselves of this heart devil."

Wow, there's so many visitors this early in the morning who want to give me offerings. ...I should visit Snow's grave more often. But what the heck is a heart devil?

***

Just what is Lucia doing out there? Why is it so loud? This isn't related to the, the medicinal pills Lucia was trying to find earlier, right? I don't think it is; I did hear her fire off a Breaking Blade. It's pretty hard to miss the giant flash of red light too. Ugh, first she woke me up to ask me such a stupid question, and now she won't even let me sleep. Didn't I explain to her earlier that I was suffering from withdrawals and she should do her best not to bother me?

Right, I, the one who criticized Lucia for being a bone addict, am suffering from bone withdrawals. In my pursuit to become a seventh-circle magician, I consumed a lot of strength bones that Lucia gave me. A lot. I wasn't planning to at first, but one day, Lucia came by and dumped a mountain of bones into my room, saying they didn't work on her anymore and that I could have them. Then she left without giving me a choice in the matter. So while I was suffering from exhaustion after practicing my magic, I consumed a bone of strength, telling myself just this one time. Before I knew it, I was using twenty bones of strength a day. On the bright side, I crossed the second wall and became an eighth-circle magician in a year. Weaning off of Lucia's divine strength bones however....

"Where do you think you're going, Sly Devil Chu!?"

Alright. What the heck was that? My window just shattered from that shout. And who is Sly Devil Chu? Chu's a really uncommon name, given or family. And sly devil? No one has that kind of nickname in Lucia's territory. Anyone brave enough to establish a name for themselves inside of Lucia's territory ends up being robbed by Lucia. She only leaves the peasants alone. Thus, there's only one conclusion I can draw: These idiots are not from around these parts.

I donned my boots that I had inscribed a flight array on and climbed out of my broken window. These boots are just a prototype that I'm making for Lucia, but I'm confident in using them without getting hurt. I can adjust the flight array in real time, but if Lucia were to encounter any mishaps, she'd have no choice but to crash towards the ground. Why are boots that allow someone to fly so special when there are already boots of flight that exist? Because these can be used even in the vicinity of a predator! It's taken a lot of my time and effort—not to mention thousands of focus bones—to revamp the system of magic circles to avoid the canceling effects of predators. It's not perfect, and my spells backfire 80% of the time, but there's no progress without failure! Unless you're Lucia. Somehow, without even trying, Lucia overcame the predators' natural effects and is able to use qi around them. When I asked her how she figured it out, her exact words were, "Eh? I woke up from a nap yesterday and it wasn't an issue anymore. Aren't I amazing?"

A massive explosion followed by a shockwave nearly knocked me out of the sky. The forest that was Lucia's backyard was set ablaze, and the night was lit up in orange lights. Below me and quite some distance away, there was a pale-looking man with tattered clothes lying by Snow's tombstone. Lucia was in pristine condition, hiding behind Puppers, who looked a lot worse for wear. And five people were standing in front of her—four of them had their arms crossed while the fifth was holding onto a stack of papers that looked like the talismans superstitious people pasted on walls to keep ghosts away.

"Ah! You spilled my hot chocolate!" Lucia shouted. She was holding a ceramic handle, but the rest of the mug was broken and on the ground in front of her. I decided to stay where I was and not approach the area of interest because the last time I spilled Lucia's hot chocolate by telling her a joke while she was in the middle of taking a gulp, she nearly suffocated me with her killing intent. "You bastards! Do you know how precious hot chocolate is!? All the health and strengthening benefits! Why would you use such a huge explosion?" As expected, reddish-black qi was rising out of Lucia's tail. Poor saps.

Down by Snow's tombstone, the injured man reached for a mug that was lying by his side. Wasn't that Lucia's mug? Why would she leave a cup of hot chocolate lying on the ground? The man downed the mug in a single gulp and gritted his teeth. A second later, he went limp and his head lolled to the side with froth coming out of his mouth. …Was it poisoned? No…, it shouldn't've been. He must've been allergic.

My attention was drawn back towards Lucia as she raised her sword into the air and shouted, "Unrelenting Path of Slaughter: Tides of Blood!" The reddish-black qi ballooned out of her tail, spreading along the ground behind her until the whole garden turned red. Her qi crawled up the side of the mansion as well, and thousands of contorted faces belonging to beasts and people—but mostly beasts—bubbled out of the qi, stretching towards the sky while letting out soundless screams. Lucia swung her sword downwards, sending the mass of qi at the five people ... and Puppers. The six unlucky fellows were submerged beneath the wave of qi, their screams cut short. The qi congealed into a single, large, quivering droplet of blood, the six figures inside trying to break free—except for Puppers. A few bubbles rose to the surface of the droplet as the talismans that the man was holding exploded one at a time. Unfortunately for them, the explosions weren't enough to break out; instead, faint images of divine beasts arose inside of the droplet and charged at the trapped people.

Their limbs separated from their bodies as divine beast after divine beast rushed towards them with claws and jaws exposed. Four of the strangers pulled round objects out of nowhere, probably interspacial rings, and crushed them with their hands. Their bodies dissolved into specks of blue light which surged up and out of the droplet before disappearing amongst the stars. Unluckily for the fifth stranger, he lost both his arms before he could crush the thing that I suspected was an instant-teleportation button. As for Puppers, he was fending off the shadows of the divine beasts without an issue. ...I thought he normally died to Lucia's attacks. Did he reach the legendary realm?

"Whew," Lucia said as she lowered her arm. The droplet of blood dissolved and disappeared, freeing Puppers and the screaming stranger. "That took a lot of effort."

What effort? All you did was raise your arm and perform a half-assed swing. You're not allowed to talk about effort, Ms. I Can Wake Up and Be Overpowered Instantly. ...Anger and bitterness are the main side effects of bone withdrawals. It seemed like it was safe to land, so I decided to check up on the person by Snow's tombstone first. I put my finger on his neck and ... he's dead. Great. The other person didn't look like he'd last long either. Two fountains of blood were shooting out of his shoulder stumps. I hurried over and performed a second-circle recovery spell to staunch the bleeding. If I restored his limbs, then he would've escaped and Lucia would've blamed me. I'm not going to take on suffering for a stranger. ...Has staying around Lucia turned me into a selfish person? Maybe I'm a little selfish, but it's fine as long as I acknowledge it. My moral integrity is a lot greater than those people who pretend to be selfless at least. I guess that's why I stay with Lucia despite her being her. She's a no good, self-centered, greedy, perverted, and immature person, but when she screws someone over, she has no idea that she's doing it, whereas a noble will pretend to help you but stab you in the back when you aren't looking. Like my grandmother from my mother's side. Ugh, just thinking about her infuriates me. I blame the withdrawals.

"So, who are you?" Lucia asked, crouching by the armless man. She prodded his cheek with a twig she had picked up off the ground, smearing his face with bloody dirt.

"S-saint-realm expert," the man said through labored breaths. "H-how?"

Lucia smacked the top of his head, causing his eyes to widen and his body to freeze. Lucia prodded his cheek again and nodded when he didn't move. "It looks like he fell unconscious. Perfect!" She rifled through his clothes and stripped him of all his jewelry. She's become extremely good at robbing people. And it seems like she doesn't want to explain what happened. It's a good thing there's a sane, sensible chaperone by Lucia's side.

"Puppers, what's going on?"

Puppers shook his head. "I'm not quite sure. It seems like our world is a miniature dimension stuck inside of a larger world called the Immortal Continent. These strangers from the Immortal Continent are here to temper themselves."

Is that so...? It's a bit unbelievable, but Cain was able to create a world inside of the coliseum for the Godking's Brawl. Maybe someone from the Immortal Continent was as strong as Cain and created a separate miniature world—ours. How many circles would that person had to have had to do something like that? Sixteen? Nineteen? Perhaps even twenty-two.

Ugh, I don't want to think about this right now. It's giving me a headache. No, that's not right. It's making the headache that I've had for the past week even worse. I..., I bet this headache would go away if I consume a bone of focus. It doesn't even have to be a large piece. Just the pinky toe bone of a divine panther.... No! You're stronger than this, Ilya! If you can't overcome a simple addiction, how can you ever hope to cross the third wall? I'll—

Lucia poked my forehead, stopping my shivering. "Ilya? You alright?"

"I'm, I'm fine." Lucia was worried about me? How can that be? She only cares about herself!

"Hm. Hmm. Hmmmm." Lucia squinted at me while rubbing her chin. Her tail twitched a few times, and I swallowed my spit as her gaze traversed up and down. She sighed and patted my shoulder twice before shoving a white mug into my hands. "Well, you were shaking, so I thought you were cold. Drink some hot chocolate!"

I glanced at the surface of the chocolate. "This ... isn't poisoned, right?"

"What? Why would I poison hot chocolate? That's such a waste." Her fingers touched my lips and pried my mouth open. Before I could squeeze out a protest, she lifted the mug and poured some chocolate down my throat. It burned a lot, but at least the pain distracted me from my headache. "S-stop!"

Lucia nodded. "See? Not poisoned."

I blinked back the tears that threatened to fall from my eyes and gestured towards the dead man by Snow's tombstone. "I saw him drink some hot chocolate out of your mug. And he's dead."

"Ah! The hot chocolate that I poisoned for Snow! Why the hell did that weirdo drink it!?" Lucia dashed over to the corpse and stared at it. She sighed before squatting beside the body and closed its eyes with her palm. She shook her head and clicked her tongue. Then she stripped the corpse of its valuables. "Well, can't let these things go to waste. I'll be sure to put your things to good use; you can rest in peace."

I'm sure his ghost would want to haunt her for saying such words. But wow, this hot chocolate really does do wonders for withdrawal symptoms. My headache's gone away. No wonder why Lucia drinks hot chocolate so often. But how come I've never—

"Ilya," Puppers said, interrupting my train of thought. "Weren't you trying to wean yourself off of Lucia's bones?"

"That's right." I nodded.

Puppers pointed at the mug. "You know that mug's made out of a divine focus bone, right…? It imbues the hot chocolate inside with—"

"Goddammit!" Lucia! You reset a whole week's worth of progress! …But it'd be a waste to dump this hot chocolate. Servants spend hours tending the cocoa trees, harvesting the cocoa beans, and grinding them into the powder before creating hot chocolate. I, I can't let their efforts be in vain! It doesn't help that hot chocolate's tasty.

Why is Puppers looking at me with such pitiful eyes?

***

It's been a long year. I would've reached the legendary realm faster if I didn't have to share Lucia's qi with Puppers, but that's not necessarily a bad thing. During this year, I've strengthened my fundamentals: power, speed, toughness, everything's gone under a qualitative change. I've abandoned the spear and reverted back to using a sword like I should've from the start. A spear was enough to defeat Lucia while I was still realms above her, but now, it's not. If I want to grow as a weapon spirit, I have to return to my roots. I've fully integrated the techniques of my fallen brothers into my swordsmanship while removing the superfluous: cutting as swift as a dagger, stabbing as sharp as a spear, swinging with the weight of a hammer, defending as if I had a shield, all the while maintaining the flexibility of a sword. Only a style as versatile as this one can hope to defeat Lucia's outrageous natural abilities.

Now, I'm taking the last steps towards entering the legendary realm. Though I've developed a path of my own, the Versatile Path of the Sword, I have no idea how to proceed to a higher realm through it, which is why I'm following in Lucia's footsteps and accumulating enough qi in my spirit seed core. My seed has been saturated for the past month, but I've been delaying the breakthrough to temper myself further. Unfortunately, today, I had a premonition that accumulating anymore qi would be counterproductive. Thus, I entered my weapon body and proceeded with the breakthrough, letting Lucia's qi remold my spirit body.

And the first thing I saw after emerging from my weapon body after breaking through to the legendary realm was Lucia squinting at a pile of items on a table while sniffing a green slip made of jade. Her ears twitched, and she raised her head to meet my eyes, her face lighting up as a smile blossomed on her lips. "Durandal! You're back!"

Though she didn't say it, I could see the question etched into her facial features. "Yes, I'm back. And I successfully broke through to the legendary realm."

As expected, Lucia's face became lewd. It's a good thing I threw away those pole-stiffening medicinal pills that I found while snooping through her interspacial ring. There was absolutely no reason for her to have those; thus, I took justice into my own hands and righted the natural laws. A crackling noise drew my attention away from her face. The jade slip in her hand was cracking near her fingers. "Lucia, you're breaking it."

"Hmm?" Lucia lowered her head, looking at where I pointed. "Ah! My treasure!" She placed the strip on the table and licked her fingers before rubbing her saliva onto the cracked portion. Of course, it didn't help. She placed the sleeve of her dress against it and wiped the saliva off, revealing a pristine, undamaged jade slip. "Phew. Just in time."

…Alright. Let's not question that. "Who'd you rob this time?"

"A weirdo," Lucia said as she placed the jade amongst the other items on the table. She met my gaze. "Oh, he's dead, so you don't have to worry about vengeance or anything." She blinked when I didn't say anything. "I didn't kill him! He drank the poison that I put in the cup, but it wasn't my fault!"

I sighed. One day, Lucia's terrible actions will catch up to her. And when that day comes, I'll be dragged into it too. Is it wrong that I'm looking forward to confronting it? Speaking of confrontation…. "Lucia. Let's spar."

"Eh? But it's almost dinner time." Lucia scratched her head and looked the other way, avoiding my eyes.

Well, when I said, "Let's spar," I wasn't giving her a choice. I drew the white sword hanging from my waist and lunged forward. "Versatile Path of the Sword: Piercing Thrust!"

"Durandal!?"

My sword pierced through Lucia's Armor of Slaughter like paper, but as the tip of my blade made contact with her skin, a large resistance pushed back against my arm as if I were stabbing into an immovable mountain. I grunted and focused all of my qi into the tip of my sword, letting out a shout as I shoved my arm forward. "Pierce!"

Instead of injuring her, my sword pushed Lucia backwards, causing her to lose her footing and fall to the floor. "Durandal! What the heck!?" Lucia bounced to her feet as she drew mini-DalDal, a reddish-black qi rising out of her skin and congealing into a ram's head behind her. Before Lucia could raise her sword, I advanced while condensing qi into the edge of my blade.

"Swift Slash!" I swung my sword horizontally, striking Lucia's elbow to break her stance, leaving her chest wide open. With a flourish of my arm, I slashed my sword downwards like a hammer. "Meteor Slice!"

My sword struck Lucia's chest and forced her to bend her knees. The floor cracked beneath her feet, but she remained uninjured. Instead, her eyes glazed over, turning completely white as she activated her path. Her free hand flashed, and she grabbed onto my sword's blade, locking it into place as she raised mini-DalDal. But I was expecting this! "Versatile Path of the Sword: Cheap Shot!"

I released my sword as I leaned in and firmly planted my lips against Lucia's, causing her to freeze. Her eyes returned to normal as they widened, and her muscles relaxed as the tension left her body. Taking advantage of her moment of weakness, I disarmed her by striking her wrist while knocking mini-DalDal away at the same time. How could a Path of the Sword be versatile if it couldn't be used without a sword? Roland had an arm-guard spirit who was an expert in grappling. I slid around to Lucia's back and positioned myself for a choke…, but Lucia's tail wrapped around my right leg and lifted me off my feet. She tossed aside my sword as she slammed me to the ground, back first, before mounting my waist. Her voice was breathy as she leaned forward and panted into my ear, "It's my turn."

Lucia knew how to grapple? When did she learn that? Her arms pressed against my shoulders, keeping my back in place. I lifted my waist in an attempt to slip out from underneath her, but her tail wrapped around my ankle and stretched my lower body out, preventing me from moving my legs. She chuckled with a flushed face as she leaned forward, her nose nearly touching mine. This, this wasn't sparring anymore! "Lu—"

My words were muffled as my lips were covered. A foreign invader assaulted my mouth, dueling with my tongue. I tried to turn my head to the side, but Lucia's hand appeared on my cheek, holding my face still. At this rate, I was going to be humiliated! Retreat back into mini-DalDal! …It didn't work. My corporeal body was still being pressed down by Lucia. Why didn't it work!? My eyes shifted towards mini-DalDal, and a sparkling blue bead attached to its hilt by a string caught my eye. Was that a spirit-restraining rope!?

…All hope is lost. Puppers, if we're companions, please, come out and save me. The door creaked as a tiptoeing, armored wolfkin opened it and slipped outside. I've been abandoned. Is this the end…? Is this how I lose my dignity as a sword spirit?

As Lucia's hands stripped off my shirt and as I was about to resign myself to fate, the floor trembled and the walls shook as cracks formed upon the ceiling. A second later, a massive booming sound echoed through the room, ripping up the floor tiles and tearing down the walls. The ceiling collapsed on top of us. It took less than a second for Lucia to clear the rubble, but killing intent was rising out of her body like smoke, her eyes red and her teeth bared. Her hair flew upwards as she whipped her head back and forth, searching for the cause of the explosion.

"Lucia!" a familiar voice shouted. It was Ilya. Was she the one that saved me? But where was she? The rubble in the distance trembled as the demon's head popped out, followed by her arms and torso. Her face was smudged with soot and tears streaked down her cheeks. "He exploded! He actually exploded!"

Who exploded? What was going on? I'm not too sure, but I know the first thing I have to do is remove that spirit-restraining rope around mini-DalDal.

"Where is he?" Lucia asked, her tail twitching back and forth, destroying the bits and pieces of the walls by her feet. "Who blew up my happy time!?"

"H-he's dead," Ilya said, swallowing visibly. Her tears also stopped flowing—it seemed like they were caused by soot in the first place. "I was interrogating him, and he told me to release him or else he'd self-detonate. I turned around to grab my pliers, and when I turned back, he was glowing while radiating heat. Then he exploded!"

"...You're sure he's dead?"

"Well, people generally die if they explode, right?" Ilya asked.

And with Ilya's brilliant timing, I managed to slip the spirit-restraining ropes off of mini-DalDal and sneak back inside. ...Or so I thought. When did Lucia place this enchanted ankle cuff around my leg? When I was pinned down and her tail stopped me from escaping? Just how many scenarios did she prepare for...? Then ... I'll accept whatever's coming to me. It's my duty as a weapon spirit to serve my master and teach her well. If, if bed stuff is required of me to bring her back onto the right track, then I'm willing to sacrifice myself!

***

Whew. That was satisfying. Super-duper extremely satisfying. "Durandal, let's do it again! ...Durandal?" Oh, right. He fainted after the fifth time. And the sun's coming up, so I guess we can stop now. Ah..., life's great, isn't it? Beautiful weather, chirping birds, and a partner in bed! What more can a girl ask for? Sure, there was that inconvenient explosion that destroyed my mansion, but that's why I have a lakeside house! ...Actually, the lakeside house is for storing guests that I don't trust, but there was nowhere else to sleep, so I had to make do. It's a shame about the pole-stiffening pills though, but thankfully, Durandal was vigorous enough without them! It must be a perk of reaching the legendary realm.

Now that there's finally some downtime, I can finish inspecting all the treasures I robbed. The thing I'm most curious about is this weird green slip. When I opened the weirdo's interspacial ring and took this out, a strange spirit came out and attacked me but died to my Armor of Slaughter. I wonder what it is. Hmm. Maybe it's money? But what would be the point of spirit stones? The weirdo had a lot of those, by the way. I squinted at the jade slip. "C'mon, stupid thing. Show me why you're valuable."

…Nope. I guess the only thing I can do is put it away for—

"Lucia? Is it over?"

Oh, it's Ilya. She has some pretty dark circles underneath her eyes. It seems like she didn't get much sleep last night, huh? Well, I'd be traumatized too if someone exploded for no reason. "Is what over?"

"Nothing." Ilya shook her head and sighed. She pointed at the slip. "What's inside?"

"Inside?" Does Ilya know what this is? It's a secret kind of treasure chest, isn't it?

"…Let me see." Ilya held her hand out.

"No! Tell me how to open it."

Ilya sighed. "Send your mind into it." She must've understood that I had no idea what that meant because she sighed again and said, "Look at it and think about entering it."

Think about entering it…? Whoa! What's this? Where am I? It's all dark and there's this floating ball of green light in front of me. Isn't this like that time I entered mini-DalDal to learn the Path of Slaughter? …I've already been burned twice by something like this! If I touch the floating light, I might learn something, but it'll hurt. And I don't like pain, so I'm just going to leave. Mhm. Just leave. …Leave. Hello? How do I get out of here?

Touch the light.

"Who said that!?" I'm all alone in this darkness! Who's creeping on me!? Was it the light? "Is there any way to get out without touching the green thing…?"

No.

Ugh…. Alright, fine. I took in a deep breath and closed my eyes while reaching for the light with my toe. Please don't hurt. Please don't hurt. Please don't hurt. Gah! Fuck! It hurts! It hurts! It … doesn't hurt? Huh? I opened my eyes. Oh, I didn't touch it yet. I'm still about an inch away from the—why is it flying towards me!? Gah! It hurts for real this time! My head's going to explode!

"Lucia? Are you alright?"

"No, I'm not alright!"

"Oh."

I could feel Ilya's stare on me as I clutched my throbbing head. "Don't just stare! Heal me!"

"Err, learning through a forced transmission can't be healed," Ilya said. "I mean, it's not supposed to hurt in the first place. Forced transmissions only cause discomfort if the recipient is an idio…. Oh. Right. That explains it."

Phew. The headache's gone. What was Ilya saying just now? Anyways, what did I learn? "Heart Devil Cultivation Technique?"

"Let me see?"

"Yeah, sure. Here." I handed over the green slip. I really wanted to break it after the suffering it put me through, but that'd be a waste. At the very least, I should sell it. "How'd you know how to use one of these things? And is there a way out once you're inside?"

"Hmm? I read about them in my father's books," Ilya said. "And there isn't a way." She closed her eyes as she placed the slip on the table. A moment later, she opened her eyes and nodded. "Like I thought. Those people are using a different form of energy than us. Otherwise, how could they cause explosions with the predators around? Most likely, I can use this knowledge to augment my abilities. But I'm not sure how well it would mix with mana…. Maybe it'll be like merging qi and mana, ruining my chances of advancing any further as a magician. I don't think it's worth it."

"So … you're saying this Heart Devil Cultivation Technique can make me stronger?" Ilya said augment, right? That means improve! See, I'm smart. Let's try it. I'm supposed to circulate my qi like this and like that and then like this, but that feels a bit uncomfortable. Wouldn't it be better to circulate it that way instead? Yes, that feels much better. Then it does a twist over here in my leg…, a loop in my arm…, three loops around my stomach? It should be four! And finally, I force it all back into my womb. Or dantian. Same thing, right?

Ilya screamed, and I opened my eyes. Why was she screaming? Don't tell me I turned hideous! Did I? Oh, there's a mirror in my interspacial ring, I'll check. …Nope, nothing's changed. I'm still beautiful. So why was Ilya screaming? Then I saw the things in the mirror behind me. Hundreds of black, worm-like things were in the sky, and they all seemed to be rushing towards … me! "What the hell is this!? Ilya!? I need answers!"

"You absorbed the knowledge too!" Ilya shouted as she ran away from me. Why was she running from me? "Stop following me! Stop! Those things are the accumulated energies your heart devils absorbed! Let me go! Lucia!"

Maybe it's a bit unfair that I'm holding Ilya over my head like an umbrella. Alright, fine. I'll swap her out with Puppers. At least he won't die if he dies.

Puppers sighed as he was held over my head. "Well. I knew this was coming." He closed his eyes and splayed his limbs like a corpse, waiting for the black, worm-like things to hit him. They drilled into his skin and came out the other side, leaving him ... completely unharmed. And then they hit me! Gah, fuck! This hurts even worse than the green ball of light!

Puppers ignored me, his dying master lying on the ground, and sidled over to Ilya. "Mind explaining what the Heart Devil Cultivation Technique is?"

Ilya sighed, her gaze boring a hole into my body. She should've warned me about this! Once this stops hurting so much, I'm going to teach her a lesson about withholding information! Ah, it's so painful. I can feel the qi inside me exploding and becoming more abundant in the process! ...Wait, becoming more abundant in the process? It's not worth it! The pain to qi-gained ratio is completely skewed towards pain!

"Right, that cultivation technique is some kind of internal energy generator," Ilya said to Puppers, ignoring the obviously dying person by her feet. I'm not bitter. Not one bit. "Apparently, everyone gets these heart devils, or internal demons, and it drains their energy while haunting their thoughts. Something like an insecurity, I suppose."

Puppers nodded. "You mean like when you confess to someone and get rejected, and five years later, you end up lying in bed unable to sleep while dwelling on that one specific instance, wondering why you're such a moron for doing such a dumb thing, and that maybe if you did it this way instead, everything would've been different?"

"...That's an oddly specific scenario," Ilya said. "I thought weapon spirits couldn't sleep."

Puppers shrugged.

"I guess those are the sentiments of a heart devil," Ilya muttered. She nodded. "And Lucia can basically harvest the energy from any heart devil she's caused another person."

"So that's why a black strand left my body," Puppers said.

"Yeah," Ilya said. "I was so surprised about the thing leaving my chest that I screamed."

Hello? I'm dying here. Why are they ignoring me!?

"Lucia! Ilya! Did you see something black fly over here?"

Was that the man in the sky? What was he doing in my territory?

"Lucia! Something black flew out of all the prisoners inside your dungeon! It flew out of me too!"

And that was Reena. Wow, everyone's here to pay me a visit, huh?

"The worldly phenomenon converged over there! The treasure must be up ahead!"

Oh, hey. More strangers from that so-called Immortal Continent. I declare today as National Tax Day! Anyone who doesn't pay up is going to jail. I'm going to be rich—especially since the man in the sky is here!

Chapter 2

Where am I? What happened? I'm lying on a bed and.... Oh. That's what happened; I remember everything now. Where's Lucia? Well, for now, I'll recover the qi that I lost. Hmm? That's odd. I'm able to draw on qi that's not Lucia's? Is this what the qi of the world feels like? I'm not sure if this is a side effect of reaching the legendary realm or a side effect of last night's activities. Either way, I'm not complaining. And it seems like I can still draw on Lucia's qi too. But it's different, like something potent and dark has been added. How did everything change so much after a single night? I feel stronger too, but once again, I'm not sure if that's because of reaching the legendary realm or not.

I finished my meditation and climbed off the bed, putting on the robe that was hanging over a chair. I left the lakeside house and frowned at the sight that greeted me. Treasures were scattered about the table outside, and two chairs were knocked over as if the occupants had been in a hurry to get away. Where is Lucia? She can't be that far since I haven't been transported back to mini-DalDal. And Lucia removed that spirit-restraining cuff too, so that's not stopping me either.

A scream coming from the nearby woods drew my attention. No doubt, that's where Lucia was. I didn't recognize the owner of the scream, so I didn't need to rush over. I strolled through the garden, admiring the thousands upon thousands of spirit seeds scattered about like dew on grass. For some reason, the trees that produce Lucia's acorns and cocoa beans have a really high rate of growing a spirit seed. They're supposed to be common in places with high concentrations of mana, but there must be something special about Lucia's lands that increase spirit seed appearance. Ilya says it's due to the predators' poop.

Lucia had been trying to create, as she calls it, super-duper soft and fluffy underwear, but every single seed she's planted into her clothes has turned out to be a male spirit, so she gave up. Now, the seeds are just left in her garden to make it sparkle and look pretty. I don't mind. It means less competition for Lucia's qi. Sure, she has an abnormally large amount, but I don't like sharing. I'm quite a selfish person, aren't I? Maybe if the world were a nicer place where strength didn't rule, people could afford to be nicer, but until then, it's every person for himself.

More screams rang through the air, but I didn't pick up my pace. While training in mini-DalDal during this past year, screams coming from outside were a weekly occurrence. Lucia's been rounding up slave traders and throwing them into her dungeons. She says she does it because slave traders are all rich, so it's a cost-effective way to make money for the least amount of effort, but I know she has a soft spot for slaves. She even frees the slaves and let them run her acorn and chocolate plantations, giving them a place to sleep and earn money. Of course, I could be wrong and this is all just her giant ploy to have an infinite supply of acorn stew and hot chocolate, but I don't believe Lucia's intelligent enough to think up something like that.

A few fireballs and lightning bolts appeared in the air above the woods where the screams were coming from. That's odd. The presence of the predators prevented magic from being used. Unless Ilya was the one casting the spells. I paused and shielded my eyes from the sun, trying to get a better view of the magic being cast. I've learned to recognize spells and their strength based on their outer appearance. After all, the best way to defeat your enemy is to know him inside and out. But a spell appeared in the sky that I didn't recognize. A massive palm made of golden light smashed past the clouds and crushed the fireballs and lightning bolts. It descended past the trees, breaking down a few treetops before disappearing from my view. What was that? A giant?

Before I could head towards the woods, a voice came from behind me. "Senior Brother, look at all these spirit seeds! There must be hundreds of thousands!"

I turned around while placing my hand on the hilt of my sword. It was a simple, one-handed sword with nothing special about it. It wasn't even enchanted. Before one relied on outer forces, one had to rely on themselves. If I could become undefeated with an ordinary weapon, how strong would I become if I used an extraordinary one? I scanned the field of spirit seeds, but no one was there. When I raised my head, there were four people standing atop swords hovering in the air. How garish. At least it made sense when Ilya created boots that allowed a person to fly. Who thought standing on top of a flying sword would be a good idea? One strong gust would be enough to knock someone off to their death.

The swords lowered, and the four people dropped to the ground. They were wearing clothes that seemed a bit out of place: long trailing sleeves, thin and robe-like, a wide cloth belt to prevent the robes from falling open. The four men gave me one glance before they crouched down and started picking spirit seeds off the grass as if they were beggars in a street. Well, there was only one thing to do, really: Kill. Lucia might not think those spirit seeds are valuable, but they're still her property. And no one is allowed to take advantage of Lucia—only I can do that. I placed my left hand on the sheath of my sword and gripped the hilt tighter. The sword flashed in the sunlight as I drew and cut with it in a single motion. "Breaking Blade."

A beam of crescent blue qi flew towards the four people. They raised their heads and glared at me, a barrier appearing around them out of nowhere, but my qi cut through the yellow light as if it was paper. It cut through their bodies just as easily, and their torsos separated from their waists, slowly tumbling forward as their eyes widened in shock. Right before my qi was about to hit Lucia's lakeside house, it ran out of energy and dispersed. I'm not like Lucia who's unable to control her power. Blood pooled through the garden, causing the spirit seeds on the ground to glisten with a red light.

A misty substance leaked out of one of the bodies, congealing into a humanoid form that tried to fly away. With a simple wave of my arm, I bisected it, causing it to disperse into golden droplets that fell to the ground. Was that a ghost? I kept my sword unsheathed as I poked around the four corpses, looking for treasure. Clearly, these people weren't from this world; I'm an expert at plundering clothes, but it's my first time seeing some designed like this. That didn't stop me from discovering four interspacial rings though. While I was at it, I picked up the swords used for flight and tested their weight with a few swings. They clearly weren't meant for fighting. Warmth flowed through my palm from their hilts and something deep inside me roared. ...Was that my stomach growling? It can't be. The first time I feel hunger, it's due to a sword? That's cannibalism. They did seem awfully appealing though, so I brought one of the swords to my mouth and took a bite. ...It was delicious. Before I knew it, the four swords had disappeared into my stomach. Warmth flowed through my veins, and I'm not sure if it was my imagination or not, but I felt stronger. There sure were a lot of strange things going on today. Even now, dozens upon dozens of people standing on flying swords were rushing to this area from the distance. ...I hope those swords taste just as good. No wonder why Lucia's ruled by her stomach.

***

The sky turned golden. No, that's not right. It's more like a giant golden hand was covering the sky. I can even see the wrinkles on the palm from here. How old would someone have to be to have that many wrinkles…? So much for immortality, huh? If some old wrinkled person said he came from the Immortal Continent, would you believe him? Immortals should be young; otherwise, there's no point in living forever.

"Lucia! Do something about that!"

Why was Ilya panicking? Jeez. The golden hand fell faster and faster, crushing the magic in the clouds that someone—I think the man in the sky—had prepared. I wonder how much the palm weighed…. I'm going to catch it. It should be a treasure of some sort, right? I could probably sell it for a lot. Maybe it's made out of real gold!

The palm crushed the treetops, and Ilya, Reena, and the man in the sky screamed at the same time. The person who summoned the giant palm laughed, and the people standing behind him had looks on their faces that were similar to the ones that the younger slaves that I freed from the slave traders had when they looked at me. Those faces turned to shock when I raised my arms over my head and caught the falling palm. Hmm, it was squishy. So it wasn't made of gold—what a shame. Could it be made out of qi? Ah, it disappeared. I feel cheated.

"Saint-realm expert!?" the man who summoned the palm shouted.

Saint-realm expert this, saint-realm expert that. I'm hearing that phrase a lot, and something about it really irks me. I'm a legend, dammit, not a saint. Legend sounds much more imposing than saint. A saint's someone like a hobbled over nun splashing so-called holy water on people. A legend's someone like me. I'd rather be me than a nun. Right, to rid myself of this annoyance, I'm going to beat these people up. But first…, I held my hand out and rubbed my thumb against my forefingers. "Pay for your lives."

The group of strangers from the Immortal Continent exchanged glances with each other. Their eyes narrowed as a weird energy flared up around them. Then pouches appeared in all of their palms from their interspacial rings. They lined up in a neat single file and approached me one at a time, handing me their bags while kneeling and knocking their foreheads against the ground. …This is not what I was expecting at all. Where was the refusal? Where were the protests? The curses? The attempts at my life while my guard was lowered? These people are terrible slave traders! Wait. They weren't slave traders in the first place. Hmm, but still. I'd feel bad if I beat someone up when they're cooperating so nicely. I guess I'll spar Puppers later to vent. When the last person paid me a tribute of spirit stones, I nudged him with my foot. "Don't you people have any dignity?"

Instead of getting angry, the man knocked his forehead against the ground again. "This junior pays respect to Senior!"

"…How come everyone addresses me as Senior?" I'm young, dammit! Senior is reserved for the elderly people in their sixties. I'm not even halfway there!

"Senior is a saint-realm expert! With this junior's mortal-realm cultivation, it would be rude of this junior not to address Senior as Senior!"

…When people brown-nose me, I usually feel good inside. So why was I getting goosebumps? This is uncomfortable. "Right. All of you can leave now."

The strangers all bowed to me again before standing on their swords and flying away as fast as possible. Moments earlier, they were screaming and killing each other to fight over some weird treasure. After the man in the sky zapped them a few times, that giant palm came down and I caught it. Then they all cooperated to give me money. I'm such a positive influence, aren't I? I turned a scene of violence into one of peace and happiness! Hmm? It was only my happiness? Well, my happiness is the only one that matters.

Right. I cleared my throat and stared at the man in the sky. He stared back at me. I rubbed my thumb against my other fingers.

The man in the sky's face cramped. "You're not serious."

"It's National Tax Day. Everyone in my territory has to pay taxes today."

The man in the sky sighed as he handed over an interspacial ring. I wonder what's inside. Barrels of … acorn stew mixed with hot chocolate…? This is simply genius! Why have I never thought about mixing those two before?

"So … about the black thing that flew over here," the man in the sky said as I tucked away the ring in a safe location.

"Lucia was practicing a cultivation technique she obtained from one of the invaders," Ilya said. "You know about the invaders, right, Mr. Thunderfire?"

"Yes," the man in the sky said with a grimace. "At first, I thought they were people from the river and thunder plane that the plants had come from. After capturing someone and interrogating him, I found out they're from an even larger world than both the river and thunder plane and our plane. Apparently, every thousand years or so, experts from the Immortal Continent open a rift to enter our world for their disciples to seek treasures and grow stronger."

Ilya nodded. "That's what I found out before the person I was interrogating exploded."

"Your prisoner exploded too?" the man in the sky asked, raising an eyebrow. "Did you find out anything else?"

Ilya shook her head.

The man in the sky nodded. "Well, I also learned that they're only going to be here for a month before they're summoned back to their realm. The most valuable item our plane has to offer are our spirit seeds. There's a massive competition amongst the invaders to see who can bring the most spirit seeds back." The man in the sky stared at me. "I'm thinking of entering the Immortal Continent in a month. What about you?"

Like I already told Puppers, I have no interest in inflicting suffering upon myself. "Nope. Not going."

"Are you sure? You'll be stuck in the legendary realm forever if you stay here," the man in the sky said with a smile. "If I leave, the next time I see you again, I'll be stronger than you."

He's telling me to beat him up now before problems arise in the future, right? Right? That was clearly a threat.

"Going to the Immortal Continent to become stronger? Of course Lucia's going. Why wouldn't she?"

…Durandal? I turned around, and yep, I was right. Durandal smiled a smile at me that sent chills down my spine. The last time I felt this way was back when Durandal was teaching me…. I know there's absolutely no chance of it happening, but why do I feel like my peaceful life is about to crumble once more? There's really no chance, right!? No matter what happens, I'll cling to this peaceful life of mine!

***

I can't wait to go to this Immortal Continent. The best way to grow is to overcome adversity time and time again. Lucia's relaxed for far too long since she entered the legendary realm. Hmm? She deserves it? Maybe, but that doesn't matter. What matters is there's a higher peak for her to climb. How can she be a true legend if only the people in a pocket realm know her name? True, I didn't know there was another world that was greater than this one. But now that I know, a new goal has been acquired. I'll make her into a legend of the Immortal Continent. It's a completely selfless goal, purely for Lucia's sake. Ignore the fact that I can also grow stronger by eating swords from the Immortal Continent. I'll be able to surpass Lucia—before, I was limited by her strength, but now, I'm able to grow on my own. If I enter a higher realm before her, I'll be able to bully, err, educate her properly! I'll finally overcome the frustrations that've built up this past year.

"Think of the predators, Durandal," Lucia said with a flustered expression. "What'll happen to them if I go to the Immortal Continent? No one will take care of them!"

"You don't do anything to take care of them anyway!" Reena shouted before shrinking back as Lucia glared at her. It was true—Lucia made Reena clean up after and feed the predators. If anything, Lucia occasionally gave the predators head pats, but that was it.

"We're going to the Immortal Continent." This is nonnegotiable. I'll never surpass Lucia if I'm stuck here. It's my duty to help Lucia grow!

"I don't want to," Lucia said, shaking her head rapidly. Her hair flew up from the motion. "You can't make me! I want to enjoy a nice cozy life and die of old age once I'm a great-grandmother!"

It's a good thing I have a trump card. I fixed my expression and spoke with my most serious voice, "Lucia."

Lucia flinched. "You're going to tell me something I don't want to hear, aren't you?"

"I'm sterile."

Lucia stared me in the eyes. Then her gaze lowered to my crotch. Then it went back to my eyes. "Really?"

"Weapon spirits are sterile."

Lucia avoided my gaze. "I wonder where I can find a sperm donor...."

If it weren't for the fact that she could beat me to death, I would've smacked her. "Lucia. There's a way for me to become unsterile."

Lucia' eyes narrowed into slits. "Let me guess. You have to become stronger, right?"

...She became smarter. Or maybe she was always this smart. But that doesn't change anything; she won't be able to resist the temptation once I agree. "That's right. And the only way for me to become stronger is to enter the Immortal Continent." Though, I'm not sure if it's true or not.

Lucia sighed as her tail drooped to the ground. "I guess I can adjust my dreams to not include children," she muttered. Then she nodded to herself. Her tail perked up as she smiled at me. "That's okay. Even if you're sterile, I won't abandon you."

Alright. That settles it. We're going to the Immortal Continent whether she wants to or not. "Ilya. How do we get there?"

"Don't tell him!" Lucia shouted and tackled Ilya to the ground before she could say anything. Thankfully, there was someone else.

"The invaders should have an item that allows them to return once the month is up," Cain Thunderfire said. "And they have an item that allows them to leave by breaking it. I've seen one use one to escape from me. They act like instant-teleportation buttons, but they leave this dimension instead." A round item appeared in his palm. "Like this."

Oh, I found a lot of those from the interspacial rings of the people I cleaned up outside of Lucia's lakeside home. There were easily forty to fifty of them. None of them got out alive. Why didn't I spare anyone? Simple; dead men tell no tales. Lucia probably won't be too happy if she finds out I killed everyone because despite being a murderer herself, she thinks she's a good person. That's why I framed Mrs. Wuffletush and had her maim all the corpses. Lucia loves the predators a lot and will forgive them for anything. To quote her, "A squirrel will never betray you unless someone offers them acorns! But no one carries more acorns around than I do."

Lucia stared at the orb in Cain's palm. Her tail flashed, and the orb disappeared. "Oh darn. It disappeared. What a shame."

"That's okay," Cain said. "I have plenty more."

"As do I. Mrs. Wuffletush killed a lot of the invaders in the field of spirit seeds. I collected all the loot on their bodies." I collected the spirit seeds as well, so no greedy intruder would ruin Lucia's home while she was gone.

Lucia's eyes widened. "A, a weapon spirit should listen to his master, right? That's what weapon spirits do, right!? Put down that orb, Durandal!"

"This orb?" The one in my palm? I wonder what would happen if I applied a teensy bit of pressure to it.

Beads of sweat formed on Lucia's brow. "Durandal.... You're, you're not angry at me, right? Let's discuss this peacefully, okay?"

"Me, upset with you? What would make you think that?" I'm not a vindictive person. I don't hold grudges..., usually. "By any chance, have you done anything that would make me upset with you?"

A dry laugh escaped from Lucia's lips as she scratched her head. "Err, no? Right?" She glanced at Ilya, who looked away, before turning towards Reena, who also looked away. She bit her lower lip as she stared at Cain, and he looked away as well. "Puppers...?"

Puppers' flat voice came out of her socks. "You didn't do anything wrong to Durandal. Nothing at all."

"See?" Lucia asked me, her eyes lighting up as her tail twitched.

Why do I enjoy seeing her desperate expression so much? Well, I do feel a bit bad for her. Almost. Right, this was for her own good. I walked over to Lucia with a smile, offering the orb. "Take it." She stared at it before slowly reaching out to grab it. Without giving her a chance to resist, I raised my palm and smashed it against hers, crushing the orb between us.

Lucia's eyes widened to the size of saucers as her body turned transparent. Before she disappeared, she reached over and grabbed Ilya's arm.

Ilya screamed, "Lucia!?"

I didn't see what happened next because my vision turned black.

Chapter 3

Gah! Durandal's so mean! Alright. Where is this? The Immortal Continent? I can't hear anything. Or see anything. Or touch anything. Hmm, I must still be in transport. Ah! The lights turned back on. This place ... is a temple?

"That's her! Master, that's her! She's the saint-realm expert who assaulted us!"

Oh, there's a lot of people sitting around a room with an altar. And I'm on top of the altar with Ilya. Where'd Durandal go? Mini-DalDal's still with me, so he's probably inside. First things first! I let go of Ilya and reached behind myself to check the state of my tail. It was soft and springy without a hint of tension. Good. That means there's no immediate danger. So what's the next step? I'm not sure; I've never been in a situation like this before. I'll ask Ilya! "Hey. What do we do?"

"Lucia! How could you!?" Ilya looked like she wanted to cry. Mm, I guess she was temporarily useless.

Someone stepped onto the platform, his weird clothes loosely fluttering around him. "Madam Fox! Are my disciples' words true?"

Was he talking to me? I looked around, but the altar was still only occupied by Ilya and me. Could Ilya be a fox beastkin? I tilted my head and pointed at my sobbing companion. "She's a demon, not a foxkin."

The man's expression darkened as slips of paper with red markings on them appeared in his hands. "I was talking to you."

"I'm a squirrel. Not a fox."

The man's brow furrowed. "Squirrel? Is that a subspecies of fox?" He looked around at the other people gathered by the altar. There sure were a lot of them, at least a dozen. Most of them looked pretty old, and they were all sitting far away from each other on the ground with their eyes closed. Their clothes' colors didn't match, like they were representing different themes. The only out of place people were the younger-looking ones with missing limbs. Their clothes were the same as the person in front of me.

An old woman who was dressed in fiery red robes shot to her feet as her eyes snapped open. "You're a squirrel!? Impossible!" A paper fan appeared in her hand, and she flicked it open with her fingers. Why does it seem like she wants to attack me?

"Oh?" An old man who was dressed in black smiled as he stood up. He sauntered over to the old lady while chuckling. The scars on his face reminded me of a slave's. "It seems like you know what a squirrel is. Why don't you tell the rest of us?"

The old lady trembled. "Stay out of this, Black Devil Shu. The greatest nemesis of a phoenix is a squirrel! If I don't kill her now while she's still weak, she'll grow into a peak sky-realm expert!"

…Killing me to stop me from growing? Just what kind of world did Durandal bring me to? Mm, well, this kind of treatment is nothing new, really. I've been discriminated against all my life. Before, the only thing I could do was give up. Abandon hope. I hated that feeling so much. But who am I now? A legend. I unsheathed mini-DalDal and raised its weight to its maximum limit: five hundred tons.

"What if I want to defend this squirrel?" the scarred man asked. Something weird was happening with his hands. Black mist was pouring out of it and congealing into claws. What did he think he was? A cat?

"Then you'll have to get through me too!"

Ah, I almost forgot about this guy. He was the master of those people who assaulted me first? They didn't even pay me tribute before leaving! I'll hit him without qi to teach him a lesson. I swung mini-DalDal, and the man shouted as the talismans in his hands flew towards the tip of my sword. Did he really think paper could stop metal? Well, they couldn't. The talismans exploded, but they didn't even slow me down. I hit the man's chest with the flat part of mini-DalDal because I'm not a murderer, and he was sent flying into the wall of the temple. He didn't even scream because I hit him so lightly. Mm, he wasn't moving either—he must've been thankful for me showing him mercy.

"Master! You killed our master!"

Whew, they sure were noisy and stupid. How could I kill someone with the flat part of mini-DalDal without even adding any qi? I didn't bother correcting them because, as Ilya always tells me when we're arguing, one should never argue with stupid people. Mm, let's ignore the small fry and focus on the woman who wants to kill me for no reason other than that I'm part squirrel. How shallow of a reason is that? Seriously, if my life were a story—which it's not—the author would be bashed for creating one-dimensional villains. Not that I'd know because I still don't know how to read despite Ilya's tutoring attempts.

"Did you see that, Black Devil Shu?" The old lady's face was a lot paler now.

Did she regret saying she wanted to kill me? That's how it should be. It's why I always keep my negative comments about other people to myself instead of saying them out loud. "Look at that idiot. I bet she peed herself." ...But sometimes, my mouth is quicker than my head and I can't help it if one or two statements slip out. Oops. But I really do think she peed herself; it smells really bad. Ah, no, it's just coming from the man that I smacked into the wall.

"I saw something, alright," the man called Black Devil Shu said. Was he related to the uh, something devil two? Chu? Probably, right? "I saw a flash of heart devil qi inside of her. If you want to kill her, you'll have to answer to the Shadow Devil Sect."

"Do you think my Star Phoenix Sect is afraid? If you defend her, you'll have to answer to my sect as well!"

Hey, hey. Aren't they forgetting something really important? Like the fact that they can't kill me? My tail's completely limp, not stiff at all. If my life really was in danger, it'd be sticking straight up. Yes, like that. The fur would puff out like a porcupine's quills. Also like that. And lastly, a shiver will run up my spine. Like this. Alright, tail, you can stop demonstrating now. ...Tail?

Someone rushed into the temple and shouted, "Tribulation clouds! Tribulation clouds are forming outside!"

...Tribulation? What's that?

The rest of the people who were sitting around opened their eyes. A few of them turned to look outside. It did look a little dark out. Was a tribulation a thunderstorm? A man dressed in pure-white robes snorted. "It's just a saint-realm tribulation."

The man who had rushed into the temple bobbed his head up and down. "But, Senior, what happens if tribulation lightning hits the array keeping our connection to the pocket realm open?"

So it was a thunderstorm. Stop being so stiff, tail. You'll make an easy target for the lightning to strike. But I'm inside a temple, right? It's not like lightning can—

BOOM!

Ah, the ceiling's gone. Holy crap! That's some really scary-looking lightning.

***

Why can't I leave my weapon body? It feels like there's something restraining me. In fact, there are tiny chains of lightning holding my core in place. At least I can still tell what's going on outside. I was expecting something different when I teleported Lucia to the Immortal Continent. Something ... friendlier. I didn't expect her to provoke someone's killing intent for being a squirrel. It's probably best for Lucia to pretend to be a fox from now on given the circumstances.

All of those people sitting around are at the legendary realm. Except for the man dressed in pure-white robes. He looked a bit like a crane—all he was missing was the long neck ... and feathers ... and wings ... and beak ... and webbed feet. He also had arms. You know, I'm not sure why I thought he looked like a crane. Anyway, I couldn't tell how strong he was, but he certainly wasn't weaker than the rest. Perhaps he was in the realm above legendary? If so, Lucia's in for some trouble. It's a good thing he's not the one who wanted to kill her for being a squirrel. Hm. Now that I think about it, aren't his clothes awfully similar to those of some of the people I killed who were trying to steal Lucia's spirit seeds? Well, it's a good thing there were no witnesses.

The crane-like man let out a shout as he raised his arms. A white barrier rose out of the ground and covered the crack in the temple's ceiling. His long hair whipped around as his robes fluttered. He shouted towards the sitting people, "Help me operate the formation!"

The other people hesitated before moving into glowing spots on the ground, sitting with their legs crossed. Energy similar to qi flowed out of them, sucked into the giant white barrier above. The sky screamed as a lightning bolt rained down, striking the white light. The faces of the formation operators turned pale as their breaths deepened.

"Foreign squirrel! This is your tribulation," the crane-like man said, glaring at Lucia. "Why aren't you helping us stop it?"

Lucia scratched her head. "Uh. I'm not sure how…. And how do you know this tribulation is mine? I'm not a lightning rod, right? If anything, it's totally the temple's fault for attracting the storm."

Another bolt of lightning, twice as large as the previous one, rained down on the barrier, causing a few of the people operating it to cough out blood. The old lady who declared her intent to kill Lucia and the man called Black Devil Shu were standing off to the side. The crane-like man grimaced. "This tribulation is a little stronger than normal. The juniors from the Star Phoenix and Shadow Devil sects, won't you help out?"

The old lady glowered at Lucia before taking a seat by the crane-like man, sending her qi into the barrier as a strike of red lightning rained down. Black Devil Shu cupped his hands towards the crane-like man and said, "Senior White is an earth-realm expert. Surely, Senior doesn't need my assistance."

The crane-like man grunted. Three bolts of red lightning struck the white light at the same time, cracking it. Everyone operating the barrier spat out a mouthful of blood, the sound of groaning accompanying the splattering of liquid. Was it just me or did that lightning have killing intent? And that killing intent was clearly pointed at me, not Lucia.

"Whew, good job, everyone," Lucia said, clapping her hands together once. "You saved the altar. That's what you wanted to protect, right?"

But Lucia. The tribulation wasn't finished yet. The storm clouds were swirling around and around, forming a vortex above the temple. Red lightning streaked back and forth across the sky, gathering in the center of the spinning clouds like a ball. Then purple lightning surged towards the vortex from outside of my view, dyeing the ball of lightning black.

"This isn't a saint-realm tribulation anymore!" one of the operators of the barrier shouted as he climbed to his feet. "If I stay, I'll die! Forgive me, Senior White!"

"Forgive me, Senior White!"

The ten or so people who were operating the barrier rose to their feet and fled, rushing out of the temple's entrance. Mm, they were spineless despite having the strength of a legendary-realm expert. Perhaps I should call them saint-realm experts? After all, when in Flusia, do as the Flusians do.

"What about your disciples!?" the crane-like man shouted. His face was flushed, and veins bulged against his skin as a storm of qi flew out of his body, reinforcing the barrier. "If the transportation array is destroyed, how will they return?"

As expected, the people who ran away didn't respond. Only the old lady and the crane-like man were operating the barrier now, and they didn't seem to be in good shape. Another two balls of black lightning had formed in the clouds. Does everyone go through a tribulation when they become a saint-realm expert? Maybe it only occurs on the Immortal Continent. It would explain why this man has a barrier specially made to counter tribulation lightning. If one of their disciples broke through to the saint realm inside of our pocket world, then a tribulation would be waiting for them when they came out. Of course, I could be completely wrong, but if I'm right, then this tribulation's for the three of us: Lucia, Puppers, and me.

And what was Lucia doing? Oh, she was going through all the treasures I stored inside her interspacial ring before I transported us here. And ... she took out an instant-teleportation button. She only has three of those, all of them taken from Cain. Lucia wrapped her arm around Ilya's shoulders and whispered into the poor demon's ear, "If the barrier breaks, we're teleporting away."

"I refuse to run away from a measly saint-realm tribulation!" the crane-like man shouted. He raised both his arms up, and hundreds of shining weapons appeared out of nowhere, surging past the barrier and towards the storm clouds. Like a provoked lion, the tribulation roared in response, sending down the three balls of black lightning at the same time. The weapons and lightning collided.

The crane-like man coughed out another mouthful of blood as all the weapons he had sent into the air were destroyed, but at least, they had destroyed a ball of lightning as well. Then the two remaining balls crashed against the barrier, shattering it and drawing out another mouthful of blood from the crane-like man. The old lady from the Star Phoenix Sect let out a pitiful scream as she exploded. She literally exploded into a bloody mist. Holy crap. If one of those things hit Lucia…! There was still one ball of black lightning left! Dodge it, Lucia! Dodge it! Too bad she can't hear me.

Lucia stiffened like a frightened squirrel, her arms jerking upwards to her chest like a t-rex. The instant-teleportation button in her hand flew towards the ball of lightning and collided against it. The lightning swallowed it up as it rushed towards Lucia's head. Doomed. She was going to—the lightning disappeared. …It's gone? Don't tell me the button teleported it away. I think…, I think it really did. But the teleportation range on those buttons aren't very far….

With a thundering crash, the temple's wall shattered as the ball of black lightning surged towards Lucia once again. Luckily for Lucia, but unluckily for Senior White, Senior White happened to be in the way of the lightning and Lucia. He screamed as the lightning made contact with his body…, and then he exploded, taking the lightning with him.

Lucia stared at the bloody puddles on the ground. One belonged to the old lady from the Star Phoenix Sect, and the other belonged to Senior White. She cleared her throat and looked up at the sky. The tribulation clouds were gone—only a blue sky could be seen. Lucia blinked and pinched Ilya.

"Ow!"

Lucia nodded. "So I'm not dreaming."

"Why'd you pinch *me* to check if *you* were dreaming!?" Tears poured down Ilya's face. "I wish this was a dream! You, you—guah!" She sobbed as she bent her legs and buried her face into her knees.

Oh, the lightning restraining my core was gone. It seems like I can exit mini-DalDal now. That tribulation really was meant for me, huh? Well, it's a good thing there were some kind strangers willing to help us out. Perhaps this world is friendlier than I thought. ...Who am I kidding? Would a friendly world explode people with lightning?

***

I nearly pooped myself. That black lightning, wow. If I didn't freeze up and accidentally throw away the instant-teleportation button, then I'd probably be dead. Even if I crushed it like I planned to, then that ball of lightning would've followed and zapped me. I mean, I was totally planning on teleporting the ball of lightning away. Aren't I a genius? ...I'm scared. What kind of world did Durandal force me into!?

"Lucia."

Speak of the devil. Where was Durandal this whole time?

"Don't look so angry." Durandal patted my head and rubbed my ears. It's hard to be mad at him when he does this. It's not fair. But I'm still mad! ...Mm, a little more to the left, please. "I couldn't come out to help you because of the lightning."

"Is that a saint weapon spirit!?"

Hmm? Who was eyeing Durandal? The people who had run away from the barrier were crowding around the entrance to the temple. What were those glints in their eyes for? Oh! The selfless senior's interspacial ring! I almost missed out on this. It's a bit bloody, but I'm no stranger to blood. I'll check what's inside after I leave all these prying eyes. "...I should remove the witnesses." Isn't that what Durandal had taught me?

Durandal stopped patting my head. Why? He drew his weapon, dashed towards the entrance, and shouted, "Breaking Blade!" Weird. He didn't use up any of my qi at all, but there was plenty of qi inside his attack. Durandal can only use qi from his owner or from spirit stones, and all our spirit stones are in my interspacial ring. Don't tell me he found a new owner.... Which bitch stole Durandal from me!? Whose qi is he using!?

"Ah! Lucia! You're crushing me!"

Oops. I squeezed Ilya's arm a bit too hard. I forgot to let go of her after the generous senior exploded. What was I thinking about before this...? Oh, right. "Durandal!"

Someone screamed, but it didn't last very long because a head flew into the air. Gah! Why is Durandal murdering people!? We just had to silence them! "Wait! Durandal! What are you doing!?"

Durandal paused, and the remaining people at the entrance froze as well. "Didn't you want to silence them?"

"Well, yeah, but we can just cut their tongues out, right?" Without a tongue, people can't speak. Then no one will know. Mhm. ...But tongues grow back, so I'll have to get Ilya to cast an anti-healing spell.

"And if they write out a message?"

Ah, right. I forgot about words. How come other people can read and I can't? Life's not fair. "Then we'll cut off their arms too."

"They can draw on the ground with their legs."

"Cut those off too!" Why are there so many ways to communicate a message!?

"They can answer questions by blinking their eyes. One blink for yes and two blinks for no."

"Pop their eardrums then." There has to be a way to silence someone other than killing them! I don't want to be labeled as an evil person the instant I enter a new world. I have to be stronger than everyone in the world first before I can be evil! Then no one can punish me. Right, I have to lie low and become stronger, strong enough to destroy that tribulation lightning with a sneeze at the very least!

"But, ah, what if they use the tops of their heads to write out a message in the mud?"

"Then cut their heads … off." Wait a minute. I feel like I've been bamboozled.

Another person screamed as his head flew into the air.

"Durandal!"

"What? I'm just following your orders."

"I didn't order you to do anything!" I was just answering questions! Those weren't orders!

"If I may suggest a solution, Madam Squirrel."

Hmm? What was this person's name again? Black devil's shoe? "Alright. Let's hear it." I'm open to suggestions, unlike Durandal. He pretends to be open to my suggestions, but he ignores them and does whatever he wants instead. For a while, I wanted to train him like I trained Puppers, but I don't want to break Durandal's soul. …I broke Puppers' soul? Who said that? I treat Puppers very nicely! I feed him a meal every other month!

"We can swear oaths to the heavens like so," the shoe person said. "I swear on the heavens that I will never let anyone know of what has occurred today. If I break my oath, then let the heavens strike me dead!" A beam of light fell down from the sky and illuminated him.

…Did he really think that'd work? "Sorry, but I don't believe in, uh, the heavens." Even Ilya can make herself light up like a flashlight. How dumb did this person think I was?

The shoe person furrowed his brow. "But it really works."

"Prove it," Durandal said. He pointed his sword at one of the trembling people. "Make an oath to the heavens and break it. I want to see what happens."

"But, Senior, if I do that, I'll die!" the man said.

Durandal sighed and another head flew into the air. Stop killing them! "Look," Durandal said. "If these oaths really work, then only one of you has to die instead of all of you. Aren't I a generous man? I'll let you decide who will make the oath between yourselves."

The shoe person stared at me with a strange expression. "Like I thought, you're perfect for the Shadow Devil Sect. No wonder why your heart devil qi is so thick."

A shiver ran down my spine. Was I being recruited? But I don't want to join a Shadow Devil Sect! It sounds so ominous! That'll definitely get me hunted down by other people for being evil! While Durandal handled silencing the people, I decided to think ahead and figure out what to do for the future. "Are there any good sects?"

"Good? The Shadow Devil Sect is one of the five fingers of Kong County. Only the other four fingers can see eye to eye with us. Everyone else is below us."

"Err, that's not what I meant by good. You know, good, like, uh, loved by the people kind of good."

"The Shadow Devil Sect is loved by the people. People love strength. Millions of cultivators flock to our sect every year for our entrance examinations."

"Millions?" Ilya asked. Hey, it looked like she finally recovered from whatever she was suffering. She just hadn't been herself recently. An Ilya that isn't doubtful isn't an Ilya at all. "That's impossible."

"I'm not lying," the shoe person said. He glared at Ilya before snorting. "Just a mortal-realm junior, what would you know?"

Ilya rolled her eyes and tugged on my sleeve. "You know, the population in our world was close to two million people. Now he's saying millions of people go to his sect yearly. Think of how big our world was and how much space is required to host millions of people." Ilya stared into my eyes. "I believe even someone like you can figure it out."

...You know, math isn't really my strong suit. But Ilya believes in me! So I'll just read her subtle hints that are yelling at me to agree with her. "Ilya's right. Do you think I'm dumb?"

Black devil's shoe cleared his throat. "Your world is a tiny one. Very, very tiny. If—"

BOOM!

Holy crap! That was loud. ...What was that? Durandal was standing by a pile of ashes, nudging it around with his sword. "Huh, interesting," Durandal said with a nod. "Those oaths really work.

Oh, those ashes used to be a person. Err, did I say I didn't believe in the heavens? Ah-ha-ha, it was a slip of the tongue! I swear! ...But not to the heavens. Please don't zap me.

***

Why me? What did I do to deserve this? I want to go home. This is all Cain's fault for telling Durandal how to get here! The instant I entered a new world with Lucia, lightning rained down and killed someone above the legendary realm. I feel like a child forced to write a thesis to graduate from an academy. I'm not prepared for this at all! Please, if there's a lord out there looking down on everyone, there's only one thing I ask: let me go home.

I sucked in my breath to gather my courage. "Excuse me, Black Devil Shu."

"Like I was saying," Black Devil Shu said, "your world is very tiny compared to this one."

"That's not what I wanted to ask about. Is there any way for me to return to the pocket realm?" Surely there has to be. If it opened once, it can open again. Besides, the people inside have to leave too, right? That definitely means there's a way back in!

"Return? Yes, of course," Black Devil Shu said. "You just need an entry pearl created by a sky-realm expert. Sky-realm experts can open pocket realms quite easily."

It's that easy? There has to be a catch. "Do you have one of those pearls?"

"No. Kong County is given ten entry pearls every five hundred years. One is used per pocket realm."

"Given? By whom?"

Shu coughed and turned his head to the side. "Kong County doesn't have any sky-realm experts. We're part of the King Province which has nine other counties the same size as ours under its governance."

This place is way too big. Though, this person could be lying to me. He does have an extremely sketchy-sounding name. "In other words, for me to return home, I need to find or become a sky-realm expert."

"Precisely."

It seems like it's going to be an extremely long time before I can see my father again. If nine circles encompass the mortal realm, then it'd make sense for each realm to be nine circles as well, right? Then I'd need 28 circles…? I guess the only thing I can do is cling to Lucia and wait for the day she becomes a sky-realm expert. I … never thought I'd be rooting for her to become stronger.

"W-we can't do that!" someone shouted.

Ugh, what was Lucia doing now? She and Durandal were standing in front of the poor natives of the Immortal Continent with their arms across their chests. She really likes copying him; I wonder if she does it consciously. Lucia snorted as she leaned forward and squinted at one of her prisoners. I describe them as prisoners because, for some reason, they don't want to run away. If they scattered, I'm sure a few of them would survive. The man gulped audibly, and Lucia patted his shoulder while asking, "And why can't you?"

"We already gave you the tribute! Please, let us off!" The man dropped to his knees and hit his forehead against the ground. The natives really like kowtowing, huh? Don't they feel any sense of shame?

"Excuse me, Madam Squirrel," Black Devil Shu said. "What seems to be the issue now?"

Lucia puffed her cheeks out and glared at her captives. "They won't give me their stuff!"

The men made noises of disagreement. "That's not true! We gave her the proper tributes!"

"Tribute smibute," Lucia said and drew her sword. "When I demand all your items, you give me all your items! Don't think I'm dumb enough to believe you only have pouches of spirit stones on you."

"Ah, Madam Squirrel," Black Devil Shu said. "Common etiquette in the Immortal Continent is to take only the tribute while robbing someone. Taking anymore can incur the wrath of the sects behind them. Or it can bring about a lifelong grudge that has to end in one person's death."

"If someone's dying, it won't be me," Lucia said. "And they swore to never speak about today's events! No one will know if I rob them."

"Madam Squirrel, the tributes are already five percent of their net worth. As a rogue cultivator, you don't want to make enemies so early on." Black Devil Shu smiled at Lucia, trying to placate her. Too bad Lucia only had eyes for Durandal. And Durandal was an even greedier monster than Lucia.

Lucia's eyes widened. "Five percent!? That's…, that's…! Ilya!"

Hmm? Why is Lucia bringing me into this!? "Y-yes?"

"Is five percent a lot or a little?"

I couldn't stop the sigh from leaving my mouth. Was five percent a lot? It depends on who you ask. If I had to give up five percent of my net worth to save my life, I'd do it in a heartbeat. So no, it wasn't a lot at all. Even fifty percent wasn't worth much. Heck, I'd give up 95% of my net worth to return home right now. "It's a little. Very, very little. You should ask for twenty times more."

"You hear that?" Lucia asked, glaring at the captives. "I want twenty times more than five percent of everything!"

It's not something to be flattered about, but I really like how Lucia trusts me when it comes to important decisions involving numbers. Would I ever betray Lucia by shortchanging her while watching over her finances? Hell no, I'm not an idiot.

"But that's demanding everything from us!"

Everything except your lives. Which are the most important things, right? I gave them a completely fair price.

"You can keep your underwear," Lucia said with a nod. "I'm not a pervert."

Durandal coughed.

"J-just our underwear?"

Lucia nodded again. "I want your clothes too. I bet I could sell them for a lot to Ilya's dad."

No. That's not right. My father has no interest in strangers' clothes. Then again, my father does buy everything Lucia doesn't need because he wants to maintain a good relationship with her. It's unfortunate my grandmother doesn't approve. Ugh, and I can't even return home to help my father free himself from her clutches. But I'm sure he'll be fine. Even if he isn't, by the time I do return home, Lucia will practically be a god, so all troubles will be solved anyway. For now, I have to look towards the future. The only thing I can do is improve myself. I have to get a lot stronger than I am now; otherwise, there's no doubt in my mind that I'll die if I'm left behind by Lucia. Once again, my fate is left in the hands of a brain-dead squirrelkin.

Chapter 4

I'm rich! Maybe. I'm not sure how much money I'd need to qualify as rich in this world. But I have about sixty interspacial rings worth of items. Sixty? Where did I get fifty others? There were only a dozen or so so-called saint-realm experts. Hmm. Well, I'm not one to question good fortune! Durandal or Puppers probably picked them up somewhere and stuck them in my ring. I also have these fancy sets of clothing that I'm not quite sure how to put on. Oh wells. Ilya's dad will buy them. He buys everything.

Now that I've stripped and silenced these people, what do I do? "Hey. Mr. Shoe, how do I go home?"

"I already asked him that, Lucia," Ilya said. She did? When? "You have to become a sky-realm expert before you can open the path home."

Uh…. "Is there an easier way?"

"No."

"Um, Madam Squirrel," Mr. Shoe said. "May I have my clothes back?"

Hmm. This person stood up in my defense when that crazy phoenix lady wanted to kill me, right? Fine. I can return his clothes. But just his clothes; I'm keeping everything else. I'm a poor defenseless squirrelkin in a foreign world that hates squirrelkin; I need all the resources I can to survive! Mm, from now on, I'm going to call myself a foxkin. I don't think they're hated here and I was already mistaken for one once.

"What are your plans, Madam Squirrel?" Mr. Shoe asked as he put on his clothes. Of course I watched. How else am I supposed to learn how to dress myself like the natives? As long as there are no weird customs where women and men wear their clothes differently, I'll be fine. "The Immortal Continent is not very forgiving towards rogue cultivators. How about you join my Shadow Devil Sect? With your strength, it's possible for you to become an elder. Not to mention the fact that no other sect can help you cultivate the heart devil qi within your body."

"Heart devil qi!? No wonder why I feel so uneasy!" one of the people I stripped shouted. Wasn't he afraid of Durandal cutting his head off? I would be.

Mm, now that Mr. Shoe mentions it, I did feel some weird sort of connection to the people I robbed. I thought it was guilt, but it turned out to be the planting of heart devils. Phew, I thought I almost became a softie. A girl has to be cold and tough to survive in a world as harsh as this! At least, that's the impression I'm getting. Though, these people are a bit honorable. How can they ignore the temptation and only receive a tribute when they can clearly take the rest? It doesn't make any sense. Maybe that's why it's called the saint realm. They're saints.

"Madam Squirrel?"

Hmm?

"About joining the Shadow Devil Sect…."

Do I want to do that? I heard from somewhere that rogue cultivators wouldn't have an easy time on the Immortal Continent. But I remember the sects from the human capital back home. They were just preachers and con artists and, truthfully, pretty weak. Then again, now that I think about it, everyone back home is pretty weak. But joining a sect…, isn't associating with other people just asking to be betrayed? Ground squirrels are supposed to be social animals, but … I've almost always lived alone. If I interact with a group of people and they treat me like family, then I might become non-selfish and grow as a person! I can't have that happen. I like my current life very much. The current life before I was transported into this world, I mean.

"Madam Squirrel…?"

"She gets like that sometimes," Ilya said.

Who gets like what?

"Try asking her again."

Ask me what? Oh! Joining the sect. Hmm. "Durandal, what do you think?"

Durandal crossed his arms over his chest and glared at Mr. Shoe. "What does your sect have to offer, and what do you expect in return?"

"…Are there no sects in the pocket realm?"

Ilya nodded. "There are, but they're not important. If anything, we have an extremely bad impression of sects back home."

Mr. Shoe's expression relaxed. "I see. Well, first and foremost, the biggest benefit of joining a sect is its backing. If you get in trouble, you can count on your sect members to help you out. If someone causes you to feel aggrieved, your sect brothers and sisters will help you get revenge. Of course, you're expected to help any sect members in return. This deterrent will aid you in traveling the Immortal Continent, well, Kong County at least."

"So it's like a gang." Right? I'm pretty sure that's how the Flopsy Gang operated before they were all hunted down. Hmm. Maybe sects are more like a country? But I wouldn't help a fellow countryman if he was robbed by a different countryman. Maybe it's not like a country. I guess it's like the relationship between Durandal and me. …Would Durandal help me if I were being bullied? He better.

"Err, maybe in the sense of camaraderie, but other than that, sects also have other benefits that joining a gang won't give you," Mr. Shoe said. "For example, exclusive cultivation techniques that can't be spread to outsiders. I'm not sure why my disciple helped you gain heart devil qi, but just by that fact alone, you should join the Shadow Devil Sect. If someone from my sect were to find out that you were using our exclusive cultivation technique, they'd hunt you down—especially since the Heart Devil Cultivation Technique is only given to the core disciples of the sect. Other than that, resources such as medicinal pills, beast blood, engraved bones, defensive talismans, and spirit stones can be exchanged for. But most importantly, you'll receive guidance and knowledge on how to break through to the higher realms."

…There's too many words. My head's starting to hurt.

"You've only been listing the benefits," Ilya said. "What's the catch?"

"There isn't really a catch," Mr. Shoe said. "You'll be expected to help out when the sect needs help. You have to accomplish tasks for the sect to continue receiving resources. An example of a task would be like what I'm currently doing, escorting my juniors to a pocket realm. Speaking of which, do you know what happened to my disciple?"

His disciple's the person who drank my poisoned cup of hot chocolate, right? "Uh, yeah. He died."

"…Died?"

"Mhm. I was having a friendly conversation with him, but then those people"—I gestured towards the scapegoats—"attacked us and he succumbed to his injuries, but not before passing on the Heart Devil Cultivation Technique to me."

"That's not true, Senior!" one of the scapegoats shouted. "It's true that I attacked him, but it definitely wasn't enough to kill him!"

Hey, don't try to shift the blame onto me! It was clearly his own fault for dying, but I can't blame a dead person, can I now? Peacefully take the fall! "They said something about ridding themselves of a heart devil by killing, uh…."

"Sly Devil Chu."

Thanks, Ilya. "Sly Devil Chu. That's right. They declared their intent to murder him."

"I, I did declare that, but I only hit him with two talismans!"

"You only attacked my disciple with the intent to kill," Mr. Shoe said. "I understand. If it weren't for the fact that Madam Squirrel is using you to grow heart devils, I would kill you. I won't even injure you. Continue to grow strong for Madam Squirrel's sake, knowing you will always be beneath her." Mr. Shoe nudged me. "You should strip them of their underwear too. It'll nourish their heart devils."

"Eh? I'm not a pervert!" Really, I'm not! "Besides, look at how small they are! They could cover everything with a blade of grass."

Mr. Shoe's eyes widened as the scapegoats coughed out mouthfuls of blood. "Amazing! With this ability to plant heart devils in people, there's no doubt you'll be a chosen of the sect! Please, join the Shadow Devil Sect!"

Mm. Chosen of a sect. I like the sound of that; it sounds special.

***

I'm on a flying boat. Yeah, I don't understand it either. How can a boat fly? Even magic isn't capable of lifting something like this high above the clouds for an extended period of time. The boat has three floors below deck and two cabins above deck on the stern and bow. It also has four masts with two crow's nests. In other words, this boat is huge. Apparently, the interspacial rings of the Immortal Continent are a lot larger than those of our tiny pocket realm. A vessel like this would never fit in a ring even if ten ninth-circle mages worked together.

Also, I don't understand the purpose of a mast. The boat's using some sort of energy to travel through the air; if anything, the sails are slowing the boat down rather than speeding it up. But Black Devil Shu says the sails are a necessity because the design on them will intimidate any robbers. But still, wouldn't it make more sense to paint the designs on the sides of the boat and remove the masts? Surely the natives of the Immortal Continent are smart, no? According to Black Devil Shu, saint-realm experts can live up to three hundred years, and earth-realm experts can live up to a thousand. A sky-realm expert's lifespan easily exceeds five thousand years. So how is it possible that the natives lack common sense?

Take this boat for example. It's huge, bigger than Lucia's lakeside guest home. But it's being used to transport a total of three people: Lucia, Black Devil Shu, and me. Before that, it was only used to transport Black Devil Shu and the poor disciple that was poisoned to death by Lucia. That's a massive waste! Why not just take a smaller boat? When I asked Black Devil Shu about this, he gave me a really, really unexpected answer: Face. The natives—who will willingly hand over five percent of their belongings while kowtowing the instant they encounter someone stronger than them—are concerned about face. And when they say face, they mean reputation. So someone with a lot of face has a really good reputation. A shameless person has very thick skin on his face. It's a weird concept, but it's not unheard of. Back in the pocket realm, people would live above their means, forcing themselves into financial debt, just to show off amongst their peers. Of course, I believe those people are mentally ill. Going even further, the Immortal Continent is a crazy-house filled with mentally unstable individuals blessed with irresponsible amounts of power. Lucia would fit in perfectly.

As for why we're on this boat…, we're going to the Shadow Devil Sect. There is definitely an ulterior motive for Black Devil Shu to recruit Lucia, but Durandal and Lucia won't listen to me. Durandal says, "A true legend must face traps head on even with foreknowledge about them," while Lucia says, "My tail's soft and springy. What danger?" I really hope Black Devil Shu's motive is something innocuous like he'll receive a promotion for finding a promising sect member, but just judging by his name, it's not going to be as simple as that. Someone with the middle name Devil can't be a good person. His first name is Black, by the way. Apparently his disciple's first name was Sly. Weird, right?

So far, we've been traveling together for half a day now. Currently, I'm eating dinner with Black Devil Shu above deck. And right now, both of us are trying to ignore the moans and grunts coming from down below.

"Durandal! Faster!"

Let's pretend I didn't hear that. Even Black Devil Shu's face is red. My lord, this is awkward. "So…."

"Right there!"

Black Devil Shu coughed. I couldn't tell where he was looking because I was staring at the plate in front of me, but I'm pretty sure he's staring at the table too. Did I mention how great the food was around here? Apparently, the food is filled with the energy of the world, similar to divine beast meat, but vegetarian. I've always been fonder of vegetables than meat. Black Devil Shu's chopsticks nudged around some beansprouts. "Does she, uh, duo-cultivate often?"

"Ah!"

"I'm not sure how to answer that." Lucia's always been holding back because of her belief that Durandal would die if he engaged in, uh, nighttime activities with her unless he became a legend. Or should I say saint? Now, I wouldn't be surprised if this became an everyday thing. "I hope you have earplugs."

"Oh."

Right. Can we change the topic? "What exactly is a chosen of the sect?" Black Devil Shu wanted Lucia to become one of those. Yes, I know what the word chosen means, but I'm not sure if Lucia was chosen to become a sacrifice or chosen to become the next sect leader or chosen to become a religious figure. There's many things she can be chosen for.

"Don't you dare faint again!"

Black Devil Shu made a strange noise before leaning back in his chair. I put my fork down and met his gaze. "Chosen of the sect…. Do you know how sects are structured?"

"No." Back in the pocket realm, there was one leader who distributed his techniques and the rest were disciples who paid the leader. I don't think it'd be the same here.

"Where do I start…," Black Devil Shu said and rubbed his chin. "I never had to explain such common knowledge before. Mm, you seem young, so I'll keep it simple."

I'm offended.

"There are sect elders and sect disciples. Amongst the disciples, there are those of the outer court, the inner court, the core, and the chosen. The closer a disciple is to the center of the sect, the more resources the sect will invest in them. With Junior Lucia's abilities, there shouldn't be any issues with becoming a chosen. Of course, she could also become a guest elder, but the sect won't nurture her as much if she does."

"So you want Lucia to become the highest class of disciple." The question is … why?

Black Devil Shu must've realized my unasked question. "I wish to sow good karma with her. On a cultivator's journey to immortality, there will come a time when they have to resolve their debts. They have to pay back what they've been given. If Junior Lucia happens to become an immortal, there's no doubt that the whole Shadow Devil Sect, including me, will be blessed by good fortune. The whole purpose of a sect is to produce an immortal."

Something that's been bothering me for a while now has been the whole concept of immortality. I still don't really believe in the longer lifespans for obtaining more circles but putting that aside…. "Do immortals actually exist?"

"Yes. I've seen one with my own eyes."

Anyone can claim to be immortal because they're alive. They're only immortal until they're dead, then they're clearly not immortal anymore. Heck, I can claim to be an immortal.

But it seems like these kinds of beliefs are deeply engrained in this society, so I'm not going to question it too much. I'll just keep it at a distance, neither acknowledging nor disregarding these delusions. After all, as a wise man once said, there are only two things that are certain: death and taxes. Which wise man was this? My drunkard teacher, Rogath Winemark. From what I've seen, he hasn't been wrong yet. For a drunkard, he's pretty smart. I wonder if I'll ever see him again. I hope not; I really didn't like him.

***

During our pillow talk, Durandal confessed something weird to me. He … eats swords. Am I married to a cannibal? Wait, I'm not even married to him. Yet. It's so weird; I never thought there'd be a day when I'd consider marriage. I don't think of the future very often, but when I do, it's about what I'm going to do for dinner the next day. Thankfully, I still have lots of divine beast corpses to eat inside of my interspacial ring. And my interspacial ring was upgraded! Well, replaced with a shinier and bigger one that I received as a tribute. But that's what upgrades are, right? I wonder if I'll be able to upgrade the quality of my dinners. I hope so. There should be plenty of legendary-realm beasts. Why do I think that? Because that crazy old lady said phoenixes exist! I bet they taste like fried chicken since they're already on fire. That settles it. I'm going to eat a phoenix. "Mr. Shoe!"

"Lucia?" Durandal asked. He was sitting in a corner of the room eating a really fancy-looking sword that I probably could've sold for a fortune. "What's up?"

"I want to eat a phoenix." I cupped my hands over my mouth and shouted at the ceiling again, "Mr. Shoe!"

A few seconds later, Mr. Shoe's and Ilya's presences were announced by the stomping of footsteps. I think they were being extra loud on purpose. Why? Hmm, well, it doesn't matter. I wrapped my blankets around myself because I'm not an exhibitionist and waited. The door to my room opened, and Mr. Shoe and Ilya peeked their heads inside. What's with that red face? Was Mr. Shoe drunk? And Ilya's face was red too! She's underage; she's not allowed to drink alcohol! What are you doing, Mr. Shoe!? You'll end up in jail!

"Junior Lucia. Did you call for me?"

"I want to eat a phoenix."

Mr. Shoe stared at me. What? Is there a problem? "Phoenixes are a very intelligent kind of creature. They make great companions, and I don't think there is a single person in Kong County who'd be willing to eat a phoenix. In fact, there are only two phoenixes that I know of that even live in Kong County, and they both belong to the Star Phoenix Sect. Is there any particular reason why you want to eat a phoenix?"

There's only two phoenixes here? Then breed them to make more! Unless those star phoenix people are as unlucky as me and ended up with only female phoenixes. But still, I'm not going to not eat a phoenix! I was a slave that became a legend; I refuse to believe I can't fulfil my goal of snacking on a fiery bird! "How strong is the Star Phoenix Sect?"

"They're one of the five fingers of Kong County. Our Shadow Devil Sect is the strongest of the five, but even we'd suffer losses if we went to war with another one of the fingers. They have four earth-realm experts, including their two phoenixes, while we have five."

That's a bit problematic. I don't think I can fight against an earth-realm expert. I mean, that selfless senior who blew himself up for the sake of my tribulation was an earth-realm expert, and he had some really scary techniques! Sorta. He could command so many flying weapons! …But they were all destroyed by the black lightning. Hmm. Maybe, just maybe, I can win against an earth-realm expert?

"You're thinking of whether or not you'd win in a fight against an earth-realm expert, right?" Ilya asked.

Don't read my mind!

"I asked him"—Ilya pointed at Mr. Shoe—"about a lot of things pertaining to the Immortal Continent to gauge our chances of survival. Right now, you're a low-ranked saint-realm expert. Before you can become an earth-realm expert, you still have to pass through mid-ranked and high-ranked."

Huh. Isn't that pretty simple? The saint-realm is a whole lot easier than becoming stronger in the pre-legendary realm! Like first I had to be a warrior, then a spirit warrior, then a divine warrior, and each of those were split into low-ranked, mid-ranked, and high-ranked. This is three times less difficult!

"And the three sections of the saint realm are split even further into three subsections, so there's a low-low-ranked and a mid-low-ranked and—"

"Stop! Too many words and I can guess the rest!"

Ilya coughed. "Not only that, but to go from one subsection of the saint realm to another is as difficult as going from a spirit warrior to a divine warrior. In other words, there are nine walls you have to cross to become an earth-realm expert."

Nine walls!? Wasn't it three times easier just a few seconds ago? How did it become three times harder!? This is why I hate info dumps! Why does Ilya always try to crush my hopes and dreams with facts? She's the worst. Hmph.

Mr. Shoe coughed. "If, if you really want to eat something like a phoenix, there's a restaurant that specializes in serving peacocks. They're a high-ranked saint-realm beast and the next closest thing to a phoenix."

...Did he just say peacock? And it's almost like a phoenix? "Say ... if I fed this peacock a pole-stiffening pill, would it become as strong as a phoenix?"

"If you fed a peacock a pole-stiffening ... pill?" Mr. Shoe's face turned even redder. Even the base of his black hair was turning red. Gosh, how much alcohol did he drink? I hope he didn't give Ilya the same amount. I wonder how a drunk

Ilya would behave. Hmm. Lucia, no! Don't give alcohol to minors. "Junior Lucia, please, can you act in a bit more refined manner? Such vulgar words shouldn't leave the mouth of a woman as beautiful as you."

As beautiful as me? And he's saying that with such a bashful expression. Like a young boy confessing his love for the first time…. This…, this…! Am I being wooed? What the hell!? I've never been wooed before! How am I supposed to react!? "M-Mr. Shoe! Restrain yourself! I'm a married woman!"

Durandal choked on the sword he was eating. I'm going to ignore that reaction.

Mr. Shoe blinked. "P-pardon?"

"She thinks you're coming onto her," Ilya said. "You haven't fallen in love with Lucia, have you?"

Blood flew out of Mr. Shoe's mouth. Ew. That was pretty gross. The nonexistent chance he had with me has become even less tangible. But why do so many people vomit out blood like that? First it was those people that I robbed back at the temple. Then it was the people who I refused to take the underwear of back at the temple. Then it's Mr. Shoe. Perhaps everyone on the Immortal Continent has an illness? What illness forces people to cough out blood? Bronchitis? Pneumonia? Eh? How do I know these terms? …I'm not sure.

"To think a junior of the sect would try to plant a heart devil into me, an elder…." Mr. Shoe wiped away the blood on his lips with the back of his hand. Beads of sweat dripped from his forehead. "To think she nearly succeeded as well."

"…How sensitive are you?" Ilya asked.

"Even if it wasn't a confession, that was the first time I have ever been rejected in my life!" Mr. Shoe's back straightened as his chest puffed out. Was he proud? He was taking pride in being rejected? Wait, what did he mean it wasn't a confession? Do people on the Immortal Continent compliment women like that for no reason? If that's the case..., I might want to stay here and never go back! Hey. I'm not a narcissist. I just love compliments as much as I love myself—a lot. There's no one in the world that doesn't like compliments, okay?

"Anyways, what are you doing, Durandal?" Ilya asked.

Durandal paused and put down a half-eaten sword. "Replenishing my energy. Lucia stole a lot."

Ilya sighed. "I shouldn't have asked." Then she sighed again while shaking her head. "I should not have asked."

What was that supposed to mean? Was she looking down on Durandal? She was, wasn't she? Before I could call her out, Mr. Shoe coughed in a really obnoxious manner that was clearly meant to draw my attention towards him. He must be a narcissist.

"The restaurant that I was talking about that served peacocks is in the city we just flew over. Would you like to turn around and drop by?"

"Yes! If I can't eat a phoenix just yet, then I'll just eat its unevolved, limper form!"

"A phoenix is not an erect peacock!"

Yeah, yeah, okay, Ilya. No need to hit me with facts. Jeez.

***

After eating over sixty swords, I've come to the conclusion that all swords were not made equal. First of all, there's me, the greatest sword in existence. And then there's these swords that I call exquisite: If I could only eat one type of sword for the rest of my life, these would be it. I can physically feel my meridians expanding when I eat them. Before, I was just a medium that transferred Lucia's qi, but ever since that fateful night—the one where I lost my dignity—I grew meridians and a dantian. The meridians are channels that transfer qi from the dantian to all the other parts of the body. It's a shame there were only ten exquisite-tasting swords amongst the ones that Lucia and I had robbed; they all belonged to the saint-realm experts at the temple.

Next, there are the delicious swords. They have the effect of a tenth of an exquisite sword. There were twenty of them; I'm not sure who they belonged to. And lastly, there's the alright swords. They're as their name implies, alright. They ease my hunger at least. Sadly, I ran out of swords.

"Durandal…. Durandal…? Durandal. Durandal!"

Hmm? "Yes, Lucia?"

"You're acting weird," Lucia said and tilted her head. Her ears twitched, and I had the urge to rub them. So I did. "Ah. Stop it! The sun's already up! …Actually, keep going. Mn."

"Can you do me a favor, Lucia?"

"Of, of course!" Lucia's eyes were closed, and her breaths were getting shorter. I should probably stop before she pushes me down and has her way with me.

"Can you help me get as many swords as you can?"

"Are you going to eat them all?" Lucia asked. Her face returned to normal after I stopped, but she was staring at my hand as if she wanted to devour it. She sighed as she met my eyes. "You're lucky I love you more than I love money."

It looks like my future supply of swords has been secured. Can I eat weapons other than swords? I should try it out. I didn't feel hunger towards them, but there were a few spears and chakrams inside of Lucia's storage ring. I retrieved a spear under Lucia's watchful gaze and tapped it with my finger. I should be able to bite through this.

…It tastes horrible. I can't do it. Before I could throw the spear away, someone that I completely forgot about appeared inside the room. It was Puppers, err, Gae Bulg. …When Lucia and I are…, does he…? Let's not think about that. "Do you want to try eating this, Gae?"

"Unlike you, I don't have my own qi." Gae sighed as he took the broken spear. He sniffed it before chomping down on the shaft. "It tastes like crap."

"Wah!" Lucia let out a sound that made me flinch. "My socks became softer!" Her eyes widened as she stared at Puppers. "Keep eating."

"Y-you don't understand," Puppers said and cleared his throat in an attempt to regain his composure. "It tastes really, really bad."

I understand, Puppers. Ah, I'm calling him Puppers again. Gae Bulg, Puppers, what's the difference? They're both two syllables long. Lucia leapt towards Puppers and tackled him to the ground before shoving the spear down his throat. Puppers was forced to bite the spear apart or choke. I'm surprised he didn't just let himself die to avoid suffering; he dies a lot under Lucia's care.

The door swung open at the same time Black Devil Shu's voice said, "Junior Lucia. We've.... This isn't a good time, is it?"

Lucia stopped impaling Puppers' face and looked up at Black Devil Shu. She was still straddling Puppers' chest with no intentions of climbing off. Lucia's tail swished, slapping against the ground. Was she angry? "Haven't you ever heard of knocking?"

"Uh, no? Is knocking the act of shoving a spear down a beast's throat?" Black Devil Shu looked genuinely confused. Was knocking on doors before entering not a custom here? How barbaric. "Is ... that beast even a beast? It's wearing armor and has quite a humanoid form."

"This is my sock spirit, Puppers," Lucia said as she stood up but not before giving the spear one last good push that made it vanish down Puppers' throat. "And knocking is when you knock on the door to let someone know you want to come in. Then that person can hide all the evidence of anything immoral they're doing, and they'll let you in afterwards."

"But how will people catch you doing immoral things if they knock first?" Black Devil Shu asked. It seemed like a furrowed brow was a universal sign of confusion.

Lucia threw a brick at Black Devil Shu, striking his face. "The point is to not catch me doing immoral things!" Where did she get a brick from? "Anyways, what were you trying to tell me before you rudely barged in?"

"Right," Black Devil Shu said, clutching his bleeding nose. "We've arrived at the restaurant. If you look out the window, you'll see it to your left."

Lucia skipped over to the window and pulled open the shutters. Sunlight flooded into the room along with some hints of gold. She squinted outside, and I walked up next to her. There was a building, nearly as large as the boat we were on, that had bright golden characters placed atop its roof. I knew how to read, but I didn't understand what the characters were at all. Now that I think about it, there were a bunch of unreadable manuals that Lucia had robbed from the natives too. So it seems like there's a written language barrier. Not like it'd affect Lucia since she was illiterate to start with.

"Hmm. Can I store the boat like this?" Lucia asked as she touched the windowsill. There was a scream as the boat disappeared and Ilya fell down from above us. I landed on the ground without a problem along with Lucia. The only one who suffered a fall was Black Devil Shu. And Puppers' face was blue with froth coming out of his mouth, but that wasn't from the boat disappearing.

A nice smell caught my attention. There was a small shop across the street from the restaurant. It looked like a weapon store. I'll have to ask Lucia to go there after she eats her fake phoenix.

***

This restaurant! It's, it's…! Kind of bland to be honest. The outside was really fancy with gold plating, but the inside is just filled with red wood. Mm? There's some weird energy coming off the wood. It feels like qi. Can I absorb it?

"Greetings, dear customers!"

Oops. The redness of the wall disappeared. Let's pretend I wasn't nearby. I'll hide behind Mr. Shoe. Hmm, this greeter person almost looks as beautiful as Snow. Actually, a lot of the women here look almost as beautiful as Snow. Are there no ugly women…?

"How can we help you today?"

Mr. Shoe gave her a mean look before gesturing towards the sash on his waist that was keeping his robe from opening. Was there something there? I didn't see anything. The greeter didn't see anything either apparently because she just stared at him with a blank expression. A dark energy rose up out of Mr. Shoe, and the greeter trembled as she took a step back. Mr. Shoe snorted. "Do you recognize me now?"

"N-no," the greeter said, shaking her head as she raised the menus in front of her face. The other customers were starting to look at us. Were they saint-realm experts too? There should be a way to check someone's realm, right? Other than smacking them over the head and seeing if they survive, that is.

Mr. Shoe snorted and lowered his head to look at his sash. The aura surrounding his body disappeared as his expression stiffened. "Oh. Right, Junior Lucia stole my badge."

His what? Oh! The jade amulet that was on his sash. It looked expensive, so I took it for myself. Finders, keepers! "This one?"

"An elder of the Shadow Devil Sect!" the greeter said with wide eyes. They bulged so much I thought they were going to fall out of her head. "Please, follow me; I'll take you to the VIP suite right away."

"Just take these three," Mr. Shoe said, gesturing towards Ilya, Durandal, and me. Puppers was still out of commission after I sacrificed a spear to make him fluffier. "I have to send a message to my sect. Junior Lucia, do you mind passing me my elder token?"

I have a feeling I won't get it back if I do. But I will since Mr. Shoe's actually been pretty nice to me this whole time. Of course, that doesn't mean I trust him. The people that you definitely can't trust in a world as harsh as this one are the nice people! No one can afford to be friendly when everyone's enemies. It doesn't make any sense. He's definitely using me somehow; Ilya says it's to get prestige with the sect if he manages to convince me to join and I end up being super strong.

"Right this way," the greeter said as Mr. Shoe left the building. He passed by the gray handprint I left on the wall but didn't say anything about it. Durandal followed behind Ilya and me, and the greeter led us to a private room in the back of the restaurant. "Here you are."

Ilya took one of the menus; I didn't bother because I couldn't read, but I wasn't sure why Durandal wasn't taking one. I stared at him, but he shrugged and closed his eyes. "I'm digesting."

...That's my excuse.

"I can't read this." Ilya sighed as she placed the menu down.

Ilya can't read it...? Then ... aren't I superior to her now? I've lived my whole life not being able to read! Whenever I had to order food, well, I just begged for scraps and never ate in a restaurant. But when I had to read things..., I didn't have to read anything, huh? "Well, that's okay. We don't have to order things on the menu. We're here to eat the cock, remember?"

"The peacock!" Ilya shouted. She covered her mouth as she glanced at the door, but the room was soundproof, so it didn't really matter. There were a lot of people outside, but not a single peep could be heard in here. I should figure out what these walls are made of and make a portable bedroom out of it for Durandal. Mhm, purely for Durandal's sake! I'm chaste! I mean, Durandal's not really a *real* person, right? He's a spirit.

Yes, it doesn't count. It's simply masticating. ...With my lower mouth.

"Yeah, yeah, same thing." I waved at the person standing in the corner. "A hundred orders of peacocks!"

The waiter's mouth fell open. "I, I don't think we have that many in stock. Peacocks—"

"Then give me all you have." I guess it makes sense. If peacocks are high-ranked spirit-realm beasts, right? That means they're rare. It's like trying to find a hundred predators back at home, but I could only find a total of five. Would I feel bad for causing the deaths of peacocks in the vicinity? Nope! I've always had a bad relationship with birds. I still remember how those scavenger crows used to play pranks on me! And then there were those stupid vultures that couldn't hurt me, so they flew overhead and constantly tried to poop on me. That was disgusting, but luckily, my Path of Slaughter dodged them all.

"Right, all the peacocks we have," the waiter said. Was it just me or was he looking at me like I was crazy? "And for your refreshments?"

"One of everything on the menu! Oh, that includes food too." I've always wanted to say that. I should have enough money, right? If I don't.... Hmm. Well, I probably do! I robbed an earth-realm expert after all. And he had a literal mountain of spirit stones.

"One of every dish, beverage, and all the peacocks we have?"

"Yup, that's right."

"Very well then, I'll let the chefs know."

The waiter left the room, and Ilya sighed as she buried her head into her hands. Hmm? "What's wrong?"

"Withdrawal symptoms."

Oh right, she had those. Oh! Peacocks should have bones, right!? I can finally engrave focus bones that actually work! This is great.

"What!? What do you mean someone ordered all the peacocks!? I came to this restaurant specifically for the peacocks! Do you know who I am? I'm an elder of the Azure Dragon Sect!"

What's going on outside? I thought this room was soundproofed? How loud was this person shouting? I opened the door and poked my head out. A man wearing a blue version of the clothes that people in the Immortal Continent liked to wear was standing by the restaurant's entrance with five people behind him: three women and two men.

"My apologies," the waiter from my room said, "the guest in the VIP suite has ordered our entire stock of peacock for the day."

"Is that so? Whoever's in the VIP suite, get the hell out here!"

…Eh. I closed the door and sat back down. The first lesson of robbing without hurting your conscience is to make sure you're the victim! No one can complain if the victim robs the bully. So while I'm sitting here cutely and peacefully, if someone decides to harass me, it's my right to beat them up!

Bang! The door to the VIP suite flew open.

And now I can freely rob more elders without feeling any guilt!

Chapter 5

There's something special about Lucia. She just has this miraculous ability to … piss people off wherever she goes—except for my father, she's an angel in his eyes. Disregarding my traitorous blood, this Azure Dragon Sect person looks absolutely enraged. I suspect he's angry because Lucia made eye contact with him before closing the door when he shouted for whoever was in the VIP suite to get the hell out. I don't know if she actually made eye contact because I wasn't watching, but it wouldn't make sense otherwise. Actually, I almost forgot the fact that I was in a nuthouse. Maybe there wasn't actually a reason other than this elder really wanted to eat peacocks.

The elder twirled his finger around his white moustache, which was wispy and long—completely unlike the thicker and bushier mustaches back home. Am I so homesick that I'm missing what facial hair looks like? A jet of warm, moist air blew past my face, causing my hair to flutter. …Was that ejected from the elder's nostrils? That's so gross! Beat him up, Lucia!

"Which sect do you three hail from?"

"That's none of your business, old man!" Lucia said, slamming her hand against the table. I thought it was going to shatter, but the red wood was a lot sturdier than I thought. Oh, there's some energy coming off of it. Perhaps it's reinforced in case fights break out? I wouldn't be surprised if that was the case. With how easily provoked people are in the Immortal Continent, fights should break out every other day in this restaurant. But why was Lucia blatantly provoking people as well? Oh, right. She's an idiot. That's why.

One of the young women that was standing behind the elder stepped forward. "Master! Look at how poorly she's treating you, an elder of the Azure Dragon Sect! Allow your disciple to teach her a lesson!"

Was it just me … or did she have the same look in her eye when addressing her master that Lucia had when she wanted to tear off Durandal's clothes? I, I think she really does. Is she a pervert or is liking older men the norm around here? The other women are staring at Durandal with probing expressions, so I guess the first one was just a pervert.

"Idiot!" The elder slapped the back of the outspoken woman's head. "If you can't sense her realm, she's stronger than you! She's a saint-realm expert that doesn't fear our Azure Dragon Sect; what should you infer from that!?"

The woman bit her lower lip and stared up at her master with teary eyes. "That she has eyes but can't see Mount Hai?"

What's Mount Hai?

"Fool!" The elder slapped the back of her head again. "Who's the one that can't see Mount Hai!? It's you! Apologize to the lady right now!"

"M-Master," the woman said, tears rolling down her cheeks. The elder snorted so hard that steam came out of his nose and instantly dried the tears on the woman's face. Yup, like I thought earlier, that's really gross. The lady put away her childish expression and glared at Lucia before lowering her head. "I apologize for my outburst."

Lucia blinked, then turned her head to stare at me, her eyes asking for help. Why was she asking me for help!? What's wrong with this scenario that you need me to help you? Knowing Lucia, she was probably thinking something stupid like robbing a group of people without guilt by becoming a victim and now her plans were completely ruined. Lucia mouthed the words, 'I wanted to rob them,' and pointed at the elder's group. …It's sad how well I know Lucia. Being around her for a year has taken a toll on my sanity.

"Won't you forgive this disciple of mine?" the elder asked as he naturally walked over to Lucia's side and sat by her. What was he doing acting like this place was his home? For the record, I'm sitting on Durandal's right while Lucia's sitting on his left and the table's a round circle with a circular bench around it. The door is directly to my right, so no one can sit beside me. Why am I sitting next to Durandal and not Lucia? Because I know how Lucia gets when it comes to restaurants. She's paranoid about being poisoned, but she constantly wants to try new food. So instead of asking me to cast an anti-poison spell on every meal because she thinks it'll ruin the taste, she'd feed me a piece of every dish to make sure it wasn't toxic. And Lucia eats a lot. Every time I'm used as an experimental poison dummy, I have to vomit three to four times in the bathroom to make space for more food.

"Um. What if I don't want to?" Lucia asked. Occasionally, Lucia can formulate a plan—but only when it comes to money, acorns, or hot chocolate—but the instant her plan goes awry, she turns into an idiot. No, that's not right. She reverts back to her idiotic self. Also, she'll forget any plan she makes if she's distracted once. It's upsetting, really. Lucia asks, read orders, me to plan things for her, but the instant something new appears, all the plans I previously set are ruined.

"Nonsense, she's barely thirty years old, you can't expect her to act maturely," the elder said. Thirty years old!? She looks eighteen! And what do you mean a thirty-year-old can't act maturely? I know some thirty-year-old grandmothers! The elder chuckled as he leaned forward and grabbed the teapot in the center of the table before pouring himself a cup. "My name is Strong Bear, but you can call me Brother Bear. What can I call you, Sister?"

"...Lucia."

Yup, Lucia's stunned because her plan failed. She's hopeless now. And Strong Bear? Is that really his name? That sounds like something Lucia would kill and eat for breakfast.

"Sister Lucia," the elder said as he stroked his equally-long-and-thin-as-his-mustache white beard. "You ordered all four peacocks the restaurant had. Surely you can't finish it all with only the three of you—especially since there are two beautiful women; how about you share with my group? What do you say?"

Was he saying beautiful women couldn't eat a lot? That's sexist. And incorrect. Lucia's stomach is unending. Lucia turned towards me, her eyes begging me for help. What was wrong with her? This is the second time in two days that I've seen her so flustered. The first time was when she thought Black Devil Shu was coming onto her. The second time is now ... when she was complimented by Strong Bear. ...Don't tell me she's weak to compliments? That can't be. Back at home, she was always complimented for being strong and heroic and brave and ... manly. Has she never been called beautiful before...? Oh my lord, she's actually weak to compliments on her appearance.

"Hmm? You want your junior's opinion? How considerate, madam," Strong Bear said and smiled at me. "What do you say?" He must've seen my hesitation because he followed up with something outrageous, "I'll pay for the whole meal."

"Deal!" Lucia shouted. Everyone except Durandal and me flinched at that sudden outburst. "No take-backs!"

***

My perfectly laid out plan to rob these people was ruined. But that doesn't matter! The only thing more enjoyable than robbing people is free food! Food always tastes a little better when it's free; it's like adding an exotic spice.

The door creaked open and the waiter poked his head inside the room. "The problem has been settled? The first dish is ready."

"Bring it in!" I'm hungry! When was the last time I ate? Last night I had snake stew for dinner. I didn't get to eat my midnight snack or before-dawn meal because of Durandal! I missed two whole meals; it's no wonder why I'm starving. Ever since I reached the legendary realm, my food requirements jumped by a humongous amount. Luckily, all that food is converted into energy that's spent somewhere and doesn't accumulate as fat. There's no such thing as a fat squirrel—they're called slow-moving treats in hawk and owl language.

"Oh? The peacock's already ready? I thought they took a while to cook due to their size," Brother Bear said. Ah! I actually ended up calling him Brother Bear without noticing! Look at how old he looks! He's balding with a white mustache and beard, and he's super thin and bony too. I wouldn't be surprised if he went to sleep tonight and never woke up. How can someone this old be my brother? I'm youthful and vibrant and beautiful! Mhm. That's right. I'm beautiful! Brother Bear said so. Ah! I called him brother again. I'll call him Grandpa Bear from now on.

"No, the first dish is a fried river crocodile," the waiter said as he pushed against the doorframe. The wall slid to the side like magic! Two people dressed in white walked into the room while holding up a lizard-like thing with a small roasted boar in its mouth. They placed it on the table before leaving the room, pulling the wall back into place. "Enjoy. Your refreshments will be ready shortly."

"Ah…," Grandpa Bear said as he stroked his beard. "A fried river crocodile. An interesting choice of appetizer. …At least it's not very expensive."

"That's an alligator," Ilya said. Hmm? Is there a difference? A fried lizard is a fried lizard. "You can tell by the snout."

"Oh, this junior must be a beast tamer," one of the women by Grandpa Bear said. What was that look of disdain in her eyes? I can tell when someone's looking down on someone from a mile away! After all, I was always looked down on for the first two decades of my life.

Ilya snorted. "I'm not a beast tamer." She met my eyes. …Then she looked like she was considering something. "Actually…?"

Hey! I'm not a beast, dammit, Ilya! And who tamed who!? If anything, you're my pet encyclopedia!

Ilya shivered, and her shivering had nothing to do with my qi threatening to slaughter her. Nothing at all. "I'm not a beast tamer. It's just common sense to know how to differentiate crocodiles from alligators."

Is it? Sometimes I'm not sure which sock goes on my right foot and which goes on my left. But that's only when I'm sleepy and just woke up! It doesn't happen any other time! I swear. Anyways, time to dig in! I summoned two forks from my interspacial ring and stabbed them into the crocodile. Alligator? Lizard. I stabbed them into the lizard and tore off a chunk of flesh the size of Ilya's head. This should be the right ratio to check for poison. If there's too little meat, then the taster might get lucky and avoid being poisoned. If there's too much meat, then there'll be too little left for me to eat! "Grandpa Bear! Try this."

"G-Grandpa?" Grandpa Bear coughed and pounded his chest with the fleshy part of his fist. "Who are you calling a grandpa!? I'm only two centuries old! If I—waguah!?"

Yeah, yeah. Only I'm allowed to call myself young when I know I'm not exactly that young. More importantly, is my meal poisoned or not? Of course, I only used one fork to stuff the head-sized piece of meat into Grandpa's Bear mouth. I have to use the other fork for myself. Only Durandal's allowed to share my spit! Wait, no, that's not what I meant—I didn't have any spit on my forks. I'll only ingest Durandal's spit! There we go. While Grandpa Bear is chewing, I'll ready a piece of the boar too.

"S-Sister Lucia," Grandpa Bear said. His face was red, and he looked a bit constipated. Hopefully that wasn't due to any poison. Now try the boar! "Th—aguck!"

"How is it?" Poison? No poison? He looks like he's about to die, but I can't tell if that's because he's choking or not.

"M-Master!" the annoying woman shouted. She glared at me. "What are you do—ingeh!?"

I've gotten really good at flinging food into people's mouths. Ilya always tries to run away from me when I need a poison tester, so I developed a separate method of distribution! I call it the Unrelenting Path of Slaughter: Food Flinging Technique. Of course, that name's a bit too long, so I don't bother saying it out loud. Besides, people will expect it if I say it.

Ilya cut out a piece of the lizard and placed it onto her plate. Why did she look so happy? That's definitely the kind of expression Durandal makes when someone else is suffering…. They're both sadists. It's sad how I'm the only normal person amongst my three companions. Puppers is a masochist, by the way, not a sadist. Anyways, time to feast!

Thirteen dishes later, Grandpa Bear and his disciples were groaning and frothing from their mouths. I tied them down so they couldn't run away, and I had the waiter bring in some buckets in case my poison testers vomited. So far, the waiter had to replace four buckets.

"The first peacock is ready; it'll be your next dish," the waiter said after I cleared away the fourteenth plate. It was a giant centipede that I mostly fed to my guests because it creeped me out how its legs were still moving even though it was dead. But it's finally time to eat my fake phoenix! Oh, and for some reason, I managed to plant seven new heart devils even though there were only six poison testers. I think I frightened the waiter.

***

This is refreshing. No wonder why Durandal and Puppers never help me out when Lucia is stuffing my face with food. The panicked expressions they make, the groans that accompany them, the desperate struggles for air, and the pale faces trying to keep the food down to preserve their dignity: It's healing to the soul. ...I've become a sadist, haven't I?

Well, this meal has been a really nice one. The refreshments and meat have some sort of intrinsic property that counteracts my withdrawal symptoms. My headache's completely gone, and my body is brimming with mana. It's a little like eating divine beast meat when I was still a fifth-circle magician. Eating saint-realm beasts is doing wonders for my development. I can feel the outline of my ninth circle taking shape.

And these peacocks…. I thought they were going to be the size of a chicken since birds don't get very large despite an increase in their strength, but I was wrong. They're huge—about the size of a cow. Lucia's poison testers weren't very happy despite the fact they came here to eat the peacocks. But that's probably because they've vomited several times now. I know their pain. Which is why I'm allowed to enjoy their suffering without guilt. Only those who've gone through hardship can mock others undergoing a lighter hardship!

"What!? The Azure Dragon Sect are in the VIP suite too!?"

That voice sounded familiar. What happened to the soundproof walls? A few seconds later, Black Devil Shu burst into the room with black qi-like energy surrounding him: Lucia continued to eat her peacock, the six poison testers were unresponsive, Durandal was still meditating, and it seemed like I was the only one available to greet the guest. "Hello."

Black Devil Shu paused and nodded. "Junior Ilya, greetings. So, uh, what's going on here?"

"These kind people have offered to pay for the meal." Though they didn't know Lucia ordered everything on the menu. I wonder how much they regret it. But I don't think they're in the right state to regret anything at the moment.

"…So why do they look so dead?"

"That's just how the cookie crumbles."

"What's a cookie?"

They don't have cookies on the Immortal Continent? "Forget it."

Black Devil Shu shook his head and walked around the table. "Stinking Bear! What do you think you're doing getting so close to a disciple of my sect?"

"D-Devil Shu, is that you?" The old poison tester was wheezing. "T-tell my sect master … that I'm sorry. I, I swore to die for the sect…, but my time has come … early."

The door to the suite swung open as the two assistant chefs pushed open the sliding wall. The last plate of peacock was placed onto the table. Lucia's eyes gleamed as she shoved all of what was currently on her plate into her mouth and reached forward with her forks. An unreasonably large piece of meat—about the size of my torso—was ripped off the bird.

"P-please, no more," the old poison tester whimpered.

Black Devil Shu furrowed his brow. "What's going on? Why…." His eyes widened to the size of saucers as the piece of meat vanished into the old poison tester's mouth.

"Oh! Hey, Mr. Shoe. I didn't see you there!" Lucia waved at Black Devil Shu and beamed at him before dragging the rest of the peacock onto her plate. I didn't take any because I was full. Even though it was just a few mouthfuls here and there, I did eat seventeen other dishes. And the refreshments left me bloated. "Did you want some?"

"Uh, that's—"

"Great! More for me," Lucia said. She opened her mouth wide and chomped into the peacock like an absolute savage. Were her teeth reddish-black from her Path of Slaughter? She was using her Path of Slaughter to eat? How hungry was she? Within a few seconds, half of the peacock vanished into her stomach which didn't seem to grow despite the ridiculous amount she consumed. Does she have a pocket dimension in there or something?

"Well, it's true that the Shadow Devil Sect and the Azure Dragon Sect have a hostile relationship with each other, but … killing them in this manner, isn't it a bit too harsh?" Black Devil Shu asked.

The dying poison tester's eyes widened. "Y-you," he said and coughed out a mouthful of vomit while pointing at Lucia. Gross. At least the vomit slid off of Lucia's invisible Armor of Slaughter and rolled into the bucket. "You're from the Shadow Devil Sect?"

"That's right," Black Devil Shu said, responding for Lucia. She was halfway through what remained of the peacock. "She's going to be a chosen."

"Chosen!?" the woman who was in love with her master shouted. Then she tilted over and puked into a bucket. If it wasn't for my tiny wind spell pushing the fumes away from this section of the table, then I'm sure the meal would've been quite unappetizing. "You, a chosen of the Shadow Devil Sect, didn't divulge something as important as this and even ate with your enemies!?"

"Ah?" Lucia stopped eating. "We're enemies?"

"Our Azure Dragon Sect has never been on good terms with the Shadow Devil Sect ever since the Shadow Devil Ancestor slept with our Azure Dragon Ancestor's wife," the old poison tester said.

Well, it seems like Lucia's idiocy disabled a potential threat before it could come to fruition. It must be very frustrating for them. I would know. Normally, I'm on the other end of Lucia's whimsical nature. Maybe coming to the Immortal Continent wasn't a misfortune. If other people suffer in my stead, then I'll have an enjoyable life from now on, right?

"Oh...," Lucia said and chewed on the tips of her fork. "But I'm not officially part of the Shadow Devil Sect yet, so we can still be buddies, right?" She laughed and thumped the old poison tester's back, causing another waterfall of undigested food to spew out.

"M-Master!"

"You're going to be a chosen! You can't be buddies with the elder of another sect!" Black Devil Shu shouted. A sword appeared in his hands, and Durandal's eyes shot open with a gleam. Black Devil Shu pointed at the old poison tester. "Leave my junior's side at once!"

"Sister Lucia and I have already become martial sister and martial brother! Who are you to say who my martial sister can or cannot associate with!?" The old poison tester slammed his palm against the table and rose to his feet. Well, he tried to, but the chain that was wrapped around his neck prevented him from standing. Where did Lucia get something that strong...?

"Ah? Grandpa Bear?" Lucia asked, her eyes widening. "You're too old to be my martial brother!" Then Lucia turned and whispered to me, "What's a martial? Is it like a partial brother? He meant to say partial, right?"

"I think he meant martial, like martial from martial arts." Maybe a martial brother is like a brother from another mother, that kind of relationship. But to treat Lucia as his sibling, isn't the old poison tester asking for his life to be cut short?

"Is that really the case?" Black Devil Shu asked Lucia with a dark expression on his face. Black qi was rising around his sword. And Durandal's eyes were gleaming even brighter than ever, staring at the carvings on the surface of the blade. Now that I think about it, where did Black Devil Shu get a sword? Lucia robbed him blind. He must've used his elder token and brought it somewhere that let him reequip himself.

"Look at how unreasonable this smelly devil is being," the old poison tester said and pointed at Black Devil Shu while smiling at Lucia. "Why don't you join our Azure Dragon Sect instead? We're one of the fingers of Kong County as well. We don't fear the Shadow Devil Sect."

Was he poaching Lucia? Why was she so wanted?

Lucia sighed and shook her head. The remains of the peacock caught her eye, and she stuffed it into her mouth. Then she cleared her throat and took on a serious expression while crossing her arms over her chest. "Then it can't be helped. Since two groups want me so badly … it's time for an auction! Give me your best offers."

***

The auction didn't take very long. Mr. Shoe won because Grandpa Bear fainted after the waiter handed him the bill. I think a second heart devil was planted inside Grandpa Bear, but I'm not sure. I'm still not that familiar with this cultivation technique, and I have no intentions of using it. The first time was painful enough. In the end, Mr. Shoe bought all the swords and spears in the weapon shop that Durandal wanted to go to. Why spears? For Puppers, of course! I'm not so biased as to forget about my precious fluffy socks. He has to eat too. Mm, I'm a fair owner. You can ask Puppers; he'll definitely agree if he doesn't want to be beaten by me.

Not only did I receive a ton of weapons from Mr. Shoe, but he also gave me a bunch of rare and precious books, according to him. Too bad I can't read. I was also promised the best treatment from the Shadow Devil Sect, and he told me that he notified the sect master about me when he went off with his elder token. I'm going to get a huge greeting befitting of a chosen! …Whatever that means; it's hard to not sound excited when I already know the Shadow Devil Sect is super-duper rich. I mean, just look at the flying boat. According to

Ilya, I can buy 100,000 barrels of hot chocolate with the amount of spirit stones it takes to operate the boat for a single day. ...And that's why we're walking to the Shadow Devil Sect.

"That doesn't look safe."

Just kidding. Mr. Shoe's trying to teach us how to fly on swords. And Ilya's the first volunteer! People might not believe me when I say this..., but squirrels can't fly. We're not birds. This is completely unnatural. I can jump really far and really high, but fleas can do that too. But fleas are named fleas and not flies because flies are the bugs that can fly. Why aren't fleas named jumps? Huh, how weird. Anyways, what was I thinking about? Right! Flying swords. Why's Ilya crouching over the sword instead of flying on it?

Mr. Shoe was clearly confused too. "Junior Ilya? What are you doing?"

"I'm analyzing the energy lines inside of the sword and comparing them to a magical array. They're extremely similar. If I copy this design for my boots, then I'm sure they'll work even in the presence of predators. I think I can do it." Ilya took out a pair of boots and grabbed the sword. Then she stepped off to the side, ignoring us.

"...You have a strange servant," Mr. Shoe said to me. Ilya's not a servant. She's an encyclopedia. And friend. Yeah, friend first. A handy encyclopedic friend. But if she's a friend first, then she'd be a handy friendly encyclopedia, no? Ah..., I need to carve out a focus bone. Good thing I stored all these bones from those meals we had! Did you know fish are extremely easy to strip of their bones? It's difficult to carve on them because they're so small, but all I have to do is squint really hard to see clearer!

Mr. Shoe cleared his throat. "Is that a dead fish?"

I'm pretty sure it's dead...? Don't tell me the fish on the Immortal Continent are immortals too! "Is it!? How do I check!?"

"Uh…, sorry. I think there's been a miscommunication."

"Miscommunication, my ass! Tell me if it's dead or not!" What if its flesh is squirming around my stomach!? All those things I ate could be competing with each other! Surely, the smallest morsel of food will consume slightly larger morsels as it becomes bigger itself, then it'll eat even the largest thing inside and end up eating me in the end too! This is a disaster!

"It's dead! Junior Lucia, it's dead! Please, please, please, watch your language." Mr. Shoe's face was bright red.

Language? Did I say something bad? "…Ass?"

Mr. Shoe's face turned even redder. If any more blood rushed to his face, it'd start leaking out of his pores. Why are people so bloody in the Immortal Continent? Coughing out blood when I state facts about their small penises, vomiting out blood when they see a restaurant bill, blood flooding their faces when they hear the word ass. Jeez. "Junior Lucia…. People won't view you in a good light if you act in such a crude manner."

"…The penis goes into the v—"

Mr. Shoe brought his hand to his mouth and coughed extremely loudly, cutting off my words. Blood trickled through his fingers and down the back of his hand. "F-forget I said anything."

This kind of reaction…. "Say, Mr. Shoe, are you a virgin by any chance?"

More blood leaked out of Mr. Shoe's mouth as he flinched. A familiar feeling welled up in my chest. This was … the overwhelming pleasure from sadism! Just kidding, I'm not a sadist. It was actually the feeling of me planting a heart devil in someone. The two feelings are very similar though. …Not that I would know! Ah, I feel a little bad now. His disciple died and a stranger, me, learned his secret technique and used it on him. I'll comfort him with words—Ilya says I'm good with words as long as I keep them to myself. But good things are meant to be shared! "Don't worry too much about it, Mr. Shoe! I'll find you a nice woman around your age, so you two can settle down. How old are you? Two hundred?"

"I'm only ninety-eight!" Mr. Shoe shouted as he took a step back, clutching his chest. "I, I already have a woman that I love!"

"But…?" There's a but somewhere in there. You don't love someone for ninety-eight years and not do anything about it!

Mr. Shoe sighed and lowered his head. "But she's married."

"Oh." Well…. "Have you tried making her husband disappear?"

Mr. Shoe's eyes widened to the size of saucers. "W-what kind of person do you think I am!?"

Hah…. This is why I don't like giving advice to people. They don't even know what kind of person they themselves are; how am I supposed to help them if they don't want to perform introspection to help themselves? He's hopeless.

"Please don't look at me with those eyes."

Did I just plant another heart devil?

"A-alright!" Mr. Shoe shouted as he whirled around. "We're taking the flying boat! I'll shoulder all the costs!"

For the rest of the journey to the Shadow Devil Sect, Mr. Shoe never left his room. But I've been in that room before and I can confirm that there's no bathroom in there. Maybe he poops in an interspacial ring. Either way, I'm not sure if I can view him the same way as I have been before today. Then again, I never really viewed him in a positive light anyway. Oh wells. Shadow Devil Sect, here I come! …I'm definitely going to have to figure out a way to rename it something less ominous.

Chapter 6

My name is Soft Moonlight. I am the only chosen of the Shadow Devil Sect. After today, that will no longer be the case. Sect Elder Shu discovered a talented individual on his trip to the sky and earth pocket realm. Apparently, this individual cultivated the Heart Devil Cultivation Technique for a single day and reached the ninth layer. For reference, I'm only at the seventh layer of the Heart Devil Cultivation Technique despite the fact I've been practicing it for over a decade. If Sect Elder Shu's report is true, then my standing in the sect will fall…, unless the individual is a man; in that case, my grandfather, the sect leader, may force me into a marriage with the new chosen.

"Isn't that Sister Moonlight?"

I nodded at the fellow disciple on the path and continued on my way. Anywhere I go within the sect, people recognize me. They flatter and heap praise upon me, hoping to become acquainted. With a single sentence, I can gather an army of willing and able men to destroy anything in my path. It's not unusual for me to receive gifts every day from my suitors. But not today. Today, everyone is preparing for the arrival of the new chosen. The gifts that are supposed to be mine are being prepared for someone else. The attention that should be mine is directed elsewhere. The gossip that should be about me is no longer about me.

"I hope the new chosen is more approachable than Sister Moonlight. She's such a frigid bit—"

"Shush! Sister Moonlight's coming this way."

Some people don't realize one's hearing is improved upon reaching the saint realm. But I don't mind. As the chosen of the Shadow Devil Sect, I have to be frigid. I have to be stoic. No matter how scared I am, I have to confront things with an unwavering heart to save face for the sect. I am the poster child, and the poster child is not allowed to cry. But after today, there will be a new poster child along with me. He or she will take half the burden off my shoulders, or even the whole burden if the rumors of his or her ability are true. And for that, I am thankful. I really, really hate my position as the chosen of the sect, but I'm the sect leader's granddaughter; it's not like I can refuse. There's nothing I want more in the world than to run away and live out the remainder of my life in a small village, free from all responsibility.

I don't need attention. I don't need suitors. I don't need gifts. Rejecting three people per day, week after week, wears down on a girl. And some men don't take rejection kindly! Speaking of suitors, here comes one now.

"Sister Moonlight! I've loved you for years! Please, marry me!"

"I'm sorry. My grandfather doesn't want me to be in a relationship. If you become a saint-realm expert, our love could truly blossom." Then I walked past him. I really, really hate rejecting people because my grandfather won't let me properly reject them! And even if I try to make my words sound as fake as possible, these men cling onto them as if they're ropes keeping them from falling into the abyss. It's all a ploy by my grandfather. He wants me to make as many men fall in love with me as possible, so that once I get married, all of them will gain a heart devil.

"I'll do my best, Sister Moonlight!"

Please don't. I'm so tired of this kind of life. I don't have any real friends. There's no one I can trust. If I told my grandfather about my real feelings, I'd be spanked and thrown into a room to meditate in seclusion for a year. After walking a bit further, I finally reached the entrance of the sect. The million sect members were separated by rank: outer sect disciples, inner sect disciples, core disciples, me, elders, grand elders, the sect leader, and the sect ancestors. That's the way it should've been, but the sect ancestors are always in seclusion, trying to break through to the sky realm. And since I'm also the sect leader's granddaughter, I'm allowed to sit by him.

"Grandfather." I lowered my head, and my grandfather patted the seat beside him.

"Come, sit."

There's something that's been bothering me for a while now. "Grandfather, why do we need to host such an elaborate ceremony for the new chosen?"

My grandfather stroked his beard. "It's … part of the terms Elder Shu negotiated with her."

"Her?"

"The chosen. Her name is Lucia Fluffytail."

It seems like I won't be getting married anytime soon. What a shame. Wait. "Negotiated?"

"She's from the pocket realm, so she doesn't understand the might of the Shadow Devil Sect. This is a show of force."

"Oh." Right. She was a bumpkin. I heard bumpkins make great friends. Could it be possible for me to become her friend…? A familiar sight in the sky came towards us. "The boat is here, grandfather."

"Yes." My grandfather nodded. He was an earth-realm expert, so he should've realized it was coming way before me. I feel silly now. "I wonder what the chosen will say after seeing this sight."

It *was* a very grand sight. A million people sat in neat rows, all dressed in the same black outfit. Everyone had taken out some spirit stones and placed them on the ground around them so that the whole place would sparkle if seen from the sky. My grandfather had even activated the grand formation that was meant to defend our sect. Of course, the formation wasn't in defense mode but in welcoming mode. Which meant translucent golden dragons and phoenixes were flying about a few characters that read, "Welcome to the Shadow Devil Sect, Lucia Fluffytail!"

The flying boat came closer and closer before coming to a stop above the gate that was the sect entrance. I squinted up at the bow of the boat. There were four figures: a handsome man who was eating … a sword, a young girl with purple skin, Elder Shu, and a woman with rounded fox ears and a very bushy foxtail. The last one must've been Lucia Fluffytail. Lucia's mouth dropped open. Was she going to say something?

"Fuck! That's a shitload of people!"

For the first time—in probably the whole history of the sect—there was not a single sound. If a pin dropped on the ground a mile away, I could probably hear it. What happened next was equally baffling. The boat did a massive U-turn and sped away.

***

"Junior Lucia! What are you doing!?"

What the hell was Mr. Shoe shouting about!? Did he not see that huge fucking crowd!? "Fleeing! What does it look like?"

"Why!?"

"Why are you shouting at me!?" I don't like it when people shout at me! I don't need his help panicking; I can do that just fine by myself, thank you very much. "No one told me there'd be that many people waiting for me!"

"I told you that you'd receive a welcoming ceremony befitting a chosen!"

"I don't want to be a chosen anymore!"

"You don't want to be a chosen anymore?"

…Wait. Mr. Shoe sounds like a middle-aged man. Durandal sounds like the sexiest man in the world. Ilya sounds like a teenaged girl. And Puppers is out of commission. So who the fuck just spoke in a grandfatherly voice!? "Who are you and how did you get on my boat!?"

The stranger that appeared out of nowhere cleared his throat while stroking his beard. "This is my boat."

"Huh?" That's not possible. It's mine. I stole it from Mr. Shoe; thus, the boat is rightfully mine. Everyone knows the rules: finders, keepers. I'm not going to let this delusional old man try to stake a claim on my boat!

"Elder Shu greets the sect leader!"

He's the sect leader? He looks like the friendly acorn-stew-selling grandpa from next door. Minus the cute ears and bushy tail, that is.

"Junior Lucia! Why aren't you greeting the sect leader?"

Eh? "Um. Hi."

"Not like that!"

"Don't worry, Elder Shu," the friendly grandpa said with a smile. "She's not from around these parts. Perhaps they aren't as stiff with formalities in the sky and earth plane. Junior Lucia…."

"Hmm?"

"Do you mind stopping the boat?"

I do. I mind very greatly. If I don't rush away as fast as I can, I'll be assimilated into that mob of people dressed in black robes. It's like attending a funeral, fuck! What welcoming ceremony befitting a chosen? It's like they were seeing a corpse off! …But judging from the look the grandpa's giving me, if I don't stop this boat, I *will* become a corpse. Is this grandpa strong? How strong is he? Should I hit him once to see how strong he is? I'm going to do it. "Receive my attack. Unrelenting Path of Slaughter: Breaking Blade!"

"Junior Lucia!?"

Mr. Shoe shouted, but the grandpa wasn't flustered at all! He raised one arm, and a black shield made of the worms that looked like the heart devil qi thingies appeared out of nowhere. I don't believe a flimsy shield made of worms can stop mini-DalDal! Full power! Five hundred tons!

Bonk.

My beliefs were wrong. How did a flimsy shield made of worms stop mini-DalDal!? The grandpa smiled at me as something pushed me away from him. "Not bad, Junior Lucia. But it'll be a few more decades before you can hope to compete with me. Let me see you channel the Heart Devil Cultivation Technique."

"...Can I refuse?"

"Refuse? Why?" The friendly grandpa tilted his head as the shield disappeared. "Didn't Elder Shu say you cultivated it to the ninth layer in a single day?"

"The ninth what?" The cultivation technique has layers? Oh right, it does. I learned everything about the technique through that glowing light, but I also mentally chose to block everything about the technique because of how traumatizing it was to learn and use it. It was really painful, okay? "Mm. Maybe I did cultivate it to the ninth layer. But it was too painful! I don't want to use it anymore."

"Painful? Ah." The grandpa nodded and smiled at me. "It's only painful the first time, Junior Lucia. The next time you use it, it'll feel pleasurable."

He wants me to say it, doesn't he? Phrasing it like that, how am I supposed to not say it? "So it's like sex?"

Mr. Shoe buried his face into his hands. The grandpa didn't say anything, but his expression was a bit stiff. Okay, it was very stiff. He set up that punchline! It's not my fault! I, I guess I'll just channel the Heart Devil Cultivation Technique to distract him. Mm. Let's do it. Hopefully, the grandpa's right and it ends up not being painful. Okay, qi, do your stuff! A few loops over there, some swivels over here, some circles around the stomach..., hmm, this doesn't feel right...? Does it change every time I do it? Well, that's okay. Five circles around the stomach instead of four! And we're done.

The grandpa was still looking at me with a stiff face. No, he was looking past me at Mr. Shoe. "Elder Shu, did two heart devils just…."

"Yes." Mr. Shoe hung his head like a dejected puppy. "She…, yes. Yes…. I want to cry."

Ooh, that tingles. The two worms from Mr. Shoe and one worm from Ilya disappeared inside of me, but unlike last time, it didn't hurt! It really didn't hurt! Fill the skies and enter me, heart devil wormies! …Any second now. No? Maybe I can't harvest heart devils from the sky and earth plane? That's a bummer. Ah, there's a few worms heading here now. One, two, three, four, five…, they're moving too fast! If I had to guess, I'd say there were twenty of them. That's so little….

The grandpa gasped. "There's so many heart devils gathered in two days! Elder Shu didn't judge your natural talents incorrectly."

Whew, so many tingles. It's a shame it's still daytime otherwise I'd vent on Durandal right now. I wonder if immortals can make the sun disappear at will. Hmm. Well, even if it was nighttime, it wouldn't be appropriate because we're back at the sect. …We're back at the sect? But I didn't command the boat to move! This grandpa's too sneaky!

The grandpa stood at the bow of the boat, his robes flapping in the wind. I have to admit, he looks cool. I bet Durandal would look even better though if he took that same pose. "Everyone, I'd like you to greet the new chosen of our sect, Lucia Fluffytail!"

"We greet Lucia Fluffytail!"

The boat shook from everyone shouting at the same time. I'm getting shivers. This … is so awesome! It's not scary at all since they're all greeting me! I, I like it. Worship me more!

"I disagree with her placement!"

Eh? Who's raining on my parade?

***

My grandfather successfully brought Lucia Fluffytail back to the sect. As planned, we gave her a proper greeting. What wasn't planned was the sudden shout that ruined the atmosphere. A core disciple stood up and pointed his sword at the flying boat. "How can we allow a stranger to become a chosen of the sect?"

My grandfather landed the boat and appeared by my side, using an instant teleportation that only earth-realm experts and above could achieve. It takes a lot of qi to shift one's body like that. My grandfather leaned over and whispered to me, "Who's that?"

"Grandfather! You're the sect leader! How do you not know?"

"There's a million people in the sect! I have trouble remembering the ten thousand essential herbs for alchemy; how am I supposed to recognize everyone?"

I sighed. "That's Flying Forest; he's the number one core disciple on the rankings. He broke through to the mid-low-ranked saint-realm level a week ago." I'll be honest; I don't know all the sect members either. I just happen to know Flying Forest because I rejected him two days ago. He's one of the people who doesn't take well to rejection, and I instantly planted a heart devil inside of him. If it wasn't for my status as a chosen, I'm sure he would've attacked me. As a cultivator of the Heart Devil Cultivation Technique, it's easy to read the emotions of someone I've traumatized.

"He's a mid-low-ranked saint-realm expert?" My grandfather raised his eyebrows. They were like fluffy white caterpillars with a little tail trailing off his face. "He didn't want to become an elder?"

"Right. When I rejected him, he told me he'd become a chosen to teach me my place." There are a lot of benefits to being a chosen instead of an elder; namely, one can practice the higher levels of the Heart Devil Cultivation Technique.

For someone to become a chosen, they have to reach the sixth layer. In other words, they have to plant heart devils in 300,000 people. ...Like I said, I have a lot of suitors. It also helps that I'm extremely beautiful—I'm not being narcissistic. I've given several thousands of women heart devils simply through jealousy.

That's not to say that someone who's an elder can't learn the higher levels of the Heart Devil Cultivation Technique, but an elder in the sect has to be partial and fair. The opportunities to plant heart devils drastically decreases. Losing to a fellow disciple that's younger can cause a heart devil to form, but what if a disciple loses to an elder? People are very frail and will find excuses to place the blame on their surroundings rather than themselves. I lost because he was an elder; it's only natural—that's how people think. I'm really curious as to how Lucia Fluffytail reached the ninth layer. Just what kind of person is she?

"Lucia Fluffytail, do you dare to duel me, Flying Forest!?"

Could she be using the same methods as me to cultivate heart devils? Pretending to be a frail and helpless young lady to charm the hearts of others? But judging from her previous outburst, I highly doubt that's the case. If Flying Forest challenged me to a duel, I'd turn him down while implying he's not qualified to even challenge me to stoke the heart devil inside of him. I think it's safe to say everyone in the sect is looking forward to seeing how our new chosen will react.

Lucia Fluffytail stood on top of the bow of the boat. Was she copying my grandfather's pose? Her arms were crossed over her chest, her dress fluttering in the wind. The sword hanging on the belt on her waist was at the perfect angle to catch the sunlight. It was hard to tell the finer details due to the distance, but from my objective standpoint, Lucia wouldn't be judged as a beauty using the Immortal Continent's standards. Her hair was brown instead of black. Her skin wasn't as pale as most cultivators, but she wasn't tan either. Evidently, she went outside a lot. And there was just something about her face—perhaps because it looked extremely angry—that made her seem unapproachable. Lucia opened her mouth, and her voice thundered over the crowd, "Unrelenting Path of Slaughter: Puppers Ballista!"

She raised one arm, and an armored person…? An armored wolfkin appeared out of nowhere on top of her palm. It was holding a spear that seemed to be made of cloth. What was she—she threw him!? Like a bolt of lightning, the armored wolfkin flew down from the boat and harpooned Flying Forest before he could react. …Are they dead? Have I just witnessed a murder in the sect? "…Grandfather?"

"Uh…. When I went to bring her back, she also attacked me for no reason whatsoever. Though she's only a low-low-ranked saint-realm expert, her physical strength was on par with a half-step to earth-realm expert. Much like a fire dragon."

Like a dragon? She had the physical strength of a dragon? So not only was she a genius in cultivating, but she was also a body-refiner. Cultivating the body is very arduous, and there aren't many saint-realm body-refiners in Kong County. Heck, there aren't that many in the whole of King Province. I wonder if our sect is a little too small for someone like her. I don't have any delusions of strength just because our sect is one of the powerhouses of Kong County. We're just the biggest fish in a very small pond. It doesn't mean much.

"Do you think Flying Forest is still alive?" The sect forbids killing between sect members. Will Lucia Fluffytail hold the record for breaking rules in the shortest time after joining the sect?

"Even if he isn't…, we'll say he is." My grandfather rose to his feet and teleported to Flying Forest's side. Then the two disappeared. What happened to that armored wolfkin?

"Who else wants to rain on my parade!?" Lucia Fluffytail shouted down from the boat. It was on the ground, but it was still three-stories tall.

"I do! How dare you sneak attack our sect's greatest core disciple? Do you dare accept my challenge!?"

Right, Flying Forest was the disciple of Elder Forest. Their similar names are not a coincidence; they happen to be grandfather and grandson. And Elder Forest is also one of the strongest elders in the sect; he's actually my grandfather's greatest rival for position as sect leader. If I'm not wrong, he wanted to make Flying Forest the next sect leader. How will Lucia Fluffytail react? Her tail was sticking straight up like a lightning rod. It seemed like that was her 'getting serious' pose.

"Oh, whew, look at the position of the sun. It's second-breakfast time! I guess we'll have to continue this challenge some other day. Bye!"

…I think I have a firm grasp on this new chosen's personality.

***

"I'll fight him."

"Eh?" Lucia looked at me with a baffled expression. "Are you sure, Durandal? He's making my tail stiff, and we both know I'm stronger than you."

…There's no need to rub it in like that. "I'm going to fight him."

"But if you die…."

"Then I'll be back in a week; there's no issue." Really, there isn't. As long as the core in mini-DalDal's hilt remains untouched, I'll be fine. The only reason I was out of commission for so long when Lucia was poisoned was due to me transferring the poison to my core.

"There's a serious issue! How am I supposed to go without sex for a week?"

This girl. Why is she so lewd? "I'm sure you'll manage. You've lasted decades without it."

"That's because I never had it before! But now that I know what it feels like, I—"

I kissed Lucia on the lips because that's the quickest way to make her fall silent. Then I retrieved a sword from her interspacial ring. This wasn't my normal sword that wasn't augmented; it was a special sword that I picked up from the weapon shop, courtesy of Black Devil Shu. When it was reinforced with qi, special formations inside of the blade would amplify the qi. There's also a function to command it from afar, but a real swordsman fights in close combat. Hmm? I said something about only using a normal sword to fight people with? Are you sure? I don't recall. If Lucia can use this excuse to retract her statements, so can I.

"You're not the one who sneak attacked my grandson." The person who had challenged Lucia was standing on the bow of the boat. Lucia was behind me, inside of the boat's uppermost cabin. Ilya was hiding behind Lucia, and Black Devil Shu was hiding behind Ilya. Why was Black Devil Shu hiding from his own sect member?

"I'm not, but I'll be the one fighting you." Since Lucia's not frightened by any saint-realm experts, there's a high possibility that this man is an earth-realm expert. He also looks extremely old, so there's that too. Normally, the older someone is, the more likely they are to be weak, but given the nature of the Immortal Continent, the norms have been reversed.

The old man snorted. "Getting in my way? You're courting death!" He raised his hand and slapped downwards even though he was standing ten feet away from me. A giant palm materialized in the sky above his head, crashing towards the ship.

Though it's true an earth-realm expert would have more qi than me, that doesn't mean I can't win. To condense something as large as that palm, the qi would be spread out equally. If I focus all of my qi into the tip of my sword, I should be able to cut through a small section of the palm. Like so!

Ilya and Lucia screamed while running away. Though I cut a small hole in the palm to prevent myself from getting hurt, the rest of the palm still crushed the ship. Well, it collided against the ship, but it didn't cause the vehicle any harm. How strong was this thing? Right, now wasn't the time to worry about that.

"Oh? You didn't die? Then how about th—"

While the old man was busy chattering away, I focused all my qi into my feet and lunged forwards; then I shifted my qi into the edge of my sword and slashed at him. I cut straight through his chest, but there wasn't any feedback. Did he disappear? A moment later, the man distorted and vanished, leaving behind a torn robe.

"How dare you sneak attack me!?"

He was behind me? I didn't even see him move. No, he wasn't behind. He was above!

"Rending Devil Claws!" The old man shouted from atop one of the boat's crow's nest. Five black lines appeared above me and screeched as they rushed towards my face, ripping apart the air in the way.

Did he think he was the only one that could disappear and reappear at will? Versatile Path of the Sword: Retreat into Mini-DalDal! Versatile Path of the Sword: Exit Mini-DalDal! And just like that, I avoided his attack. Is this cheating? That's up to the winner to decide! I focused my qi into my feet and stepped against the boat's mast. Then I charged vertically up. A Breaking Blade might have long range, but it'd be easily blocked. My attacks can only pierce through his defense if his qi is spread out.

"You're an earth-realm expert? That can't be! How did you disappear like that?"

Of course, I answered his question with a slash of my blade. The only time you should speak while fighting is never! Unless you're Lucia, who likes shouting out the names of her abilities. Or if you're a magician who needs to chant his spells. It seemed like the old man learned his lesson about my slash. He condensed a shield made of black worms like the one the sect leader had created to block Lucia. Unfortunately, my attacks aren't as straightforward as hers! Versatile Path of the Sword: Curving Like a Whip! My blade traced the edge of his shield and curved towards his shoulder like a serpent, drawing blood.

"You—!"

I thought he'd learn by now to not speak so much. I stepped forward, placing my leg behind his and wrapped one arm around his waist. Then I leaned forward while kicking my free foot against the mast in the crow's nest. Like that, both of us tumbled towards the deck of the ship. A fall from this height won't harm either of us, but the most important part is removing his leverage. Versatile Path of the Sword: Biting Like a Beast!

"Grah! You're biting my neck!?"

"How dare you bully Durandal! Unrelenting Path of Slaughter: Swing as Hard as I Can!"

A humongous force crashed into me and the old man from below. Like a fountain, spurts of blood shot out of the old man's mouth and splashed over me. I didn't feel much of it because I was soaring through the air and the wind was cutting my face. Since the distance I was from mini-DalDal grew too great, I was transported back inside it. I exited mini-DalDal just in time to see the old man create a small imprint amongst a faraway cloud. Perhaps there was a certain requirement to using his teleportation technique and flying through the air wasn't it.

"Phew, that was scary. I freaked out when I saw you bleeding!"

But I wasn't the one bleeding…. If anything, her attack was the one that injured me the most. I sighed and ruffled Lucia's hair, making sure to rub behind her ears. "Thanks." At least my master cares for me.

"Where's Elder Forest!?" …Wasn't the sect leader a little late? He did drag away that poor harpooned disciple, so I guess he can be forgiven. "I heard he attacked the chosen?"

Lucia pointed at the cloud with the person-shaped hole inside of it. "I smacked him far, far away."

The sect leader stared at the cloud. Then he looked at Lucia and me. "What happened while I was gone?"

***

That was incredible. The man by Lucia Fluffytail's side actually competed with Elder Forest without giving an inch. Clearly, he was just a saint-realm expert, but he managed to stand toe to toe with an earth-realm expert. Amazing people are bound to be surrounded by amazing people, huh? I guess that's why I'm all alone. …That was a joke. Even mediocre people are surrounded by mediocre people. I don't even have a mediocre friend. I'm so lonely.

"Little Moon, come up here."

Little Moon? That's me. Why was my grandfather calling for me? I rose to my feet and retrieved a flying sword from my interspacial ring. My grandfather was standing atop the bow of the boat, waving at me to come over. For some reason, I have a bad feeling about this, but what can happen to me as long as my grandfather's there? In the first place, why do I have a bad feeling about this? Just what is making me so uneasy? It must've been the breakfast I had. It definitely has nothing to do with the new chosen who's superior to me in nearly every single way.

"This is my granddaughter, Soft Moonlight. She was the only chosen of the sect until you came along." My grandfather introduced me to Lucia Fluffytail. She's ... not imposing at all. It looks like my nerves were just getting the better of me. She looks so friendly! It must be the ears and tail. They remind me of my grandmother's pet fox.

"Whoa," Lucia Fluffytail said. Her tail twitched a few times as she stared into my face. "She's as beautiful as Snow!"

As beautiful as snow? That's a compliment I've heard about two hundred times from all my suitors. Usually I'm compared to an untouched field after a night of snowfall though. Or as beautiful as moonlight softly streaming through silk curtains. My suitors think they're original because my name's Soft Moonlight, but they're all the same. It's almost depressing how similar they all are.

"She's a lot like Snow," the man beside Lucia Fluffytail said. He wasn't handsome by the Immortal Continent's standards, but there was something about him that drew my gaze towards him. His muscles were toned like a farmer's, and his skin was as tan as Lucia Fluffytail's. Most men in the Immortal Continent are pretty, not handsome. Was this man interested in me? I tried to look into his eyes, but his gaze was directed elsewhere, namely, my chest.

"Yeah! You're right!" Lucia Fluffytail said. She was looking at my chest too. "She's just as flat as Snow!"

...I will neither refute nor give a reaction to that statement.

"Are you going to...?" The purple-skinned girl by Lucia Fluffytail hesitated and gave me a look filled with ... pity?

"Let's bet, Durandal!" Lucia Fluffytail's eyes lit up as she completely ignored me and my grandfather. What did my grandfather think about this situation? He was looking away, pretending not to notice. Well, it wouldn't be appropriate for my grandfather to comment in this situation, so I can't blame him.

"Bet? On what?" the man asked. So his name was Durandal. It sounded very foreign.

"I bet Soft Moonlight's a man!" Lucia Fluffytail said while puffing her chest out.

I, what, no! I'm a woman! "N—"

"What are the stakes?" Durandal asked. His voice overpowered mine, and I thought he gave me a signal with his eyes to keep silent. "I bet she's a woman. If I win, you have to let me rest during the night for the next three days."

"What!? Three days!?" Lucia Fluffytail's tail slapped the floor of the boat. "Well, I'm not going to lose, so fine! If I win, you're not allowed to faint even if we do it thirty times!"

…What are they talking about?

"You!" Lucia Fluffytail pointed at me. A reddish-black mist was rising out of her tail. It reeked of blood. I'm scared.

"Y-yes?"

"Are you a man or a woman?"

"Didn't I introduce you as my granddaughter?" my grandfather mumbled from beside me.

Yes, yes you did, Grandfather. "I'm a woman."

"That's impossible!" Lucia Fluffytail shouted, and the reddish-black mist exploded outwards. "You're definitely a man!"

"I'm a woman!" What was wrong with Lucia Fluffytail's head? Even a buddha will get angry if provoked three times! I'm not an easy person to bully! And I also have to save face for the sect, but that's not even why I'm mad. I've never been mistaken for a man before. This is a matter of personal face!

"Looks like I win," Durandal said.

"Not yet!" Lucia Fluffytail said as she pounced towards me. Was she going to attack me? If she does, no one can blame me for being ruthless! "Hold still."

Hold still? For wha—!!!

"Eh? There's really nothing there? No! That can't be right."

H-her finger's going deeper! "S-stop!"

"Sister Moonlight!"

"The new chosen is assaulting Sister Moonlight!"

"Wife Moonlight!"

"Sister Moonlight!"

Who called me their wife just now!? I can't tell over the thousands of people shouting at once! And what is my grandfather doing!? Save me! Your granddaughter is being violated right in front of you! "G-Grandfather!"

My grandfather cleared his throat and turned his head away. ...I've been forsaken. Lucia's probing hand disappeared, but I could still feel her touch down there. I've never felt more uncomfortable in my life. I, I...

Lucia Fluffytail sighed. "Fine, you win, Durandal. She's not a man. You said three days, right? Why do you need to rest for two days? I'm perfectly willing to yield one day to you. I guess I'll fulfill my end of the bargain and leave you alone for an hour."

Durandal smacked the top of Lucia Fluffytail's head with his palm. "Shouldn't you apologize? She's crying."

I'm not crying! A chosen is not allowed to cry! ...I'm a failure of a chosen.

"Sister Moonlight! The new chosen made our goddess cry! Sister Moonlight!!!"

Stop wailing, people! It's annoying!

"H-hey," Lucia Fluffytail said to me with an awkward expression on her face. "Did I really scar you that badly? I just planted over a thousand heart devils.... It can't be healthy living with a thousand heart devils, so cheer up, okay?" She bit her lower lip. "S-sorry."

A thousand heart devils...? She only planted one!

"I'm so jealous of the new chosen!"

"My precious Moonlight's first time was taken from me!"

"Wife Moonlight!!! How could you betray me like this!?"

This goddamn peanut gallery. I'm my own person! Why are you getting heart devils when I'm the one that was violated!? "As you can see, those heart devils were planted in my suitors and secret admirers, not me."

"You have a thousand suitors?" the purple-skinned girl asked with wide eyes.

"I have a little over half a million secret admirers and over a thousand publicly announced suitors."

Lucia Fluffytail stared at me with the gaze of a hungry fox. …Did I say something wrong? Or did I look so tantalizing with tears decorating my face that my beauty transcended genders? "So … you're saying if I grope you again, I can plant up to half a million heart devils?"

"N-no! That's not what I'm saying at all! S-stop!" Then her hands…, her hands…, they…. To preserve my sanity and remove the heart devils within myself, I've mentally sealed off the next course of events.

Chapter 7

Ilya was kidnapped! She was taken away by an old lady who claimed Ilya was going to be her disciple! And Ilya willingly went with her after I refused! Mm, maybe kidnapped is the wrong term. I was robbed! Someone stole Ilya from me! She's my friendly encyclopedia that knows the answer to everything, but she's gone now. Hah. Well, there's a new encyclopedia who knows more about the Immortal Continent than Ilya does, so maybe it's not an overall loss?

"I'll visit you often, so don't make that face, Lucia." Ilya sighed from the old lady's side. She should be by my side instead! I'll remember this, old lady! I might not know your name, address, position in the sect, or anything about you, but I'll remember this!

"My grandmother will take good care of your friend. Please don't stare at her like that," Softie said. Softie is Soft Moonlight, but Soft is such an awkward name, and Moonlight is also such an awkward name, so I just call her Softie. She's a big ol' softie with lots of tears inside of her. It's a fitting name.

After I planted an additional hundred thousand or so heart devils by thoroughly marking Softie as mine in front of the whole sect, the sect leader brought us to a mountain. According to him, only chosens of the sect are allowed to live on this mountain, and no one's allowed to visit without the chosens' or sect leader's permission. That's why I'm saying goodbye to Ilya here.

"Do get along with each other now," the sect leader said. He patted Softie's shoulder. "Take her to the impurity-cleansing pool when you have the chance. I have to accommodate the elders from the other sects for the cultural exchange."

"Grandfather…." Softie had tears in her eyes. I knew her name was fitting. "Y-you're going to leave me alone with, with her? Are we even related? How could you do this to me?"

Oi. What's wrong with being left alone with me, huh? Huh? I'm a very friendly person. Everyone tells me I'm nice, and if everyone thinks it, then it can't be wrong! Besides, we're not really alone. Durandal and Puppers are here too.

"I'll see you soon, Lucia," Ilya said and waved. Then the old lady by her side smiled and nodded at me before grabbing onto Ilya and disappearing. She didn't even give me a chance to say goodbye. What if I never see Ilya again? That'd be so sad. Two friends parting without a proper farewell. Ah. I hope Ilya won't be too miserable without me around.

Once Ilya and the thief were gone, the sect leader disappeared as well. It's just me and Softie now. Softie's supposed to be my guide in the sect. Softie's shoulders shrank back as she lowered her head and looked up at me. "U-um, are you tired after your journey? Shall I show you the residences, Sister Lucia?"

"Just call me Lucia." All these sister and brother and elder and grandpa titles are so annoying to deal with.

"Eh? Are you sure? How about Chosen Lucia?"

"Lucia."

"Miss Lucia…?"

"Lucia!" I'm going to smack her.

"Y-yes! Lucia! Y-you can call me Sister Moonlight or—"

"Softie."

"Pardon?"

"I'm going to call you Softie from now on, okay, Softie?" She's a bit slow, isn't she? Mm, but that's okay. I'm used to slow people. For some reason, it takes a long time for most people to understand what I'm saying.

"Isn't that a pet's name...?" Did she have a problem with my naming sense? "Hiih! Softie it is! I like the name Softie a lot!"

Mm, that's better. It looks like Durandal's intimidation tactics work perfectly in the Immortal Continent. "What was that about residences?" The place that they're going to let me stay is bound to be filled with riches and luxuries, right? That's the whole point of being a chosen. We get special treatment. And judging by their simple transportation vehicles, a giant flying boat, their architectural standards are really high! I'm looking forward to this.

"R-right, I'll show you the way," Softie said. She couldn't look me in the eyes. Was she waddling? Why was she waddling? She probably peed her panties, huh? Oops.

This mountain looks like ... a regular mountain. There's trees, grass, dirt, rocks, an evil waterfall that's threatening to claim my soul, and a deadly river with some monstrous creatures that Softie calls koi. And there are absolutely no signs of any residences. I'm not being cheated, right? This isn't some sort of elaborate scam to harvest my organs? Well, it's not like I have any valuable organs to harvest anyways since I don't have a penis. Just like Softie.

"Lucia? Hello?" Softie's voice was really soft. One day, she won't be so nervous around me. "Is something wrong?"

"No. What's up?" Why'd we stop? We reached halfway up the mountain, but there still aren't any buildings in sight. There's only a few holes dug into the ground, but since the mountain's sloped, maybe it's more appropriate to call them caves?

"We're here. You can pick any residence you like." Softie bit her lower lip and stared at me with wet eyes. They were pleading, trying to tell me to do something. But what the heck am I supposed to do in this situation? Don't tell me the buildings are invisible.

"Where...?"

Softie bit her lower lip and pointed at the caves. "There."

"…Is this a joke?" I know I'm a squirrel, but I don't actually live in a burrow! I'm being racially profiled! I thought people didn't know about squirrels on the Immortal Continent. Wait, no, foxes live in burrows too, but still, this is wrong! "I'm more human than fox, damnit. I'm not going to live in a hole!"

"S-sorry! Please don't hurt me!" Softie covered her head and crouched down. She was shaking a lot. Hah. Why is she so timid? Isn't she supposed to be a chosen? I almost feel bad for her. She's a sheltered princess who's lived all alone and was spoiled by her grandparents. No wonder why she hasn't faced any hardships. Me being mean to her is for her own good! She has to toughen up or she'll be bullied by someone even worse than me one day. And I'm not even trying to act scary. Jeez.

"Alright. How about this. Take me to where you live." I don't know if the sect leader told her to bring me here because he thought a foxkin would like living in burrows, but I can't live in a cave. There's not even a door for privacy!

"O-okay," Softie said. She sniffled and walked forward before looking behind herself to make sure I was following, which I was. Then she walked up to one of the caves. "I live here. Um, would you like to come inside?"

Maybe I'm missing something here. There's surely another dimension inside of these caves, right? Like a personal pocket realm! That must be it. I poked my head into the cave and saw a beautiful world made of … dirt. And a dirty red carpet with a pillow. I've been scammed. This isn't a rich place at all!

***

For the first time in my life, I'm doing manual labor. I've never built a house before; I never realized how difficult it was. Those poor people in the mortal realm who have to exert all their strength doing menial tasks, I'll never judge them again. But somehow, I think I have it a bit harder even though I'm in the saint realm. For one, I don't think normal people build ten-story houses by themselves. Well, I'm not really working alone. There's the wolfkin spirit that Lucia summoned here with me. He's very friendly. Compared to Lucia, who I'm terrified of, and Durandal, who is aloof, I think I get along with Puppers the best. After all, misery loves company.

"I got more wood!" And Lucia's back with more building materials.

At least she's not making me gather the materials to build the house too. After Lucia cut down three trees, I told her we couldn't cut down trees on the chosens' mountain because they're thousands of years old and exude qi, making the place a holy ground for cultivation, so Lucia went off to the core disciples' mountains before I could stop her. I hope she didn't harvest too … many!?

"Sister Moonlight! Please, save us!"

Lucia…, Lucia was carrying … a mountain. With one arm. "Um. Lucia? Weren't you going to get wood?"

"Ah? Yeah," Lucia nodded as she tossed the mountain peak to the side. People screamed as it crashed into the ground. Why are people screaming!? "You know how sometimes you're too lazy to pick acorns off a tree one at a time so you decide to cut the whole tree down? This is similar."

No. I don't know anything about picking acorns. "Um. No."

Lucia sighed and looked at me as if I was an idiot. Am I an idiot? I don't think I am. But people wouldn't tell me even if I was since I'm so pretty. They wouldn't want to offend me. …Maybe I *am* an idiot.

"Look," Lucia said. "If I cut down all the trees, then I'd need to pick them up one by one. But if I cut down the mountain they're all on and drag it over, then once I cut down a tree, it'll already be here. See?" She grabbed a tree on the broken mountain peak and tore it off with her bare hands before throwing it in front of me. I think I understand now. She's a natural disaster.

"Sister Moonlight!"

"Shut your traps!" Lucia shouted and kicked the mountain peak, causing a ton of trees to shake and fall over. "Sister this, sister that. Aren't there any other words in your vocabulary?"

Lucia really doesn't like formalities. I'm not quite sure why, and I'm too scared to ask, so I guess I'll never know. Anyway, back to building this mansion. Luckily, I can cover my hands with qi to prevent callouses from forming, and since the chosens' mountain is a holy ground, I recover my qi faster here. And I'm not sure if I'm right, but I think the trees have been producing more qi ever since Lucia came here. Perhaps her cultivation technique draws upon qi from the earth, which is a little weird since most cultivators from the Immortal Continent draw upon qi from the stars. What about heart devil qi? It has a higher purity than star qi, but it's too hard to obtain for it to be reliable. To reach the earth realm, I'd have to plant fifty million heart devils.

"You guys can scram." Lucia was kicking away the core disciples that had been dragged along with their mountain peak. Speaking of their mountain peak, where did it go? There's only a massive pile of trees in its place. Did Lucia store it? Why? "And if you call out for Sister Moonlight one more time, I'll rip your tongues out, got it?"

The core disciples fled from the chosens' mountain without a word. Lucia's never threatened to rip my tongue out before. Perhaps she's actually treating me nicely? Maybe she noticed I don't really like being bothered by the peanut gallery all the time. "You didn't have to threaten them for me, you know?"

"Eh?" Lucia tilted her head. "But how else am I supposed to grow heart devils?"

So it wasn't for me. That's okay. I'm not disappointed.

"D-don't cry! Damnit! Why do you cry all the time!?"

"I-I'm not crying!" Even if I am, I'm not allowed to admit it. I have to be a stoic chosen. Deep breaths. In. Out. In. Out. Phew, okay. That's better.

Lucia sighed. Did I disappoint her? "One day, there's going to be someone who'll attack you, and your go-to defense of crying isn't going to save you." She flicked my forehead, and it felt like an explosion went off in my head. "Ah, that was a bit too hard. Anyway, stop crying so much, got it?"

Was this her trying to be nice to me? I'm not sure if I should take that as advice or as a threat. Maybe it's both? But I really have the feeling that she's trying to be my friend—or maybe that's just the wishful thinking of a lonely person. I'm not sure why she'd try to be friends with me. Men only want to court me. Women hate me for attracting all the men. Sometimes I wonder if I have any redeeming values that aren't my beauty or status in the sect.

"If you're tired, then you should rest. Drink this," Lucia said and placed a cup of brown liquid into my hands. What's this? It's hot. "Don't you dare slack off, Puppers! I know you don't get tired."

It's sweet! "W-what is this!? It's amazing!"

"It's hot chocolate," Lucia said with a nod. "They don't have it on the Immortal Continent, right? I ordered every beverage back in the flaccid phoenix restaurant and it didn't show up."

"The flaccid phoenix restaurant...?" Why..., why does that sound so dirty?

"Mhm. Speaking of restaurants, where do I get some food around here? It's time for my noontime snack. And then I have to eat lunch in an hour."

"Ah, you're hungry?" Finally, something I can properly help her with! "Here." I handed her a grain of cooked immortal rice that I pulled out from my interspacial ring.

Lucia stared at the rice. "…What's this?"

She doesn't know? "It's rice…?"

Lucia stared at me instead of the rice. I-I'm not eatable! "This is all? Really?"

"R-really!" One grain of rice will keep someone full for a month! "I'm given thirty grains a year, so you don't have to worry about me running out."

"…What else do you eat?"

What does she mean? "That's it."

"You're given thirty grains of rice to eat every year…?"

"I also receive a cup of the highest-quality spirit water every month." One cup of highest-quality spirit water is the equivalent of cultivating for three months. Only chosens are allowed to drink it because it loses its effects the older one is. It won't do anything for the ancestors of the sect.

"Don't you eat anything else?" Lucia's tail was slamming against the ground over and over again, cracking the earth. She's clearly agitated. Did I say something wrong?

"Ah? No. Eating and drinking causes impurities to build up, so my grandparents don't let me. This is my first time tasting something that isn't spirit water or rice." I wonder how many days I'd have to spend at the impurity-cleansing pool to rid myself of this single cup if I drank it. My grandfather says it's a painful process. That's why I only dipped my tongue into the cup and didn't swallow anything.

"Drink it!"

"Huh? I can't. My grandf—!" S-stop! It, it burns! But it tastes so good! Why am I so conflicted!? I, I have to hurry to the impurity-cleansing pool!

"Where are you going?"

"Impurity-cleansing pool!" I might not be able to fight as well as Lucia, but I'm confident in my movement techniques! Even an earth-realm expert will have a hard time catching … me!? How is she so fast!? She's almost as fast as I am!

***

There's something wrong with this sect. Something seriously, terribly wrong. They're abusing their chosen! One grain of rice and one cup of water every month for food? Fuck! I had a better life when I was a slave. At least I had a quarter of a carrot every day! And I could drink water whenever I wanted even if it was a bit muddy. "Stop running from me, damnit! Let me feed you properly!"

"I can't ingest impurities!"

"Whose cooking is impure!?" How dare Softie not accept my goodwill! I don't offer hot chocolate to just anyone! Gah, why do I care so much about this crybaby anyway? She has nothing to do with me. But I just hate how weak she is! She reminds me of a slave with no free will, but she has the power to change that! Grr, I don't know why I'm so pissed off at her, but once I catch her, I'm going to shove a barrel of hot chocolate and acorn stew down her throat.

"This isn't about your cooking, Lucia! Please, stop chasing me!"

So far, we've run down the chosens' mountain, through a plaza of people, past a marketplace of sorts where suspicious-looking things were being sold. We ran past a field of rice, a couple of mountains with people on them, a few fancy-looking buildings that I should steal on my way back, and an enclosure filled with animals. There's clearly plenty of animals to be eaten! What's this one grain of rice a month nonsense!? Now we're running past a forest of bamboo, and I think I just stepped on a really precious flower because someone screamed when I did, and Softie still hasn't shown any sign of slowing down. Is she speeding up? This is nonsense! There hasn't been anyone I haven't been able to catch since I became a legend. Is it time to bring out the Puppers Ballista?

"H-how are you still following me?" Softie was slowing down! She stopped in front of a building that looked like a red tower with frills. She swallowed as she inched backwards and pressed herself against the door. "T-this is the impurity-cleansing pool. There's no violence permitted. And, and you can't use qi either."

Oh really?

"It's against the sect rules! Please, stop radiating like that!" Tears fell from Softie's eyes as she whirled around and pulled on the door just as I grabbed her shoulder. "Elder who's on duty! Elder who's on duty! Save me!"

"What's going on!?"

Ah? This voice. I recognize it. Like I thought, it's Mr. Shoe.

"Elder Shu, please, save me!" Softie was squirming in my hands, but I wasn't going to let her go! She's extremely hard to catch, but extremely easy to restrain.

"Ah. Junior Lucia. Junior Moonlight. Is something wrong?" Mr. Shoe was inching backwards, and the door to the tower was slowly closing. "Like I thought, there's no issue, right? Ah-ha-ha." Then the door closed before Softie could say anything.

"E-Elder Shu…. Elder Shu! My grandfather ordered me to bring Lucia to the impurity-cleansing pool! If you don't help me out right this instant, you'll be disobeying the sect leader's wishes!"

Ah? Softie became brave all of a sudden? That's good! She's less spineless now.

"The sect leader may have ordered such a thing, but have you asked Junior Lucia whether or not she agrees? It seems like she's unwilling or there wouldn't be such a racket at the door, no?" Mr. Shoe was talking through the door. It sounded like he was standing really far away and getting even further with every word. I also felt the heart devil inside of him growing. Hmm. Is he that frightened of me? There must be something wrong with this Heart Devil Cultivation Technique. It must be making me seem scarier than I actually am!

"N-no way." Softie became limp in my arms and her head hung down. Did she lose her spirit? What happened to the spine she just grew? "Why do you have more face than my grandfather...?"

That's a compliment, right? I was totally complimented just now. I'll go a little easier on Softie. "Mm. So what's this whole impurity thing you were talking about?" Of course, if I don't like her answer, the punishment of a barrel of hot chocolate will resume!

"You really don't know what impurities are?" Softie asked. Her lower lip was quivering, and there were tears in her eyes. ...I'm jealous of how pretty she is. I'll pinch her cheeks to make her face puff up. "Ahwah!? Luciwah? S-shtop!" Ooh, this is pretty fun. Smoosh, smoosh. They're so squishy and elastic. And I thought squirrels had the softest cheeks.

"Sister Moonlight is being violated again!"

"Wife Moonlight!!!"

Who's violating someone!? I'm not a pervert, and only perverts can violate people! I'm just playing with her face! "Unrelenting Path of Slaughter: Puppers Ballista!" Mm, I'll have Puppers deal with the annoying people who don't know when to shut up. Back to kneading Softie's cheeks. Smoosh, smoosh.

"Brother Forest's been attacked in the sect's no-attacks-allowed zone! He's being murdered!"

It's a good thing I have Puppers or I'd be the one blamed for attacking someone in the no-attacks-allowed zone. It looks like Softie really wasn't lying about that rule. A large sect must have a lot of rules, huh? There's absolutely no way I'm going to remember all of them. Can there be a rule to exclude me from all the rules? I'm going to petition the sect leader for that rule.

"C-can you let go of mwai face?"

Ah. I was still holding onto Softie. What were we talking about? Right. Impurities. I know what those are! Those are the things that Durandal said would build up if I continued consuming beast cores like I did while completely ignoring his advice to use them one at a time! Mm. Why didn't I remember earlier before pinching Softie's face? …I'm not sure. Sometimes weird things jostle my memory.

"Pwease?"

Oh. I forgot to let go.

Softie sniffled and rubbed her cheeks. Then she spoke really fast as if she was afraid I'd interrupt her. "Why do cultivators cultivate? For immortality. Cultivators want to transcend the earthly lands and become a part of the heavens. And if we want to do that, we can't eat earthly foods or it'll hold us back. We call these earthly shackles impurities. That's why we have the impurity-cleansing pool. If someone bathes in the pool, their impurities will be cleansed. But prevention is always the best solution, so it's better to never ingest impurities in the first place. Please don't hurt me."

"So what you're saying is … you want me to take a bath?"

"Ah? A bath in the impurity-cleansing pool, yes. Why are your eyes so scary!?"

Me, scary? Maybe. Me, bathe? Fuck no! I'll drown!

***

My grandfather has set me on an impossible task. Lucia is vehemently against bathing. I'm not sure why. And it's not like she smells funny or anything from lack of washing. That's right. How does she wash normally? "Lucia...? You wash yourself, right?" If she says she licks herself clean like a cat, I'm not sure how I'll respond.

"Mm. Of course. Why? Do I smell?" Lucia released my shoulder and sniffed herself. Couldn't she release my other shoulder too? She was pinning me to the door of the pagoda that the impurity-cleansing pool was located in.

"Cleansing your impurities is like washing yourself." On the journey to immortality, impurities are a major hindrance. They slow your qi circulation which slows your cultivation and the speed at which your techniques come out. Impurities can cause health problems. In short, impurities are the bane of every cultivator's existence. That's how it is according to my grandfather. Lucia seems like she'd have a lot of impurities since she eats earthly food, but she still reached the saint realm just fine, which is a little weird.

"Hmm. Promise?" Lucia's eyes narrowed at me. She looked like a fox eyeing an unsuspecting rabbit. That makes me as pitiful as a rabbit. ...Just what have I been doing as a chosen? Why am I so worthless? Compared to Lucia, I'm nothing....

"Oi."

Ow! It really, really hurts when she flicks my forehead. "Y-yes?"

"You didn't promise me and started crying instead. Are you trying to trick me?"

Before I could respond to that, Lucia tripped me and grabbed my waist. Then she slung me over her shoulder like a sack of potatoes. This, this is humiliating! "S-someone, help!"

"My Wife Moonlight's being swept off her feet by someone other than me!"

The door flew open, no, it flew off its hinges with a bang as Lucia kicked it down. Elder Shu was nowhere to be found even though he was supposed to be on duty. As a saint-realm expert, there's no way he didn't hear the banging noise! I'm going to report him to my grandfather when I have the chance.

And who keeps calling me Wife Moonlight!? "L-Lucia. What are you doing?" There's no point in struggling. Grandfather said Lucia had the strength of a fire dragon. Besides, this is a no-violence zone too.

"I'm going to look at your impurity-cleansing pool," Lucia said. Her tail kept brushing against my face, and I had to fight the urge to sneeze.

"As you should. Our daily spars aren't challenging enough for you to ingest beast cores properly. I wouldn't be surprised if those dragon cores are still lying dormant inside of you." Durandal appeared out of nowhere and walked alongside us. It must be nice having spirits you can summon at will. If I had a few weapon spirits, I don't think I'd be as lonely. But weapon spirits aren't very reliable according to my grandfather. They require a constant upkeep of qi even if they're dormant which greatly slows one's cultivation. And most weapon spirits have a lifespan of less than a decade. That's nothing in the eyes of an immortal.

"Eh…. I'm a very pure person though." I could feel Lucia nod since my hip was right next to her head. "How many impurities could I have possibly built up?"

"You eat a lot."

"That doesn't mean anything! If I ate a lot, then I'd be fat, right? But no, I'm not fat. So there! I'm eating the proper amount a girl my age should be eating." Lucia's tail smacked my head a few times as it swished back and forth. I heard foxkins' tails telegraphed their owner's feelings. It seems like that was true. It's very easy to tell when Lucia's upset. I just wish I knew why. It seems like Lucia's displeased by everything I do…. No one's ever displeased by what I do. Is it a problem with everyone else, or is it a problem with Lucia?

"Mm. If you say so."

"Durandal! What's that supposed to mean!?"

"Nothing. I was agreeing with you."

What's this buzzing sensation by my hip. Lucia's ... growling? Is she going to attack Durandal? I hope not; this is a no-violence zone! "Ah, Lucia. The top floor of the pagoda is reserved for chosen." There's so many people here. It's embarrassing to be carried around like this, but at least, I won't have to wait in a line. Even though there's an appointment system to use the impurity-cleansing pool, a lot of sect members take more than the allotted time and a line is formed. But chosens have benefits such as using the purest water at the top without having to wait for anyone else.

"The top? Isn't that too far for a chosen to walk? I thought chosens were special; shouldn't we get the most convenient spot like this room right here?" Lucia knocked on a door nearby, and it fell open. A few women screamed. I think she broke down the women's changing room.... "Ah, oops. Why's everything so flimsy here?"

"Only your mansion's reinforced to handle your strength," Durandal said and patted Lucia's head. Lucia reached over and covered his eyes while dragging him past the room of panicking women. I hope they don't develop heart devils from this. While planting heart devils amongst each other is encouraged in the sect, it's a great way of making enemies. Lucia might be a chosen, but her backing isn't that great. She may have the elders of the sect watching over her now, but if she ever falls from grace, all the people she built animosity with will be waiting to tear her apart. This doesn't include me, by the way. I'm not going to attack someone who sent Elder Forest flying no matter how far that person falls. My grandfather says I'm too nice.

"That's another thing I need to petition the sect leader for then," Lucia said and sighed. Another thing? What else was she going to ask of my grandfather...? "I take those stairs to go up, right?"

"Those stairs only lead up."

"I was asking Softie!"

"Y-yes. Those stairs lead to the top of the pagoda." Is the relationship between Lucia and Durandal not good? I wouldn't be too surprised, honestly, considering how she treats Puppers....

***

When Softie said impurity-cleansing pool, I assumed it would be an actual pool filled with impurity-cleansing water. That'd make the most sense, right? But this is it? It's very long and wide, but it has the depth of a metal pan that Ilya uses to bake cookies. Even I can't drown in something like this. I could probably drink all the water in the pool in a single breath.

"This is the impurity-cleansing pool. Can you please let me down now?"

Mm. I held onto Softie because I thought this was a conspiracy to drown me and I was going to use her as a hostage to escape, but it looks like I don't have to!

"How does it work?" Durandal stepped to the edge of the so-called pool and crouched down. He touched the surface, and it rippled, but nothing else happened. "Is it broken?"

"N-no," Softie said once I put her down. "Spirits don't have any impurities. Um, Lucia, you have to take off your clothes and wash yourself with the water. Usually, I jump in right away, but if you think that's too crude, you can wipe yourself with that towel."

Of course, I'm wiping myself with the towel. That's how I always bathe! There's no risk of drowning with a towel. And no evil monsters are going to appear out of the depths of the water to nibble on my ankles, ultimately causing me to fall over and be consumed completely. Why is water so scary? Water's like the dark; you don't know what's out to eat you inside of it. Time for my first bath since coming to the Immortal Continent!

"W-wait! Why are you stripping now!?"

"Huh?" What's wrong with stripping? Wasn't she the one that told me to take off my clothes? And once all the clothes are off, I'm not putting them back on.

"I-I'm still here! A-and Durandal's a man!"

"...So?" Ah. I understand why Softie's so flustered now. "Oh. Don't worry! Yours are still growing."

"Still ... growing? What are you talking.... That's not it!" Softie's face turned bright red. Was she going to spit out blood too? I hope she doesn't spit it in the pool. That'd be gross. I have to use this water to bathe, you know? "H-here!" Softie shoved the towel into my hands and ran away. Well.... That's okay too.

"Durandal! Eh? Durandal?" Where'd he go?

"I'm not going to watch you wash, Lucia."

Why not!? I guess I'll drag Softie back in here. What if something weird comes out of the water and tries to drown me? Like a tentacle. Or an azure dragon. Mn, the Immortal Continent's filled with danger. Can't be too careful. "Softie! Help!"

The door to the pool room creaked open. Softie's head poked inside, but only half of it. "Y-yes?"

"Come here for a second."

"I.... Do I have to?"

"Yes."

Softie took in a deep breath and—then I pounced on her! I wasn't going to let her flee! How do these robes come off? It should have something to do with this sash, right? Right. Let's remove this real quick and..., there we go! All done.

"L-Lucia! M-my clothes!"

"Silly. You're not going to wash yourself while wearing clothes, right?" Wearing wet clothes is almost as bad as having wet fur. At least clothes can be taken off. Well, I guess a tail can be taken off too, but it'll be painful to regrow. No one's allowed to cut my tail off! Hmm, Softie's body is really soft. I guess her name's very suitable. Now, let's drop her into the pool and see what happens…!? How did she disappear!?

Softie's head broke through the surface of the water. "Pwah! You dropped me too suddenly!" She…, she was treading water like an evil sorcerer practicing some sort of black magic. This water seemed to be a lot deeper than I thought…? No way, the water was playing tricks on me! Softie looks super long underneath the surface! What I thought had the depth of a baking pan was actually as deep as an ocean! …It's a good thing I dropped Softie in first or I would've drowned, huh?

"You're not going to put Durandal and Puppers into your interspacial ring?" Softie's face was bright red. She was clinging to the edge of the pool with everything except her head submerged. Some black things were leaking out of her body and mixing into the pool, but they disappeared when they went far away from her.

"It's cruel to store weapons and armor with spirits inside of interspacial rings!" Mm, after Durandal told me all about his bad experience inside of the Godking's treasure trove, I promised myself I wouldn't put him in a similar situation.

"Is it…? I don't think that's the case…." Softie's voice was really soft. It seemed like she was afraid again. Hah. The plan to make Softie grow a spine seems like it'll take a lot longer to implement than expected. When was there a plan to make Softie grow a spine? It was always there! I hate weak people. Hate them. So if I'm going to be keeping Softie as a portable encyclopedia, she has to grow a spine!

"Anyways, time to wash off the impurities that I don't have." I'm still technically chaste since Durandal's just a spirit! There's nothing about me that's impure. I grabbed the towel and squatted next to the pool. Here we go. I dipped the towel into the water. Oh, it's warm! Eh…?

"Wah!?" Softie's eyes widened as she scrambled out of the pool that was rapidly turning black. "L-L-Lucia! What's happening!?"

Why is she asking me!? "Stop panicking so much! You'll make me nervous too!" Okay. Let's evaluate this situation. Ilya always says I need to slow down and think even though it may be difficult. …Was Ilya saying slowing down would be difficult? Or was she saying it's difficult for me to think…? Gah! I'm going to add hot peppers to her hot chocolate the next time I treat her. Mm, but what was…, oh! Right. The impurity-cleansing pool…. "So, it's not supposed to turn black, right?"

"N-no." Softie took in three deep breaths before finally being able to speak. The pool turned completely black without any ripples. It looked like the surface of the inkwells that Ilya always used. "I-impurities are cleaned out right away by the impurity-cleansing fishes. They're really tiny, so you can't see them unless you look underwater. They eat the impurities, and their waste turns into new impurity-cleansing water."

"…You wanted me to wash myself with fish pee?" I knew it! There were unseen monsters lurking inside the water!

"But it's very clean fish pee!" Softie's face turned red again. She covered her chest and crotch with one arm each before waddling over to the edge of the pool. She crouched down and I resisted the urge to push her in. I'm not that mean! "But what did you do to the water…? I saw you dip your hand and towel inside, and then the whole pool was filled with impurities."

"Mm. There's only one explanation: The pool's broken." Ah, there's some tiny bubbles appearing on the surface of the water. Is that a bead?

"Ah! That's the belly of an impurity-cleansing fish! Is it dead!?" Softie waved her hand, and I felt some qi leave her fingers. It wrapped around the bead and lifted it into the air before coming back to her hand. "It, it's dead." She swallowed and pointed at the pool. Hmm?

Thousands of bubbles were popping on the surface of the pool, and thousands of little beads soon followed. Were those all dead fish? Someone must've held a serious grudge against me for violating Softie in front of the whole sect! They actually poisoned the impurity-cleansing pool that I was going to use! How vicious! The Immortal Continent is a scarier place than I thought. People even poisoned your bath water.

"Wait…." Softie swallowed as she rose to her feet. "The water at the top is the purest and it trickles down to the lower floors of the pagoda. If that's the case—"

Screams filled the room, coming from outside the door. "I can't see! Everything's black!"

"Brother Forest's skin is melting off!"

"Another toe is growing out of my foot!"

"My belly button turned into a nipple!"

"H-help! I'm dying!"

"What's going on!?"

"The Great Poison Sect must be attacking us! They came here for the cultural exchange! Brothers and sisters, we must band together to wipe them off the face of the Immortal Continent!"

"To the cultural exchange!"

"They'll pay for turning my belly button into a nipple!"

Wow, this place is a little hectic, huh? Especially since the sect has over a million people in it. Like I thought, once one person starts panicking, everyone else starts panicking too. "Let's go with them to beat up the Great Poison Sect!" I haven't beaten anyone up in a long time! That person who Durandal fought doesn't count. All I did was swing once.

"Um. But I don't think the Great Poison Sect was responsible for this…?" Softie lowered her head and looked up at me through her eyelashes. Gah! Why's she so pretty!? I'm jealous! "L-Lucia? Hiih! Yes, yes! The Great Poison Sect is completely responsible for this! Let's go destroy them immediately!"

Ah, oops. My jealousy frightened her. But that's okay! Once the problem with the impurity-cleansing pool is solved by wiping out the Great Poison Sect, I'll finally be able to wash properly. Mm, it's good to have goals. They're great motivation.

Chapter 8

Lucia's officially a chosen of the sect. As one of her companions, I was given the choice to stay by her side as a servant or become a disciple of the sect. This choice required absolutely zero thought. Of course, I became a disciple of the sect! And I was promoted right away to core disciple because of my relationship with Lucia. The wife of the sect leader volunteered to become my master, so it's safe to say I have a pretty stable backing. If the sect leader is similar to an emperor, then his wife is the empress. Compared to a duke, an empress has a higher status. Thus, I should have more face in the Immortal Continent than I did back at home. The only problem is Lucia didn't really like my parting, but I tried to act as reluctant as possible so her anger would shift onto my new master instead of me. It should be fine since my master's an earth-realm expert. …Right?

Currently, I'm attending the sect's cultural exchange with my master. If I had to describe it in a single word…, then it'd be hectic. Apparently, in Kong County, there's over a thousand sects. A lot of them are as large as the Shadow Devil Sect, but the disciples of those sects aren't as gifted. It really makes me wonder how big the Immortal Continent is exactly. Over a thousand sects with a million people each. That's already a billion people. And that's not even mentioning the fact that only one out of ten people will have the qualifications to join a sect, which means there's nine billion regular people, adding up to a total of ten billion. And that's in Kong County alone! King Province is made up of ten counties, each of them the same size as Kong County. That's a hundred billion people! There was a food shortage in some parts of the sky and earth plane, and we only had a population of two million. I can't even imagine how difficult it'd be to create residences for a hundred billion people let alone feed them all.

But I digress. The cultural exchange is basically a giant male-organ-measuring contest between all of the sects, and it's currently hosted by the Shadow Devil Sect. It happens once every three months because the sects really like competing or something. My master says it encourages growth due to rivalry. Right now, I'm watching a bunch of middle-aged men play with fireballs. That's right, the same kind of fireball created by a first-circle spell. And everyone's amazed. I don't understand.

"Aren't you interested?" My master was the grandmother of Soft Moonlight, but she didn't sound old at all. If she hid her face behind a veil, anyone would think she was still a young woman if they heard her voice. "It's not every day you can see alchemists flaunt their techniques."

"But didn't you say the cultural exchange lasted for three months? And that it'd be set up again in another location after the three months were over? If I followed it around, I could see these alchemists flaunt their techniques every day, but that's not the point. Even a child can do what they're doing." I was playing with fire since I was eight; my father didn't really approve though. All that these so-called alchemists are doing is adjusting the temperature of the flames in their hand.

"Really?" My master raised her eyebrows. "Is it that simple? Only one out of ten thousand people are born with a flame essence."

"Fireball." A ball of fire hovered above my palms. What else were those alchemists doing? Increasing the temperature? All I have to do is layer on another fireball. "Fireball. Fireball. Fireball. Fireball. Fireball." There, now my flames are hotter than all of those alchemists' out there combined.

"You…, have a fire essence?" My master looked around. Was she making sure no one else was watching? But what's this fire essence she keeps talking about?

"I don't think so?"

"But you can control flames! You have to have a fire essence to convert qi to fire."

Really…? "What other essences are there?" Like if I were to change these flames into ice by casting Frost Ball, would she say I had an ice essence. I don't think this is anything impressive, honestly. "Frost Ball."

"Ice essence!"

"Earthen spike…?"

"Earth essence!"

"Gust."

"Wind essence!"

"Lightning Bolt."

"Thunder essence!"

Hmm? Shouldn't that be lightning essence? Thunder's the sound that accompanies lightning, you know? Well, whatever. "Chaos Orb."

"Origin essence!" My master's eyes widened to the size of saucers as she covered her mouth with both her hands. But it was too late because everyone else heard. And they were all staring at me. Even the people who hadn't heard were staring at me because of herd mentality. Once they saw other people staring, they had to stare as well.

"She has origin essence!"

No. I have mana. And any magician in the pocket realm could do this with enough mana.

"If we dissect her, we could each have a little bit of her to study!"

Oi! What the hell!? Is this what I get for showing off? Save me, Lucia! Wait. Lucia's not here. "M-Master."

"Ahem!" My master climbed to her feet while radiating qi. She was imposing, but I don't think she's as threatening as

Lucia. Lucia's qi has a bloodthirst mixed inside of it. My master's is gentler even though it's thicker. "Which one of you has designs on my, Bright Moonlight's, personal disciple?"

All the alchemists, elders, and perverts who had their designs on me backed off under my master's glare. When everyone averted their gaze, my master turned to me and swallowed. "Can I have a portion of your liver to study? Just one tiny portion and I'll heal you right away!"

…I think I'm in more danger here than I was with Lucia. Is this what people mean when they say the grass is always greener on the other side? I miss Lucia already and it hasn't even been a day since we separated. What is wrong with me? If Lucia were here, she'd have done much more than just threatening. Those people who coveted me would be robbed.

"You Greedy Poison Sect bastards tried to poison me! Prepare to pay with your life or all your life belongings!"

Like that. Exactly like … that. Lucia?

***

Whew, there's a lot of people gathered here. Softie said this was the cultural exchange, and I think she explained what it was to me, but I wasn't listening. Instead of the monotonous scene of people wearing black robes, there were all kinds of colors. Apparently, only the Shadow Devil Sect is allowed to wear black. Other sects had their own colors, and the weaker sects sometimes used the same color, but black was unique to the Shadow Devil Sect. And Softie told me only the Star Phoenix Sect could wear red after Durandal asked. I almost forgot the Star Phoenix Sect was my mortal enemy until Durandal reminded me. But I'm a fox now! So there's no reason for the Star Phoenix Sect to want to kill me at all.

"Outrageous! Who do you think you are!?" a man in purple stood up and shouted at me. Around him, there were a bunch of other people wearing purple too.

"Those are the Great Poison Sect members, Chosen Lucia! Please, avenge my belly button!"

This guy has a serious attachment to his belly button. Since the greedy..., great? Since the Greedy Poison Sect tried to kill me by contaminating the impurity-cleansing pool that I was going to use, they impacted a whole lot of people! At least thirty. I'm sure there's more, but I didn't want to spend time counting them and thirty seems like a lot. And as a chosen of the sect, those impacted people—like the guy who had his belly button turned into a nipple—flocked around me because Mr. Shoe was the elder on duty at the time, but he ran away somewhere. Since I'm a naturally charismatic leader, I decided to lead this righteous cause!

Durandal nodded at the purple-robed person. "Once we rob them, I want all their swords. They look like they'd have exquisite swords."

...Robbing people is a righteous cause! Hmm? How? Simple! I'm doing it out of love for Durandal, and any act done out of love is righteous. The bonuses that come with the swords are the world's way of rewarding me for being a good person. Mn. This is justified.

Softie coughed. Was she sick? Don't tell me the poison got her too! My encyclopedia can't die on the day I meet her! That's really bad luck. "Lucia? You're not going to respond to them?"

Respond to who? Ah! Right. "I'm Lucia Fluffytail, chosen of the Shadow Devil Sect! And you're the bastards who tried to assassinate me!"

"Us? Bastards? Assassinate? You?"

Hah. It looks like these people were even slower than Softie. He only spoke four words, but all of them were questions! "Yes, you. If you're not bastards, then what are you? Assassinate means to kill. And me is I!" Or would it be I is me? Hmm. Well, they get the point. At least, they should.

The purple-robed man crossed his arms over his chest, and qi billowed out of him. My tail rose and puffed out, but it wasn't completely stiff. If I fought him, I wouldn't die, but I might not win either! How strong is this person? "Sect Leader Moonlight! What is the meaning of this? My Great Poison Sect might not be one of Kong's five fingers, but I won't let your disciple slap my face with false accusations! We're not that easy to bully!"

The sect leader, who was sitting next to the person who kidnapped Ilya, oh! It's Ilya! I waved at her. Wait, what was the sect leader doing? Right, he stood up and rose into the air. Then he landed in front of me. "Junior Lucia…. Do you mind explaining what's going on?"

"Sure!" I pointed at the people in purple. "Those people tried to poison me."

The sect leader followed my finger with his gaze. Then he turned to Softie. "Little Moon, do you mind explaining what's going on?"

Hey! Don't blatantly ignore me like that! I'm going to hit him. Breaking Blade! …Darn. How come his shield's so strong? I'll have to get Durandal to teach me how he managed to injure that other person with the shield. If I can't hit someone, how am I supposed to solve my problems? This is a disaster that needs to be addressed immediately!

"I brought Lucia, err, Sister Lucia to the impurity-cleansing pool like Sect Leader asked. While we were there, the whole pool became contaminated and the impurity-cleansing fishes all died. Even now, the pool is filled with toxins that caused my fellow disciples' skins to melt. The—"

"And my belly button turned into a nipple."

"Yes, there's that too. Along with melting skin, mutations occurred upon contact with the toxins. I think someone grew another toe." Softie stopped speaking and nodded at her grandfather. She whispered, but I could still totally hear her, "I think it was Lucia's fault."

How was it my fault!? All I did was dip a towel into the pool! I only touched it with my fingertips. It can't be my fault. She was making a jab at me, right? Right? Once the sect leader's not around to defend her, I'll teach her to call someone impure. Hmph.

"Junior Lucia." The sect leader smiled at me. It looked friendly, but I'm sure the intent behind it wasn't friendly at all! It was like Durandal's sadistic smile! Did I join a sadist's sect? Wait. They get qi from making people suffer heart devils; of course, this is a sadistic sect! I-I'm surrounded by perverts! "Do you have any proof that the Great Poison Sect did it? You seem extremely sure."

"Ah, yeah. One of the disciples said it was the Greedy Poison Sect people." I turned around. "Which one of you was it?" No one said anything. "Who. Was. It?"

"I-it was Brother Mint, Chosen Lucia!"

Everyone pointed at one person in the center of the crowd. He swallowed and walked up to the sect leader and me with his head hanging down. "Right." I patted his shoulder, and his knees buckled. He was as scared as Softie. Does no one have a spine? "This person personally saw some Great Poison Sect people poisoning the pool."

"P-personally...?"

Hmm? Did he say something? No, it must've been the wind.

"Is this true, Junior Mint?" The sect leader gave the junior an encouraging smile that looked completely inappropriate now that I know he's a pervert, and the junior raised his head. "If you're wrong, then you'll be punished. Naturally, if you're right, you'll be handsomely rewarded."

The minty person's eyes shone. "Y-yes! With my own two eyes, I saw a Great Poison Sect disciple contaminate the impurity-cleansing pool!"

"There you have it! That's my proof." See? I knew it couldn't be me. Now I can plunder everything from those people in purple, right?

"That's preposterous!" the purple-robed people's leader shouted. "Why would my Great Poison Sect wish to kill your chosen?"

"It doesn't matter why! It only matters that you did!" Hasn't he ever heard the phrase actions speak louder than words? "Eat my sword! Unrelenting Path of Slaughter: Breaking Blade!"

Softie sucked in a deep breath and a whip appeared in her hand. I knew she was a sadist! "Support Chosen Lucia!" Her whip cracked like lightning, and a black snake made of the heart devil worms appeared from the whip's tip. It chased my Breaking Blade and opened its jaws wide to swallow the purple-robed people. I thought Softie was supposed to be weak!

"Support Chosen Lucia!" Every Shadow Devil Sect member rose to their feet, and many, many colorful techniques flashed through the air! Just kidding. All the techniques were composed of the black heart devil worms. There was no color at all. And just like that, the group of purple-robed people were forced into dire straits, but all of them were still alive somehow. Ah, there were tons of broken defensive-looking equipment on the ground; that must've been how they survived. Well, it's not like I wanted to kill them in the first place! Everyone just jumped in after I attacked. I should've expected it since all the Shadow Devil Sect members are sadists who wouldn't give up a chance to see someone else suffer. But they supported me right away—even if it was for their own perverted nature. This must be what it means to have the backing of a sect!

***

I'm not sure why I attacked the Great Poison Sect members right after Lucia. Is this what people call a woman's intuition? I felt like if I didn't support Lucia, my future would be very grim. For feeling like this, I'd like to apologize to the elders of the Great Poison Sect. At least the grudges won't be very strong; the attacks of Shadow Devil Sect disciples aren't tailored to kill. They're designed to plant heart devils. That's why there's only three dead disciples amongst the Great Poison Sect … members…. Why are there three dead disciples!? Their bodies were completely cut in twain at the waist!

"Hmm. Since they all lived, should I attack again?" Lucia tilted her head to the side while her tail relaxed completely and swished along the ground. What do you mean they all lived!?

"Um, Lucia. You see those three with their bodies cut into two parts?"

"Yeah. What about it?" Lucia blinked at me.

Okay. I've confirmed the fact that between me and Lucia, I'm not the stupid one. I was seriously worried that I might be an idiot that no one had the heart to break the news to. "They're dead, aren't they?"

"From that? That's just a flesh wound." Lucia nodded twice and propped her sword up with her shoulder. …There was blood dripping down the edge of the blade. Why was there blood? Her sword didn't even connect with them. "They'll be perfectly fine in a few hours if someone holds their two halves together."

That's not how people work…. "I, I don't think you should attack them anymore."

"Hmm? Ah! You're right!" Lucia sheathed her sword and patted my shoulder. It felt like a boulder landed on my back, and I was nearly forced into the ground. "If I break their defensive items, that'll be like breaking my own defensive items! I almost broke my own possessions, phew. I knew you were a smart encyclopedia."

An encyclopedia? Is that what Lucia sees me as? Qi rose up from behind us, and I swallowed the words I was going to say. "G-Grandfather?"

"Chosen Lucia!" My grandfather glared at Lucia. Was he going to punish her? I think she deserves punishment. The cultural exchange is a peaceful tradition that's been carried out for millennium. The last time someone died at a cultural exchange was over a thousand years ago. But punishing the new chosen on the day she joins the sect…, isn't that ruining her face? "Good job! You uncovered a plot that seriously endangered the foundation of our Shadow Devil Sect. It seems like my Shadow Devil Sect is no longer feared? Is that it?" My grandfather's qi billowed towards the sky, separating the clouds. His voice boomed through the crowd, and tingles ran down my spine. "Because the tiger doesn't roar, you think it's a kitten? You think you can trample on the dignity of my Shadow Devil Sect!? You slimy frogs from the Great Poison Sect, cripple your own cultivations or die by my hands!"

"Dark Devil Moonlight! Don't you think you're being too overbearing? This is the cultural exchange!" An elderly man dressed in white rose to his feet. Only White Crane Sect members are allowed to wear white robes. And judging by the three blue stripes on his sash, he must have an important position as an elder. The qi coming off of him is nothing to scoff at either. If I wasn't a chosen, I'd have already hidden behind my grandfather like Lucia. …One day, Lucia will understand the responsibilities that come with being a chosen. I hope.

"As the host of the cultural exchange, I freely allowed your sects inside of mine! And the Great Poison Sect repays my hospitality by poisoning my impurity-cleansing pool? I have every right to be overbearing!"

The elder from the White Crane Sect scoffed. "Trillions of years of peace shouldn't be ruined by one disciple's accusations!"

"Trillion years…, how many thousands is that? That's a lot of thousands, right, Durandal? At least a thousand-thousand thousands."

I couldn't help but look at the foxkin hiding behind my grandfather who was counting on her fingers. "Err, Lucia, it's just hyperbole." There haven't been trillions of years of peace. There was a war between two sects just last week.

"Hyperbole?" Lucia tilted her head. "Is that a final attack?"

Durandal hit her forehead. He actually hit her! "It's an exaggeration to make people feel more outraged than if he just spoke the truth."

"Oh! So he's a liar." Lucia nodded and rubbed her forehead. "I understand now!"

"I'd rather trust my disciple than an elder of another sect!" My grandfather puffed his chest out, and heart devil worms rose out of his back, creating a giant hand above his head. "Is the White Crane Sect going to stand in my way today? Shall the five fingers of Kong County become the four fingers?"

A crane's clear cry rang through the air as white qi rose out of the White Crane Sect elder. "You're crazy! The other fingers of Kong County won't allow you to do this!"

"Don't drag the Green Lotus Sect into your problems," a woman wearing green said. Her voice wasn't very loud, but I could hear her as if she were standing right next to me. She snorted as a green barrier rose up around her sect's section.

A woman wearing red shot to her feet and yelled, "The Star Phoenix Sect stands by the White Crane Sect!" Flames burst into the air, and a few sects near her scrambled away.

Boom! A beefy man wearing only a blue loincloth slapped his thigh, causing lightning to strike the gourd in his hand. "Ha-ha! If the Star Phoenix Sect is joining in, then you can't leave our Azure Dragon Sect out of this. Whoever the Star Phoenix Sect stands by, we'll help the other side!" He raised the buzzing gourd to his lips and drank a deep gulp before spitting out a mist filled with electricity. He wiggled his eyebrows at my grandfather. "It looks like we're allies for today, Sect Leader Moonlight."

Something nudged my side. What was this? A disc with brown spots on it?

"It's a cookie." Lucia nudged me again with the disc. "You eat it."

"I, I thought I told you I don't eat—!" She shoved it into my mouth! Again! Why is she always forcing impurities into me!? Oh? This tastes ... amazing. Unbelievable!

Lucia pulled a couch out of her interspacial ring and plopped down, leaning back into it while sipping on a mug. "There's a good show to enjoy!" She patted the space beside her. "Sit."

...Am I a dog? Wait, no. How can Lucia be so relaxed after causing tensions to rise between four of the five fingers of Kong County? A great war can break out in the next moment because of her!

***

I love drama. It's great. Life's boring if there's no drama to be had! As long as the drama doesn't involve me, of course. That'd be bad. I can't enjoy a good meal if I'm in the middle of a drama, but I can enjoy one if I'm just a spectator.

"Lucia? What are you doing?" Softie was sitting on my couch, munching on the cookie I gave her. It seems like she's fallen victim to the charm of pastries. As for what I'm doing....

"I'm setting up the grill." Naturally, barbequed meat and acorn ale are necessary to watch a war break out in comfort! What's acorn ale? It's exactly what it sounds like. And it tastes like acorn stew but bitterer but better too. On my way back to the cultural exchange from the impurity-cleansing pool, I passed by those fields of animals again. And once I passed by the field, there were no more animals left. I wonder why. Hmm. Maybe if the sect offered more than one grain of rice per month to their chosens, the animals wouldn't have disappeared. That's just my hunch. Anyways, what was I grilling? These unique beasts that I picked up from somewhere! A single one of these aurochsen, as Softie called them, seems like it can fully fill me up for a whole meal. They look like skinny cows, which is why I'm going to barbeque them.

"Do you really intend on killing these Great Poison Sect members today if they don't cripple their cultivation?" That person wearing white reminded me of that selfless senior who exploded for my tribulation. I wonder why. Mm, must be my imagination. Anyway, a quick cut to this aurochs' belly and a few tugs to its organs and … it's ready! Onto the grill it goes.

"My words have more weight than gold! I mean everything I say!" The sect leader's really overbearing. But he's a really good guy. He supported me right away! I just don't understand why he abuses Softie so much if he's so partial to chosen. After all, Softie lives in a hole in the ground and is fed rice and water without any condiments. Maybe there's a reason he's willing to cripple a bunch of people for the chosens but not feed the chosens properly. Is food that expensive here? I wouldn't know since Grandpa Bear paid for my restaurant bill. But there were so many aurochsen around; that can't be it. Not to mention that wouldn't explain the horrible living conditions. "The question is, do you dare declare war for the sake of a single sect!?"

Whew, I love this grill. Ilya made it for me. It has a seventh-circle heating spell that cooks meat evenly even if only a single part of the meat is touching the top. Ilya tried to explain how it worked to me, but it was too complicated and unimportant. After all, the most important thing was that it did its job. And if it breaks, Ilya can fix it for me, so it's not like I need to know. Mm, let's add some salt and pepper. One can never go wrong with salt and pepper when cooking cow-like creatures. I bet acorn paste with garlic would be great on it too.

"Before I answer that question, may I ask what your chosen is doing?"

Hmm? What the chosen was doing? Softie was eating a cookie while sitting down, nothing special about that. Anyways, let's add the stuffing to the aurochs. A benefit of reaching the legendary realm is that all my wounds recover really fast, so I can touch this really hot piece of meat directly and not care about getting burned since it'll heal in a few seconds. Is the drama about to start? The food's about ready.

"Chosen Lucia. What are you doing?"

I looked around the grill. The sect leader was staring at me. Couldn't he tell? "Making a light snack."

The sect leader stared even harder. "Is that one of the sect's battle mounts...?"

"...No." There's no way cows are battle mounts, right? They were only a little bit stronger than Mrs. Wuffletush, which meant they still died in one hit. And their beast cores didn't even improve anything of mine, which means they're weaker than dragons. Right. Even Snow had a dragon as a battle mount and the plant possessing him was from a pocket realm like mine. There's no way my snack is combat worthy in any way, shape, or form.

"S-Sister Lucia killed all the aurochsen." Softie swallowed the last bits of her cookie and nodded at her grandfather. "She, um, said they'd sate her hunger for at least a year."

"She killed all hundred thousand aurochsen?" The sect leader was looking a bit scary.... And my tail was getting uncomfortably fluffier. Is it going to stiffen? I'll grab onto Softie to make sure I have a hostage. Just in case. "What do you mean sate your hunger for a year?"

I didn't say they'd sate my hunger for a year. "At least a year." I'm sure it was more, but the math to figure out how much more was too annoying to figure out, so I didn't bother. Who has time to sit down and crunch numbers during casual conversations? Besides, I was too busy killing the aurochsen to think. Sheesh.

"Didn't Little Moon offer you immortal rice?"

"Ah, I'm a foxkin, yeah? Yup. Totally a foxkin. Foxes don't eat rice, sorry." Since I'm pretending to be a foxkin, I have to fully commit to that role. Mhm. And this sect leader's already let me get away with touching his granddaughter in front of him, so I didn't think he'd be so mad about a few cows. I knew Softie was being abused. How can this man care more about cows than his granddaughter? I'm not a hero, but seeing Softie being so blatantly bullied leaves a foul taste in my mouth. At the very least, I have to show her the good parts of the world like food and slaughter and sex. …Maybe not sex. I'm not sharing Durandal. But food and slaughter are necessities in life! Without food, people die. Without slaughter…, where else are you supposed to get penises to sell for money?

"Is now really the time to eat…? There's going to be a battle unless the Great Poison Sect members choose to cripple themselves."

No, it's not the time to eat right now. I have to wait for the fighting to start so I can watch! Then it'll be the right time to eat.

"Psst. Lucia."

"Hmm? Durandal? What's up?"

Durandal cleared his throat and leaned closer. His breath tickled my ears. "Since there's bound to be a fight breaking out, can you drag those people wearing the silver robes into it? It seems like they're cultivators who live and die by the sword."

What!? What kind of person does Durandal think I am? I can't just implicate people for no reason! Those people in silver robes look so righteous and dependable. But one of them's looking at me funny. Right. That's a good enough reason to implicate someone.

Chapter 9

Those people in silver robes are definitely sword cultivators. There's something about them that resonates with my blood. There's no doubt in my mind that I'll gain good fortune by robbing them of their things, whether it's by a new qi-circulation technique or exquisite swords to consume. I just hope Lucia's able to fulfill my request; there's no doubt in my mind she's thinking of a way to help me. Except for when it comes to nighttime activities, Lucia always listens to me.

"Chosen Lucia?" The sect leader waved his hand in front of Lucia's face. "Are you feeling unwell? Your face looks pale."

"Hmm? No! I'm just thinking! Don't bother me."

When Lucia concentrates on something, her expression seems like she's being mortally wounded. It's cute, really. It's a shame she has no sense of timing for when she should think or not. Everyone's waiting on her to decide the fate of the county. It's not really appropriate for anyone else to speak right now. As for what I'm hoping for…, I wish a war would break out. A weapon spirit lives for battle after all. I'm not a nanny spirit.

Should I amp up the tension and accelerate the outbreak of war? First, I'd have to evaluate the danger that Lucia would be in. Since this is the Shadow Devil Sect's home ground, our side will definitely have the advantage if a battle starts. There may be a lot of sects, maybe a thousand, but they only brought a small group of maybe a hundred each. And I assume each finger of Kong County has the same number of lesser sects underneath them, so not every sect will be fighting against us—some will help us. As long as we can cleanly wipe out all our enemies, no one will bring back news to the main sects. From there, we could sweep everyone up with surprise attacks if the whole sect mobilizes. But that's for the future. I'm only interested in the moment, and I see absolutely no disadvantage to Lucia if my arm suddenly slips and happens to perform a Breaking Blade. Or if my mouth opens and words uncontrollably spill out of my mouth like, "I am Chosen Lucia's weapon spirit! My will is her will! My actions are her actions! Support Chosen Lucia with your strongest attacks! Breaking Blade!"

Oops. My arm slipped. A Breaking Blade is accidentally flying towards that elder from the White Crane Sect. But where's my support, hmm? Let's glare at Softie. …Lucia's naming sense is rubbing off on me.

"S-Support Sister Lucia!" Softie's whip cracked like thunder and a black snake roared out of thin air. I really like her choice of weapon. It's odd that her personality doesn't match it though. As far as I can tell, Softie's a masochist. Why else would she willingly let herself be bullied by Lucia?

"Support Chosen Lucia!"

The scene from before repeated itself. Thousands upon thousands of attacks rained down on the White Crane Sect members. During this, Lucia was still lost in thought. I rubbed her ears to distract her. "Mm? Ah? Durandal?" Her eyes widened as she looked around. "What's going on!?"

"It seems like the Shadow Devil Sect could no longer tolerate the White Crane Sect's actions." I leaned closer. "Quickly, take this chance to rob those people dressed in silver with me."

"Mm? Right! Let's do it."

Under the chaotic atmosphere where everyone started attacking one another, Lucia and I slipped through the crowd and made our way to my original target. They were actually engaging in combat with those Great Poison Sect members who were already severely injured earlier. It seemed like they wanted to get rid of a rival under the guise of chaos. Well, I'm not a cruel person. Once I thoroughly take what I want from them, I'll do the same to the Great Poison Sect. Then it'll be fair.

With Lucia's expertise in stealth, she ran up to the silver-robed people while shouting a drawn out Breaking Blade. Of course, Lucia has zero expertise in stealth despite being part squirrel, and everyone on the battlefield noticed her. But noticing her didn't equate stopping her. She bulldozed through the silver-robed people and Great Poison Sect members alike, blood and limbs flying into the air. She sincerely believes her attacks don't kill people. If she can survive with all her limbs cut off at once, then other people can survive with all their limbs cut off at once too—that's how she thinks. She's like a child that way. Well, I can't blame her for lacking a proper education while growing up.

Surprisingly or not, there weren't many earth-realm experts. Well, I was under the impression that they were hard to find in Kong County. I remember hearing from somewhere that even the five fingers of Kong had less than ten earth-realm experts each. And this meant Lucia was free to go on a rampage as one of the strongest people attending. I didn't even need to help her, but that doesn't mean I'm not going to. There's no reason not to gather combat experience while I can.

Truthfully, after killing a few so-called elders of the lesser sects, my impressions of the Immortal Continent aren't very good. They're weak, so pitifully weak that it makes my stomach churn. Every single one of them hesitated at critical moments. It was as if they had zero experience fighting for their lives. Were their techniques just for show? There was no substance behind them, no killing intent. How disappointing. Compared to Lucia, these people have never struggled a day in their lives. No wonder why they belong to second-rate sects. Perhaps it's a cultural thing. If people can live forever, then why would they expose themselves to danger before they're immortal? It's ironic that that way of thinking is the greatest obstacle on the way to immortality. Well, as long as I get easy access to flying swords to eat, I'll stomach this uncomfortable feeling that's similar to doing chores.

***

Swing, swing, swing. Chop, chop, chop. Mince, mince…, eh? I shouldn't mince. Right. No mincing. Slice, slice, slice. Whew, this is really easy. What am I doing? Planting heart devils, of course! Every time I harvest a limb, a heart devil blossoms. Sometimes multiple heart devils appear with a single swing of mini-DalDal. It's great! Why am I working so hard to plant heart devils? Because the more heart devils I plant, the more pleasurable it is when I cycle the Heart Devil Cultivation Technique! Oh, and I guess it can help me become a sky-realm expert to go home. Yeah, that too.

But there's just one issue…. Some of the heart devils are disappearing. A lot of them, actually. And that doesn't make any sense. A heart devil is only resolved by death or by overcoming whatever was plaguing their hearts. And if I'm terrorizing people by chopping off their limbs, then they shouldn't be able to shrug off these heart devils that easily. Obviously, they can't be dying either. So there's only one conclusion. Mm. I have to traumatize my next heart devil seedbeds thoroughly, so thoroughly that they'll see me every time they close their eyes.

There's so many people to plant heart devils in; this is the perfect environment for the Unrelenting Path of Slaughter. I can shut off my hearing to drown out all the screaming and the begging for mercy. And qi that is rushing towards me is super easy to notice. Mm, and since red lines mark the best place to cut someone to kill them, all I have to do is not follow the lines to not kill them. I'm so generous. With the help of my Path of Slaughter, this is an extremely easy and carefree task, which is why I love it. Only a combat junkie would want to fight something stronger than herself. No matter how many paths there are, I will always take the one of least resistance! And if the path of least resistance has too much resistance, then I'll give up. These are my principles. I'm a principled person, not a lazy one. Mhm.

Of course, Puppers is following behind me and looting everyone. Durandal went off somewhere after robbing the silver-robed people that looked at me funny. And Softie plus a small army of Shadow Devil Sect members are tailing me. At least, I think that's Softie…. I'm colorblind with the Unrelenting Path of Slaughter active. Huh? What if I accidentally plant heart devils in Shadow Devil Sect members? That doesn't matter! I already planted so many in Softie's suitors that a few more won't hurt. According to Softie, planting heart devils in fellow sect members is totally allowed. And the other sects that are supposed to be our allies can use a few heart devils too.

But wait, why aren't I killing people even though there's no doubt a lot of sects that want me dead? That's simple! Dead people can't have heart devils. Err, I mean, I'm not a murderer! I don't kill people even if they want to kill me! I'm like a saint, super-duper forgiving and nice and stuff. Besides, my Unrelenting Path of Slaughter still grows despite no one dying. I'm not sure why, but it does. Maybe it's the amount of blood I spill? I'm sure it gets a little bit stronger for every five liters of blood I extract from a person. I'm not sure how many liters of blood people have but losing five isn't enough to kill them! I think. Anyways, it depends on the size of the person since some beasts have a lot of blood.

Whew, it's been a while since I've had such long and continuous unbroken thoughts. This is all thanks to my engraving skills and the flaccid phoenix bones I took from the flaccid phoenix restaurant. Since I became the owner of a large territory of land, I've learned something called resource management from Ilya! Mainly, don't overindulge on non-renewable resources. Like bones of focus that actually work on me. That's why I'm only using them when I have those annoying headaches or when I really need their effects. And a slaughter like this requires a lot of my undivided attention. Besides, there aren't any trees in this place, so there can't be acorns or cocoa beans. I could probably do this without any focus bones!

The lack of danger greatly pleases me too. My Armor of Slaughter is enough to stop every attack aimed at me, but even if it wasn't, Softie and the army behind me are canceling out attacks heading towards me with their own. No doubt, I'm a very important person. Joining this sect was a great idea. It was my idea, right? It definitely wasn't Durandal's. Right, Durandal's ideas are my ideas anyways. I have such great ideas! Nothing can stop me. This is the life! Doing whatever—ow! Fuck! What was that!? Did something just…, gah! There's an arrow in my heart! What the fuck is this!?

There! It was that bastard with the bow! I'll rip him to shreds! "Unrelenting Path of Slaughter: Tides of Blood!" This technique is my new strongest attack, even stronger than Breaking Blade. I developed it all by myself. Unlike Breaking Blade where I gather all my qi into mini-DalDal and swing, I focus on my target and gather all my qi directly on top of it! There's something inside my qi that doesn't like other people, so if they're surrounded by it, they get attacked by that something. I'm not sure what it is. But it's a lot more effective than Breaking Blade! I ran repeated trial runs on Puppers with Ilya's help as a researcher. Of course, once I focus all my qi on the target, I'm left wide open, but all I have to do is consume a bone of strength, like this one, and I'm back to full health. Of course, there aren't any consequences to using bones of strength like tainting my body with impurities; they're a completely overpowered item which let me use repeated Tides of Blood if the target survives. Like this fucking bow user. How dare he shoot an arrow into my heart? If two or three Tides of Blood don't work, then I'll drown him in an ocean of blood! I have lots of strength bones!

***

Well, the cultural exchange is ruined. I thought I could experience foreign customs without an issue, but no. I should've known the instant I heard Lucia's voice targeting those poor Great Poison Sect members that something was going to happen. Lucia was shot in the chest by an arrow. And now she's gone berserk. Everyone between her and the archer that shot her is dead. Luckily, there weren't any Shadow Devil Sect members ahead of her. They learned their lesson and trailed behind her when she cut off some of their limbs.

But I guess this puts me in an awkward situation, huh? My master told me not to worry since she's an earth-realm expert and she could defend me, but I can't help but feel that I have to worry considering I'm the person here who knows Lucia the best. It'd be nice if I could give up feeling responsible for her. But why did she have to tell Durandal to attack those White Crane Sect people? Ugh. This whole battlefield is a disaster.

"Unbelievable! Chosen Lucia is forcing back Thirtieth Prince Yi!"

…Thirtieth? There's at least thirty princes? Wait, there are princes? "Who's Thirtieth Prince Yi?"

My master tore her gaze away from Lucia's battle and smiled at me before turning back towards the archer that shot Lucia. Was she not going to answer me? "The Yi family has ruled King Province for the past hundred millennia. Emperor Yi is a sky-realm expert who's fathered over a thousand children. Thirtieth Prince Yi is an earth-realm expert who enjoys scouring through cultural exchanges for talents that he can recruit for himself."

A thousand children.... Well, if sky-realm experts really live for a thousand years, it makes sense for them to have a lot of children. I mean, after a few hundred years, I imagine life would get pretty boring and what's a better pastime than copulation? After all, Lucia enjoys it a lot.... I really wish she'd keep it down at night. Wait. What would happen if...? "Say Lucia kills this prince. What'll happen?"

My master sighed. "Honestly, it depends on Emperor Yi's mood. Since he has a lot of children, he's not really attached to any of them. But he'll think of the murderer as someone not giving him any face. If he's in a terrible mood, our Shadow Devil Sect could face the wrath of the royal family. If he's in a good mood, then nothing will happen."

Is that normal? That's not normal at all, right? It can't be normal. "Out of curiosity, how many children do most people have?"

"Hmm? As many as their resources can support. A rich man can easily have up to a hundred children. A poor man can easily die a virgin. Of course, cultivators are a bit different; some vital essence is lost while creating children, so cultivators won't have offspring until they feel like they can progress no further in their cultivation."

Well. I guess the fact that the emperor can't keep it in his pants is pretty normal then. And it's not *too* unreasonable if I try to justify it. Some animals have lots of offspring with very little care given to each one: spiders, frogs, clams. Some animals have very few offspring with lots of care devoted to each one: monkeys, dolphins, whales. It just so happens that this Emperor Yi is similar to a frog. After all, there can only be one successor to the throne; he can't care about all the princes. But there's still the risk of retaliation simply from the blow to his reputation he'd suffer if someone killed a prince. Despite knowing this, not a single person from the Shadow Devil Sect is trying to stop Lucia from killing Thirtieth Prince Yi. "Shouldn't someone save the prince?"

"Hmm? Why?"

"Didn't you say our Shadow Devil Sect would suffer the wrath of the royal family…?"

"That's the worst-case scenario. And the wrath of the royal family can easily be settled with a payment of spirit stones."

…I'm starting to feel bad for these princes and princesses. Their lives are worth so little simply because their father's an unfaithful person. I'm sure he's unfaithful. There's no way one woman gave birth to over a thousand children by herself. But I don't feel bad for this Prince Yi. He's the one who had to shoot Lucia with an arrow. Of all the people he could've shot, he shot Lucia. I bet all the arrogance he has as an earth-realm expert is being washed away at this very instant. There's no way anyone would feel good after being swallowed by over a hundred of Lucia's Tides of Blood. Well, taking a second look at him, it seems like more than his arrogance is being swept away. Like his skin, flesh, and bones. And … he's dead. Lucia's killed royalty of the Immortal Continent in less than a week.

"Chosen Lucia's killed an earth-realm expert!"

"As expected of the one brave enough to violate my Wife Moonlight in front of me!"

"Chosen Lucia! I'm proud to be in the same sect as you even though you terrify me!"

"Chosen Lucia!"

And everyone's treating it as a momentous event. Jeez. What is wrong with people here? They have zero common sense. Their personalities are twisted too. How can they celebrate someone's death but not expect to die during a fight? It's clear that many of the people here don't have any experience with actual combat. I've been watching a lot of the fights out of curiosity because I've already seen what Lucia could do, so there was no point in watching her. A standard fight, from what I've observed, goes like this: two natives lock eyes with each other, they bluster and curse at each other while hurling insults, one or both of their faces turn bright red and they both start radiating qi, both of them perform a single technique, whoever spits out blood first instantly surrenders and offers up the tribute interspacial ring, and then the fight is over. There's no desperate struggle. It's like ... watching the mating dance of a bird. If the discrepancy between two natives' strengths is too great, then after locking eyes, they disengage and find someone else. If they spit out blood at the same time, they nod at each other and shake hands before disengaging. There's some unwritten agreement to not kill. And that's not a bad thing at all, really. Unless you throw in someone like Lucia who doesn't even know the meaning of the word customs. Even though these natives won't kill anyone, they get extremely happy and riled up when someone dies. That's the weird part. The Shadow Devil Sect members behind Lucia have been whipped up into a frenzy.

"Assist Chosen Lucia!"

"Chosen Lucia! Please, marry me!"

"No! Marry me instead! I'll let you do whatever you wish to me!"

...These people are hopeless. They're literally courting death. My lord, why was I even remotely worried about their mental health? It's clear they're too damaged to be helped. Hmm?

My master nudged me. "You're not going to take part in this battle? It's a good time to obtain experience."

"No. I'll pass." This isn't the kind of experience I need. After facing down death by staying with Lucia in the desolate mountains, this kind of battlefield isn't stimulating at all. ...Wait. Wait a minute. Am *I* the broken one? I'm turning down a perfectly safe and good chance to experience the techniques of the natives because it's not dangerous enough for my liking? Ilya! Clear your head! This is a golden opportunity to see how you compare to others! Before Lucia fully clears the battlefield, I'll harvest as much experience as I can! "Actually, I'll take part. Please, watch over me. I don't want to be hit by a stray earth-realm expert's attack." Lucia got shot by that prince because she was attracting too much attention. Thankfully, I even have a master to aid me in times of trouble. Right?

"Yes, I'll watch over you carefully, disciple."

She's so much nicer than Teacher Winemark and Lucia….

***

"What's this? What's this?"

Lucia held out an opaque glass bottle of immortal pills and shook it in front of my face. I sighed. Ever since that battle that day…, I've been stuck inside Lucia's unfinished mansion appraising items for her. Thankfully, she didn't force me to build the mansion anymore, making Puppers do it without me. "That's a bottle of mortal-realm immortal pills. It clears meridians and helps qi circulate better, but it's only effective for those under the saint realm."

Lucia sighed as her tail drooped. "So it's worthless. Got it." Then she stuck it into her interspacial ring. Another item appeared in her hands: a jade slip. Her eyes lit up as her tail rose once more. "What's this? What's this?"

…When I see her excited expression that looks like a dog that found a bone, I really find it hard to believe she's the same bloodthirsty slaughterer from that day. Which personality is the real Lucia? I took the jade slip from Lucia and inserted some qi into it. A few golden characters lit up on its surface. "This is the Great Poison Sect's core cultivation technique, Immortal Poison Body. It's not worth cultivating. It makes you immune to all poisons of the same rank that you cultivate it to, but the impurities that build up will slow your cultivation to a halt. No one's ever gotten past the saint-realm while cultivating this technique, which is why the Great Poison Sect is a second-rate existence."

Lucia snatched the jade slip out of my hand. Her eyes widened as she hugged the slip to her chest. "Did you say it'd make me immune to poisons?"

"Your cultivation will also slow to a halt...."

"Just learning it won't hurt, yeah? As long as I don't cultivate it, it'll be fine, right? Mm. Right. I'm just taking a peek." Lucia took in a deep breath and squinted at the jade slip. "This is going to hurt a lot, but for the sake of eating food without being poisoned, it'll be worth it!"

...I did say it wasn't worth cultivating, right? I'm sure I said it. But Lucia only cares about the facts I can tell her and not my opinions. To her, I'm nothing more than an encyclopedia. Hah. I know this is supposed to make me feel sad, but I'm a little happy that I can be useful to someone. As long as there is a relationship that ties us together, even if it's one between a person and her encyclopedia, there's a chance that it can develop into a friendship. I'm sure of it! ...I hope I'm right. Maybe I'm wrong. I should just give up....

"Gah! It hurts! Fuck! Ow! Guuuuh...." Lucia clutched her head and rolled around on the ground. Her body hit the wall, and then she rotated the other way until she hit the opposite wall. This wasn't the first time that this has happened. Other than the Immortal Poison Body, Lucia also learned the Great Earth Sect's technique, Footsteps of the Giant, and the Longevity Turtle Sect's technique, Impenetrable Shell, along with the Evil Flame Sect's technique, Madness Strike. I tried to tell her that learning too many techniques wasn't advisable and that she should focus on a single technique before learning more, but Durandal told her otherwise and Lucia completely ignored my advice. In the Immortal Continent, it's common sense to hone a single technique to the pinnacle, but Lucia doesn't abide by common sense. I just hope she doesn't bite off more than she can chew and suffer from any qi deviation.

Lucia stopped rolling around and sat up. "Whew. It's over." She stuffed the jade slip into an interspacial ring and materialized another item. "What's this? What's this?"

"That's a sword."

"Durandal! Snack!"

Durandal grunted. "Put it to the side." Durandal was cultivating the Righteous Sword Sect's core cultivation technique. I wasn't aware that spirit weapons could increase in rank by cultivating like a person, but apparently Durandal can. Puppers can't though. I wonder why.

Lucia tossed the sword to Durandal like she was throwing a dart, and the blade sank into the floor by Durandal's feet. Another item materialized in Lucia's hands. "What's this? What's this?"

Does she not look at what she's taking out of her ring? "That's a spear."

Lucia tilted her head up. "Puppers! Dinner!"

"I don't need to eat…," a gruff voice said from beyond the ceiling.

"Nonsense! If you don't eat, how are you going to get fluffier?"

Puppers is an amazing fighter, but Lucia really doesn't care about that. I feel bad for him. But I don't understand why she feeds him spears. If Durandal is a sword spirit that eats swords, wouldn't it make more sense for a sock spirit to eat socks? I'll ask. "Lucia? Why do you feed Puppers spears instead of socks?"

Lucia stared at me without moving. Durandal's eyes shot open, and a chill ran down my spine. There was a thumping sound as something fell off the mansion and onto the ground outside. I assumed it was Puppers. Did, did I say something wrong…? I don't think I did….

"You're a genius, Softie!" Lucia rose to her feet and tackled me. Is, is she hugging me? Is this how a hug feels like? It's … warm. And I can feel the softness of her tail from the backs of my arms. My heart feels so fuzzy right now. I've never been hugged before. "Uh. Softie. Hello? Softie? You can let go now."

"R-right. S-sorry." Ah, my face is on fire! I'm so embarrassed. Did I really just embrace someone before marriage? What if my grandfather finds out…? I hope Lucia doesn't tell anyone. Deep breaths. In. Out. In. Out. Ah! My heart won't stop pounding! I, I've heard about symptoms like this before! Am I suffering from qi deviation!? If Lucia's filled with impurities like I suspect, then is it possible they were transferred to me during that short period of contact? I'll send a message to Elder Hadrian; he's the doctor of the sect.

"Puppers! Eat these socks! Stop pretending to be dead, dammit!"

Why do I want to groan? Why do I feel like my stomach is trying to jump out of my throat when I hear Lucia's voice? Could it be because of the heart devils she planted in me…? This, this is bad. Please reply soon, Elder Hadrian!

Beep.

A message! It's from Elder Hadrian! "Chosen Moonlight, these symptoms that you're describing are not a result of qi deviation. Rather, it sounds like you're in love. Don't worry. I won't tell your grandfather about this message."

…Me? In love? With Lucia? N-no way! It's true that I've never been interested in any suitor that's ever pursued me despite their topnotch looks, status, and wealth, but, but…! I, I'm a woman! I'm sure I like men! I just haven't met the right one! And, and … Lucia's violent! And bloodthirsty! And wicked! And she violated me in front of the whole sect! No one could possibly ever love her except for Durandal! Yes. Elder Hadrian is wrong. That must be it. Even elders can make mistakes.

"Softie! What's this? What's this?"

Why's Lucia so close!? "T-t-t-that's a cauldron for alchemy."

"Hmm? Why're you stuttering more than usual? You alright?"

"I'm alright! Yes! Absolutely perfectly normally alright!" I, I have to get away from here! "Forgive me! I lied! I'm not alright! I, I have to check with my grandfather to make sure I'm not suffering from qi deviation!"

Chapter 10

Life is suffering. I am living. In conclusion, I am suffering. Why is Durandal's training so brutal!? I'm already the best! Let me slack off! Please. ...I wish I didn't learn these techniques when he told me to. "D-Durandal. I'm tired."

"If you have the strength to speak, you have the strength to do another thousand Madness Strikes."

Speaking doesn't require that much energy! "If I do any more Madness Strikes, I'll go insane! I haven't eaten for the past three hours!"

"Excellent. The more unstable you are, the easier it'll be to learn Madness Strike properly."

This is abuse. Durandal tricked me and stole my interspacial rings and buried them somewhere. So I don't have any food! Or focus bones! Or strength bones! Or, most importantly, food! And every time I try to attack Durandal to beat the location out of him, he slips into mini-DalDal and I can't do anything! If I had my spirit-restraining ropes, I could stop him, but the ropes are inside the interspacial rings. I'm so hungry that I could probably eat Softie, but she ran away to her grandfather! Why don't I just stop practicing and go find some food to eat? Because Durandal threatened to kill himself to withhold sex from me for a week. Like I said, I'm being abused. Durandal said he'd give me food only if I'm able to do 60,000 Madness Strikes in a day. I'm going to starve to death. This is how the legend of Lucia Fluffytail ends: Died of starvation. Huh? I could just find food anyway and not have sex for a week? Not possible. I'd die even faster.

Well. The only thing I can do is Madness Strike this board. Yup. This board. I pulled it out of an interspacial ring, and

Softie told me it was a Madness Strike practicing board. It's a giant square that's about as tall as me, and it has a lot of spikes organized in neat rows and columns. All I have to do is stick a spirit stone inside of a hole, and the board lights up with fancy colors. The light creates a snake-like pattern through the spikes, and I have to swing my sword as hard as I can while following the colorful path. It's maddening. What kind of sword slash doesn't cut in a straight line? Sheesh. And every time I hit one of the spikes on accident, they screech really loud and hurt my ears.

Five thousand six hundred thirty-two…. Five thousand six hundred thirty-three…. Five thousand … seven hundred…? Fuck. I lost count. "Durandal! I lost count! I can't focus without focus bones or food!"

"I guess you'll just have to start from the top."

"…Durandal."

"Yes, Lucia?"

Don't smile at me like that, you sadist! I'm going to cry. I, I wonder how tasty dirt is. Would it be immortal dirt since this is the Immortal Continent?

"Don't eat the ground, Lucia."

I wasn't going to! I was just digging. Sometimes people bury acorns and forget where they buried them; I might uncover a treasure trove if I dig in a random spot. Oh!? I found a barrel of wine! I don't know what kind of wine it is, but it smells like a gift from the heavens! Anything's a gift from the heavens when you're starving!

"Lucia. Are you going to drink that?"

Gah! Look away, Durandal! "N-no. Of course not." I'll distract him and drink it really quickly. "Look! It's a really kickass sword over there!" He didn't fall for it! It's my barrel of food! I earned this! "Stop! Let go!" Eh? It vanished? Did he store it inside of the interspacial ring? Hah. This isn't fair. The heavens sent me a drink, but the devil stole it away.

"Don't be like that, Lucia." Durandal patted my head and rubbed my ears, but my stomach growled instead. There's no pleasurable feelings from this at all! I'm going to cultivate the Heart Devil Cultivation Technique. How did it go? Some qi over there, some over there, there too. Loops and squiggles. Some more loops and spirals down to the stomach. And all done! Come to me, heart devil wormies!

…That's a lot of them. The sky turned completely black. Jeez. Are there that many people who have me in their hearts? It's nice to know there are that many people who care about me, even if it's a murderous kind of care. It's no different from Durandal's so-called personalized and specialized training that he created out of love just for me. …Who says I'm bitter? Ah, all my feelings of frustration and annoyance are being washed away by these cute little wormies. And replacing it is … more frustration. Why does Durandal insist on being a monk?

"Junior Lucia!"

"Eh?" Oh. It's the sect leader. "Hey. What's up?"

"I forgot to pass you the higher levels of the Heart Devil Cultivation Technique. Seeing your … cultivation reminded me." The sect leader handed me a jade slip. He raised an eyebrow at the Madness Strike practicing board. "Isn't this the Evil Flame Sect's? No, never mind. I suppose you have a lot of spoils after, uh, what you did. Please, never do that again. Dealing with all the lesser sects and the headache it's given me…."

It's Durandal's fault for starting the battle. I didn't tell him to do anything, but everyone thought I did. I'm being framed! Now that I think about it, Durandal's not a very good person, huh? He's a no-good, mean bully. If it weren't for the fact that I'm in love with him, I would beat him up! Wait a minute. If Durandal can torture me under the guise of training me out of love, can't I do the same to him? I'll beat him up in the name of love! "Durandal! Madness Strike!"

The essence of the Madness Strike is anger. The angrier I am, the more effective it becomes. According to the knowledge I gained from the green light in the slip, anger constricts everyone's meridians and slows qi circulation. When I get angrier and angrier, the pressure on my meridians builds up. At the peak of my anger, I forcibly channel all my qi and explode it outwards! It synergizes really well with Breaking Blade, doubling the power at the very least. And with the Madness Strike practicing board, I can control the trajectory of my strike like a whip! …Just kidding. If I do that, the muscles in my arm tear and that's painful, so I'd rather not. It's okay if I do it during practice, but it's definitely not okay in a real fight. Not like I'm fighting Durandal seriously though; this is a love tap! That's why it's okay to rip my muscles apart to avoid his guard. This is to vent all the frustrations that've built up!

…And he disappeared into mini-DalDal. Goddammit. I need some catharsis before I die of frustration! "Sect Leader, spar with me! Madness Strike!"

***

Once a heart devil worm flew out of my chest, my grandfather left to chase after it. I didn't even get the chance to ask him if I was suffering from qi deviation. My heart still hasn't calmed down, and my blood is circulating a lot faster than normal, especially to my cheeks. I guess the only thing to do is chase after him…. But that'll bring me back to Lucia. I, I'm not scared of Lucia or anything—I'm just nervous about seeing her. It's because she's a horrible, horrible person. I'm nervous out of fear, not shyness!

On the way back to the chosens' mountain, there were a lot less people than usual roaming about the sect. Normally, people would be exchanging pointers with one another, and sometimes people would market some goods. Disciples would take missions and go out and about, but it's strangely quiet. It's not silent, but it's still eerie. I've lived in the sect for my whole life, but I've never experienced it quite so desolate before. It must be because everyone's recovering from the mishap at the cultural exchange. People are calling it the Shadow Devil Sect massacre because Lucia wiped out six hundred sects by herself. Well, not whole sects, but the people that attended the exchange. I don't know how my grandfather's going to mend relationships with the sects. It's possible a large number of people are missing because he already declared war.

War used to be a common occurrence, or so I've read. The fight for resources is brutal. To become an immortal, a lot of spirit stones, medicinal pills, treasured weapons, and other resources are necessary. And there's simply not enough to go around for everyone. It's also why the people of Kong County don't have any sky-realm experts. Kong County is relatively barren when compared to the whole of the Immortal Continent. The real holy land of cultivation is smackdab in the center of the Immortal Continent. I wish I could go there one day, but I'd probably only qualify as a simple outer sect disciple at one of their weaker sects. Well, struggling is a natural part of becoming an immortal.

"Madness Strike! Madness Strike! Madness Strike!"

…What did I just walk in on? Lucia's whaling on my grandfather, and it looks like my grandfather's losing…. How did Lucia become so proficient with Madness Strike in the time it took me to gather my senses and go to my grandfather? It couldn't be that I took a really long amount of time to settle my excited heart, right? I don't think I spent very long, but time is like flowing water to a cultivator. A year could've passed…, but I don't think I meditated for that long. I didn't have to eat anything after all. Right, not much time has passed. That just means Lucia is abnormal.

"Madness Strike! Madness Strike! Madness Strike!"

Madness Strike is an explosive attack that can transcend ranks during a fight, but it comes at a great cost: torn muscles, damaged meridians, loss of sanity. It's why the Evil Flame Sect hasn't risen up to the position of one of the five fingers of Kong County. The recovery period is extensive unless medicinal pills are consumed to rejuvenate the user's health, but Lucia doesn't seem to require any rest. And it isn't as if she's holding back, judging by the foam pouring from her mouth. She looks like a rabid animal; though, I've only seen pictures of them in books. Maybe Lucia has rabies?

"Madness Strike! Madness Strike! Madness Strike!"

To be able to force out that much qi repeatedly..., the difference between her and me is too great. Where is she getting that much energy from? I'm not sure if I should just be watching like this, but I don't think I'd be able to help my grandfather. If a high-low-ranked earth-realm expert is being pushed back like this, I wouldn't be able to do anything as a mid-low-ranked saint-realm expert even if I have a few techniques that can transcend ranks. But it's good to see Lucia's fighting style so clearly for the first time. ...Yes, I followed behind her during the great massacre and should've seen her fight then, but all the blood made me nauseous and unable to focus. Now that I can see Lucia up close without worrying about dying, my heart's beating even faster than it was during the massacre. Why...? There's just something about her that makes my blood boil. She's so ... heroic.... I've never met a man as fierce, domineering, and aggressive as Lucia. Wait! That makes it sound like Lucia's a man, which she isn't! She's a woman like me..., but she's not very feminine.

"Madness Strike! Madness Strike! Madness Strike! Damn you, why won't you die!?"

"Wait, you're trying to kill me?" My grandfather let out a grunt as he stomped his foot and raised his hand into the air. Heart devil qi surged out of him and crashed into Lucia, but it went around her as if she were a rock in a river. "Oh? Then how about this? Heart Devil Apparition!"

It seems like my grandfather's trying to end this as fast as possible. Heart Devil Apparition is the strongest technique an earth-realm expert can use if they're utilizing the Heart Devil Cultivation Technique.

"Ah?" Lucia paused as the heart devil qi around her drew back and congealed into a blob. It twisted and rose up while taking the shape of a…. Lucia sliced it in half. "Like I'd wait for something to happen! Madness Strike!"

It's a shame slicing heart devil qi doesn't do anything. A massive black hand reached out from one of the halves and grabbed Lucia. "H-hey! Stop that! The worms tickle!"

Right. The Shadow Devil Sect specializes in planting heart devils, not in killing opponents. The most efficient way to place a heart devil in someone is to traumatize them. And what's a better way to traumatize someone than to cover their whole body in wriggling worms that try to burrow into their skin?

"Why isn't my Armor of Slaughter stopping this!?" Lucia struggled and squirmed, but the heart devil worms were relentless and crawled towards her ears. "W-wait! I-Impenetrable Shell!"

That's the other technique she stole; don't tell me she's proficient in that too. If she is, then what exactly have I been doing with my life? She's able to learn two techniques in the time it takes me to calm my nerves. Wait, no. A heart devil worm just crawled into her ear straight past her defensive technique. Phew, she's not unbelievably talented. But I should stop my grandfather's Heart Devil Apparition from going any further or Lucia will have to deal with a heart devil. …Why do I feel pity for someone who planted heart devils in me after violating me in front of the sect? But my chest feels oddly painful when I see her suffering. There's definitely something wrong with me. "Grandfather, stop!"

***

"So Lucia's been training the Madness Strike by continuously using it without rest…, and you want her to do this how many times?"

"Sixty thousand." It's a reasonable amount. If she does one every second, she'll still have seven to eight hours of free time left in the day. She can spend six hours eating, one hour doing nighttime activities with me, and the last hour for rest. It's upsetting that I have to motivate her by denying her pleasure, but I've already come to accept the laziness and lack of ambition from Lucia.

The sect leader stroked his beard. "That's a completely unreasonable amount. The sect elders of the Evil Flame Sect only practice the Madness Strike three times a day. Any more than that, and their bodies will break down. It doesn't matter if Lucia's a body practitioner; unless her meridians have been strengthened as well, she'll likely suffer permanent injuries from doing this."

After Lucia's little spar with the sect leader, Lucia went back to practicing against the training board. There is no doubt in my mind that she's picturing the light on the board as the sect leader's face. She didn't take very kindly to the heart devil worm crawling down her ear, but it did increase the strength of her Madness Strike by leaps and bounds. As for Lucia being injured from attacking…, I don't think that'll happen. Call it a hunch. "Lucia will be fine. Trust me." I have no basis for this statement, but I don't think I'm wrong. Maybe it's because Lucia's dumbfounded me so many times before. "Isn't that right, Lucia?"

"Fucking die. Madness Strike!"

Yup. With that much anger inside of her, there's no way she's suffering from any injuries. "See? She's perfectly fine."

"Well..., I can't deny she's done a lot more than should be possible," the sect leader muttered. His hand shifted from his beard to his moustache. "Alright. I shouldn't judge her with common sense. But why are you, a weapon spirit, overseeing her training? Doesn't she have a teacher?"

"I am her teacher." Yes, I'm a weapon spirit. That's all I have been, and that's all I will ever be, but I'm a damn good weapon spirit. I think. Of every weapon spirit I knew, I was the best, so that's pretty damn good if I may say so myself. "I've brought her this far." Right. Lucia's merits are my merits. Without my teachings, Lucia would still be a luggage carrier back in the Ravenwood army. Would she? If one day, she happened to learn about qi, I think she'd have developed quite nicely without me, but I *did* impart multiple techniques to her. Regardless, I was the one who brought her up when no one else saw her worth. Disregard the fact I only picked her as my master because she was the only beastkin amongst the people who found me.

"Really? You?"

What was that raised eyebrow about, hmm? It's like a wiggling caterpillar taunting me. "Are you looking down on me?"

"Ah? No, no. It's just that ... it's like the blind leading the blind? You're weaker than her, but you're her teacher. It makes sense for an immortal to tell someone how they became immortal, but for a mortal to explain to a mortal how to reach immortality...? Do you see what I'm getting at?"

...His words make sense even if I don't like them. "What are you trying to say?" Is he just here to criticize me? Or is he telling me my methods of teaching Lucia are wrong? I don't think my methods are wrong at all. Lucia's been upgrading her strength via beast cores and repetitive actions; if something isn't broken, then you don't need to fix it. Lucia managed to get a ton of beast cores during that little scuffle, but I'm still sorting through them all before I let her consume any. She wanted to consume them all at once, but I don't want her to experience a sudden growth. She has to establish a firm foundation first. Hence the practice.

"Quite frankly, it seems like Lucia needs someone to guide her," the sect leader said. The small smile on his face made me want to punch him. "A master, if you will. One of the ancestors of our sect has taken an interest in her and would like for her to become his disciple. What do you think, Junior Lucia?"

"You fucking die too. Madness Strike!"

"E-eh?"

Well, it seems like Lucia's sincerely upset. I don't think I've ever seen her this angry before. It's true that she throws tantrums and whines a lot and gets irritated when someone touches her food, but she never lets her anger stew like this. Maybe I pushed her a little too far with this training? But I have to push her at least this much; this Immortal Continent is a very dangerous place. Lucia has no sense of urgency, no drive. Even after facing the bow-wielding earth-realm expert, the first thing she wanted to do was eat instead of train. She should want to grind earth-realm experts underneath her feet without breaking a sweat! Or is that just me? Am I the one that's too hasty? No, that can't be. I'm training just as hard as Lucia is. But I do eat those exquisite swords while cultivating…. Alright. Fine. "Lucia. Take a break and have something to eat." I unearthed the interspacial ring that I buried in a top-secret place. When I turned around, Lucia was directly behind me, staring at me with wide eyes. Her tail flickered back and forth as her gaze dropped to the ring in my palm, and her nose twitched as she sniffed the air.

I held my palm out, but instead of taking the ring, Lucia flinched and stepped back. Her eyes narrowed as her tail straightened. "…What's the catch?"

Really. Am I that untrustworthy? "If you don't want to eat, then that's fine too. You still have 53,000 Madness Strikes to go."

"Eat! I'll eat!"

I couldn't see Lucia's movements clearly, but the next moment, she was holding the interspacial ring and hugging it to her chest while staring at me with wary eyes. I asked, "What are you looking at me like that for?"

"You're being nice. And that's infinitely scarier than when you're being mean." Lucia's head bobbed up and down. "You poisoned my food to help me train in the Immortal Poison Body like the green light said, didn't you?"

"I did no such thing." I really didn't. Just what exactly have I done to earn this distrust? Let's think back to the very beginning. I taught Lucia by placing spikes underneath her while she sat in a horse stance. I trained Lucia by shooting arrows at her while she danced atop bamboo spears. I encouraged Lucia with lots of head pats. I transferred poison from Lucia to myself when she was dying. I sparred with Lucia to help her incorporate her beast cores faster. I trained Lucia's Armor of Slaughter by throwing her out of a carriage and had her chase after it. I broadened Lucia's horizons by forcing her to come to the Immortal Continent. Looking back on all this…, I see way more positives than negatives. There's no reason for such a bad relationship between me and her to exist.

"I'm going to eat ten aurochsen."

You don't need to tell me how much you're going to eat. "Then eat ten aurochsen."

"Are you sure you're okay with me eating fifteen aurochsen?" Lucia bit her lower lip as she took a step back, still holding the interspacial ring to her chest.

"Eat however much you need to replenish your strength."

"Are you really Durandal?"

"If you're done eating, then give me back the ring."

"Eating! I'm eating!" Lucia ran away and instantly set up the grill that Ilya made for her. She placed an aurochs on top of it, and then she created an additional fifty bonfires. She skewered some aurochsen and positioned them over the flames with experienced movements. There wasn't a single wasted motion. If only she could be that dedicated towards training….

"…Is she cooking our battle mounts? I know I've seen this before, but I just want to make sure." The sect leader and Softie stood off to the side, just staring at Lucia. "How many days will she have to spend at the impurity-cleansing pool to purge all of this…?"

"The pool's still out of commission, Grandfather."

"Don't worry. I sent the two remaining Great Poison Sect members to nullify the poison. And I've already made a deal with the Azure Dragon Sect for more impurity-cleansing fishes."

Softie looked like she wanted to say something, but she held it back. Lucia thinks Softie is being abused by her grandfather, but from what I can tell, he shows his care in a very strict manner. He just has to encourage her more often. I wonder how he does it. It's easy for me to boost Lucia's morale by rubbing her ears and tail, but Softie does not have a tail. She has ears though. Hmm. Well, taking care of Softie's not my problem. I already have my hands full with Lucia.

**

Phew. I can't move. I ate too much. A whole 200 aurochsen disappeared into my stomach. I'm not a glutton! I just have no idea when I'll be able to eat again; that's why I ate until I was about to explode. Right now, if I eat even a single grain of salt, my stomach will rupture. That's how bloated I am. There's no way Durandal will force me to do anymore Madness Strikes in this condition! My plan is foolproof!

"Alright, since you're done, it's time to resume training."

...My plan is foolproof.

"Lucia. Closing your eyes and pretending to be asleep isn't going to work."

Foolproof.... I'm going to cry. Gah! Don't move me! I'm extremely fragile right now! "Wait! Wait! I'm awake."

"I had a feeling you'd do something like this." Durandal patted my head and smiled at me. ...That's his scary smile. I didn't do anything wrong! It was his fault for threatening to take away my food in the first place! "But don't worry. Even if you can't perform Madness Strikes, wasn't there another technique you picked up?"

Hmm. There was Madness Strike, Impenetrable Shell, Footsteps of the Giant, and Immortal Poison Body. I clearly can't practice Madness Strike in my current state. If I mess up Impenetrable Shell and get hit, I'll likely vomit everything out, so I don't think Durandal will make me train this one. Footsteps of the Giant requires me to stand, so that's already ruled out. Then the only thing left is....

"It looks like you figured it out." Durandal's smile turned even more sinister! "The Immortal Poison Body."

Wait. How was I supposed to level up Immortal Poison Body? If I recall correctly..., I have to be exposed to—is that a snake!? Ah! It bit me! It went straight through my Armor of Slaughter and it bit me! What the fuck!? "Durandal!? Where did you get that snake!? Wait, no! Why did you let it bite me!?" My arm hurts! It hurts, it hurts, it hurts!

"Calm down and channel the Immortal Poison Body."

"You have to warn me first!" Gah! Immortal Poison Body, do your stuff! Pain, pain, go away. Please. I can't feel my arm. I'm not sure if that's because the Immortal Poison Body technique is circulating or if it's because the snake venom killed my nerves. But most importantly.... "Why are you still letting it bite me!?" If I weren't so bloated, I'd get off my ass and kill it! But, but I can't! And all my qi is focusing on circulating this technique. "Softie! Save me!"

"Um, D-Durandal. Is, is this a good idea?" Stop being so soft, damn Softie! Kill the goddamn snake! Why are you asking Durandal questions when immediate action needs to be taken!? If I could open my mouth to yell at her, I would, but I just found out my throat is swollen and I can't speak. I'm going to die. I'm sincerely going to die. At least I had a decent last meal. I can die without regrets. Mm. …Fuck! Who am I kidding!? I'm not going to die a worthless death like this! Channel faster, you stupid Immortal Poison Technique!

"Of course. The Immortal Poison Body clearly said it required the user to be exposed to poisons." Durandal's voice was coming from everywhere. It was spinning too. By it, I mean everything. And I'm sure the snake was still biting me, but I just couldn't feel it anymore.

"But, um, you know poison is ingested, right? A snake's bite is injecting venom into her, not poisoning her."

…What. Did I hear that properly? I better not have. The snake's *poison* had better be messing with my hearing.

"But the Immortal Poison Body said it covered venoms too." Durandal leaned over and picked up the snake. Then it disappeared. Where'd it go? Why's Durandal looking more like a blob and less like a person? I, I think I'm going to faint. Or die. Is there a difference? Isn't fainting just a miniature death? Mm. By extension, sleep is death too. I die every day. Right. If I close my eyes now, then this'll just be like … sleeping….

Cold!?

"No, there's a footnote next to that statement. It only covers venoms if cultivated in conjunction with the Immortal Venom Body. I'm sure Lucia has it in one of the rings she retrieved."

Was Softie making me drink something? What is this? I'll vomit if I drink anymore. I really will. There's absolutely zero space left inside my stomach! I guess it can float around in my esophagus first. That should work. Ah, I'm losing consciousness again.

"Is this it?"

"No."

"This one?"

"Are you ... unable to read?"

"That's right. Look through this ring and find the Immortal Venom Body for me."

Is this heaven? I'm dead, aren't I? The world's black. It's so dark. So, so very dark.... I can't feel my body. Am I floating? Where am I floating? Ah. I see a green light. It's so colorful.... I'm going to eat it. But where's my mouth? Mm. I'll eat it with my thoughts. Come closer, little green light...!? It hurts! Gah! Fuck! I was bamboozled! This isn't heaven; this is hell! Urgh. I'm dying. No. I'm already dead. I'm suffering. I said life was suffering, but death is suffering too. Everything is suffering. I, I don't want to exist anymore. Ah. The pain's gone. Did my wish come true? Wait; if it did, then I wouldn't be able to think right now. Then something else must've....

"Well, she stopped groaning in pain, so I think she learned the Immortal Venom Body. Lucia, can you hear me? Channel the Immortal Venom Body if you want to live."

But living is suffering.... So I shouldn't channel the Immortal Venom Body? But I don't want to die either! That's suffering too. There's, there's just no good choice, huh? Mm, but if I die, I'm sure Durandal would be sad. Right...? The person who put me into this perilous situation would definitely feel sad if I died, right!? Gah! I should die just to spite him! But then I won't be able to eat if I die.... Mm. Alright. I'll channel the Immortal Venom Body. Ah. I can feel my limbs again. And I can feel pain again. Ow. It hurts. Why am I so sore? Oh, I can see again.

Softie's face was hovering in front of mine. It was bright red. "How are you feeling, Lucia?"

I have very, very mixed feelings. But right now, all I want to do is hug something soft and take a nap. And there's a perfect candidate hovering over me. Don't struggle, Softie! Any sudden movements and I'll really puke. Ah. She really is soft. How can she feel like this without any fur? I'll thoroughly inspect her … one … day….

***

Alright. So I made a mistake. Who told the creator of that jade slip to add footnotes to his teachings? It's pretty important to mention that the Immortal Poison Body only works on venoms if used in conjunction with the Immortal Venom Body. That's seriously something that shouldn't have been added as an afterthought. Yes, the information was directly seared into my mind, but it's still easy to gloss over certain parts that are only mentioned once as if the creator were trying to hide them. At least Softie was here to save Lucia with that antidote. This mishap could've ended a lot worse. I even might've been forced to extract the venom out of Lucia again and disappear for an extremely long while.

"So … about the ancestor seeking to make Junior Lucia his disciple…, looks like Junior Lucia could really use another teacher, eh?" There's something about the smug look on the sect leader's face that makes me really dislike him. It's probably the fact that his eyebrows look like white caterpillars. "Since Junior Lucia's not really in any position to respond, how about you decide for her? After all, your will is her will, as you said before you started a massacre."

Would Lucia be better off with another teacher? If she did have another teacher, he'd have to learn her quirks. He'd soon find out the best way to encourage her was through ear rubs. Then when she looks at him with her lewd face, the ear rubs would turn into tail rubs, and eventually into massages. From there, slowly, ever so slowly, they'd become more and more intimate with one another until Lucia receives a happy ending from him. Before she knows it, she'll be tricked into nighttime activities with him! There's no way I'll allow Lucia to have another teacher! I may be a weapon spirit, and weapon spirits don't have feelings, but I refuse to allow anyone else to have Lucia! This isn't jealousy; nor is this pride. It's…, it's…, it's just not going to happen!

"Right. Lucia's will is my will. And you heard her earlier. The answer is no." Well, it was a lot cruder earlier, but I'm a refined weapon spirit. Such crass language is below me.

"Hmm. Well, I can't force her." The sect leader shrugged. "It's just unusual for a chosen not to have a master. Even the core disciples all have a master. A lot of higher ups in the sect won't like that, so you'll have to prove to us that Junior Lucia is worthy of receiving our support as a chosen."

"Grandfather! Are you going to make her do that…?" Softie still hadn't escaped from Lucia's embrace. I don't think anything that can't teleport can get away actually. I've been on the receiving end of that death-grip-like sleeping hug. It's scary: Her arms lock her target's arms and torso into place. Her legs lockdown her target's thighs. Her tail coils around her target's feet. If the target tries to move, everything tightens. And if Lucia happens to curl up and the target is positioned in a poor manner, there's a serious chance of a few bones breaking. Thankfully, since I can get away by slipping into my weapon body, Lucia's only been going after Ilya. I wonder how that little girl is doing anyway. I saw her having fun during the massacre, but I didn't see her after it was over. …And I sidetracked myself. What was Softie talking about when she said that?

"That? No, of course not." The sect leader shook his head. What was that? Why were they talking so cryptically? Something bad's going to happen to Lucia, I can tell. Mm, well, lots of good things have happened to her since joining as well, so it's only fair. "The simplest way for Junior Lucia to show how valuable she is to the sect is to help solve some of its problems. Namely the issue of placating the sects that lost people during the cultural exchange."

Hmm. What does placate mean? It rhymes with exterminate. The definition should be similar. "And you want Lucia to take care of that?"

"Right. After all, she was the fuse that started it all." The sect leader smiled and nodded. I didn't like his smile either. It was a friendly smile, but every time Roland gave me a friendly smile, I'd always end up in a horrible situation. Nothing good comes from a friendly smile. That's why I always smile at Lucia when I'm about to begin strenuous training with her. "Of course, I don't expect Junior Lucia to accomplish this by herself. Chosen Moonlight here will be going with you as well as a few elders from the sect. There will also be a mission in the task hall for any disciple to volunteer too."

Softie whispered, "I-I'm going too, Grandfather?" But I don't think the sect leader heard her, or if he did, he pretended not to.

Anyway, this task seems simple enough. "Let me get this straight. Since Lucia refuses to have a master within the sect, you feel she's not completely trustworthy. To gain your trust, she has to placate the sects that were caught up in the massacre that she started during the cultural exchange." Hmm. Something's off. "But earlier, it seemed like you were willing to do anything to incorporate Lucia into the sect. Why does she suddenly have to prove herself now?"

"Like you said"—the sect leader nodded—"she's refused to take on a master. That's refusing to give our Shadow Devil Sect face, and many elders won't like her disrespectful actions. Personally, I don't mind, but for a tranquil future in our sect, Junior Lucia has to show the sect her worth. Of course, if she takes on a master, her master will be able to vouch for her and all of this won't be necessary."

Well, it seems like Lucia's going to placate some sects. I'm not refusing a master for her out of jealousy or insecurity; placating sects seems like a good method of training. As Lucia's teacher, I have to provide abundant opportunities for her to grow. And exploring the Immortal Continent should provide plenty of experience. Besides, Lucia has to go to the four sects she learned cultivation techniques from to rob..., appropriate them of resources necessary to advance those skills. Cultivating the Immortal Poison Body will be a lot easier if she has access to the Great Poison Sect's poisons. After all, I can't get lucky all the time and find pouches with live poisonous beasts inside of them. Apparently, the satchel that I have on my waist belonged to some beast-taming sect's elder. Inside was a snake, the same one that bit Lucia, and an eagle. I'm not sure why those two beasts haven't killed each other yet, but I'm not going to separate them. I only have one satchel.

"Have you thought it over?"

"Yes. Lucia will placate the sects."

"Very well." The sect leader nodded and a rolled-up scroll appeared in his hand. "This is a list of all the sects we've caused issues with. Chosen Moonlight's received an extensive education and should know where they're all located. Take good care of her. You will depart in a week."

Chapter 11

This past week was hell. There's simply no other way to describe it, and I'm very good at describing things! Not only have I been practicing Madness Strikes, but I've also been working on my Impenetrable Shell and Footsteps of the Giant. Durandal said I only had a week to improve my strength, so he decided to, as he calls it, expedite my training. That means practicing all three at the same time.

Footsteps of the Giant is actually a pretty neat technique that I like a lot. When the giant walks, who dares bar its path!? That's the technique's motto. Doesn't it sound super-duper awesome and perfectly tailored for me? Anyways, it's really useful. I extend tendrils of qi out of my feet as if I'm a tree and my qi tendrils are roots, and by doing so, I'm firmly rooted into place and can't be moved. Actually, I can extend qi tendrils out of any part of my body and stick them into any object other than the ground even though Softie said that wasn't supposed to be possible unless I had really, really large meridians. Supposedly, the meridians in normal people's feet are large, so it's easy to send qi out of them. I guess that means I have really, really large meridians, or I'm special. I knew I was special. Only a special person could find the Godking's legacy! …Bryant wasn't special because he died.

Ahem. Anyways, like I was saying. I can walk on walls and on ceilings with the Footsteps of the Giant. Eh? I wasn't saying that? Well, I just said it. I can firmly root myself in place by spreading my qi into the ceiling. So of course, Durandal's had me perform everything upside down, including Madness Strikes, eating, sleeping, and even nighttime activities. It's extremely difficult when only one person is able to glue themselves to the ceiling. I'm really glad I have a tail that works like an extra limb. Who wants to be a weak-tailed crowkin anyway?

As for Impenetrable Shell..., it's like an Armor of Slaughter that I have to focus on using. It's hard. I can barely follow a single train of thought; how am I supposed to multitask with an active shield too? But to train the Impenetrable Shell, Durandal's been helping me. Helping.... Right, he's definitely helping.... Gah! He's just using this *practice* as an excuse to beat me up and test his techniques! I've been hit by more sword techniques in this past week than I've taken shits in my life! And I can't even kill him because then I'll be punishing myself if he disappears for a week. Life's not fair. Humph.

Why haven't I been practicing the Immortal Venom Body? That's simple! When Durandal tried to get the snake to bite me again, I bit its head off. Mm. Squirrels and snakes have a very volatile relationship. The one who doesn't want to be bitten must bite first! I'm sure that's a saying somewhere in the world. If not, then it's a saying now. Softie's been throwing a lot of sayings at me, stuff like: What's seen can't be unseen; please don't strip me. And, there is no medicine for regret; please stop stripping me. And, the strongest steel is forged in the hottest fire, stay strong, Soft Moonlight; please stop touching me, Lucia. All these sayings are so profound. I wonder what Softie's trying to tell me. I'm sure I'll figure it out one day.

But who cares about one day? The hellish week is finally over! It's time to set off and placate some sects! Durandal told me I received a mission to eradicate the sects, but Softie corrected him. I have a list of four hundred sects to visit and fully infest with heart devils. People can't be angry at you if they're completely terrified of you, right? Terrorizing when brought to the extreme is also a form of placating. Mm. Softie told me it would be a good experience, and from what I can tell, since the whole Shadow Devil Sect is filled with sadists, a good experience for them is defined as torturing others to plant heart devils in them. Clearly, they want me to torture the lesser sects.

"You're thinking too hard again, Lucia. Steam's coming out of your head."

Eh? It's Ilya! "Ilya! Why are you here?"

"You ... crushing me...."

Hmm. After eating over a thousand aurochsen, my physical strength increased again. I can't be blamed for hugging Ilya too hard. "Oops."

Ilya sighed and cast a healing spell on herself. It's been a while since I've seen one of those. I've asked Softie if she had any healing spells because the snake also bit my tongue when I bit its head off, but apparently healing techniques aren't very common amongst Immortal Continent natives. They use drugs instead. Lots and lots of drugs.... During this week, I've seen Softie eat seven whole bottles of pills, and all she did was sit cross-legged in her cave. Of course, I couldn't let her live life like that, so I dragged her out every so often when it was time to eat. For some reason, she gets really annoyed when I do that, and she even spat out blood once, but all her resentment disappears when I stuff her face with food! As a trustworthy food peddler once told me, the fastest way to cheer someone up is through food! Now that I think about it, every time I asked that peddler a question, the answer was always buy more of my food. Well, food's never not solved any of my problems, so she was right!

"Did you hear any of what I just said?"

...Was Ilya talking? "Uh. You said I was crushing you. Mm."

Ilya sighed again. "You never change. I'm not sure why I expected you to." She shook her head. Did she grow a little taller? Maybe I shrank.... "Are you listening now?"

"Yes! Loud and clear!" I'm paying attention. Mhm. Focus, Lucia. Pretend you consumed a focus bone. How does that feeling feel like? Hmm. Ah, Ilya's mouth stopped moving. I'll just nod and pretend I heard. "Uh-huh. Sure. Got it."

Ilya slapped her forehead with her palm. Then she sighed again. That's three sighs in less than two minutes! She must be feeling pretty sad, huh? I wonder if it's because she misses her dad. How does it feel like to miss her parents? I'm sure I felt it way back when but repressed those memories because they were too miserable. Mm. I'll rub her ears to cheer her up.

"W-what are you doing?"

There's no way Ilya can escape from my grasp! Ah, but I still haven't figured out what she was here for. "So. Why are you here?"

"Can you let go of my ears?"

I can, but I won't. So I shook my head.

"My master forced me to volunteer for the sect-placating mission that you're in charge of. Besides me, there's another hundred thousand disciples who've signed up."

Wait. "I'm in charge of the mission?"

"Aren't you?"

"Am I?" I thought I was just a bystander! If I'm in charge…, then that makes everything better! "That means everyone has to listen to me, right?"

"Well, yeah. Listening to the chosens was part of the task description." Ilya's face changed. What kind of expression is this? It's hard to tell because I'm playing with her ears and the skin around her eyes keeps moving. "Please, order the disciples around responsibly."

"Hah? You think I'm not a responsible person?"

"No, I don't think that. I know you're not responsible."

Hey! I'm very responsible! If I wasn't, would I have been put in charge of this mission? Hmph, hmph. I'll show Ilya what it means to be a chosen of a sect! As a chosen of the sect, I have to…, uh, be responsible or something. Yeah. Softie tried telling me, but I was too busy trying not to die from Durandal's attacks so I wasn't listening. But the sect leader trusts me to teach these lesser sects their place! And I can't betray that trust. Well, I could, but I wouldn't gain anything from it, so I won't.

***

This is my first time leaving the sect! I'm excited and nervous at the same time. I wonder what the outside world is like. I've read many, many books and seen a lot of images, but I've never experienced it for myself. My grandfather always kept an eye on me and never let me take any tasks that'd bring me outside. Since my parents died before I could even remember them during a skirmish against the White Crane Sect, my grandfather pays extra care towards me. I was shocked when my grandfather said I'd be accompanying Lucia. But it's not like he left me alone without any protection. "Elder Sky, you don't have to watch over me when I'm in my room…."

Elder Sky didn't respond. He was cultivating in the corner of my room on the flying airship that Lucia was driving towards the Little Clam Sect. Was he even paying attention? What if I left right now? I stood up, and Elder Sky's eyes instantly snapped open. "Did Junior Moonlight need something?"

"I wanted to stand on the deck…." If it's my first time leaving the sect, it doesn't mean anything if I'm stuck inside the airship the whole time!

"The sect leader sent me to guard over you, Junior Moonlight. I can't guarantee your protection on the deck, but this room is reinforced with many defensive formations. You're safe here. It'd take three earth-realm experts to force their way—"

Bang! The door flew off its hinges and crashed into the wall beside me. A corner of the door was firmly embedded in the hardwood next to my head. If the door had flew a little more to the right, I would've died. "Softie!"

"H-how did you break through the defensive formations!?" Elder Sky staggered to his feet and pointed at Lucia, the culprit who barged into a girl's room without knocking.

"Eh? You're not Softie. Did I get the wrong room?" Lucia blinked twice before her gaze landed on me. "Ah! There you are! Help! I followed Durandal's instructions and now we're lost."

But I was the one who told Durandal which way to go…. How are we lost?

"C-Chosen Lucia! The defensive formation!" Elder Sky looked like he wanted to strangle Lucia. I used to feel that way about her, but then I realized how hopeless it was. Besides, she's a little cool and valiant when she kicks open doors like that. Though I'd appreciate it if the doors would stop ending up so close to my head.

"Defensive formation…." Lucia tilted her head to the side. Her tail twitched a few times, and the qi that was powering the formation crackled around her fur like lightning. "Are we under attack?"

"Why are you asking me!?"

"Cause you're the one who brought up defense!" Lucia's ears perked up as her shoulders inched upwards. "Why are you yelling at me!?"

Lucia doesn't like being yelled at. She told me it reminds her of the times when she'd be whipped for not following directions properly…. At first, I didn't believe her because, well, who in their right mind would offend Lucia? But then I saw some scars on her back when she was changing. …It's not like I was watching her strip! S-she just took off her clothes in front of me without warning! Nothing happened between us! She just changed clothes and that's it!

"Mm. That's what I thought." Lucia nodded at Elder Sky, who seemed to be paralyzed out of shock. Then she ran up to me and lifted me by my waist. Before I could even scream, wind was blowing my hair into my face, and I was on the deck of the airship. And it wasn't like Grandfather's instant teleportation. Lucia just ran really, really fast. My stomach's nauseous. Lucia dropped me onto the floor without warning, and I had to channel some qi to land on my feet properly. "Okay. I brought her, Durandal! Get off the steering wheel!"

This is what it's like outside the sect! It's ... the same exact sky as inside the sect. And the people on the airship outside of the sect are the same people that I'd see inside the sect. I think my expectations may have been too high. Well, I'll figure out where we are since that's what Lucia requested of me. Judging by the position of the sun, clouds, and endless sea of green beneath us..., I have no clue where we are. If the stars were out, I would know, but it's not nighttime yet. But Lucia's counting on me! And shuffling me towards the steering wheel....

"Alright, Softie. Do your stuff." Lucia's eyes were like brilliant dewdrops: so clear, so enticing.... If she puts on such an expectant face, I can't tell her I don't know where we're going!

I took in a deep breath and looked behind myself. There were nine hundred ninety-nine other airships following ours. We should've arrived at the Little Clam Sect by now if we were heading the right way. But since we haven't and we haven't run into any other sects, that can only mean we've gone the complete opposite direction and headed towards Hong County instead. Then to get to where we want to go, we have to do a complete about-face. That's a massive loss of face for us as leaders.... The first hour of the expedition and we completely reverse directions? I, I guess it can't be helped.

After making a giant loop around, it took around two hours for us to reach the first sect. Thankfully, it was also the Little

Clam Sect. I managed to salvage Lucia's mistake.... Phew. I didn't betray her expectations. "Lucia, we're here."

"Whoa!" Lucia ran to the edge of the airship and leaned over the side. I sincerely thought she was going to fall off, but she—did!? Oh, she caught the railing with her tail. I thought she was going to die. "Ilya, look! It's a giant testicle!"

...A what?

"That's a clam, Lucia."

"Which mortal dares insult this great clam!?" Well, that's the guardian beast of the Little Clam Sect. The Little Clam Sect was founded by the offspring of a sky-realm clam. It's still not fully mature, so it's only a high-high-ranked saint-realm expert. With Lucia's nonsensical physical strength and Elder Sky's cultivation, there's no way the guardian beast can defeat us. Unless it decides to sacrifice its lifeblood and boost itself to the earth realm.

"Clam.... That's seafood, right? That means it's edible?" Drool was pooling in the corner of Lucia's mouth.

"I will not stand for such disrespect!" The guardian beast of the Little Clam Sect was glowing. It seemed to be gathering qi. Does it not see the fleet of a thousand ships in the air? Why is it acting so rashly? Could it be the, the tes..., test..., the insult that Lucia called the clam caused...? Oh! Lucia must've planted a heart devil in it since she's already cultivating the tenth layer of the Heart Devil Cultivation Technique.

***

I learned my lesson. Clams taste horrible. They're so chewy and slimy and gross and exactly what I'd expect something that looked like that to taste like. At least killing the clam planted heart devils in every single one of the people who worshipped the clam. Why would they worship something so weak anyway? It couldn't even take thirty Madness Strikes before its shell broke apart, and once I got a good hit on the soft and squishy parts, it died instantly. Eh? I'm a murderer now? That's impossible. Clams aren't people. You can only murder people. It doesn't matter if the clam could speak; it simply doesn't count.

Anyways, I distributed the rest of the clam meat to my underlings—there was a lot of it; everyone got at least two servings—and I kept the beast core to myself! Of course, I instantly absorbed it before Durandal could take it away like the other beast cores I found during that cultural exchange. Surprisingly, it got easier to control the Impenetrable Shell technique after doing so. It's a shame there was only one clam. If I could master Impenetrable Shell, Durandal wouldn't have an excuse to hit me anymore! But alas, there was only one. Woe is me. On the bright side, the clam said something about its sky-realm father coming to hunt me down once its death was discovered! I'm looking forward to it. Its beast core will definitely improve my Impenetrable Shell to levels where Durandal can't pierce it. Mm. Too bad clams can't walk though. The father clam will probably never be able to find me.

And I didn't forget to accomplish the task that the sect leader handed me. I completely and utterly robbed the evil sect blind. I didn't even leave a single tree behind because I remember what Softie said to me about trees on the Immortal Continent. They're apparently really good at producing qi, so I had to take them all. They fit perfectly inside of these pouches that can hold living things. Let me repeat that, these interspacial pouches can actually hold living things! That means I can store Ilya and take her with me no matter where I go! But she keeps crawling out after I stuff her inside, so I'll only store her when it's necessary. Softie says I didn't understand the purpose of the task, but I'm the leader here! My interpretations are the correct ones.

So now we're heading to another sect with Softie driving the flying boat. And Durandal's forcing me to cultivate because he says I've been slacking for far too long. I only spent a day cleaning out the clam-worshipping sect and he claims I'm slacking! This is abuse. Well, at least the Heart Devil Cultivation Technique is fun to do. So many tingles. And it's really effective! Every few minutes or so that I circulate that technique, the amount of qi that enters me is the same as a dragon's core. But after cultivating for a couple of hours, there were three popping sounds coming from my stomach that really concerned me. Durandal and Puppers have no idea what they're about, and Ilya didn't either, which is why I'm off to find Softie!

And she's at the steering wheel. She's such a dedicated underling; I want to keep her. "Softie!"

Softie flinched before locking eyes with me. "L-Lucia? You, you broke through three ranks at once!?"

I did what? Hmm. "Speak in terms I can understand without using my head."

"You became a low-mid-ranked spirit-realm expert in the two hours that you were gone!" Softie was staring at me with the same kind of look that the acorn-picking servants back at my mansion gave me when I met them. "Wait. It makes sense if you deeply planted heart devils in all the Little Clam Sect disciples.... That's at least 900,000 heart devils to draw qi from.... Right. It makes sense, but why do I feel like it's unfair...?"

So, in other words, I'm amazing. Right? That's what Softie's trying to tell me? "That's right. I'm the best!"

Gah!? Durandal pinched my tail! "You say that, but you haven't practiced any of the practical skills that accompany the Heart Devil Cultivation Technique. Since you're so amazing, you'll learn those without any problems, right, Lucia?"

Please. No more learning. Learning makes my head hurt. "I, I have to practice my Madness Strikes. Mm. Right. Busy, busy."

"Weren't you telling me how sick of Madness Strikes you were just a few days ago? Let's take a break from them. Why don't we start with the easiest technique, the Heart Devil Apparition?"

That's the most difficult technique! I received the knowledge first, Durandal! You can't trick me! Normally, I'd protest out loud, but Softie told me I shouldn't quarrel with people in public to protect my face. And she's right. If I'm quarreling, then my guard will be down and I might suffer an unexpected arrow to my eye! I was already shot in the heart once when I wasn't paying attention. That wasn't very fun. What was I saying? Right. "But look, we're so close to the next sect. It'd be a waste to have to cut practice short. It's better to not start it in the first place. Mn. Besides, it's been two hours since I last ate! I deserve a snack."

Durandal rubbed my ears. It felt good, but I wasn't going to be tricked! Stay vigilant, Lucia! "Yeah, you're right. You should eat first."

…What the hell? Durandal's being nice about practicing? What is this!?

"I'm nice all the time."

Don't read my mind, please. "Are you okay, Durandal? You're not feeling sick or anything, right?" Can weapon spirits even get sick? I don't think that's possible. Maybe he's poisoned. But he hasn't eaten anything but swords, so I don't think that's the case.

"Are you going to eat or not?"

"Eat!" I was sincerely concerned about his health! There was no reason for him to glare at me like that, jeez. What food do I have in my ring for second lunch? More aurochsen. Hmm. I'm going to be eating aurochsen for a long while, huh? Oh wells. At least they're tasty.

"Softie, are all the sects going to be as easy to ruin as the first sect?" Durandal went over to Softie's side while I prepared my grill. "Aren't there any sects that'll provide a challenge for Lucia?"

Softie shook her head. "None on the list we've been given, no."

That's great! I love easy tasks. Everything should be easier so I can live more comfortably.

Durandal sighed. "Then I guess there's no choice but to artificially increase the difficulty for her."

Say what?

***

"During this sect's subjugation, you're only allowed to use your tail to attack."

Lucia froze mid-bite. "Say what?"

Lucia has so much potential, but she doesn't draw it out. I suppose that's a fault with the environment she's staying in—it's too weak to encourage her growth. That's why I'm imposing some limits on her while she goes about placating the sects. And the first thing that she should work on is using her tail. She only ever thinks to use her tail when she's in a situation where she can't use her hands and feet. To get her to use her tail in a fight more often, I'll threaten her by refusing her nighttime wishes if she uses anything other than her tail to attack the sect waiting below us. And since sects have upwards of a million people in them, I think Lucia will get the hang of using her tail really quickly after smacking around that many victims, err, target dummies. "While you subdue this sect, you're only allowed to hit people with your tail. If you don't listen, the usual punishment applies."

"That's not fair!"

"Um, Durandal." Softie didn't seem like she was intending on stopping the boat. "We're just passing over this sect. They're subordinates of the Azure Dragon Sect, our allies."

What? I've already established a plan, and I'm not going to let some feelings between sects change that. Once a man decides on doing something, they should accomplish their goal! Disregard the fact I'm a weapon spirit. "Nonsense! Allies support each other in times of need, and Lucia needs to hone her techniques! This will simply be a friendly exchange where she might happen to plant heart devils in her friendly opponents."

"Wait, wait, wait." Lucia put down the drumstick she was holding. "We should leave allies alone. Mhm. It's not because I'm lazy and don't want to fight or anything like that. I'm a principled person! I won't beat up my allies."

If that's the case..., I guess it can't be helped.

"D-Durandal...?" Why was Lucia inching away from me, hmm? "W-what are you planning?"

Why is Lucia so suspicious of my intentions? I'll look away to lower her guard and ask Softie a question. "Hey, Softie. What's the name of the sect we're flying over?"

"...The Raging Wind Sect."

Darn. It's not a sect founded by an animal. "I suppose they don't have any guardian beast that I can insult to trigger a skirmish?"

Softie gave me a strange look. She's not as easy to read as Lucia—it's hard to tell what she's thinking. "...No. The Little Clam Sect was named after the clam that founded it, but the Raging Wind Sect is named after their signature technique."

Alright. It looks like I'll have to trigger this the old-fashioned way. I'll borrow Lucia's and Softie's reputations and attack the sect. Am I evil for doing this? The only thing that's evil is not pursuing one's potential to their fullest! This is all for the sake of Lucia's growth. I'm willing to become hated if it means Lucia will become stronger; this is what it means to be a weapon spirit. I walked over to Lucia and hugged her from behind while resting my cheek against the side of her head to distract her. I used my gentlest voice to whisper into her ear, "Lucia...."

"Y-yes?"

I could feel her body rapidly heating up in my embrace. Before she gets too excited, I should hurry up and accomplish my goal. I whispered, "Don't forget to get me exquisite swords while you're down there," and then I threw her off the side of the flying boat.

While Lucia was screaming, I stood atop the railing and fired a few Breaking Blades at the Raging Wind Sect before shouting, "Follow Chosen Lucia! Attack the alliance breakers!" And that's all it took to convince the Shadow Devil Sect members. They leapt off of their boats and flew after Lucia on flying swords. For some reason, Softie stayed behind.

"T-that's the second time you've done that...."

"Done what?" What is she accusing me of? All I did was ignite the morale of our troops.

Softie bit her lower lip. "Started a massacre using Lucia's name." Tears formed in her eyes. Why was she crying? "Y-you can't keep using her like that.... It's, it's wrong."

"Huh?" Lucia really picked a good name for Softie. She cries so easily. It's wrong to force Lucia to grow? Impossible. Ah, maybe she's crying over the injuries people will suffer if a fight breaks out. But getting hurt is a natural part of life.

"I-it's wrong to treat Lucia like you do. Haven't you seen her scars? She..., she deserves to be treated better!"

...What was with this girl? "I'm not mistreating her. Lucia's a lot stronger than you think—she's just lazy. All I'm doing is giving her the push she needs."

Well, it seems like Lucia reached the ground since screams started rising up. Surprisingly, after eating a ton of exquisite swords, I can stay further away from my weapon body without instantly being transported back inside of it. The boat's at least fifty feet above the sect and I'm still materialized up here, but

I'm bound to be taken away as Lucia travels deeper in. Along with being able to stay further away from my weapon body, I found out something else that changed. I can't absorb as much of Lucia's qi as I used to be able to. I'm not sure if it's because I'm incompatible with the qi she's getting from the Heart Devil Cultivation Technique or if it's something else, but there's no doubt that I'm receiving less than usual. At least I have the swords to eat to keep up with Lucia's monstrous growth, and I can gather my own qi by circulating the Silver Sword Sect's cultivation technique that Lucia obtained for me at the cultural exchange. It's great that I can cultivate on my own, yet it makes me feel a little lost, like I'm slowly slipping away from Lucia.

"What...," Softie said and raised her head. "What is Lucia to you?"

What is Lucia to me? I'm not sure of the question's intent. "What do you mean?"

"Is she your student? Your owner? Your friend? Your ... lover?" Softie took in a deep breath and glared at me with teary eyes. "What is she to you?"

Hmm? Why was Softie so interested in the relationship between me and Lucia? Well, I suppose it wouldn't hurt to give her an answer. "Lucia's my sole reason for living. I want to see her reach the very top, the very peak of existence, whether that be an immortal or a god. I want everyone to know the name Lucia Fluffytail, and I want her legacy to live on forever. I made her a promise."

Softie exhaled. "So ... you're not her lover?"

"...Why are you so fixated on that?"

"N-no reason!" Softie's face flushed an extremely bright shade of red as she shook her head. "I, I was just—"

The world turned black before I could hear her answer. It looks like Lucia went too far away and I was transported back into mini-DalDal. But for Softie to be so concerned about

Lucia's lover and that over-the-top reaction.... There's no way, right?

Chapter 12

It's been a long, long, long year…. At least, I think a year passed. It's hard to tell when every day's the same. And there's no changes in seasons! It's always spring here. Or maybe spring is just really long. Hmm. Well, that doesn't matter! I've finally completed that stupid task the sect leader handed me! I've thoroughly terrorized, robbed, and planted heart devils in every single sect of Kong County except for the five fingers. Softie said we finished the real task a few months ago, but Durandal insisted on overachieving. Why should we only terrorize the sects on the list? Why not terrorize every sect? …Yeah. Durandal's a serious slave driver. I haven't gotten a good rest in a whole year. Attacking three to four sects every day, eating for seven hours every day, cultivating the Heart Devil Cultivation Technique and Immortal Poison Body and Immortal Venom Body instead of sleeping every day…. There was practically no time for decent foreplay!

And now I'm finally taking my well-deserved break…. Not. There's a horrifyingly scary cloud floating above our boats. It's very, very big. Like very big. It stretches as far as the eye can see, and there's no speck of blue anywhere in sight. If it weren't for the purple flashing lightning, I'd have thought it was nighttime. Now, this isn't the first time I've seen a scary cloud like this. During this year of plundering, a lot of my underlings jumped from the mortal realm to the saint realm with their stolen goods, and clouds similar to this one appeared on an almost daily basis to rain down tribulation lightning. I say similar because this one is a lot larger than any from before, and more importantly, it's making my tail stiff. Which means I'm the target. Shit.

"Lucia…? Is that, um, your tribulation cloud up there?" Softie was inching away from me. Just a few seconds ago, she was cultivating the Heart Devil Cultivation Technique next to me near the steering wheel. "I think I felt you break through to the earth realm…."

"I'm pretty sure that's mine." What to do? A stiff tail is no good. Despite the Thundering Heavens Sect's name, they gave me absolutely zero practice in fighting tribulation lightning!

"That's really weird. According to the technique, it should only take someone fifty million heart devils planted to reach the earth realm if they have no impurities," Softie was muttering to herself in the corner. "But Lucia eats a lot"—hey! I do not!—"so maybe it was possible for her cultivation to slow down by that much due to her impurities. It's still ridiculous to reach the earth realm in a single year though…." Softie stopped muttering and raised her head. "Hey, Lucia? How many heart devils have you planted? I want to know before you undergo your tribulation, just in case it kills you."

…Softie's gotten a lot braver during this year. Is it about time to strip her again? Though the heart devil inside of her seems to stop growing so much after every time I do it. Maybe she's building up resistance. Hmm. Anyways, how many heart devils do I have planted? One…, two…, three…. There's too many to count. "At least four."

Softie sighed. "This is why you're the perfect fit for our sect."

"Thanks for the compliment." I've never been a perfect fit anywhere before. Except for when I made my own place and became an empress. That was pretty fun. I should do it again once I get strong enough. But first, this tribulation's still gathering more power! I can feel it sucking up the qi from beneath the boats. This is sincerely scary. Maybe if I hide inside one of the interspacial pouches, it'll go away.

"What are you doing?"

"Hiding."

"You can't hide from the tribulation by entering a pouch. Only metal-spirit kangaroos can do that."

A what? Why wasn't I born as a metal kangarino or whatever? This isn't fair. "Then what do I do!?"

"Um." Softie nodded. Did she have an idea? "All the earth-realm experts who've survived their earth-realm tribulation have one thing in common. They all lived. So all you have to do is not die. Right. I'm going to evacuate the boat now! Good luck, Lucia!"

"W-wait!" Which bastard taught Softie such stupid logic!? To survive a tribulation, all I have to do is live? No shit! Ah, but she's already gone, and all my underlings are fleeing from my boat. Hmm. I'll put the boat away for now and … Ilya? "Huh? What are you doing here? You'll die to the lightning!"

Ilya shrugged. "Judging by the previous tribulations, you still have a good thirty minutes before your tribulation starts."

Right. Ilya went through a tribulation too when she became a tenth-circle magician. I'm not sure how she advanced so fast in a year, but she did. "Are you here to help?" Since Ilya's been studying for a year, she has the answer to nearly all my questions again like an updating encyclopedia! She has to know a way through this tribulation. I've seen how my underlings got through theirs, but I don't like it. They sacrifice too many items. Items are my blood! Without things to sell, I'll be poor. And being poor sucks. So I won't throw my stuff at the lightning unless I have no other choice.

"Yes. Here."

What's this? A piece of paper?

"It's fake money Immortal Continent natives burn for the dead."

...Huh? Fuck! "What is this!? Bully-Lucia-with-false-hope day!? Get over here!"

"W-wait, wait! I have an actual plan! S-stop! It hurts!"

Humph. "Alright. What's the actual plan?"

Ilya wiped away the tears in her eyes before glaring at me. All I did was give her a noogie. "The Star Phoenix Sect is only ten minutes away. If you fly there and hide inside one of their buildings, then they'll surely help you out once the tribulation starts breaking things. Remember all those formations you had to break through for every sect? The Star Phoenix Sect should have a massive defensive one since they're a finger of Kong County."

What? Using other people to beat my tribulation? That's an excellent idea! I knew Ilya was the best answerer around. But wait, will they let me in? "But to get in, I have to go past the defensive formation myself, no? Can I do that before the lightning falls?" For the weak sects, the formations took at least five minutes to break apart. Some sects even took up to twenty minutes!

"Don't worry about that. All you have to do is wear their robes. Only Star Phoenix Sect members can wear red. So wear these"—a red robe appeared in Ilya's hand along with a sash that had a name stitched on it in gold—"and run over there saying you saw the person undergoing the tribulation nearby and you wanted to hide inside the sect."

"You're a genius, Ilya! Help me put these on! But where did you get these?"

"One of the sects we attacked had a visitor from the Star Phoenix Sect, so I stole her stuff."

Stealing the clothes right off a woman. I taught Ilya well!

"You're thinking something stupid, aren't you? Hurry up and go before the tribulation starts." Ilya patted down my clothes after she finished tying the sash. "You better not die, Lucia. You're the only hope I have of going back home."

I managed to make it to the entrance of the Star Phoenix Sect. I say entrance, but it's actually a space between two bamboo poles that says, "Entrance." There's nothing on either side of the poles, and there's one person in red robes standing between the poles. What would happen if I tried to enter the sect from the not-entrance space? Apparently, I'd get fried. I sent Puppers through to test, and he instantly combusted into a pile of ash. So … now I'm here. In front of this disciple. In my not-suspicious outfit. "Hi."

"Returning to the sect?" The person in red stared at my sash. Then his brow furrowed. Did he know the person this robe belonged to? Ilya didn't steal this from a famous person, right? "Sister Hapless, is it? Your parents have an odd naming sense."

"Mm. Yeah." Actually, everyone's naming sense in the Immortal Continent is weird. People here name themselves after adjectives and nouns. There aren't any proper names like Puppers or Mrs. Wuffletush. Sheesh. "Let me through? The tribulation's scary."

"Hmm." The red-robed man squinted at me and stroked his chin. "Those ears…. That bushy tail…." His eyes narrowed even further. Was he going to see through my disguise!? "Ha-ha! You almost look exactly like Heart Devil Lucia, but there's no way she'd be here. Go on in."

…It worked! And what's with the weird nickname they gave me? Heart Devil Lucia? Jeez. It's so tasteless. "Yup, yup. There's no way Lucia would be here at all. I bet she's busy doing busy stuff. Yup." Now I'll just walk past him with my impeccable acting, and … I'm in! That was easier than I thought. According to Ilya, I still have a few minutes to find a place to seek shelter before this tribulation starts. It's a good thing sects are so large; I wouldn't be able to do this in a sect with only a few people. I'm glad not knowing fellow disciples is an extremely common thing. Heck, I traveled with a hundred thousand Shadow Devil Sect members for a year and I can only match Softie's name with her face. Everyone else is just 'black-robed fellow' or 'hey, you'. Ah, I'm getting distracted. Hmm. Safest building…, safest building…. The cafeteria! It'd be a disaster if the food was … wait. Cafeterias aren't important in the Immortal Continent. Then the next safest place is the ... treasury! Treasures should have a lot of protection..., which means it'll be hard for me to enter. Darn. This is a lot more difficult than I thought. Eh, whatever. I'll head over to that pagoda over there because it's the biggest building and it looks like a lot of people are gathering around it. Whew, there's really a lot of people surrounding a stage. Is there a play going on? I want to see!

"Fellow brothers and sisters! The time to declare war on the Shadow Devil Sect is now! For the past year, they've terrorized Kong County! They've slaughtered hundreds of sects!" ...We did? "They've robbed trillions of spirit stones!" What!? I only got several thousand thousand thousand thousands! "They've stolen billions of companion beasts and ate them in front of their crying owners!" ...Guilty as charged. "Are we going to let them continue terrorizing the county!?" But there's nothing left to terrorize. "We attack in three days! Let us herald the summer with the blood and tears of the Shadow Devil Sect! We'll exterminate every last one of those bastards and display their chosens' heads on our sacred artifacts!"

Wow. That's a bit ... excessive. I prefer to have my head attached to my body, thank you very much. It's a good thing they don't notice me. I'm starting to think I shouldn't have come here based on the cheers of support the crowd's giving the speaker who wants to impale my head on a golden pike. Mm. Welp, it's too late now. I'm already here, and the lightning's about to fall. I hope this works out! I'll slip inside the building and then I'll—

"Excuse me, Junior. What are you doing?"

Me? "I'm digging."

"This is the skill-storing pavilion. You're not allowed to dig here." The person at the front desk didn't seem to like the fact I took out a shovel and started tearing through the tile. Well, it doesn't matter if he doesn't like it! There's a huge thundercloud up there and I don't want to get zapped by lightning. "S-stop! Didn't you hear what I said!? How are you digging so fast!?"

Dig. Dig. Dig. Mm. This should be deep enough. Now, I'll take out this cylindrical building and use it as my first layer of protection. It should be sturdy since I stole it from the armadillo or whatever sect. Apparently, it was a trial tower or something like that, but I'm sure it definitely works better as a shield. Should I keep digging? I don't think one building will be enough.... Alright, it's settled. I'll keep digging downwards! I have to increase the distance between me and the lightning as much as I can. My tail's so stiff I could use it to kill someone. Err, easily. I could kill someone with a non-stiff tail, but it'd be harder. Oh? Red light's coming out of the ground. Did I discover a treasure? That'd be super neat! I remember I dug up a wine barrel back in the—gah! I'm falling!

"What's this!? Who dares intrude on the forbidden ground!?"

The forbidden what? First, I'll pick myself up off this really warm floor. And ... there's four scary-looking people staring at me! Just judging by the qi coming off of them, they're about as strong as the sect leader. And behind them, there's two big bright-red eggs. "Uh. Hi. Wait, no! I mean, uh, Junior Lu—Hapless greets the, err, elders?"

...I don't think they're falling for it. The four elders looked at each other and—

Bang!

Eh!? The ceiling's collapsing!

"What did you do!?" The four elders dove towards the eggs and created a barrier over them. Of course, I followed the elders! I feel safer next to them than I do by myself when tribulation lightning is trying to kill me! My tribulation finally started. I can tell because there's purple lightning everywhere.

"Is ... this an earth-realm tribulation?"

Boom!

Lots of screams came from outside the red barrier that I was hiding in with the four elders. I thought I dug really far down. How can I hear the screams so clearly?

Kaboom!

"T-this is a disaster!"

Well, that tower that I placed as a shield didn't last very long. Neither did the skill-storing building of the Star Phoenix Sect. There's a giant hole leading to the surface and I can clearly see the tribulation clouds above me. It's a little like looking up a chimney at the sky, but the chimney's a giant tunnel and the sky's trying to kill me.

"Look!" One of the elders beside me pointed up. All I saw was a red speck amongst a sea of black and purple. "The ancestral beast is resisting the lightning! We have to help it!"

"Wait! What about Junior Hapless? Doesn't this tribulation look like it's hers!?"

"Is it yours!?"

Uh…. "No?"

"Shit! Who are you trying to fool!?" One of the elders lunged at me, but I dove towards the eggs and hid behind them. They're definitely protecting these for a reason! I'm sure they won't try attacking!? Why are they trying to set me on fire!? The eggs are fireproof! No wonder!

"Wait!" I grabbed mini-DalDal and raised it over my head. "If you don't stop, I'll break these eggs right now!" The four elders paused and I took that chance to store the eggs into an interspacial pouch. Hostage acquired! "Help me pass the tribulation and I'll return the eggs!"

"Y-you!" One of the elders pointed at me. His face was red and it looked like he was about to … he spat out blood. As expected.

"Do you know what you're doing!?"

Of course! I'm surviving! But before I could respond, lightning rained down onto the red barrier, causing cracks to form. One of the elders screamed and vomited out a fountain of blood. Then he fell onto the ground while clutching his chest. While the other three elders stared at him, I pointed at the sky. "Questions later! Tribulation now!"

The elders, except the one on the ground, cursed before summoning a bunch of fancy artifacts outside the barrier. There were swords, shields, axes, handcuffs, whips, shovels, and more. One of the elders called out a giant cone that he held to his mouth. "All sect members shall work together to surpass the tribulation! Activate the defensive formation, Sect Leader Feather!"

Gah! That hurts my ears! So loud. His shout was even louder than the tribulation thunder. I think my ears are bleeding. Well, they'll heal quickly. Mm, but Ilya had a really good idea when she had me come here. There's definitely no way in hell I could've suppressed this tribulation by myself. I guess that just means I'm not strong enough.... Maybe if I ate these eggs I'd get a super boost to my strength. Hmm.

***

This year's been a productive one. I've learned a lot about the Immortal Continent while accompanying Lucia on her reign of terror. It's a pretty nice place. Occasionally, people have a hard time pronouncing my name even though it's only two syllables, but other than that, I can't really complain about how I've been treated. I'm not discriminated against for having purple skin, and I'm pretty sure people are extra aware about their manners around me because I'm Lucia's companion. Being the disciple of the sect leader's wife helps too, I'm sure.

Over the course of the year, I've been heavily studying alchemy. It's interesting and not too different from the alchemy I've seen back at home, but that's only referring to the fundamentals. The alchemy here is much more developed; there's thousands upon thousands of more formulas and raw materials and effects that pills can produce. But at the same time, the alchemists here aren't as innovative. They're still using cauldrons that they have to control the heat of manually. I've developed a grill that can be set to—and maintain—any temperature up to a thousand degrees that'll evenly cook whatever is placed on top of it. Lucia already has one of these. With this magic tool, the obvious thought comes next: why not use it for alchemy? With this, anyone can become an alchemist even if they can't control fire.

Other than my progress in alchemy, I've also crossed over the third wall to the tenth circle. Mana is massively abundant in the Immortal Continent. Maybe it's because no one uses it; I don't know. I've also washed out my impurities in one of those impurity-cleansing pools that the lesser sects had, and my speed at accumulating mana greatly increased. I tried to convince Lucia to wash herself too, but she says she doesn't want to bathe in fish pee. I'm not sure how fish pee is related to cleansing impurities, but I've already become numb to Lucia's nonsensical replies. The tribulation that I had to go through when I became a tenth-circle magician wasn't a very difficult one. My fellow disciples helped me in exchange for pills. I've become something of a drug dealer; I'm not too proud of that, but a girl's got to make a living somehow, eh? The Shadow Devil Sect members hand me raw materials, and I convert them into pills for spirit stones; it's a lucrative business.

Speaking of tribulations…, there's a massive one going on right now: Lucia's. It's … going well, I assume. At least, it hasn't ended which means Lucia didn't die. For the past three hours now, it's been going on and on and on. There's been hundreds of boats flooding into the area, all of them belonging to the five fingers of Kong County. I suppose the birth of an earth-realm expert isn't a very common thing, and the tribulation clouds span an extremely long distance. The sects must be coming out to scout and seek an opportunity to ingratiate themselves with the new earth-realm expert. It's weird to think Lucia's already at the top of the food chain of Kong County when she's only been here a year and everyone else that's as strong as her has been cultivating for at least a hundred years or so. She's just that naturally gifted. It's really not fair. But she had a rough past, so I suppose it evens out. …A little.

As for my plan to use the Star Phoenix Sect to surpass her tribulation, I'd say it's going pretty well. Although I can't see the whole sect from my vantage point on the boat, as far as my vision extends, it's pure destruction. The buildings are burnt to the ground. There's charred corpses everywhere. Charcoal and ashes are fluttering about. The lightning's continuously pouring down like rain, and the remains of whatever's left of the surface is slowly eroding away under the pressure. Did Lucia dig underground perhaps? There's massive craters everywhere, and the lightning seems to be traveling further into the sect. But sadly, I can see it striking down, but I can't see the ground it's hitting. According to Softie, we're not allowed to intrude in another sect's airspace—like we've been doing for the past year. It was okay to do it to the lesser sects, but the Star Phoenix Sect has earth-realm experts to stop us. I really want to see what's going on though, but I guess I'll wait. I don't believe Lucia will die—wicked people live forever.

"Sister Ilya, are you worried?" Softie asked. She was standing next to me on the bow of the boat. I've started calling her Softie after hearing how Lucia and Durandal called her; though, I should be calling her Chosen Moonlight or Elder Sister Moonlight. Titles and etiquette weren't too difficult to learn, but it's a little awkward calling middle-aged men junior brothers, so I tend to avoid talking to them.

"Lucia's the last person I'd be worried about."

Softie pursed her lips and stared beyond the horizon. "I can't help but feel nervous. What if she becomes seriously injured? Or what if she doesn't make it? She's in enemy territory all by herself...."

"She has Durandal and Puppers, remember?"

"Puppers died instantly before Lucia even entered the sect."

That's true. Who knew there'd be a vaporizing formation? Well, it makes sense. It'd be impractical to build a wall around the whole territory seeing as it's constantly expanding—not to mention the cost of materials and labor. But Durandal's still there with Lucia. Though he's weaker than her, so I guess that doesn't matter. Speaking of which, I wonder if he'll undergo a tribulation as well when he reaches the earth realm. Wouldn't it be horrible for the Star Phoenix Sect if right after Lucia's tribulation, Durandal's occurred? But the chances of that happening are close to nil. And I don't wish that kind of misfortune on anyone. "Well, either way, I believe in her."

Softie sighed. She lowered her head and clutched her necklace. Which was made out of a focus bone that Lucia gave her. For some reason, I have the sneaking suspicion Softie's feelings for Lucia are beyond a normal friendship. There's these little things that Softie does for Lucia: wipes off her sweat during training, offers to feed her during mealtime, offers a lap for her to rest on. ...Yeah. They even meditate together at night after Lucia and Durandal conclude their nighttime activity. It's a bit weird, and I feel like I've lost my place next to Lucia's side. But I really don't mind. I'm free from Lucia's nonsensical whims *and* I get to use her reputation? That's a great deal.

"Say, Softie, how long do earth-realm tribulations normally last?"

"Lucia's should end soon. The final lightning is building up, see?" Softie pointed up at the black cloud. The lightning that was purple was now red, and a giant vortex was forming. It looked a little like an eye. "If she survives, then our sect will be the strongest in Kong County. Maybe we'll even win the upcoming King Province Exchange."

These people in the Immortal Continent sure have a thing for exchanges, huh?

***

"It's ending! There's one last bolt!"

Is it finally over? The elders beside me had tears in their eyes as if they had witnessed their family dying in a natural disaster and were unable to do anything to help. But it's not over yet! There's still that vortex in the sky that's building up a really, really big thunderbolt. I can sense it. My tail's telling me by standing erect. I've only used up that single tower so far during this whole tribulation; I think it's been pretty successful. But the Star Phoenix Sect…, yeah. They must hate me. The heart devils inside of them agree with me.

"Reinforce the formation!" the elder next to me shouted into the cone that amplified his voice. We were in a crater surrounded by a whole bunch of Star Phoenix Sect members. The tribulation had destroyed almost the whole sect. The formation that the sect members were using to defend against it required a lot of qi in the area to power, and every time it blocked a strike, the area would be void of qi. So we've had to traverse through the whole sect, absorbing every ounce of qi while leaving behind a path of destruction. Once, a sect member said the easiest way to stop the tribulation was to kill me, but the elders were afraid of their eggs being broken. I knew hostages were the way to go. Hmm, this reminds me a little of the Godking—he tamed a phoenix, right? Should I try? Well, I don't think I'll be able to considering I'm surrounded by a whole sect and the only thing that's keeping me from being mobbed is the tribulation. If only there could be another tribulation after this one….

"Lucia."

Hmm? "Durandal? Why'd you come out?"

Durandal's forehead wrinkled as he rubbed his chin. "I think I'm about to break through to the earth realm…. There's this strange feeling I'm getting."

"Really?" How come Durandal cultivates so much faster than Puppers? I know Puppers spends more time being dead and all, but the disparity shouldn't be this great. I think Puppers is still somewhere in the mid-ranked spirit realm. Or maybe he's high-ranked now. Hmm.

"Yeah." Durandal pulled a sword out of my interspacial ring and munched on it while looking up at the tribulation clouds. There was a red dome covering us, and a thread of qi extended from every sect member up to the barrier. The vortex in the clouds was still getting larger and larger and it was rumbling a lot. Even though it was just sound, the ground was trembling and the barrier fluttered. "I'm going to hide in mini-DalDal before that lightning falls."

I wish I could hide too.

"It's coming! Brace yourselves!" the elder with the cone shouted. With a boom, a pillar of lightning that was wider than a small town crashed onto the barrier. The whole world turned red, and I couldn't see anything. Did I die? I tried to say something, but no sound came out. The roar of the thunder was too loud. I'll pinch myself. Ow! Alright, I'm still alive unless I can feel pain after dying too. This…, if I didn't have the Star Phoenix Sect volunteering to help me out, how the hell was I supposed to survive this!? How long has it been? Ten seconds? Twenty? Hmm. Maybe my eyes are broken? Everything's still red. Oh! Unrelenting Path of Slaughter! There we go; I can see again. Eh…. Are those cracks on the barrier? And are they getting … bigger? The barrier broke! Gah! It hurts! Shit! It feels like my face is melting off! Impenetrable Shell, Armor of Slaughter! It, it's not enough! I'll pull random houses and buildings out of my interspacial ring to use as makeshift shields! They're disintegrating, but at least they provide a little over a second of shelter each.

I didn't count the number of buildings I went through, but the final pillar of lightning finally went away. My clothes had melted off, so I donned my pink and black robe that the Shadow Devil Sect had provided me. They had insisted I wear all black, but I didn't want to look like an ordinary mook, so I requested a pink top to differentiate myself. It's much comfier than the Star Phoenix Sect's robe, but that's probably because Ilya stole those tight robes from someone whose proportions didn't match mine. I'm not fat! I deactivated my Path of Slaughter and looked around. Hmm. There's a lot less people than I remember....

"Are the eggs safe!? W-wait! That pink and black robe..., those ears and fluffy tail! You're Heart Devil Lucia!" The elders seemed to have survived; though, they looked a bit ragged. Now, while they're still injured, I'll take this chance to escape! Flee!

A fireball flew past my head and nearly burnt off my ears. "Stop right there!" If you want someone to stop, don't throw fireballs at them! "Seize that foxkin!"

It's a good thing that final pillar of lightning lasted for so long. I bet most of the disciples are blind right now and their ears should still be ringing, so it'll be harder for them to notice me as I slip by. Why didn't Durandal let me learn any stealth techniques? There were so many! The Slippery Loach Sect, the Fast Cockroach Sect, the Unseeable Sect, all of them had skills that I could use to steal food from places unnoticed, err, I mean, to escape from a mob of angry people! Durandal said it'd take ten times the effort to achieve half the result if I practiced a stealth technique because of my giant tail. I can be sneaky if I tuck my tail into my robe!

Speaking of Durandal..., he came out and grabbed me before I could run away from the crater. "It's starting." He pointed at the sky. "My tribulation."

...Well, shit.

"Whoever catches that foxkin will receive—" The elder stopped midsentence and stared at me. I was back by his side as if I had never left at all. It seems like I can run faster after reaching the earth realm. "Uh. You came back? Are you going to return the holy eggs now?"

I copied Durandal and pointed at the sky. "It's not over."

The elder frowned at me before looking up. Then his face paled. "H-how?" He lifted the cone and brought it to his lips. "R-ready the defensive formation!"

A collective groan rang through the air. The Star Phoenix Sect members seemed to be in no position to do anything, much less ready a formation. One of the members knelt at the elder's feet. "Ancestor! We're in no position to defend against the rest of this tribulation! The whole sect is in ruins and over half of our disciples have perished! The ancestral beast has already fled! This, this isn't an earth-realm tribulation. It's a sky-realm's!"

"We have no choice!" the elder lifted the cone and pointed it straight at the kneeling person's face and yelled into it. "Disciples? We can always get more! Buildings? We can rebuild! Phoenix eggs? Fuck! Can your wife give birth to phoenixes!?"

"A-Ancestor...."

The elder raised the cone and whipped it across the kneeling person's face. ...Ouch, that must've hurt. The poor fellow went flying. "We defend this foxkin to the death! If the eggs are destroyed, our sect will cease to exist!"

Ah, I love being defended. It makes me feel like I'm wanted. The Immortal Continent's been really nice to me.

***

The clouds have shrunk. They're not nearly as thick and wide as Lucia's were. I'm a little offended. Did this heavenly tribulation regard me as weaker than Lucia? Even though it's true, I'd rather face an equally terrifying or even stronger tribulation than hers. But wishing for it won't make it happen. I sighed as I placed my hands on my hips while chewing on an exquisite sword.

"Don't worry, Durandal!" Lucia smacked my back, almost knocking me over. "You'll be fine! We've got the whole Star Phoenix Sect backing us up. Well, what's left of them at least." She coughed and looked around before making a threatening gesture towards the pouch at her waist with mini-DalDal. "Isn't that right? An unfortunate accident might happen if this tribulation fails!"

"R-right." The ancestor with the cone had a smile on his face that looked more pained than excited. "We'll do our best to help you pass your tribulation. You can count on us."

The thing is … I don't really want their help. When I really think about it, aren't these tribulations trials of sorts? These are meant to be passed on your own! Did the first saint-realm expert in the Immortal Continent have people helping him pass his tribulation? Who would've helped him? Mortal-realm novices? No! He must've used his own strength to surpass the lightning. And that's what I want to do. I'm not lazy or fearful like Lucia. Sure, I avoided my first tribulation because I had no clue what was going on, but I'm ready for this one. I've specifically cultivated techniques from all the lesser sword sects around that are effective against tribulations. And compiling them all, I've created my very own sword formation. How effective it'll be against the tribulation…, I'm not sure. But I have to try.

I reached into Lucia's interspacial ring and pulled out a thousand exquisite swords. Sending my qi into them, I had them hover around me in a neat circular formation that created a cylinder with the swords pointing away from my body. There were ten circular layers, with a hundred swords in each layer. It was a little difficult to sustain this many swords with my own qi alone, but I'm not going to draw on Lucia's unless it's absolutely necessary. The road to the peak is supposed to be one of solitude after all. Or should it? It's not like I can leave Lucia.

"Durandal? What are you doing?" Lucia pushed aside some swords with her bare hands, not minding the metal edges, and tilted her head to the side.

"Getting ready to face the tribulation."

Lucia's head tilted even further to the side. "But … why?"

I snorted and rubbed Lucia's ears while ruffling her hair. "Because I want to."

"But what if you die?" Lucia grabbed my sleeve with wide eyes. Was she that worried about me? No. She was most likely worried about how she'd take care of herself at night if I died and went missing for a week. After all, as long as she protects my core, nothing can happen to me.

"Then I'll make it up to you later." I pinched her nose, causing her to cry out. "Don't worry, Lucia. Do you think I can't handle a little bit of lightning? Look at the tribulation clouds. They're not as ominous as yours."

"This … isn't her tribulation?" The ancestor had a strange expression on his face. "It's yours? You're a weapon spirit." A familiar flash appeared in his eyes. Was that greed? I've seen Cottontail covet a lot of treasures, and her eyes always glinted the same way. But if this man thinks he can take me away from Lucia, he's in for a rude awakening. "An earth-realm weapon spirit…." The ancestor lifted his cone and shouted, "This tribulation will be easier than before! Don't lose hope!"

Hmm. If it weren't for the fact that Lucia and I were isolated in a small space surrounded by enemies, I really would've faced this tribulation by myself. But since we're in this situation, I might as well let the Star Phoenix Sect weaken the tribulation before taking part myself. It wouldn't be good if I exhausted my energy and something unexpected happened that'd lead to a disaster. Though I want to overcome this trial by myself, Lucia's safety is the most important thing. It's still a shame. Suppressing my desires for the sake of Lucia, she's not even going to praise me for this. But it's my duty as a weapon spirit; why do I want praise? Hmm. The emotions that I shouldn't have have been a bit unstable ever since I entered the saint realm.

Before I could think of an excuse to face the tribulation alone, the first bolt of lightning rained down. It collided against a barrier that the ancestor threw up and dispersed. The ancestor's roaring laughter filled the air as he raised his cone to his lips. "This is a normal tribulation! A normal one! There are eight bolts of lightning remaining! Only the disciples will power the formation for the second and third strikes. Elders will power the formation for the fourth to sixth strikes. And everyone will power the formation for the last three strikes!"

It seems like there's a science to tribulations. Another bolt of lightning crashed down. It was a little thicker than the previous one, but not by much. It crashed against the defensive formation that had reactivated, and the disciples powering it trembled. Lucia looked around with a disappointed expression on her face. "What's this? Why isn't it chaotic at all?"

This girl. When did she develop such a strong sense of schadenfreude? It's wrong to derive pleasure from other people's misfortunes. Who taught her such immoral things? Sheesh. I looked up at the barrier which was clearly weaker than it had been when Lucia's final tribulation lightning fell. It seemed stable: no cracks, no fluctuations. Perhaps my tribulation would pass just like this. How disappointing. The third bolt of lightning rained down and crashed against the barrier, crackling with a bang before dispersing. The disciples who were powering the formation coughed out mouthfuls of blood as the barrier dimmed. Then the elders connected threads of qi to the barrier, causing it to brighten again. Did they not have to move around to gather more qi like they did with Lucia's tribulation? Just what was wrong with Lucia to provoke such a huge one?

Lucia poked my side after waltzing through my formation of swords. "Is it just me, or is your tribulation a lot easier than mine? It's not fair."

Even Lucia realized the difference. That's how obvious it was! "Mm. Well, I think it's safe to say I'm favored by the heavens while you're not."

Lucia narrowed her eyes at me. Then she snorted before turning her head away. "Humph. Fine, be like that."

Did I say something wrong? A crashing sound echoed through the dome. The fourth bolt of lightning was purple instead of white. The barrier didn't even tremble as another two bolts of lightning rained down in succession. Before the elders could orient themselves or the disciples could add on their qi to the formation, a seventh bolt of red lightning roared like a dragon as it crashed against and pierced through the barrier like a spear through paper. I manipulated the swords around me above my head and into a pyramidical formation like a metal umbrella. The lightning surged against the wall of swords before crashing into the ground around me, spreading out like red snakes once they touched the earth. A few disciples screamed as they were slowly corroded away as the snakes lashed out at them. A few snakes of lightning crawled towards Lucia, but she punted them away with her tail, burning a few of her furs.

The Star Phoenix Sect didn't have time to reactivate the formation, and the eighth bolt fell. Metal shattered as the swords above me snapped apart, causing the qi inside me to become turbulent. I coughed out a mouthful of blood as I snatched more exquisite swords from Lucia's interspacial ring and had them replace the broken ones. The air hissed and the sky crackled as a vortex formed in the clouds. Dirt and ashes were lifted into the air, floating an inch above the ground as some sort of force prevented them from falling. The hairs on everyone's heads spread outwards like afros, and a tingling sensation surged through my limbs. The final strike was coming!

"Hey, hey! Activate the formation, you bird worshippers!" Lucia kicked the ancestor with the cone before reaching into her pouch and pulled out a phoenix egg. She raised mini-DalDal over it, ready to break it apart with my weapon body's hilt. "If anything happens to Durandal, I'll smash this egg!"

The ancestor glared at Lucia, his eyes glinting at the egg and sword hovering over it, before shouting into the cone, "Ready the Soaring Phoenix Formation!"

The Star Phoenix Sect's leader, who was next to the ancestor, widened his eyes. "T-the Soaring Phoenix Formation?"

Was there something wrong with the Soaring Phoenix Formation?

"Hurry up!" the ancestor shouted, his amplified voice causing my ears to ring. "We don't have much time! Focus the formation on the weapon spirit!"

Fire sprang into life beneath my feet. What was this!? Wait. It wasn't hot. Qi surged through my veins, and the swords above me took on a red hue. This clearly was a formation that amplified my strength. Perhaps the ancestor thought a defensive formation would be too dangerous if it were to break? Well, regardless, with this much support, I could take out another thousand swords to defend myself. It's a shame not all of them were exquisite; despite the numerous number of sects we robbed, exquisite swords were hard to find.

The vortex in the clouds rotated faster and faster as it sucked in the surrounding clouds, shrinking the whole tribulation. The remaining lightning was condensing and spinning around, roaring like a trapped tiger. This is it! One man versus the heavens! Alone, I shall surpass this final strike of the tribulation! I forced all of my qi into my sword formation and launched it towards the vortex. The first to strike has the advantage! The swords howled as they split apart the air, flying upwards like a massive metal spearhead. As if provoked, the tribulation cloud flashed twice and roared before striking down with its condensed ball of red lightning. Like throwing paper into a fire, the swords at the forefront of the formation disintegrated as they made contact with the crackling ball, but I believed my sword formation could overcome it! In an instant, half the swords were gone and half the lightning had dispersed. But at that very moment, a fierce pain engulfed my chest and exploded outwards, setting my meridians ablaze with agony. I screamed as I lost control of my sword formation, and the ball of lightning crashed down unimpeded, filling my vision as it grew larger and larger until all I could see was red.

The next moment, when my vision finally returned, I was floating in a vast empty space filled with red light. Ahead of me, there was an animal that looked like a featherless chicken. It was pink and around the same size as me. Once it saw me, it's eyes widened and it let out a shriek before dashing at me. What the hell was going on? Was this part of the tribulation? Whatever! It doesn't matter! I'll overcome any adversary even if it's a featherless chicken!

**

Durandal died! That's not too big of a deal, but mini-DalDal shattered! The tribulation lightning bolt ate Durandal's spirit body and then his weapon body went crack! Then mini-DalDal broke to bits! Before I could do anything, Durandal's spirit seed dropped out of mini-DalDal's hilt and fell right onto the phoenix egg! Then it merged into it instead of bouncing off! This is a disaster of epic proportions! What's going on!? "Hey! Durandal!" I'm going to smash this stupid egg and take him out!

"Wait! If you break that egg now, the spirit seed will disappear as well!"

…Huh? What was this elder saying…? I glared at him and stuffed the egg into my pouch. This was all his fault! "It was your formation, wasn't it!? You caused Durandal to die!" That's right! Durandal suddenly flared up and stopped mid-attack during the final lightning bolt. His swords just fell out of the sky! I reached for my waist and grabbed…, grabbed…, right. Mini-DalDal broke. What do I fight with now!? "Breaking Tail!"

The hateful man in front of me didn't react as my tail swept from underneath and in between my legs. With a muffled thump and squelching sound, it crashed into the man's jewels. His eyes widened as he vomited out a mouthful of blood and fell onto his face.

"Ancestor!" someone shouted. I didn't know who, and I didn't care either! I grabbed the fallen man by his neck and hoisted him into the air. If I didn't have mini-DalDal, then I'd use a substitute blade! All of these bastards were responsible for that filthy trick that killed Durandal. I'm going to tear every single one of them to pieces!

My vision turned white, black, orange, and red as I activated my Unrelenting Path of Slaughter. I infused all my qi into my temporary weapon and swung him as hard as I could. Disciples went flying and my weapon lost a few limbs, but I kept bashing people with him. Bash, bash, bash. Bash, bash, bash. Bash, bash, bash. Bash, bash, bash. Bash, bash, b…. He broke. A twitch caught my eye and I looked down. Someone was trying to crawl away from me, so I grabbed his leg and replaced my weapon with him. People were running away from me, but when I had the thought to run after them, I teleported in front of them instead. What was this sorcery? Well, it didn't matter!

I'm not sure how long I activated my Path of Slaughter for. I'm not sure about anything really. I just wanted to vent my anger at these bastards for killing Durandal like that! But once I was done, there was no one left. Just blood and bones and bits of mangled flesh floating around. The crater that was created by the tribulation was covered by a layer of knee-deep blood. Ah. Durandal…. I pulled out the egg and hugged it to my chest. Was Durandal really in here? If, if it hatches, will Durandal come out?

An ear-piercing screech rang through the air, and I quickly stuffed the egg back into my pouch. A phoenix was flying above me, circling overhead. This stupid bird. How dare it lay an egg that absorbed Durandal! I'll go up there and strangle it with my bare hands! …But I can't fly—I teleported!? Caught it! The erect peacock plummeted to the ground and I landed on its back. It let out a strangled cry. Oi, I'm not fat. What was it crying for? Wait a minute…. I shouldn't kill this bird just because it annoyed me. I need it to incubate the Durandal egg. If Durandal hatches as a phoenix…, I think I'll cry. Durandal…, please be okay. Please, don't leave me. You promised not to leave me. Why? Why did you leave me again? Again! I hate you, you stupid sword spirit! Durandal…. Durandal…. Durandal…. My chest hurts so much.

"L-Lucia?"

Who was that? Ilya? And Softie.

"Lucia? Are you alright?"

"No." I'm not alright. How can I be alright!? Durandal just died a stupid death! I could've saved him if I tried. If I didn't threaten those stupid bird people to help him with a formation! I should've used all my treasures to block the lightning for Durandal instead! If I weren't so greedy, Durandal would still be here, hugging me and patting my ears! Why am I so greedy!? Why!? Why…? …Durandal's worth much more than every treasure I have. And I lost him. I fell to my knees and smacked the bird in my hand against the ground. It stopped moving, and I shoved it into the pouch. The blood covering my legs and waist was warm and wet. A very, very familiar feeling.

"Lucia...." Something soft pressed against my back. Arms wrapped around my waist, and a cold cheek pressed against my neck. "What happened?"

"S-Softie?" It's hard to speak. My nose is stuffy. My eyes are watering. My lips won't stop trembling. I don't deserve to live. I let Durandal down. I'm such an idiot! Stupid, stupid, stupid, stupid greedy squirrel!

"Stop!" Softie grabbed my forehead, but that didn't stop me from slamming it into the ground again. She hissed in pain, but she didn't let go. Why wasn't she letting go? Why was she even here? What was she doing? "Lucia…. Tell me what happened. Everything's going to be okay. Do you hear me? Everything's going to be okay."

"D-Durandal broke a-apart and merged into an e-egg." I'm ugly crying. But that doesn't matter. Nothing matters if Durandal's not around.

"Can I see the egg? If his core didn't break, I might be able to save him," Softie whispered. She stroked my back and patted my tail. There was something so comfortable about her embrace. It was warm and soft and perfect to cry in. I sniffled and reached into my pouch. Where…, where did the egg go!?

Softie yelped as I bolted to my feet and tore the pouch off my waist. I took out a bed from my interspacial ring, and then I flipped the pouch over and emptied its contents onto the soft mattress. An unconscious phoenix fell out. Then a red egg. Then a red pearl that looked like a … spirit seed! I grabbed the spirit seed and stared at it. This was Durandal. It *had* to be Durandal! I need a weapon! But all the exquisite swords Durandal had were broken….

"Congratulations, Lucia." Softie smiled at me and patted my arm. Hmm? What was she talking about? "That's Durandal, right? Sometimes, spirit seeds can absorb treasures; though, most of the times, they're absorbed by the treasures instead. It looks like Durandal became stronger after fusing with a phoenix egg."

"Then ... he's not dead?" Durandal's alive! Well, he's still in seed form, but he's alive! I need to get a super-strong sword to stick him into! "Softie! Where can I find the best sword available?"

"Hmm? In Kong County, any sword in our Shadow Devil Sect's treasury can be counted as a top-tier sword." Softie nodded. Was it that easy? "But they're only at the peak of spirit realm. If you want an earth-realm-ranked sword, then you might be able to find one at the King Province Exchange. Or ... if you're really feeling up to it, you can look for a sky-realm-ranked sword in Kang Country's Imperial City."

Hmmm. I think I'll plant Durandal into one of the Shadow Devil Sect's swords. The sooner Durandal reappears, the less stressed I'll feel! "Do you have a good sword on you right now?"

Softie shook her head. "I only use whips. But I'm sure Elder Sky has a few nice swords with him."

"Then it's settled! Give me—"

Don't you dare stick me in anything other than a sky-realm-ranked sword!

"...A second." What was that? "D-Durandal?"

That's right.

"You're really alive! I'll stick you in a sword right away! Then we can break you later and stick you in a better one, yeah?"

Stop! That won't work. I can't speak for long. Promise me you'll put me in a sky-realm-ranked sword.

"Eh...."

Promise me!

"Eh...."

Lucia! If you don't promise me, I won't have sex with you ever again!

"Promise! I promise! I'll stick you in a sky-realm-ranked sword!"

Good. It's time for me to ... hibernate. I believe in you, Lucia.

…In the end, he left me again, huh?

Chapter 13

It's amazing how much can change in a year. That's how long I've known Lucia. Just one year has passed and my world is completely different.... I've left the sect for the very first time. I've accomplished my first mission. I've had my first kiss ever with Lucia. I've led my first expedition. And I progressed by three whole ranks! Huh? What do I mean by my first kiss with Lucia? It's exactly like it sounds like! I was meditating on the boat as usual in Lucia's room while Lucia was sleeping. Then she suddenly stood up, walked over, and fell on top of me while muttering, "Durandal." And that's when we kissed.... Even though she was the one that was asleep, I feel like I'm the one who was taken advantage of.... It, it's not like I enjoyed it! I-it was just really weird. Yeah. Weird.

"Softie, what's up? Your face is redder than Lucia's when she exercises." Ilya sat next to me and tilted her head. Right now, I was sitting on a bench facing the side of the boat, staring off the edge at the sky. The boat was flying back to the Shadow Devil Sect. It hasn't even been two days since Lucia completely eradicated the Star Phoenix Sect. Right, that's another thing that's greatly changed in a year: The five fingers of Kong County are now the four fingers of Kong county.

"Oh, nothing! Nothing at all!" It took forever to separate from Lucia. She hugs really tightly when she's asleep!

"If you say so." Ilya raised an eyebrow before shrugging. "So, be honest. How bad is it that Lucia destroyed the Star Phoenix Sect? Is anyone going to come after her? Do they have a backer that we should know about?"

I sighed. "Yes, they do. The Star Phoenix Sect is a small branch sect of the Rainbow Phoenix Sect. They're located within the imperial capital of Kang Country. Most certainly, they'll send someone to investigate the destruction of the Star Phoenix Sect, and since there were so many witnesses wanting to see who the new earth-realm experts were, they'll be able to find out it was Lucia. Of course, the Shadow Devil Sect won't abandon Lucia." Even if the Shadow Devil Sect faces annihilation in the future, I'll convince my grandfather to save Lucia. She's our sect's greatest hope of advancing in the world. It, it's not like I have a personal bias that wants to help her—this is purely for the sect!

Ilya's brow furrowed as she pursed her lips. She seemed a lot older than she actually was when she did that. "Does our Shadow Devil Sect have any backers?"

"Um. Sort of. We're under the umbrella of the Immortal Devil Sect. Kind of." It's hard to explain. "Long, long ago…, no, that's not right. How do I put it…? There's basically two factions in the Immortal Continent—well, two major ones— the light faction and the dark faction. A long time ago, there weren't any factions but separate sects. One sect, the Greedy Devil Sect, provoked the ire of nearly every single sect; as a result, they were besieged from all sides and eventually slaughtered. Then, the sects that slaughtered the Greedy Devil Sect decided to form an alliance to annihilate every sect that shared the same principles as the Greedy Devil Sect. Because—"

Ilya raised a hand. "Let me guess. Then the sects not in the alliance stuck together and formed the dark faction."

"T-that's right." Ilya catches on a lot quicker than Lucia. At the very least, I know she's always paying attention. Lucia doesn't.

"And our Shadow Devil Sect belongs to this dark faction. If the Rainbow Phoenix Sect attacked us, then the dark faction would step in, is that it?" The creases in Ilya's brows smoothed out as she took a notebook and magical writing utensil out of her interspacial ring. I took a peek at her notes, but they were written in an unknown language.

"That's the theory...."

"Why's it only a theory?"

"Well, there hasn't been a large conflict in an extremely long time. A full sect annihilation hasn't occurred in over a thousand years—even if it was only a tiny branch sect." No one ever completely eradicates another sect; that'd be wrong! It's etiquette for the losers to subordinate themselves underneath the victors and pay tribute. These were the rules that the two factions had set up to prevent a perpetual cycle of revenge. Now that our sect has broken that rule, a sky-realm expert from the dark faction might pay us a visit. "Mm. There might be trouble, now that I think about it more."

"Trouble? What trouble?" A head with furry round ears appeared between me and Ilya from behind.

"L-Lucia!?" Where did she come from? "G-Good morning!"

"Hmm?" Lucia tilted her head, her hair brushing against my neck. I wanted to hide myself in a corner somewhere and cover myself with a blanket. "What's up with her? Why's she so jumpy?"

"I'm not sure," Ilya said. "Did you do something to her this morning?"

"I don't think so?" Lucia's hand clapped against my shoulder. Heat flowed from her palm straight through my clothes and into my skin. My neck started to itch. "Softie? Are you okay? And what trouble were you talking about?"

"I, um, it's, err—"

"You wiped the Star Phoenix Sect off the face of the earth," Ilya said, interrupting me before I could gather my thoughts. Why am I so flustered!? L-Lucia doesn't even remember doing anything to me, so it never happened! It never happened. "Usually, killing a million people brings about trouble from their family, lovers, allies, and whatnot. In this case, there might be another sect coming to look for you."

"Me? Kill a million people? When did I do that?" Lucia blinked and recoiled while pointing at her own face.

"Y-you don't remember?" How can she not remember? When Ilya and I found her in the Star Phoenix Sect, she was standing in a lake of blood filled with mangled corpses. There were no survivors! Could it be that she blocked off the memory due to trauma? Many cultivators choose to lose memories to rid themselves of heart devils, but if they suddenly encounter a trigger that makes them recall what they chose to forget, then the consequences will be dire. I hope Lucia hasn't done something similar. I'll force her to remember now to mitigate the damage. "The Star Phoenix Sect. Doesn't that ring a bell?"

"Of course," Lucia said and nodded. "Those selfless volunteers who sacrificed themselves completely for me to pass my tribulation. They were good people. Ah, I should burn some fake money for them. That's a custom, right, Ilya?"

"You actually remembered something I said?" Ilya asked, her eyes widening. She bit her lower lip and shrank back and away from Lucia while hunching her shoulders. "You already gave me a noogie!"

I don't understand. "Huh?"

"Lucia only remembers grudges," Ilya said and hid behind me. "I didn't think she'd still be upset over a little joke I played on her."

Lucia snorted and raised her head into the air while puffing her chest out. "I'm not upset. I'm a very magnanimous and merciful person. Why would I hold a grudge against you?" Then Lucia summoned a grill from her interspacial ring and placed it down by the bench. "Anyways, it was my tribulation that destroyed the Star Phoenix Sect. It can't be blamed on me! They were just in the wrong place at the wrong time. Mhm."

Lucia's words would be a little more convincing if she wasn't busy trying to cook a struggling phoenix on her grill. But since she was, I couldn't believe her. I guess if she eats the phoenix now, when the sky-realm expert comes to check on us, she won't eat it in front of him then. Now I'm curious—what does a phoenix taste like?

***

Phoenixes are magical creatures. No matter how high I turn up the heat on the grill, the phoenix simply doesn't cook! Mm. Oh wells. I've cut it apart a few times, but it always turns into a pile of ash and reforms. So now I have a very upset phoenix and a pile of raw phoenix wings that can't be cooked. There goes my dream of eating a phoenix. I don't eat raw food; I'm not a savage! During my attempts to cook the phoenix, Ilya kept saying something about a Rainbow Phoenix Sect. I thought phoenixes could only be red. Are there green and yellow phoenixes too?

Anyways, now that Durandal's in his spirit seed form, I don't have to work hard anymore! I can finally slack off and rest. After all, I don't have a sword to perform Madness Strikes with anymore. Mhm. This is justified laziness. And since the Impenetrable Shell needs a sparring partner to train and my usual sparring partner turned into a red bead, I don't have to train this one either! As for the Footsteps of the Giant, well, that's fun to use since it lets me walk on walls and ceilings, so I'm always using it. I've really been thinking about wearing pants instead of this robe since my clothes are still affected by gravity if I want to romp around upside down. But it's great to finally relax after this hellish year of training! The only downside is Durandal doesn't have a penis in his current state. Oh! And I'm an earth-realm expert now! I've learned how to teleport! All I have to do is focus really hard on the place I want to go and ... poof! I'm behind Ilya now!

Ilya sighed and shook her head. "The last thing Lucia needed was the ability to teleport. She's hyperactive enough as is. Now, if she's bored, she'll blink away somewhere and ruin something. She ruins everything she touches. How am I supposed to keep an eye on her now? This is a nightmare."

Oi.

Softie made a strange expression, and Ilya stiffened before sighing. "She's behind me, isn't she?"

Softie's head bobbed up and down.

Ilya screamed when I grabbed her and ground my knuckles against her head. "Who's a disaster, huh? Who ruins everything she touches, huh? Say that to my face." For an encyclopedia, she's gotten awfully brave over this past year! It's because she reached the saint-realm by breaking through to the tenth circle, isn't it? I have to teach her not to be arrogant since her dad's not around to watch over her. She needs a responsible adult—say, a cute squirrelkin girl like me—to keep her from straying on the wrong path.

Speaking of the wrong path…, it's quite unfortunate about the Star Phoenix Sect. If they helped Durandal pass his tribulation properly, I'm sure they would've all survived. But since they tried to kill—wait, no. Since they actually killed Durandal by interrupting him at a crucial moment, they were struck by divine punishment and wiped off the face of the Immortal Continent. Right. It was divine punishment caused by the heavens and not an individual. As the only witness, my words are law. Anyone who disagrees with me wasn't actually there, so they're wrong since I'm the only one who witnessed what happened. …And this phoenix, but phoenixes can't talk. Maybe they can talk to other phoenixes, but the other phoenix died while helping me pass my tribulation so that doesn't matter.

"Mm. Anyways"—I released Ilya—"how do I get to Kang Country? That's where you said I could obtain a sky-realm-ranked sword, right?"

Softie nodded. "I said Kang Country's imperial capital. We're in Kang Country right now. King Province and Kong County are a small part of it." Softie's brow furrowed. "I'm sure I told you this before when Ilya asked."

"Even if you did tell me, you'd have to tell me at least ten times for me to remember something as boring as that." Mhm. I only remember important things! Like how to cook stuff and miscellaneous things about Durandal like his favorite color. It's blue, by the way. What was I doing? Right! "Okay, so how do I get to the imperial capital? I'm rich, right? I can just waltz in and buy a sword there, yeah?"

"You're rich...?" Softie tilted her head. "Oh! It's because you stripped all the resources from Kong County. But that's not enough to purchase a sky-realm-ranked sword."

What!? "A whole countysworth of stuff can't buy me a sword? Then how do I get one?" Durandal's set me on an impossible task! I should just stuff him into a normal sword. Right, even if he swore to never have sex with me if I did, it's better than never seeing him again because sky-realm-ranked swords are impossible to obtain. Besides, it's not like he can uphold that promise. All I have to do is shackle him with a spirit-restraining rope and tie him to a bed. Right. It's settled then. I'm sticking Durandal into the first sword I find.

"W-well, a smith who can create a sky-realm-ranked sword is obviously overflowing with riches; there's no need for them to worry about money." Softie grabbed my sleeve, her face bright red. What was up with her? Did she think I was going to run away? "The only way to convince them to forge you a weapon is as a favor. For normal people like us, that means we have to appeal to the people who are capable of receiving the smith's favor."

"...Appeal to people? Like prostitute ourselves?" I'm not doing that!

"N-no!" Softie's hair whipped my face as she rapidly shook her head. "Not like that! The imperial family of Kang

Country can give you a sky-realm-ranked sword if you establish good connections with them."

"Is that the one that Lucia killed a prince of?" Ilya asked. I killed a prince? "He was the thirty-somethingieth archer at the cultural exchange."

"No, that's a different one." Softie pursed her lips. "They're the imperial family of King Province. The imperial family of Kang Country rules over them, and they aren't related by blood."

"Okay." My head's starting to hurt. "Tell me the easiest way to get a sky-realm-ranked sword, but make sure you explain it in such a way that a five-year-old can understand." Right. Thinking too far ahead isn't my strong suit. I just want to know what I have to do! I don't care about any family or dead princes or any of that stuff. And if there's no satisfactory answer, then Durandal's going into a normal sword. Mm.

"Um. Win the King Province Exchange that's coming up soon. Then volunteer for the imperial army. Accomplish their tasks and gather merits until the imperial family acknowledges you." Softie ticked the three things off with her fingers. "That's it."

Now that seems simple enough. But I'm the successor of the Godking! There's paths available for me that normal people can't take! "Isn't there an easier way, say, like kidnapping the smith's son or daughter and exchanging them for a sky-realm-ranked sword?"

"Um. Yes, I suppose that could work, but then every expert who wants a sword from the smith will hunt you down in exchange for the smith's favor."

Hmm. That's a bit problematic. Wait! If I can get the smith's favor by rescuing his child, then doesn't that mean…? "So you're saying I should pay someone to kidnap his child and become the hero who earns the smith's favor?"

"That's not what I said at all!"

"Mm. Alright. I like this plan better!" Right. Now all I have to do is find someone willing to and capable of kidnapping a famous weaponsmith's child! Where am I going to find someone like that? Hmm. I lowered my head to think … and made eye contact with the grumpy phoenix. Perfect!

"W-wait!" Softie said. "At least participate in the King Province Exchange first in case your plan goes awry, which it will!"

Hah. When have any of my plans ever gone awry? I'm a strategic genius! …But I'll do that exchange as a just in case. Strategic geniuses always have backup plans.

Chapter 14

Today's the day of the King Province Exchange. Not much has happened since the time Lucia destroyed the Star Phoenix Sect until now. We successfully traveled back to the Shadow Devil Sect without a hitch—not like anyone would try to stop an armada of flying boats branded with the Shadow Devil Sect's crest. Arriving back at the sect however….

My grandfather was shocked to put it simply. I've never seen him make the expression he made when he saw Lucia and me step off of the boat. He had heard of Lucia's feats, but there wasn't any time for information about Lucia becoming an earth-realm expert to reach him before we arrived. I think his heart stopped for a moment when I told him about Lucia's tribulation exterminating the Star Phoenix Sect. Right. Everyone on board the boats agreed to swear an oath, with Lucia's persuasion, saying it was her tribulation that wiped out the sect. She's such a horrible person; I don't know why I like her so much. As a friend! Like her as a friend!

Afterwards, there was a lot of unrest as the disciples that accompanied Lucia challenged the disciples that didn't. The disciples that followed Lucia completely dominated their challenges as a result of the experience and loot they obtained over the past year, and they completely occupied all the core disciple spots. The days passed by in a blink of an eye, and the time to leave for the King Province Exchange came before I could completely settle down. Also, the impurity-cleansing pool had been fixed, but Lucia snuck in to play a prank on Ilya and contaminated it. …Again. I knew it was her fault the first time! But really, what kind of earth-realm expert has the time to prank a saint-realm junior? Lucia hasn't cultivated at all since she passed her tribulation. She..., she's making a mockery of cultivation.

Regardless, mockery or not, Lucia is representing us for the disciple portion of the King Province Exchange. Even though she's as strong as an ancestor, she's able to sign up as a disciple because she's young, less than a hundred years old. The King Province Exchange takes place in the imperial city of King Province, which is in the center of the province, between the borders of the strongest three counties, Hong, Long, and Yong. The seven counties that surround those, including our Kong County, is objectively weaker by a tiny margin. There's—eep! "L-Lucia? Please, don't poke me like that!"

Lucia tilted her head, her cute tail twitching. "But don't you like it when I poke you there?" She shrugged and looked around, her eyes glistening as they widened. "Whatever. You've probably told me already, but I forgot; what are we doing here? And why is that wall so huge!? What's it made out of?"

Right now, we were standing at the edge of our airship as it descended towards the space reserved for us since flying isn't allowed in the imperial city. I've never been here before; I've only heard rumors about it. The walls of the city are monstrously high. I bet if I stood on top of it, I'd be able to touch a cloud if I raised my hand. "Legends say the imperial city's walls are made out of a giant's femur. An immortal diced the giant into pieces, and part of its femur fell to the earth. Eventually, its marrow was absorbed by the earth and the bone became hollow. Then people dug into it and created what is now known as the imperial city."

Lucia's jaw dropped open as her tail stiffened. "That's just a portion of a giant's arm!?"

"A femur's a leg bone," Ilya said and rolled her eyes. She stuck to Lucia like glue these days. I think she was avoiding my grandmother. "And do you really believe that? Honestly, it'd be impossible for a giant of that size to ever exist. Think of how much food it'd need to sustain itself. And oxygen is extremely sparse the higher up you go. The giant would have to practically crawl on the ground to keep its head at acceptable breathing levels."

"Giants really exist!" They do!

"Have you seen one for yourself?" Ilya asked. She placed her hands on her hips. "I've been going through the books that I borrowed from the library, and quite frankly, a lot of things don't make sense. As a researcher, there are some things I can believe and other things I can't."

"Hmm? But don't you use magic, Ilya?" Lucia asked, still staring at the giant wall. "Besides, there's an easy way to prove if that's part of a leg or not."

"Magic has a very logical system! So does qi!" Ilya glared at Lucia before sighing. "You can't believe everything you hear, Lucia. The wall is definitely artificial. Sky-realm experts can move mountains, creating something like this is easy in comparison." She squinted at the wall and rubbed her chin. "If you gave me a month or two, I could create something like that with earth magic too."

I'm not a liar…. And I don't like Ilya correcting me in front of Lucia! She's slapping my face when she does that! Besides, I'm the native; Ilya's not. "Lucia, what's your method to determine if the legends are true?"

"I'll just carve some engravings on it," Lucia said and chuckled, her tail finally relaxing. "Then I'll try to absorb it! If it disappears, then it was a bone. If it doesn't disappear, then it wasn't. It's as simple as that."

"…Won't that get rid of the wall?" Wait. That's destruction of property. Wait, no. It's even worse than that. If the wall disappears, then it can be taken as a sign of attack. Only an invader would want to destroy the imperial city's defenses. "Lucia…?" I looked away for a second and she's gone!? "Where—"

"She teleported over there." Ilya pointed straight ahead. I squinted my eyes and shielded them from the sun. There was a brownish speck halfway up the imperial city's walls which I thought was Lucia.

"Where's Lucia?"

I jumped from the voice suddenly appearing in my ears.

My grandfather smiled at me before looking around. "Isn't she usually with you?" he asked.

"She's on the wall, Grandfather." I pointed at what I thought was Lucia. "She's testing something."

"Testing something?" My grandfather's caterpillar-like eyebrows wiggled as they rose upwards. "I was under the impression she never tested anything in her life. What's she…?" My grandfather's jaw dropped open, and a sense of unease gripped my stomach as I turned my head to follow his gaze. The imperial city's walls were gone. Hundreds of people were falling from the sky, screaming before they were silenced by the ground. Perhaps they were on top of the wall before it disappeared…. Then, without warning, a surge of qi struck me and forced me to my knees. Ilya gasped and my grandfather groaned as they both fell down too.

"Sky-realm expert!" my grandfather hissed, his eyes widening. Though it was hard to see, my vision distorted due to the qi filling the air, I could make out a figure standing above the imperial city's buildings. It was wearing purple robes and a golden crown—the emperor.

***

Whew! I feel so refreshed after consuming the giantest bone of focus ever! Hmm? Giantest isn't a word? Nonsense! Big, bigger, biggest. Giant, gianter, giantest! After all, the only adjective one can use to describe the bone of a giant is giant. It only makes sense. But now that I know I feel refreshed, where am I? What happened last? I carved the rune of focus, absorbed the bone, then I fell from the sky. Logically, I should be on the ground outside of the city, but I'm not. I'm surrounded by corpses and cripples. What the heck happened? Well, for once, these people weren't injured because of me, so it's not my problem! Now, there is one thing that may be an issue, and that's the purple-robed person in the sky radiating a massive amount of qi. Who did he think he was? Flying's not allowed in the imperial city; Softie told me that! As a law-abiding citizen, I have to take the law into my own hands! "Hey! You stupid nitwit! Flying isn't allowed in the imperial city!" I'll hit him with a Breaking Blade and…. Right. Mini-DalDal's gone, and I didn't find a new sword to replace it!? What the heck have I been doing!? And all the swords Durandal used for his tribulation turned into piles of molten crap…, except for this one. Isn't this just a normal sword? I guess it is.

"Are you talking to me?"

Fuck! How did he get so close!? Right, teleportation. At least he's on the ground. "Hey! Mister! Teleporting isn't allowed either!" I quickly ran to his side and wrapped my arm around his shoulder and placed my lips close to his ear. I whispered, "Listen, I'm telling you this because you're clearly not from around here. Flying, teleporting, or doing anything that shows you're an earth-realm expert isn't allowed in this city! According to my friend, if you're caught doing those things, the royal family will take you out behind a shed, tell you to close your eyes, and bam! You're dead."

"Is that so?"

What was that look on his face? It's like he's looking at an idiot! I'm smart when I'm focused! I raised my hand and smacked his forehead with a satisfying thwack! But why was he wearing a crown? What an odd sense of fashion. "Right. That's exactly so! Well, I think it is, but I haven't actually been here myself. It's just what I've heard. And I only remember important details! Since I've remembered those rules, it's definitely true! I'm telling you this for your own good!"

The purple-robed, crowned fellow seemed to be in a daze. Did I hit him too hard? He rubbed the bump on his forehead and scowled at me before asking, "By any chance, do you know who I am?"

Shit! I really did hit him too hard! "Gah! Sorry! I hit you so hard that I gave you amnesia!" What do I do? Ilya! She knows the answer to everything! I'll take him to her. Gosh, why am I so quick-witted? "But don't you worry! I have a friend who can patch up your memory in no time! You'll even remember the screams of your mother on the day you were born."

The young man tried to say something, but I looped my arm around his waist and ... right. I didn't know where I was. But that's not an issue! I'll teleport up into the sky, look around and figure out where I am, and then teleport back down before anyone notices me! Here we go! Up. Oh, there's the boat! It's a good thing there's fancy markings on it. And I'll teleport there instantly! Bam, done. I dropped the young man in my arms onto the ground. "Whew, no one saw me, right?"

"Didn't you say teleporting and flying wasn't allowed?" the young man asked and raised an eyebrow.

"It's okay! I was only up there for a second. It's impossible for those scary nobles to have noticed." Right. Even I wouldn't notice someone flying over my territory back at home if they were only up there for a second. And if I can't do it, then no one else can. Mhm. It's as simple as that. "Look, there's my friend. Ilya! I hit this person on the head too hard and he lost his memories. Can you fix him?"

"E-Emperor Yi!" the sect leader, who was standing by Ilya, shouted. He bowed his head and cupped his hands at the young man.

...Emperor? I stared at the person in purple. Then I pointed at him while looking at the sect leader. "This dude's the emperor?"

"J-Junior Lucia! Err, pointing at the emperor is a serious crime. Hurry up and apologize!"

...Well, it looks like the sect leader's finally gone senile. It's about time too. I heard he was over a hundred years old. I laughed and patted the purple-robed man on the back repeatedly, causing him to stumble forward. "Don't listen to this dotard. There's no way you're the emperor! You look like you're sixteen years old! The emperor has thousands of concubines and thousands of children! There's no way someone with your looks could possibly attract so many women."

"...Am I not attractive?"

"Nope!" Everyone, when compared to Durandal, is unattractive. Well, men, at least. Softie's attractive, but she's a woman. I'm not jealous! "Besides, you look even younger than that prince that shot an arrow into my heart!"

The man in purple coughed, and I thought I saw blood leaking out of the corner of his mouth, but his hand wiped it away before I could confirm. It certainly smelled like blood. Was he injured? He glared at me. "Thirtieth Prince Yi? What happened to him after he shot you?"

"He died. Unfortunate accident, really. It's a shame." I shrugged. It wasn't my fault! I only wanted to tear off his limbs, but one of the beasts inside of my Tides of Blood tore his head off instead. Bad, dragon! Bad! "Anyways. Ilya, hurry up and cure him before he really thinks he's the emperor."

Ilya stared at me, unresponsive. Softie had a frightened expression like a deer being stabbed by my sword. And the sect leader's face was cramped. "What's wrong with you three? Don't tell me you have food poisoning." But we all ate the same thing. Oh! It's because I cultivate the Immortal

Poison Body, huh? Have the aurochsen in my interspacial ring gone bad? That's impossible!

The man in purple rubbed his chin before smiling at me. "I came out to find the expert who retrieved the great wall, but I found a much more interesting toy instead. Little girl, what's your name?"

Little girl? Was he talking to me? I don't want to be called little girl by someone who can't even grow out facial hair! "I'm Lucia Fluffytail, chosen of the Shadow Devil Sect. But you have to call me Lucia. If you call me little girl again, you'll regret it!"

"Oh? What will you do, little girl?"

This bastard. He's only as old as Ilya, but he's so much cockier than her! I'll give him a noogie. Oh? He's trying to push me away with his qi? Footsteps of the Giant! Neither of us are going anywhere until I'm done!

"R-release this emperor at once!"

Tsk. Why did the sect leader have to go around planting false memories into people? It'll be troublesome if the real emperor heard. Supposedly, he's a sky-realm expert. I wonder how strong he is.

***

I'm not sure how, but it seems like Lucia has mistaken the emperor for … someone not the emperor. She even embraced him with her arms and rubbed her knuckles against his head! Why does my chest feel so stuffy? I'm not jealous of him! He's being tormented by her, but…, but…. No, it's nothing. Breathe in. Breathe out. Phew. "E-Emperor Yi. Are you alright?"

"What kind of person is this foxkin!?"

Lucia's loving knuckle rub was still ongoing, and Emperor Yi was pouring out more and more qi, but none of it was working! Lucia was like a steady mountain, holding onto the struggling teen while completely unconcerned. It seemed like every knuckle rub of hers was interrupting the emperor's qi from gathering. All he could do was emit it from his body. "Hush! This is your own fault for calling me a little girl. Repent for your crimes and call me big sister!" Lucia's hands suddenly stopped moving. "Wait. No. Don't call me that; I hate honorifics! Call me Lucia."

"Unhand me this instant! I'm the emperor!"

"Gah! Look at what you taught him, you unthinking sect leader! He really thinks he's the emperor." Lucia rolled her eyes as her knuckles ground even harder against the emperor's head. I couldn't help but feel bad for him. I wish it were me…. That was able to subdue a sky-realm expert like that! I didn't wish to suffer under Lucia's punishment! T-there's no way.

"I am the emperor! I really am! Look at my crown!"

Lucia's knuckles stopped grinding against the poor man's skull as her hand flashed. The crown disappeared as her fingers touched it, and then she resumed grinding his head again. "I don't see a crown."

"L-Lucia…. Stop. Please."

T-the emperor conceded! How could a sky-realm expert bow his head so easily!?

"Mm. That's better," Lucia said and dusted off her hands after releasing Emperor Yi. She patted his back twice, planting his face into the ground with her overwhelming strength. I've been on the receiving end of that palm once. It's not pleasant. "Ilya, hurry up and mend him."

"Okay…," Ilya said with a sigh. She rolled her eyes and sauntered over to the fallen emperor before placing her hand on his head. It glowed white with what she called mana, and then she retracted her hand. "All done."

Mana was a curious thing. It behaves a lot like qi. It's almost as if the person who came up with the concept had a firm grasp on qi and attempted to traverse his own path. I wonder if there are any sky-realm experts who use mana. I haven't heard of any, but then again, I'm just a frog in a well. The world is vast, and I've only stayed in my sect for the vast majority of my life.

"Do you remember who you are?" Lucia asked, picking the emperor off the ground. She blinked at him and tilted her head, her tail twitching. "You must've been someone important since you know how to fly and teleport. Only earth-realm experts and above can do that! And this old man's over a hundred years old, but he hasn't reached the sky-realm yet. You're, like, sixteen or somewhere around there and your qi is much thicker than his. Thus, you're some kind of chosen from an important sect!"

Ilya's eyes widened. "Lucia's deducing things? What is the world coming to?"

"I always deduce things! I'm an intelligent person!" Lucia stamped her feet and glared at Ilya. "I just have a lot of focus right now. Very, very, hyper focused."

"Enough of this farce!" Emperor Yi shouted. His feet lifted into the air, but Lucia tackled him back onto the floor of the boat in an instant.

"I already told you, you can't fly here!" Lucia growled. "Damn. Idiots these days. They can't appreciate any goodwill!"

"Look at this!" Emperor Yi pulled something out of an interspacial ring as he struggled. The royal crest!

"And that is...?" Lucia leaned over the emperor and smelled the crest. Her brow wrinkled before she licked it. "Hmm. No idea."

"Y-you licked the royal crest...." Emperor Yi looked crestfallen. He stared at the single wet droplet crawling down the lines of the bow and arrow engraved on the metal. "B-barbaric! How dare you try to seduce me, fox!?"

"...Seduce?" Lucia blinked. "I already said you weren't attractive! Why would I seduce you?"

The emperor choked and coughed out a mouthful of blood. "Which part of me isn't attractive!?" He roared and let out a massive fluctuation of qi. The floorboards cracked underneath him, and Lucia was blown up into the air as if she were hit by a geyser. A bow materialized in the emperor's hand, and he drew back the string, an arrow made of white qi forming at his fingertips. With a twang, the arrow vanished and instantly reappeared embedded in Lucia's chest.

"Lucia!" I couldn't stop myself from shouting as Lucia coughed out a mouthful of blood, her tail stiffening as her eyes widened.

"This crazy person!" Lucia teleported beside the emperor and smacked the bow out of his hands. Surprisingly, he couldn't resist! Just how strong was Lucia's physical strength? Her physique was beyond my comprehension. Wasn't she only at the strength of a red dragon? Wait. She did eat over a thousand aurochsen which are famed battle mounts known for their strength. But could it make that much of a difference? The impurities she accumulated from eating them isn't worth it! "Who shoots someone in the heart!? What if my boob scars!?"

"You licked my royal crest first!"

Emperor Yi has absolutely no dignified manner…. Is he really the emperor? Maybe Lucia was right. He's clearly an individual who lost his memory.

"Don't say it like that!" Lucia's arm once again wrapped around the emperor's neck. Then, with smooth, practiced motions, Lucia's hand slid around Emperor Yi's body like a snake, and everything that looked valuable was stripped. I, I don't think he even noticed. "Sheesh. People will misunderstand!"

"Father!" Who was that? Dozens of people were soaring through the air, heading straight towards us! Of course, with the wall disappearing, all the princes and princesses would come out to investigate once their father's aura went missing.

Lucia's jaw dropped open as she released the emperor. She looked down and plucked out the arrow in her chest before tossing it aside, blood spurting from the gaping hole. In a second, her flesh wriggled and healed, leaving behind her tanned skin underneath a partially torn robe. "Hey, Mr. Not Attractive," Lucia said and pointed at the incoming crowd. "Those people are calling you father. And they're wearing the same thing that thirtieth prince was wearing…." Her eyes widened. "Are you actually the emperor!?"

"That's what I've been trying to tell you," my grandfather said as Emperor Yi glared at Lucia.

Lucia tilted her head. "But then why's he so weak? How could he have so many women with no looks, no money, and no power? Don't you think he looks like the kind of person who'd die alone?"

Emperor Yi winced and clutched his chest, blood leaking from his lips.

Lucia blinked and scratched her head. "Ah. Another heart devil gained. Which poor fellow was it this time?"

***

Hmm. Maybe, just maybe, I messed up. And Ilya says I don't know how to admit my mistakes. I made a teensy-tiny misjudgment about this man who's currently being choked by my arm. It turns out, he was actually the emperor. Who knew? There's no reason for an emperor to wander around looking like a sixteen-year-old! That's just asking to be mistaken for someone he's not! Right. This isn't my fault. This is the emperor's fault. I'm sure he's not sixteen; he's using some kind of disguise that makes him look younger. …I wonder if he'll teach me it—not that I look old enough to need it.

"Father, is this the expert who stole our wall?"

And now there's a giant group of princes and princesses hovering nearby the boat. If all of them shot me with arrows at once, then I'd be screwed! It's a good thing I have this human shield.

"No! Don't be stupid. This foxkin's merely an earth-realm ... expert." Emperor Yi struggled in my grasp, so I tightened my grip. I can't let my only safety insurance escape!

"But she's suppressing you...." One of the princes at the front, that didn't resemble Emperor Yi at all was leading the pack and doing all the talking. Emperor Yi's so lucky to have this many children. Even after trying with Durandal for over a year, I'm not even pregnant! It can't be that I'm sterile, right? That's impossible. I can be shot in the heart and regenerate! Surely my eggs are just as sturdy. Then is it Durandal's issue...? Maybe I should have a doctor see him. Mm. I'll do that as soon as I plant him in a sword. Oh! Sword! Emperor Yi's a sky-realm expert. Surely he has a sky-realm-ranked sword. I'll check through the interspacial ring I stole later. I might not even have to kidnap a blacksmith's child. Hmm. Emperor Yi's such a long name. I'll call him Yiyi from now on.

"This isn't suppression," Yiyi said and glared at his son. Honestly, his son looks like the father, and he looks like the son. Maybe women in the Immortal Continent like childish-looking men? How else would Yiyi have so many women? Clearly, everyone's an immoral pervert. Ah, it's tough being the only normal person, but thankfully, I already have a lot of experience ignoring everyone's looks. "This is friendly skinship."

That's right! This is a friendly gesture totally not meant to incapacitate people! I nodded twice to play along. But why was Yiyi helping me out? I know! This is all about face! He can't go around saying he, a sky-realm expert, lost to me, an earth-realm expert. That's.... Holy crap. I'm amazing, aren't I? Are all sky-realm experts this weak?

"Then ... you're courting her, Father? Is now the time? The great wall has gone missing!"

"Hey, Yiyi. Are you really courting me?" I'm taken! And I already told him he was unattractive!

"Court your mother! You're the one who tried to seduce me first!" Yiyi glowered at me. I could feel his gaze piercing me. Literally. Lasers of qi were shooting out of his eyes and burning my skin. "And what did you just call me? Yiyi? Only my first wife, the empress, can call me that!"

"What action did I take to seduce you, damnit!? I know I'm beautiful, charming, naturally attractive, and irresistible, but I didn't even give you a single hint of affection!" It looks like I have to rename Yiyi. How about … Quick Shot? Right, it has the same number of syllables and accurately reflects his nature. It's perfect! "But fine. I'll call you Quick Shot from now on, alright?"

Quick Shot twitched and blood flowed out of his mouth like vomit. "W-who's a quick shooter!? Just because I have a lot of children doesn't mean I have no stamina!"

What does children have to do with stamina and shooting arrows quickly? There's something wrong with Quick Shot's head. I might not have wiped out his memories when I smacked him, but I certainly addled something. Mm. I even planted a heart devil into him just now. For some reason, planting heart devils in people always makes them vomit out blood. Maybe the heart devil literally resides in the heart like a lump and forces out excess blood? Nah. Even I know the heart isn't connected to the mouth! I learned that through a lot of dismembering of beasts. "Yeah, yeah, okay, whatever. Just tell your children to go away, okay? They're really intimidating with all their bows drawn." When I gave Quick Shot an extra squeeze, all the princes and princesses drew their bows.

"What are you unfilial children doing, pointing a bow at your own father!?" Quick Shot shouted. Qi flew out of his mouth like shockwaves, pushing back his children and causing their faces to turn red. Wow. I wonder if I can do that. I'll try it! I'll call it Breaking Shout!

I'll put all my qi into the back of my mouth and.... "Testing!" It worked! Qi flew out of my mouth like the shockwave from an explosion and collided into the group of flying people. They were knocked so far away that I couldn't see them anymore. Whew. If I do this every time I shout out a sword technique, I'll get too tired too fast. That took up a lot more energy than expected.

"You ... copied my royal family's secret Dragon Roar Technique...." Quick Shot stared at me in awe. I'm sure that's awe and not fear. And what secret technique? How is it even close to a secret!? Anyone can figure it out in one glance!

"If you wanted to keep it a secret, you shouldn't have done it. Mm." I nodded. Damn. I'm so wise when I'm focused. Well, I'm always wise, but only when I'm focused am I able to enlighten other people with my wisdom.

Quick Shot's face fell. "...It took me ten years to learn that."

What? Really? "Uh, I know I'm a genius who learns really quickly, but, um, maybe you're just an idiot?" Oh! The heart devil grew even more! It's just begging me to harvest it. I wonder how strong I'll grow from a sky-realm expert's heart devil. I haven't been cultivating the technique because it's too upsetting to use when Durandal's not around to relieve the frustration that comes with it.

"...You're really infuriating, do you know that?"

Me? Infuriating? That's a first. "I think you mispronounced infatuating." Mm. That must be the case. Anyways, I have a mission to accomplish! "Quick Shot, when are you going to start the King Province Exchange? I need to win it as a backup plan!"

***

With the power of Lucia, somehow, we were invited into the imperial city's royal palace. The royal palace is larger than my father's territory back at home in terms of overall acres, which just goes to show how large that giant's femur bone fragment was. I still can't believe a giant of that size existed and walked the earth. I mean, seriously, just a portion of its femur reached the clouds. That's a walking disaster! Surely, if giants were common and had places to live in, then I'd be able to see those structures from anywhere on the Immortal Continent, but I can't. Ugh, forget it. I'm only obsessing about the giant because I was wrong and the wall was actually a bone.

We, the whole dozen people who made up the Shadow Devil Sect representatives, were shown a place to stay while the royal family prepared the King Province Exchange and cleaned up the mess caused by the wall disappearing. Luckily, one of the previous emperors had foresight and set up a substitute defensive formation over a thousand years ago just in case the wall was destroyed. I don't know why they're so trusting of something from that long ago in the past, but it's not just the royal family who's like that. Apparently, all the sects adhere rigidly to tradition, believing that the things left behind by their ancestors were greater than anything they themselves could ever come up with. It's such a stupid train of thought! Innovation is key! Without innovation, magic wouldn't exist! It's funny how the Immortal Continent is the one that's stuck in the past despite my home being the one that's the pocket dimension. Well, it's not like I can't understand their logic. Some of these sects' ancestors became immortals. If they follow in those immortals' footsteps, then won't they become immortal themselves?

And now Lucia's staring at a ring that suspiciously looks like a royal crest. "Lucia, what are you doing?"

"I'm trying to figure out how this interspacial ring works," Lucia said and squinted at the bow-and-arrow design. She flipped it back and forth, up and down, before sighing. "It's a mystery."

No. You're just an idiot. When did I become so bitter? Ahem, anyways…. "If you're trying to open it like it's an interspacial ring, and it's not opening, then what should that tell you about the ring?"

"That there's a secret mechanism that needs to be unlocked first!" Lucia growled at the ring before biting it, breaking off the tip of the arrow with her teeth. "Hmm. That didn't work either."

I'll try to slowly guide Lucia to the right answer. If I tell her it's not an interspacial ring straight out, she won't believe me. But if she comes to the conclusion herself, then she'll realize it really isn't an interspacial ring. "Are all rings interspacial rings?"

"They can be." Lucia stopped fidgeting with the royal crest and stared at me. "You can turn this into one, right?"

Well, yes, I could. But creating interspacial rings leaves one completely drained of mana for a while, so I've avoided it ever since doing it the first time. "I can, but I won't. Alright, so if every ring has the potential to be an interspacial ring, then that means some rings currently aren't interspacial rings, right?"

"Right…." Lucia furrowed her brow. Was she going to understand soon? Her head tilted to the side as the wrinkles on her forehead disappeared. "But it's impossible for this ring to not be an interspacial ring. Why would they make such a fancy ring and not make it hold stuff too?"

Well, I tried. "Some people like useless things. It's like assigning value to gold because it's shiny. Gold's worth has nothing to do with its capabilities. That crest isn't an interspacial ring, so you can stop trying to open it now." Seriously, for the past three hours, she was making strange clicking noises while puzzling over it. She consumed the largest bone of focus ever in existence, but it doesn't matter if she's focused so intently on something that's wrong.

"What? No way! It has to be an interspacial ring!"

"Is that ring on your finger an interspacial ring?" I pointed at the ring Lucia wore on her left ring finger. She made a matching pair for herself and Durandal a while back.

"No. It's a disguise! When people want to steal my stuff, they take it instead of the real ring that's hidden."

"Right. And why can't other people do that?"

Lucia's eyes widened to the size of saucers. "I was tricked! Quick Shot is such a slimy bastard! How dare he fool me with a fake ring!?"

A soft cough echoed through the room. Softie opened her eyes and smiled at me with a look of disdain. I was being looked down on? "Actually, Lucia was right. It's an interspacial ring. It's just bound to Emperor Yi and Lucia's qi isn't condensed enough to shatter a sky-realm expert's sealing mechanism." Softie walked over to Lucia and placed her hand on top of the interspacial ring. "Don't listen to Ilya, Lucia. She's wrong."

This bitch. Now I remember why I became so bitter over this past year. She's trying to steal my spot by Lucia's side! Everything she says about me is to discredit me. She never says anything good about me. Phew. Calm down, Ilya. Softie's just a jealous, selfish child because of her upbringing. Since I became her grandmother's disciple, she thought I was taking her place in her grandmother's heart. You're mature and responsible, Ilya. There's no reason for you to be mad at someone who's so immature.

Lucia's brow wrinkled. "But Ilya's never wrong."

Softie's voice softened as she whispered into Lucia's ear like some kind of courtesan in bed, "Wasn't she wrong about the wall not being a bone? Don't you believe me? Once you become a sky-realm expert, you'll be able to open this ring." Softie's eyes narrowed for a second as she gave me a sly glance without turning her head away from Lucia. A little smirk appeared on her lips that quickly went away as her face softened once more when Lucia turned to face her.

That settles it. I'm going to murder her in her sleep one day. It'll be tough since she's technically stronger than me, but I'm resourceful. There's plenty of ways to go about it. I could pretend to be Lucia, sneak into Softie's bed, and stab her in the throat when she tries to do immoral things to me. Don't think I don't know how you look at Lucia, Softie! And Lucia won't believe me if I try to expose Softie's crafty nature. No, she might believe me, actually, but she'll say something stupid and fuel her narcissism like, "It's only natural for Softie to fall so in love with someone as perfect as me that she became jealous of you!" Well, it's not like Softie's trying to harm Lucia. The only person she's trying to get rid of is me. But I'll teach Softie her place with this newfound skill I picked up.

"Ooh, whatcha doing, Ilya?" Lucia ears perked up as she turned her head towards me. I had taken out the cauldron that my master had given me.

"Crafting immortal pills that taste like chocolate." That's right! I know all of Lucia's vices! There's no way Softie can ever hope to compete with me.

"Make me a batch! No! Make me two batches!"

"Of course."

"You can't eat those, Lucia!" Softie tugged on Lucia's sleeve. "The impurities inside of them are too high!"

Lucia snorted. "Impurities this, impurities that. You always say the things I do build up impurities, but nothing ever happens to me!" In a flash, Lucia appeared by my side and stared into the cauldron, drool leaking from her mouth as I added the component that made it taste like chocolate, which was, well, chocolate. A cold gaze caused a shiver to run down my spine, and I raised my head to take a look at Softie, who was glaring at me like a snake. I gave her a smug smirk in return. Don't dish out what you can't receive! Wait. I'm supposed to be mature. Mm. Oh wells, I *just* turned sixteen. Cut me some slack.

***

Ilya's a genius! Through some sorcery and black magic, she created chocolate that can recover my qi! Anyways, right now, I'm following this princess who's supposed to be leading us to the exchange. It was delayed by a couple of hours because the wall went missing because of a certain someone, but those hours passed really quickly for some reason. I was trying so hard to open that stupid ring that I lost track of time. This giant bone of focus is amazing!

"Oh? If it isn't the Sniveling Devil Sect. Here to embarrass yourselves again?"

Hmm? From a different passageway, a group of people dressed in golden robes were following behind a prince. I learned to recognize princes and princesses by their crests! It's a useful skill to learn, you know, just in case an emperor feels like masquerading as a sixteen-year-old again. Thank the Godking that the crests are pictures of bows and arrows instead of writing. The Immortal Continent apparently uses a different written language than back at home. I had enough trouble trying to learn one! I've accepted my fate as an illiterate. It's a good thing my encyclopedias can read. Ah? If I focused really hard on trying to learn the language, then I'd learn it in no time? Of course! I could definitely do it if I tried, but I'm a very busy person with too little time. Mhm. I'm not making excuses!

"That's the Righteous Buddha Sect," Softie whispered to me and grabbed my hand. Why did she have to grab my hand? Did she think I was going to hurt them? I don't need my hands to do that. Well, Softie's hand is soft and warm, so I'll let her do what she wants. I haven't held anyone's hand in a while since Durandal unbirthed himself…. "They don't like us, and we don't like them. We get stronger by planting heart devils in people, but they get stronger by cleansing people's hearts."

The sect leader snorted and glared at the bald and fat golden-robed person. "This year, we will grind you beneath our feet and pay you back for the last exchange."

"Oh? I will look forward to it. I can't wait to see the look on your face when your sect is ranked last again." The bald and fat man gave the sect leader a gentle smile before he turned his head towards me. His eyes were narrowed and arched into tiny crescents. He also didn't have any eyebrows. I wonder if the friction between the Shadow Devil Sect and their sect was caused by this man being jealous of the sect leader's caterpillar-like eyebrows. Nah. It can't be. "Is this Heart Devil Lucia?"

Ah? "You know me?"

"Yes. Your exploits have become quite widespread." The bald and fat man nudged the other bald and fat man behind him. They look exactly the same! "This is my grandson. He's a mid-low-ranked earth-realm expert participating in the disciple portion of the exchange. He's only ninety-eight years old." The fat grandson smiled at me.

"Holy crap!" Ninety-eight! How large is that? Hmm. That's nine tens and an eight. So…, two less than ten tens…. That's two less than a hundred! The fat grandson's smile was even wider than before. "You're ancient!"

The grandson's smile stiffened.

"Don't smile at me like that! I know I'm beautiful and infatuating, but I'm young enough to be your great-great-granddaughter!" His smile suddenly turned a lot creepier once I figured out how old he was. Ugh. Even my tail has goosebumps. Seriously, everyone needs to stop with their age-disguising trickery. Hmm. Now that I think about it. "Hey, Softie. How old are you?"

"Mn? I'm nineteen."

Phew. She's normal.

"Too bad you act like you're twelve," Ilya muttered.

Hmm? Did something happen between the two of them?

"Ahem! I'll crush you during the exchange, Heart Devil Lucia." The fat grandson glared at me before turning away. Then their group left first. It seemed like the princess that we were following knew not to walk alongside them.

"You have to watch out for him," the sect leader said to me and patted my shoulder. Why? I subdued Quick Shot! A measly earth-realm expert is nothing in my eyes! "The Righteous Buddha Sect's techniques are direct counters to ours. They'll destroy the heart devil worms that you've cultivated, causing you to directly drop in strength."

Eh…. Heart devil worms are a supplement for me. My real strength comes from my Breaking Blades mixed with Madness Strikes! It's a super-duper strong ultimate technique that I've named Breaking Madness Blade Strikes! Oh, I've also learned the Heart Devil Apparition which was supposed to be the strongest attacking skill of the Heart Devil Cultivation Technique, but I don't use it much since it summons something to beat up my enemies for me. There's just something satisfying about cracking open someone's skull with your own sword, you know? It's like opening an acorn! It tastes better when you break the shell yourself. Mn. Of course, I don't eat the contents inside the skull. It was just an analogy! Ah. That reminds me. I still don't have another sword that can manipulate its weight like mini-DalDal could. Well, I still have my fists.

"Anyways. What exactly is the exchange?" Crushing people and grinding them beneath our feet. It sounds like we're making blood wine. It can't be a wine-making competition, right? "Like, what do I need to do?"

"You didn't tell her?" the sect leader asked Softie.

"I did, but she wasn't listening or she forgot," Softie said.

Hey. Well, that's probably true, but there's no need to place the blame on me! If you know I'm not going to listen or forget, then you just have to make sure I'm listening and not forgetful at the time. Jeez, it's not that hard. "Right. So what do I do?"

"You just have to beat people up," Ilya said. "It's an exchange, but it's really just a show of strength. The overall winner of the exchange receives a token that lets them form a squad with a hundred people of their choice for the Kang Country Army."

What? How come Ilya knows this?

"Yes," Softie said. "Not only that, but if our sect wins, a hundred disciples will have a chance to move up in the world, further establishing our sect's foundation. You have to do your best, Lucia!"

Ilya gave Softie a dirty look before snorting. Mm. There's definitely something going on between these two…. But no one's said anything to me, so it's not my problem! "Got it. Beat people up. I can do that. It's actually what I do best."

***

This is my first time attending the King Province Exchange! There's less than a thousand people gathered, about ten for each sect attending. The King Province Exchange isn't a public event. Some techniques should be kept a secret from the populace. Lucia, Ilya, and I were following behind the elders of our sect, entering the competition grounds which looked like a giant circular arena. Though I said it was my first time attending, it seems like everyone knows me already….

"Miss Moonlight, won't you sit by me?"

"So that's Chosen Moonlight of the Shadow Devil Sect. She's even more beautiful than the rumors say."

"A woman of Miss Moonlight's caliber can only be matched by me!"

"Miss Moonlight met my eyes! Did you see that brothers? This is fate!"

"Idiot! She was looking at me!"

"Whoa." Lucia wrapped her arm around my shoulder. "You're so popular, Softie! Which one do you like the best?" Her eyes narrowed as she pointed with her free hand. "It's definitely that man, right? He's totally frail-looking and as soft as you! Hmm. Maybe that's actually a woman. Never mind."

The disciple she singled out from the White Tiger Sect coughed out a mouthful of blood. Condensed qi that could only belong to an earth-realm expert rose out of his body. "Who's frail and looks like a woman!?"

"L-Lucia! Please don't do this. I, I don't like him." This is so embarrassing. Lucia knew I had a lot of suitors from the start, but this may be the first time she's seen them act so brazen! Back in the Shadow Devil Sect, no one would approach me when Lucia was around, but now these people are openly gossiping about me. What would Lucia think about me? I, I don't want her to see how many people like me. What if she grows discouraged and chooses not to pursue me…?

"Eh? I was wrong? So it's not the girly catlike man." Lucia nodded at me. She, she didn't look displeased at all. In fact, she looked happier that I rejected her choice! "Then it must be that one! The translucent fellow with the sharp fangs and narrowed eyes."

The disciple from the Vampire Bat Sect's eyes lit up as he smiled at me. A shiver ran down my spine. "Lucia! Please! Stop. Why are you always choosing the ones I'm least likely to be attracted to?"

"Eh…. I thought I knew your taste." Lucia furrowed her brow as she squinted at the crowd. "Then that man over there? The fat one with the wrinkles and grey skin. If skinny and pale is the opposite of your taste, then clearly fat and not-pale people are your type!"

The Vampire Bat Sect disciple glared at the Rampaging Elephant Sect disciple before issuing him a duel by throwing down a glove. Did Lucia just start a battle between two sects with me as the prize!? "None of these people here are my type!"

"…Then what is your type?" Lucia tilted her head to the side. "You're so stupidly beautiful, but you don't have a man! Not that I'm jealous of your looks or anything."

"I, I like people with, um, big bushy tails and furry round ears." My face was burning! I can't look Lucia in the eyes! I, I can't believe I'm confessing to her like this!

"Oi! Puppers! What the hell have you been doing to Softie!? Why's she in love with you!?"

"T-that's not it! Puppers isn't my type! I swear!" I've caused a huge misunderstanding. If Lucia thinks I like Puppers, then she'll definitely be dissuaded from pursuing me! "The person I like has a brown tail and brown ears!"

"Ah." Lucia stopped strangling Puppers and shoved him back into her socks. "Then it's him?" She pointed across the stage that was built for the exchange. I followed her finger, and my gaze landed on a blushing foxkin. He had a big bushy brown tail, and his ears were brown as well. They weren't as rounded as Lucia's, and his tail wasn't as luxurious as Lucia's either. He was flatter than Lucia too…. Wait. No. That's normal.

Wait! No! "It, it's not him! I swear!"

"Mm. Yeah. Okay." Lucia nodded and wrapped her arm over my shoulder again. "Your face is bright red, and you're speaking in a really high voice right now. But if you say you don't like him, then that's that, right?" She winked at me before chuckling. N-no! There's a serious misunderstanding! The foxkin across the stage turned an even brighter shade of red as he shot furtive glances at me. I…, what have I done?

"People with a bushy brown tail and brown furry ears are your type, huh?" Ilya said, suddenly appearing by Lucia's side. She coughed. "There's another person with a bushy brown tail and brown furry ears, you know?"

"Eh?" Lucia asked. "Who?"

"You."

Lucia burst out into laughter. "Ilya, you're normally so smart! There's no way Softie likes me. I'm a woman!"

Ilya smiled at me. Underneath that angelic face, there was a devil! A seriously sadistic devil! "Yeah, what was I thinking?" Ilya asked. "There's no way Softie likes you, Lucia. Isn't that right?"

Why did Grandmother accept this villain as her disciple!? There's no reason for this third wheel to be hanging around me and Lucia! "T-that's not true. I like Lucia a lot."

"Did you hear that, Lucia?" Ilya asked before Lucia could say anything. "Softie likes you a lot as a man."

"I didn't say as a man!" Is she really younger than me!? How is she so adept at twisting my words!? The traps she laid out for me…, these aren't things a normal teenager should be able to prepare! Just what kind of upbringing did she have…?

"Oh. My mistake. Softie likes you a lot as a friend, Lucia."

I've never really understood why people killed each other out of anger. But I'm starting to understand now—just by a little.

"Well, that's a given. Everyone likes me," Lucia said and puffed her chest out.

"We greet Emperor Yi!"

Before I could respond, everyone—except Lucia, Ilya, and I—chanted at once. Did they rehearse that? Why didn't Grandfather warn me? Anyways, after the greeting, Emperor Yi took his seat which was near the front of the stage prepared for the exchange. He folded his hands in his lap and leaned back. "It seems like we're missing one of the fifty sects this year." Right. The Star Phoenix Sect that Lucia completely exterminated. "No matter. The exchange will proceed as planned. Compete fairly. Don't kill each other. Remember what you're fighting for. With that being said, let the exchange begin."

***

This exchange is ... boring. Well, at least Ilya seems excited. Right now, we're watching alchemists performing alchemy. There's fire and cauldrons and ingredients…. This is exactly like watching someone cook without the good smells that accompany roasted meat! At least I won't get hungry. Well, I will, but not from this. Ilya's master is up on the stage competing against all the other sects' alchemists. I've decided to forgive her for temporarily taking Ilya away from me because she taught Ilya how to make qi-regenerating chocolate orbs. Aren't I magnanimous? I forgive people very easily! But I'm bored! This focus bone requires me to focus on something! I'll finally finish organizing everything I've gathered over that year of terrifying sects. Hmm? I didn't do it earlier? Of course not! Each sect I robbed gave me close to a thousand thousand interspacial rings! Where was I supposed to find the time to go through all my loot? I barely managed to find time to eat during that hellish year of training! But Durandal had skimmed through the stuff and picked out appropriate things for me while taking all the swords for himself.

"T-this again?" Softie asked when a pile of stuff appeared by my feet. "Are you looking to learn new techniques?"

"Nah, I just want to organize this." I've hidden an uncomfortable number of interspacial rings on my body! If it weren't for the fact that these rings have a massive amount of space inside of them, I wouldn't be able to carry around all my spoils. Some rings have more space than others—Ilya says it's because the people who created the bigger rings were better at it, but Softie said the rings were made out of a higher-quality space ore. Why do they always give me conflicting information? Sheesh. "Ilya, want to help?"

"No, this is a pretty useful learning experience for me," Ilya said without taking her eyes off the stage. Maybe she'll be able to make acorn stew that recovers qi later. I look forward to it!

"Alright, Softie, what's this?" I picked up the thing on top of the pile. It was round and kind of looked like an oddly shaped ball.

"That's a clam shell."

"Oh. That testicle-looking thing." I remember clams! I know not to eat them because they taste horrible. "Why was this in an interspacial ring?"

"It's an ingredient commonly used in alchemy," Softie said. "You grind it up into powder and add it to things. I'm not sure on the specifics."

"Okay, so this goes in the useless pile." I shoved it away into the designated useless-stuff ring and grabbed the next thing. It would be annoying to have to ask Softie what everything was every time, so I'll just stare at her with expectation until she identifies what I'm holding.

"That's a bundle of talisman paper. If you inscribe formations on it, you'll be able to use techniques at no cost to yourself, but the talisman will burst into flames. They're commonly used by mortal-realm experts. A saint-realm expert doesn't need a talisman to set up a formation."

So these are the things that those invaders liked throwing back in the territory when I first met them. Into the useless pile it goes since I have no idea what a formation is. I picked up the next item.

"Those are undergarments."

Well, yeah, I can see that. "But what does it do?"

Softie's face turned bright red. "Um. Hide the important bits in case your clothes are destroyed? I don't know what you want me to say, Lucia."

"I know what underwear is! I was just asking if these were special or not."

"T-they're not."

Softie becomes weird at the strangest times. It's odd. Whatever. Time to put these into the useless-stuff—

"Hey."

Hmm? I turned my head, and this man was standing right next to me! When did he get here!? He was wearing pink robes and had long, flowing hair. Maybe he was a she? What's with people and their ambiguous genders!? "What?"

"I was just wondering. Where did you get those?" The pink-robed man pointed at the panties in my hand that I hadn't yet stored away.

"Hmm. I think I stole it from some kind of oyster sect disciple in Kong County." Why did this person need to know?

"They're emitting quite the fragrant scent."

…He's a pervert. How sick and depraved! I should shoo him away before people start to think I know him.

"I'll buy them from you for ten spirit stones."

But I'm not one to turn down free money! "It's a deal."

Softie stared at me, the person who was now ten spirit stones richer, and shook her head before sighing. "He's from the Seducing Succubus Sect. Their cultivation techniques are a bit … deviant."

The pink-robed man laughed. "That's a nice way to put it," he said and smiled. He tried to walk closer to me but stopped when I growled at him. "I'm willing to buy any kind of used underwear you may have, Heart Devil Lucia. It seems like the rumors of you plundering Kong County were true."

"What about unused underwear?"

"I have no need for such unscented things."

He's a true pervert through and through. "Alright, you weird stranger, I'll sell you all the underwear that I don't need."

The pink-robed man blinked and drew his head back. "Stranger? Didn't I introduce myself?"

"No."

"Oh, right. I didn't. My name is Blooming Rose, but you can call me Brother Rose."

"I'll never acknowledge you as a brother." Seriously! I can't associate with perverts! Isn't there that famous saying? Tell me who your friends are and I'll tell you who you are? That's why I surround myself with smart people like Ilya and Softie. People will think I'm smart too! Aren't I a genius? And that's why I can't associate with people like this pervert. At most, I can only sell used underwear to them. With that, I decided to stop going through my rings one at a time. Instead, I went through all of them to find the underwear! The pervert even bought men's underwear. I can't believe Durandal didn't get rid of these while he was looking for swords. What's he doing, making a young and chaste lady like myself touch such grotesque items? By the time I finished scouring through all the rings for underwear, the alchemy portion of the exchange had ended ... along with another three portions that I'm not sure what they were because I was too focused on my current task. And I finally sold all the underwear for a nice tidy sum of ... too much to count. I'll make Puppers count it later.

"Junior Lucia, it's your turn to go up on stage."

Oh! It's finally my turn! Wait. Why does the sect leader have two black eyes? "What happened to your face?"

"You weren't watching?" the sect leader asked. His expression changed, but his cheeks were swollen too, so I couldn't tell what he was feeling. Actually, his whole face was swollen like a pig's.

"Nope. I was selling used underwear."

"...The people I planted heart devils in during the last exchange all plotted against me. I fought thirty-eight rounds in a row."

"Ooh. Did you win?"

"No." The sect leader sighed. "I lost to that old fogey from the Righteous Buddha Sect. Chosen Lucia! As your sect leader, I am giving you a mission of utmost importance! Beat that old fogey's grandson until he's a millimeter away from death! Do you understand?"

"I understand!" But not really. I only said I did because his attitude was saying I couldn't not understand. What the heck is a millimeter? Mm. I'm supposed to be smart. A meter is a unit of distance. And he wants me to beat the grandson a lot. I got it! "You want me to inscribe runes on every bone in his body and absorb them without killing him!"

"Can you do that?"

"No clue. I never tried."

"Well, don't do that. That's cruel and unusual. Just hit him until even his mother won't recognize him anymore. Oh, and there's no pressure, but you better get first place."

***

While Lucia engaged in her questionable sales, the King Province Exchange continued as planned: My grandmother obtained 42nd place in the alchemy portion. Elder Iron obtained 46th place in the smithing portion. Elder Shu obtained 45th place in the testing portion. And my grandfather obtained 29th place in the challenges portion. During the previous King Province Exchange, our sect brought a disciple who ended up thoroughly in last place—I wasn't old enough at the time to participate. And the greatest amount of weight is placed on the disciple portion of the exchange because the best way to measure a sect is through its future potential. But this year, there's a chance at victory because we have Lucia! For some reason, it doesn't really feel like Lucia's a part of the sect. Maybe it's because she grew up outside of the sect. I wonder what she thinks about us. Well, it doesn't change the fact that she's representing us now. "You can do it, Lucia!"

Lucia sauntered up to the stage while counting spirit stones. She counts awfully slow for an earth-realm expert. I actually don't think I've ever seen an elder count before....

They normally sweep their qi over the objects and instantly know the amount. And at the rate she's counting, it'll take her literal years to count up to the billions of spirit stones she obtained. I think she drained the Seductive Succubus Sect's spirit stone reserves dry. ...Isn't Lucia richer than the whole Shadow Devil Sect?

"And let the disciple portion begin," Emperor Yi said. He was resting his cheek against his palm with his elbow propped up on his seat's armrest. I don't blame him. He's already a sky-realm expert; this kind of event must be tedious for him to conduct. But it's his duty as the ruler of King Province. If he doesn't fulfill his obligations to the ruler of Kang Country, he'll be replaced by someone else.

"Wait!" Lucia shouted. "Aren't you going to explain the rules, Quick Sh—"

Emperor Yi violently coughed as he sat up, muffling Lucia's voice. "Everyone will fight everyone else in a duel. I don't care how it's done. Normally sects challenge other sects." That's how my grandfather was forced to fight thirty-eight times in a row. "Your placement depends on your wins and losses. The only rules are to not interfere with other fights and don't kill each other. Do you have any other questions, Jun..., Lucia?" It seems like Emperor Yi hasn't forgotten his lesson of addressing Lucia as Lucia and only Lucia.

"No questions!"

"Then let the disciple portion begin." Emperor Yi sighed and slumped back into his seat, resting his cheek against his palm once again. I wonder when he'll confront Lucia about her stealing his royal crest? There's absolutely no way he hasn't noticed its absence.

"I challenge the bald, fat grandson!" Lucia hopped onto the stage before anyone else could react and pointed at the chosen of the Righteous Buddha Sect. For a brief moment, the peaceful countenance on the chosen's face flickered as his eye twitched. He sighed and climbed to his feet before walking up onto the stage.

"Challenging me so early? Truly, the ignorant have no fear." The chosen pressed his palms together and smiled at Lucia. "My name is Smiling Pig. Are you—"

"Wait." Lucia raised her hand. "Is that a nickname or is that your actual name…?"

Smiling Pig puffed his chest out. "It's my actual name."

"Jeez, and I thought my parents were bad for selling me off," Lucia said and scratched her head. "I'll feel bad if I beat up someone who was hated by their parents…." She sighed. "Ah wells. There's nothing that can be done."

Smiling Pig's smile stiffened. "How dare you make fun of my family?" he asked as his eyes shot open. Before, they were just crescent moonlike slits. "Even a buddha will get angry when you provoke him three times!" A golden aura appeared around him as he pulled out a bell. Wasn't that…?

"Lucia! Cover your ears!" I shouted before covering my ears with my hands. Everyone from the Shadow Devil Sect did as well. That was the Sin-Devouring Bell, the strongest treasure of the Righteous Buddha Sect! It was actually entrusted to the younger generation! And it seemed like Lucia didn't listen to my advice….

Lucia hunched over and vomited out a fountain of black blood before falling to her knees. The golden aura faded as Smiling Pig stowed the bell. I uncovered my ears, and immediately, Ilya tugged on my sleeve. "What was that?"

"That's the Sin-Devouring Bell. It draws the sins out of a person!"

"Isn't that a good thing…?" Ilya asked. "Wouldn't that mean Lucia would become less greedy and mean?"

"No matter who you are, there's always some sin inside of you. With the Sin-Devouring Bell, the Righteous Buddha Sect can draw out their enemies' sins, then destroy it with their mantras, but everyone's sin is a part of them. Suddenly having a portion of your personality destroyed can do catastrophic damage to your mind, sometimes halting one's cultivation permanently. How could that sect claim to be righteous when using such heavy-handed techniques!?"

"Then you're saying, that thing is Lucia's sin?" Ilya pointed at Lucia. A black mist was rising out of her, leaking from every one of her pores. A cultivator shouldn't have many sins since cultivation is all about diligence and separating oneself from mortal pleasures. But Lucia's different....

"W-what's going on!?" Smiling Pig asked as he took a step back, his face pale. He turned around and shouted, "Grandfather! Is the Sin-Devouring Bell broken!?"

The mist pouring out of Lucia completely obscured her body from view, becoming denser and denser while expanding at the same time. As if night were spreading from the ground, the mist around Lucia continued to grow, devouring all the light in the area, filling up half the stage. It bubbled and rose upwards like a pillar, but its ends split into four upon reaching the clouds. Emperor Yi had set up a barrier to prevent the mist from affecting the audience, but at the same time, he had trapped Smiling Pig inside the arena with Lucia. A golden aura was keeping the mist away from his body, but it was rapidly dimming.

"Is it just me, or is that a really big predator's claw?" Ilya asked and pointed up at the clouds. The four branches of the pillar had curved, their tips narrowing into sharp points that could tear the sky. Black, billowing fur blossomed along the pillar as some kinks appeared, bending the pillar like an arm. Without warning and without a sound, the claw descended and shattered the barrier that Emperor Yi had erected. The Righteous Buddha Sect members screamed as their region of the arena was covered by the misty claw. The claw clenched, and the screams stopped. Then, as if it were all an illusion, the mist fell apart and was sucked back into Lucia, who was lying face down in the center of the arena. There was no one else on the stage.

"Lucia!" Ilya shouted.

Lucia's tail twitched once. Then it twitched again. Her torso suddenly shot straight up, and she blinked a few times. "What happened?" she asked as she looked around. "Mm. There was that annoying sound. And then I fell asleep. A lullaby? But where did he go?"

***

I can't believe I was lured to sleep! So much for a giant's focus bone, huh? It couldn't even keep me awake during a battle. I demand a refund. I should've made it into a strength bone. But why's everyone looking at me so strangely? Mm. As usual, it's because I'm special, isn't it? Ah-ha-ha. No, seriously. Please stop staring. It's unsettling. "Um. It looks like he surrendered while I fell asleep! And his cheering squad left too. Wow." No one's saying anything. Someone, please respond. "Hello? Anyone? Quick Shot?"

"Don't call me that!"

Mm. The world is right again. Everyone's moving and chattering now! For a second, I was afraid I broke apart common sense. Wait a minute. What if this is an illusion caused by the bell!? Then I'm screwed. I don't have any techniques to counter illusions…. I really should learn one. I'm sure there was some kind of technique that caused hallucinations in one of my interspacial rings. When the leader of that illusion sect used it, I really thought I was killing people by ripping off their limbs! Anyways, I'll ask Ilya a personal question. If she answers correctly, then this isn't an illusion! I knew I was a genius. "Ilya! What kind of books do you keep underneath your bed!?"

"Why is that the first thing you ask me!?"

Okay. I don't think I'm in an illusion. Then that means…? "I challenge the next person! I don't care who you are, just c'mon up here." The faster I get this over with, the faster I can eat lunch. For some reason, I'm really hungry. Maybe it's because I didn't eat anything while selling those panties? Hmm. No, then I would've been hungry before the first match. I know! I collapsed and fell asleep out of hunger. Why is my body so inefficient? It needs way too much food. Hah. At least I'm super-duper strong. But no one's coming to fight me. "Anyone? You." I pointed at a chosen—well, I think it was a chosen—and pointed at the ground by my feet. "Fight me."

"I, I surrender!"

The hell…?

"Emperor Yi!" someone shouted. It was an old lady with her hair tied up in a massive bun that extended towards the sky like a few bowls of stew stacked upon each other. "The rules! She broke the rules!"

Mm? Me? Rules? What were they again? I forgot. But I'm pretty sure I didn't break any! All I did was fall asleep, and there definitely wasn't a rule against falling asleep. "I did not!"

"You killed Smiling Pig! You killed the whole Righteous Buddha Sect convoy!"

Wow. These accusations are quite brazen, huh? I think I'd remember doing something extremely evil like murder. And if I don't remember doing it, then I didn't do it. It's that simple. "Oh really? Prove it. The fat baldie rang a bell that put me to sleep, then he and his cheering squad ran away. You must've fallen asleep because of the bell too."

"You don't remember anything, Lucia?" Quick Shot asked me. Is it just me or was that fear in his eyes…? Mm. Well, it's natural to be intimidated by me! With all the noogies I gave him, it'd be weirder if he wasn't.

"He rang the bell. Then I dreamed of something. But I almost never remember my dreams. So nope, don't remember." I don't remember many dreams. Usually they're nightmares anyways, so it's a good thing I don't. Ah? What kind of nightmares? Well, I'm usually trapped in a cage while someone's cooking right outside of my reach and my strength is too weak to break open the cage. Or I'm young again and being whipped for eating a cookie. Or I'm about to have fun with Durandal, but he suddenly disappears into mini-DalDal. Wait, no. That's reality. Mm. Once Durandal settles into a new sky-realm-ranked sword, I'm going to make him permanently wear a spirit-restraining rope.

"Alright. Well, due to unusual circumstances, I won't disqualify Lucia. The Righteous Buddha Sect used a technique that they obviously couldn't control, and they suffered the consequences." Quick Shot shrugged. "The exchange shall continue with the remaining forty-eight sects."

"That's outrageous!" the woman with the giant hair said. What was her problem? I'll teach her a lesson.

"I challenge the chosen of her sect!" For some reason, I'm really irritated. It's probably because I'm hungry. But I feel restless, like my heart wants to jump out of my throat. Or like something deep inside of me woke up after taking a long nap and wants to exercise. Hmm. Yeah, I think I'm just hungry. I'll munch on these chocolate pills that Ilya gave me.

"Don't worry, Sect Leader," one of the people behind the woman said. "It doesn't seem like she can use that technique at will. It was the result of her sins, but the Sin-Devouring Bell is gone now." The person leapt onto the stage and drew a sword. He wore a green robe that had brown markings on it near its legs, a little like little roots. "My name is Firm Sapling. Let us have a fair fight, Heart Devil Lucia."

…Parents in the Immortal Continent must really hate their kids. Firm Sapling? Really? Well, I'm not here to judge people's names. "Heart Devil Apparition!" Since I don't have a sword and I don't want to stop eating, I'll make the heart devil wormies fight for me. The apparition I summon takes on the shape of Durandal, including his sword, most likely because Durandal's the scariest thing I know. ...But what the hell is this? This apparition isn't Durandal! It's, it's a predator? And the heart devil wormies seem a lot glossier than usual.... Did I break my technique? Before I could cancel it to try again, the heart devil predator pounced towards Firm Sapling and swallowed him in one bite. It chewed a few times, and then it disappeared. Firm Sapling fell to the ground, screaming. The heck was that all about? Oh! It planted a heart devil. That was faster than the Durandal apparition. But is Firm Sapling okay? I'll inspect him real quick.

"Don't come closer! I surrender! I surrender!" Tears and snot and piss and poop escaped from Firm Sapling all at once when I took a step towards him. Gross. "Sect Leader, save me! Save me!"

Mm. I don't know what happened, but it seems like my Heart Devil Apparition technique leveled up! This calls for a roast aurochsen celebration. ...I'm not making up an excuse just to eat.

"What did you do to our chosen!?" The nagging woman teleported onto the stage by Firm Sapling's side. Hey. I thought teleportation wasn't allowed in the city? "Die, you wretch!"

Huh!? What the heck? Branches shot out of the ground like spears. This is like Ilya's dad's spell. I know how to counter this! All I have to do is position myself in this strategically superior position, brace myself for the incoming impact, and give those spears a good whack! But I don't have mini-DalDal.... But I do have this hammer! Hmm? Where'd I get this hammer? From the Bloody Bull Sect, of course! This was their sect leader's weapon. It's way too bulky and not nearly as heavy as mini-DalDal can be, but it still weighs ten tons, so it's not too bad. "Unrelenting Path of Slaughter: Breaking Madness Blade...? Hammer! Breaking Madness Hammer Strike!"

Kaboom!

Ah. Half the stage disappeared. I know I haven't practiced since reaching the earth-realm, and I have no idea what my new capabilities are, but isn't this too exaggerated? The stage is huge! But one strike disintegrated it. Hmm. That nagging sect leader woman didn't even have time to scream when she was sent flying with her chosen. I wonder if she's dead. Nah. There's no way! I didn't even make direct contact with her. But wow! That really was a lot stronger than I expected it to be. No wonder why earth-realm experts were so annoying to beat up when I was a saint-realm expert. Their qi is much more condensed! My Madness Strike is at least a hundred times stronger than before. Breaking Blade too. If I knew I'd automatically get this strong just by reaching the earth realm, I wouldn't have practiced so hard! Well, it's not like Durandal would let me not practice. Hah. Durandal needs to learn how to relax and appreciate the little things in life. Like food and sex and sleep. Speaking of Durandal…. "Who's next!? I don't have all day!"

***

Lucia thoroughly crushed every single chosen competing against her … and their respective sect leaders and elders. The way she hit them with her hammer made me think she was venting her grievances—whatever grievances someone as carefree as her could have. The elders of the sects were involved after Lucia repeatedly poked fun at the sect names and insulted their disciples in the way that only she can manage to do. I'm a refined individual, so I won't repeat the things she had said. And Emperor Yi didn't step in because he thought Lucia's antics were amusing.

There's just one thing I was wondering about…. "Hey, Ilya?"

"Whoa. You're taking the initiative to talk to me? What happened?" Ilya raised an eyebrow at me.

…Is that odd? I suppose I don't really like her, but I thought I was hiding it pretty well! Besides, aren't we supposed to display a harmonious façade in public lest other sects think there's discord within our Shadow Devil Sect? Arguments are meant to be held in private. There's no need for her to be so snarky! "You seemed to recognize Lucia's sin. What did you call it? The arm of a predator?"

"Yup." Ilya nodded then looked away.

Hey. "Elaborate, please."

"Oh? There's something the mighty Softie doesn't know? I bet if Lucia asked, you'd suddenly figure out what it was." Ilya rolled her eyes and stood up.

…I don't like her very much. "Where are you going?"

"To Lucia. That was her forty-eighth victory."

My legs straightened and I stood up before I even thought about it. "I'm coming with you." I can't let Ilya be the only one at Lucia's side! Lucia needs a loving wife to greet her when she comes back from a long day at work, not someone mean and rude like Ilya! Wait. There's something wrong with that thought. Ah! But I don't have time to revise it! "Lucia! Good job!" I took a handkerchief out of my interspacial ring to wipe away Lucia's sweat…, but she didn't have any. So I wiped away the grease stains on her lips that were left behind by the cooked aurochs that she was eating during one of her duels.

"I trust no one has any complaints if I declare the Shadow Devil Sect as the winners of the King Province Exchange?" Emperor Yi asked, his voice echoing through the stage. No one responded. I would be more surprised if there actually was a response, seeing as Lucia's beating disfigured everyone's faces and chests. It must be hard for them to speak when they can barely breathe. "Since that's the case"—Emperor Yi teleported next to Lucia—"I present to you the proof of victory."

Lucia blinked and looked around. "Where is it?"

"You stole it from me."

Lucia stiffened. "...Did I?"

"Right. It was the ring I was wearing." Emperor Yi smiled at Lucia. Hmm. Maybe that royal crest wasn't actually a sealed interspacial ring? Then it turns out Ilya was right. But Lucia probably forgot the conversation already, so it won't reflect poorly on me.

"Oh...." Lucia scratched her head. "Then where's your actual interspacial ring? Just wondering, you know, out of curiosity. Mhm."

"I'd be a fool to tell you that," Emperor Yi said with a snort. "Regardless, all you have to do is present it to the guard captain at Kang Country's imperial barracks and you'll be able to join the army." Emperor Yi hesitated. "You still have it, right?"

"Of course!" Lucia reached into her pants from the front and took the ring out from somewhere.... "It's right here."

Emperor Yi's face turned red. "You damned foxkin. Stop trying to seduce me." He sighed and shook his head before clearing his dirty thoughts, his face reverting back to normal. "Why's the tip of the arrow broken?"

Lucia beamed before wetting her lips with her tongue—did I miss a spot of grease? "I bit it off."

Emperor Yi shuddered and retreated back by a step, lowering his hands towards his groin in a protective manner. "A-anyways! This concludes the King Province Exchange! I ask all of you to leave as soon as possible. Since an unknown expert took away the great wall, some final defensive touches have to be implemented."

"Wait!" Lucia grabbed Emperor Yi's arm before he could teleport away. "I was promised an earth-realm-ranked sword for winning this. Could you make it a sky-realm-ranked sword?"

Emperor Yi coughed and glared at Lucia. "Do you know how valuable a sky-realm-ranked sword is? Even I don't have one! And you'll receive the earth-realm-ranked sword when you speak to the guard captain at Kang Country's imperial capital."

Lucia tilted her head, her tail twitching. I wanted to grab it and play with it, but I restrained myself. "You don't have a sky-realm-ranked sword? I thought you were an emperor. How are you so poor?"

Emperor Yi winced. "You know I have thousands of wives and thousands of children, correct?"

Lucia's hair fluttered as she nodded. "Right."

"Women and children cost money to maintain."

"So you're poor because you couldn't keep it in your pants."

Emperor Yi coughed again; this time, blood leaked out of the corners of his lips. "I'm not poor! I'm just not as rich as I would be if circumstances were different! Now if there's nothing else of importance, I hope to never see you again." A sword made of qi materialized in Emperor Yi's free hand. Was he going to attack Lucia!? With a swishing sound, Emperor Yi's sword descended and cut off his own arm, the one that Lucia was holding onto. Then he teleported away before anyone could say anything. H-he actually cut off his own limb to escape from Lucia….

Lucia stared dumbly at the arm she was holding onto. Then she looked at me and blinked. She folded four of the arm's fingers and poked me with it. Gross! "Do you want this?"

"N-no!" Even if it's a gift from Lucia, I have no need for a severed arm!

"I'll take it," Ilya said and snatched the arm away. "It's the arm of a sky-realm expert. I'm sure the blood and bones will make decent alchemy materials. Besides, it's not like it was forcibly taken away—there's no guilt or immorality involved at all."

…I still think it's gross.

Chapter 15

I've spent more time on a flying boat than I have on land in the Immortal Continent. It's not too bad of a feeling, honestly. The scenery's nice. The rocking of the boat can be soothing at times. And there's no chance of being attacked. What would threaten us this high up in the sky? Birds? I suppose there are some earth-realm avian beasts, but why would they expend any effort to hunt down something mostly made of wood? It doesn't make any sense.

"Stop your ship! This is a raid! Behave yourselves, and no one has to get hurt!"

Okay. I spoke too soon. Well, Lucia or Softie will take care of it. I'll just continue refining this sky-realm expert's blood. Refining blood is an interesting process. If you heat it to the right temperature, it congeals instead of evaporating. After adding some bone powder, I'm able to create a gelatin-like substance. And then I ... have no clue what to do with this. Maybe I should eat it…? No. That's cannibalism.

"Oh! What's that?" Lucia appeared out of nowhere and snatched the final product out of my hands!

"Stop teleporting around like that! And give that back!"

Lucia brought the gelatin up to her face and sniffed it before wrinkling her nose. "What's this? Blood? Human blood? I didn't know you were a cannibal, Ilya."

"I wasn't going to eat it!"

"I said everybody up on deck!"

Lucia and I both stopped and stared up at the ceiling. Lucia was still holding the gelatin over her head, keeping it just out of my reach. How come she's taller than me? This isn't fair. "Shouldn't you go do something about those bandits?"

"A hero always arrives at the last moment! That's how they sway people's hearts! Imagine the emotional moment when you're about to die, but out of nowhere, a handsome prince swoops in and saves you. Mhm. That's what I'm going to do," Lucia said. She lowered her arm and held the jelly towards me. "Anyways, here you go."

I reached out to grab it, but a red blur blew past and snatched it away! Lucia's hand extended as fast as lightning, and she caught the offending phoenix by its neck. The gelatin was already halfway down its throat. Lucia squeezed, and the jelly slipped inside instead of out! That phoenix ate my final product! "Lucia. Let's cut it open."

"What!?" Lucia's eyes widened. "You can't kill Mrs. Feathers!"

"It's a male. But that's beside the point!" That was jelly made out of a sky-realm expert! I could've sold it for a fortune! How many sky-realm experts are there to make jelly out of anyway? The answer is not a lot!

"Then you can't kill Mr. Feathers. He helped me during my tribulation!" Lucia nodded and patted the phoenix's head, causing it to wince. "Isn't that right? But hurry up and barf out Ilya's thingy."

"You tried to eat Mr. Feathers…." Ah. I did it again. I called Lucia's random wild beast by the name she gave it. "Alright…. There's a spell that I can use to force my gelatin out of him." I'll just grab this stick and jam it down this stupid bird's throat. If it would stop struggling! "Lucia! Hold it still!"

"Lucia! Help!" That was Softie's voice. And Lucia disappeared along with my final product…. Alright. I'm upset now. I spent two whole days creating that without sleep! Which idiot bandits came to rob our ship!? I'll teach them a lesson they won't forget.

After stomping up to the deck of the boat, I saw limbs and blood and gore coating the wooden floorboards. It seems like they already learned a lesson they wouldn't forget…. And what was Lucia doing!? "Don't cut them off!"

"Eh?" Lucia stopped taking off a person's pants. "I was just taking their underwear. It's worth ten spirit stones! I don't cut off people's penises. They don't sell for anything, silly."

…Don't call me silly when I was just trying to predict your nature. Hah. Staying with Lucia is so stress-inducing unless one stops caring. Right. I should stop caring too much. Lucia's pretty much guaranteed to stay alive; there's absolutely no reason for me to care about her. But her stupid bird stole my jelly! Softie was trembling in a corner of the boat's deck. Were the bandits that strong? "I thought no one was stupid enough to rob a ship with the Shadow Devil Sect's sign."

Softie stopped trembling and raised her head. Wasn't she used to Lucia's butchery? And these disciples were all chosen to be part of the army. How come they lost to some bandits? "There are some people brazen enough." Softie stood up and clutched her robe. Part of it was torn. "Their leader was an earth-realm expert."

"This one?" Lucia asked, raising a limp person with one arm. He wasn't wearing any pants.

Softie's eyes narrowed as she drew a dagger out of her interspacial ring. "Yes. That's the one." She stepped towards him and swung her arm down. An ear-piercing shriek escaped from the bandit leader's mouth as blood spurted everywhere, shooting out of his groin like a fountain. Softie swallowed and gripped her hand tighter on her dagger. She was trembling. "What did you s-say you were going to do to me? Can you still do it now?"

Lucia blinked and looked at me with wide eyes. She dropped the crying bandit chief and appeared by my side. "Hey, uh, Softie's not as soft as I thought she was…."

"I was clearing a heart devil, Lucia," Softie said with a shaky breath as she exhaled. She looked at the dagger in her hand and paled before dropping it. There were tears in her eyes. "You don't have to be afraid of me."

Hmm. I think Lucia's wrong. Softie's just as soft as she thought she was. Anyone would be unsettled after, err, doing something like that. I'm used to witnessing torture because of my father and his dungeons, but I've never done any torture myself. I haven't killed anyone either. For some reason, I think it's better to keep it that way or I'll end up like Lucia, delusional and living in a fantasy land where I'm a saint who can do no wrong.

"So, who were these people?" Lucia asked. "There weren't any crests or things that usually mark a faction."

"These are rogue cultivators, sectless people," Softie said in a soft voice. She bit her lower lip and walked over to Lucia. "C-can you hold me? J-just for a moment."

"Hmm?" Lucia tilted her head but hugged Softie anyway.

"You came at the perfect time. You were like a hero from the stories," Softie said, burying her face into Lucia's chest.

…Well, Lucia did say this was what she wanted. But I think she forgot who her audience would be if she saved them like that. It's not like Durandal was up there calling for help.

Lucia patted Softie's back and glanced at me. Then she gave me a thumbs-up and a smile. She moved her lips, but nothing came out. I could still make out what she was saying though: It worked!

Maybe she did intend to steal Softie's heart. As if she hadn't done that already.

***

Softie totally fell for my charm. I'm not sure how that worked since I'm a woman, but I'm a hundred percent certain that Softie's totally smitten with me. With this, I've thoroughly solidified the heart devils inside of Softie's suitors! I'm sure Softie will get over me and find an appropriate person in time. She's a jealousy-inducing beautiful person. It's impossible for her to not find someone.

As for the bandits that tried to rob us, we stole their clothes, their spoils, their pride and dignity, and their boat! They've been stripped completely naked, and Softie took out these ropes that could bind an earth-realm expert. I tried pulling one to test my strength, and it broke apart pretty easily. But the bandit chief was already basically dead, so there's no chance of him escaping. Softie said we could drop them off at Kang Country's capital and receive a reward; though, Ilya thought it'd be easier to just kill them. But murder's the one thing I won't do!

We're traveling to the imperial capital to join the army. Or at least report to the guard captain for my fancy sword. Then I'll find a smith who can forge sky-realm-ranked swords and make this phoenix abduct his child. If he doesn't have a child, then I'll find a different smith. Mm. There's absolutely nothing that could go wrong with this plan. I've been wondering though, just what's so special about the army? "Hey, Softie." Right now, we're cuddling! It's been too long since I've cuddled someone cause Durandal had to turn into a tiny ball.

"Yes, Lucia?"

"What's the point of the army again?" I'm pretty sure someone said some time ago that there were no wars going on.... I might just be imagining things though. Hmm. "Are there wars?"

"Well, yes. There's always wars, but not civil wars. Kong County belongs to Kang Country. There's no reason for a war to exist in one of a country's counties. But there are other countries that are at war with Kang Country. The army exists to patrol borders; there hasn't been any serious fighting in a while—only a few skirmishes here and there." Softie paused and snuggled closer. "Actually, there's one section between Kang Country and Fang Country that has a perpetual battlefield. I've only heard about it. I think you should go there if you're looking for as many merits as possible. …Unless you're really planning on following through with your kidnapping plan."

"Of course I am! Isn't that right, Mr. Feathers?" I reached towards the pouch by my waist and grabbed onto … Mr. Feathers? He's limp…? Ah! He ate Ilya's weird thing and I forgot to get it out of him! "Mr. Feathers!"

Mr. Feathers twitched. His eyes fluttered open weakly. His beak widened as if he were a turtle slowly chomping away at food. His feathers rustled as his wings barely rose off the blanket. A faint cry came out of his mouth. "Meow…."

…What? Did I hear that correctly?

"Did a phoenix just meow like a cat?" Softie asked, her eyes wide as she stared at Mr. Feathers. Mr. Feathers stared back and hissed at her before his head collapsed onto the soft silk. …Maybe I shouldn't eat Ilya's alchemy products without testing them first.

"Hmm. I'll shove him back into the bag, and maybe he'll get better." If he doesn't, I can always make someone else kidnap the child. Like Puppers…? Right! Puppers can definitely do it. He just has to never show his face again. Mm. I'm not sure he'd like that, so I'll be sure to dye his fur to disguise him before the deed is done. I think Puppers would look great with pink fur. Everything looks great in pink. "Ahem. Anyways. After I pick up that sword from the guard captain, I'll go straight to finding a smith! Do you know where one lives?"

"No. If people knew where they lived, then there'd be an endless stream of people hoping to meet them." Softie sighed and lowered her head back onto the pillow. "If you choose not to join the army, then … I'm going to follow you."

Yup. I definitely captured Softie's heart. Even though I'm not a prince, I *am* extremely charming. "Great! I was planning on kidnapping you anyways." But to make sure Softie's safe while traveling with me, I have to overcome some of my weaknesses! "Do you know any techniques that can stop illusions?" Yup. Illusions are the bane of my existence. Ilya trapped me in one as a prank once. *Once*. Then she learned her lesson.

"Why did the topic suddenly change like that…?" Softie asked before sighing. "Yes. The Nine-tailed Fox Sect has multiple manuals on dealing with illusions. Why? Are you interested? Our sect's Heart Devil Apparition is actually an illusionary technique as well."

"Huh? Really?" I thought it just summoned heart devil wormies in a solid shape to beat things up for you.

"That's right. It traps its target in an illusion with all of its heart devils. If someone was scared of spiders, then they'd be confronted with thousands of spiders inside of the apparition's attack." Softie pursed her lips. "But it doesn't seem like you're looking for something like that. You want to break free from others' illusions, right?"

"Mhm."

"The Clear Heart Mantra is the…, actually, no, that wouldn't suit you at all." Softie's forehead wrinkled. "Then the Mind at Peace…, no. Um, there's the Unfettered Thoughts that … also won't work."

"What's wrong with those three?" Wasn't she going to say the Clear Heart Mantra was the best one out there?

"Many illusion-countering techniques require, um…, yeah. They're just not suitable for you."

Require what!? "Say it! What do they require!?"

"L-Lucia! S-some people are blessed with great strength! That's you!"

Mm. She's not wrong. I'm extremely strong; I've noticed I haven't met anyone who can lift as much as I can. The closest was that bull person whose hammer I stole.

"And some people are blessed with great intelligence and wisdom, like Ilya."

That's true too. Ilya's really smart, and she's younger than me. It's not fair.

"And people with an emphasis on strength usually don't have great times with illusions." Softie nodded repeatedly like a frightened rabbit.

"So ... I can't learn those illusion-countering techniques because I'm too strong?" That's weird. It doesn't seem to make very much sense…, but Softie's the encyclopedia. If she says that's true, then I guess it must be true. "You're not lying, right?"

"Eep! I'm sorry! I'm sorry!" Softie shrank back and shivered. "Please, put your apparition away. I'm sorry I lied! You're just not smart and virtuous enough to learn illusion-countering techniques!"

…One day, people will recognize me for my intelligence. Mm. That's a fine goal. I'm going to accomplish something so ingenious that everyone will be in awe of my brain's thinking power. Let's see who'll try to call me an idiot then! I'm sincerely smart! It's just hard to prove sometimes. Hmph.

***

How much longer will it be before I can return home? I've already been stuck in the Immortal Continent with Lucia for over a year now. Sure, she became an earth-realm expert in a year when it takes the average person over a hundred, but there's no telling how long it'll take her to reach the sky realm. I wonder how my father is doing; I hope he's not worried. He may be one of the stronger people back at home, but there was that issue with the plants possessing people from the other plane. Ah, worrying about it now won't do anything. I have to focus on the tasks at hand.

"Ilya!"

...So much for focusing on tasks at hand. "Yes, Lucia? Haven't I told you repeatedly not to teleport into my room like that?"

"I vaguely remember you saying something like that," Lucia said, her head bobbing up and down once. "Anyways. I have a very, very important task for you."

Another task...? The first time she said she had a very, very, super-duper important task for me, she forced me to increase the production of her acorn stew and hot chocolate factory through magic. "What is it this time?"

Lucia clapped her hands onto my shoulders and stared me in the eyes, unblinking. "I want you to help me become smarter." A wrinkle appeared on her forehead. "Wait, no. I want you to help me express my already high intelligence in a manner that lets more people think I'm smart." Her head tilted to the side. "Can you do that?"

"Did someone call you stupid again?"

"Softie said I'm not smart enough to learn illusion-countering techniques!"

Well..., if she's saying that, then there must be a reason behind it: like it's true. "Alright. I can help you."

"Eh? Really!? You can!?" Lucia's eyes lit up and she lifted me into the air. It was uncomfortable because she was lifting me by my shoulders in an overhand grip. "Why haven't you helped me earlier!?"

"I have. Put me down, please." I really have. It's just that Lucia always got distracted. "Have a seat."

Lucia sat down on the floor, her tail twitching back and forth as she beamed at me. I retrieved some things from my interspacial ring and placed them onto the floorboards in front of her. "Ilya...," Lucia said as her face crumpled. "Is this what I think it is...?"

I don't know what you think it is, Lucia, because I can never know what you're thinking. "If you want to express your intelligence, then you should learn how to read and write. Writing will allow you to immortalize your words. Even after you die, people will remember what you've said if it's written down."

Lucia deflated. Her tail slumped, followed by her shoulders, and then finally her head. The rest of her body slid down like a wet noodle while she let out a drawn-out sigh. When her chin touched the floorboards and her body was flattened like a pancake, she made a strange whining noise. "Isn't there an easier way? Not all smart people are literate!"

"But the ones that everyone knows about are."

"But, but … what about people like Durandal? Yeah! Durandal's super smart and well-known, but he's illiterate!"

"Durandal can read…."

Lucia froze. "…He can?"

"Did you not know…?"

Lucia scratched her head. "I must've forgot."

I stared at Lucia and she stared back at me. This continued for a while. What was she waiting for? "If you're looking for easier ways to become smarter, then I don't have any. Learning to read is the simplest way I know. Not only does writing allow you to share your ideas with others, you can even digest the ideas of other people, including dead people's."

Lucia wrinkled her forehead. "That sounds like magic. And I can't do magic."

It's not magic! It's reading! "Lucia. You can do it. With that giant bone of focus, there's absolutely no reason for you not to be able to."

"But it's hard," Lucia whined. "And it makes my head hurt."

"Wasn't it hard when you first started training your Madness Strikes? Didn't your body hurt? You carried on despite that, didn't you? Your brain is like a muscle. The more you use it, the easier it becomes to use it more."

"When you put it that way...," Lucia muttered to herself while stroking her tail which had curled around towards her chest. She sat up and straightened her back. "But is it true? Brains are squishy compared to muscles! They definitely don't work the same way."

"You'll just have to take my word for it." Lucia came to me begging for help, but somehow, I'm the one begging her to take my advice. This is usually how interactions with Lucia end up. "Are you going to learn or not?"

"Not!" Lucia shook her head back and forth. "I can't do it. It's simply impossible. Give me another way."

I sighed. "You just want to counter illusionary techniques, right?" Was this because of that one time I trapped her inside of an illusion? I was testing out a defensive formation I picked up from the Nine-tailed Fox Sect and Lucia walked into it because she entered my room without knocking. She thought I was pranking her…. My butt still hurts just thinking about it.

"I mean, that'd be nice, but I want to be smart too!"

"I have a way for you to counter illusionary techniques." As for making her smarter, I don't think that's possible. There's the saying you can't teach an old dog new tricks. Well, there's the second part of that saying which is you can't teach Lucia. Anything. Unless you're Durandal, but even he's failed at teaching her how to read and write.

"Really? But what about making me smarter?"

"Right. See, people are innovative creatures. If we're lacking in scales for defense, we make armor. If we don't have claws, we create swords. If you're susceptible to illusionary techniques, then you just need an item that prevents them. Here you go." I took out an item that I had retrieved from the Nine-tailed Fox Sect and passed it over to Lucia. I was studying it, but I don't need it anymore, and I forgot about it until now. "You just wear it and it'll prevent illusionary attacks below the earth realm. It'll stop an earth-realm expert's illusion too, but it'll break."

"Ilya. How do I wear this?"

"It's a veil. You wear it like a hat and it covers your face."

"...But then how will people recognize my beauty?"

When did Lucia become so vain...? Or was she always like that? "Do you want it or not?"

"Can you turn it into something else? Oh! What if I tear it a bit and make it into a ribbon?" Before I could stop her, Lucia tore the veil. It exploded. Qi rushed through the room, ruining my furniture. It's a good thing all my important research materials were kept safely in my interspacial rings. I have to keep every valuable item hidden away from Lucia or she'll break it without intending to. Like that veil. "Ilya! Why didn't you warn me!?" Lucia's hair was frayed and messy from the explosion, but other than that, she was unhurt.

And this is why I feel like there's no hope for Lucia's intelligence. "I'll make you a necklace that counters illusionary attacks."

"Will it make me smarter too?"

I'll redirect her attention instead of answering. "It'll be ready in a week."

"But will it make me smarter!?" Lucia disappeared and lifted me up from behind.

That stupid bone of focus makes her fixate on the stupidest things! "Yes! It will! Please, let me down! Believe in me!" Alright, it won't, but maybe the placebo effect will work. As long as she sincerely believes it'll make her smarter, then maybe, just maybe, she'll become a little more intelligent.

***

Ilya made me a necklace of intelligence! It also counters illusions, but that's whatever. This necklace makes me smarter! It's only now that I can appreciate how smart Ilya is.

She's so smart, she can make other people smart too! I can feel my thoughts moving faster already. "Thanks, Ilya!"

"You're welcome," Ilya said and sighed as I hugged her. "You're squishing me. And don't tell anyone about its effects, or I'll be swarmed with requests to make these."

"Got it!" If everyone had a necklace of intelligence, then I'd only be at an average intelligence. There's no way I can let anyone else know; that way, I'll be smarter than everyone else. Wow! This necklace is working already!

Before I could go off to find Softie to bug her, the boat tremored and thudded. The table in Ilya's room shook, but I didn't move because I was rooted in place by my Footsteps of the Giant. What was that? Were we under attack again? I focused my thoughts onto the deck of the ship, and poof! I reappeared next to a startled disciple. How come I always appear next to startled people? Hmm. Even with this necklace of intelligence, it's still a mystery. Oh wells. "What's going on?" Why did we land?

"Chosen Lucia!" the startled disciple said and bowed at me while cupping her hands. "We've reached the border of Kang County. This is a no-fly zone."

"Kang County? Not country? Weren't we going to Kang Country's imperial city?" I'm pretty sure that's where we were going. No, I'm definitely sure!

The disciple kept her head lowered. I could feel the heart devil inside of her wiggling. When did I traumatize her? Don't tell me she was one of Softie's suitors. "Kang Country's imperial city is located in Kang County which is located in Kang Country. Our Kong County is also a part of Kang Country."

...Whoever made this confusing naming system deserves to be taken behind a shed and put down. "And no one's allowed to fly here? Then how the heck are we supposed to travel around?" I've gotten too used to this boat! It's a moving mansion! I can go anywhere in the world without leaving my house! Taking away my boat might as well be taking away my life!

"There's a city ahead that we can rent carriages to travel in." The disciple raised her head and pointed over the edge of the boat. I squinted because the sun was too bright. Ah, there really is a city. It doesn't really look too impressive. There's no giant wall. There's no phoenixes or giant clams. There's no raging bulls or disciples flying in the air. How boring. I guess sects really were richer than cities, huh?

"Fellow brothers and sisters. We've arrived at the border of Kang County. Get ready to dismount."

That was Softie! The boat has this formation that you can speak into and everyone on board will hear it. It's fun to whisper into it at night pretending to be a ghost. I planted two heart devils that way! Ah. Maybe one belonged to this disciple. Ahem. It wasn't me! It was a ghost. Anyways, I really don't want to walk. I like this boat. A lot. "I have an idea!" I teleported to the talking formation and appeared next to Softie, who was startled. "Don't get ready to dismount! We're riding this boat all the way to the capital!"

"L-Lucia?" Softie asked. "We're not allowed to fly in Kang County."

"Yeah, I know. But I have a plan because I'm smart!" I pictured the tree that I saw off the side of the boat and teleported there. Whew, it was bigger than I thought, but that's okay. With a good thwack of my hammer, it fell over. Then I knocked over the other tree next to it. I dropped them into the interspacial ring and made my way back to the boat. I didn't teleport because it'd be faster to get where I wanted by jumping once. I landed on the ground next to the boat's bow and pulled the tree out of my interspacial ring. Now how do I do this…? Hmm. Rope! I tied the tree to the boat before teleporting to the boat's stern and attached the other tree.

"Lucia? What are you doing?" Softie asked from up above. She was leaning over the side of the boat.

"I attached wheels to the boat to make it into a carriage!" Aren't I a genius? The boat's as big as a three-story building, so it might be a little conspicuous, but I'm sure I can convince people into believing it's a carriage with a little persuasion.

"But the way you tied the trees to the boat make it so that they can't function as wheels…. They can't spin."

"They don't have to spin, silly! We just have to pretend they do! Just fly the boat along the ground and no one will know." This necklace of intelligence is the greatest thing Ilya has ever created. I can't believe I didn't get her to make me one earlier. Do you know how much easier my life would've been if I could've come up with these brilliant ideas all the time? I teleported back onto the boat and sent some qi into its steering wheel. "Full speed ahead!"

"W-wait!" Softie shouted as she ran up to me. "We can't do this!"

Hmm? "Why not?" My plan's perfect.

"No one will ever believe this is a carriage. I-it's clearly still a flying boat."

Pshaw. "And who's going to stop us?"

"Halt!" A group of people appeared out of nowhere! Don't instantly answer my question, world! "Flying is prohibited beyond this point!"

Softie lowered her head. "S-sor—"

"We're not flying!" I spent so much effort attaching those wheels to the boat! I'm not going to let that effort go to waste. "This is a carriage. You can see the wheels in the front and back."

"…Those are trees."

"And what are wheels made out of? Dead trees!"

"…Please stow your boat."

"This is a carriage." I accidentally retrieved my ten-ton hammer from my interspacial ring and accidentally waved it at the group of people in a threatening manner.

"Are you threatening us?"

"...No." Hey. It's embarrassing if you call me out like that. I thought Immortal Continent natives were all about subtlety and face. Jeez. "Anyways, this is a normal-sized carriage shaped like a normal-looking carriage being driven on the road like a normal carriage with normal wheels. There's nothing out of the ordinary here, right?"

The person at the head of the group looked at the people behind him. They all nodded. "Start the sealing formation."

Did my persuasion fail? But I'm so charismatic! Alright, let's give them a few whacks since they can't recognize greatness when they see it. "Unrelenting Path of Slaughter: Breaking Madness Hammer Strike!" And … they're gone. Perfect! I smiled at Softie and stowed my hammer. "You see that? With a little bit of persuasion, you can convince anyone that you're right. Now, full speed ahead!"

Softie stepped towards the edge of the speeding boat and looked in the direction those people flew. "Those were imperial soldiers…."

***

I, Soft Moonlight, have been a law-abiding citizen all my life. I've never committed any crimes. I've never broken any rules of etiquette. I'm the model of a goody-two-shoes. Yet, here I am, a wanted criminal. Lucia's smacked everyone who tried to stop our boat: imperial soldiers, mercenaries, robbers, citizens. When I told her she'd spread a bad name for our Shadow Devil Sect if she did that, she promptly switched out the crests, sails, and flags with the bandits' that had tried to rob us earlier.

"Chosen Lucia!" the disciple on the boat's crow's nest shouted. "There's a fully armed squad of soldiers heading our way!"

Lucia paused from her feast of aurochsen and looked up. "Does it look like they want to talk?"

"Actually, yes…," the disciple said, his voice faltering. "They're waving a white flag."

"Oh?" Lucia nodded. "That's great! It means I can keep eating."

A white flag? I don't think the army will have any face if they surrender like this. But Lucia's practically as strong as a sky-realm expert albeit a low-ranked one. All the earth-realm experts that have tried to intercept us so far were beaten and stripped of everything before being tossed aside. Ilya even shaved them to take their hair as an alchemical ingredient. I really wish to see Lucia and Ilya's home plane. How dreadful are the conditions in there that they learn to not waste a single bit of anything?

It didn't take long for the squad to reach the boat because the boat was heading straight for them without pause. Lucia did finish her lunch though. When she was done, she sauntered over to the side of the boat and rested her arms against the railing while leaning over. "Is that them?"

"Greetings, Shadow Devil Sect." The leader of the group cupped his hands towards us. He was wearing a grey robe with a crest that looked like a shield on his chest. The group exchanged glances, and then they ran after us because the boat wasn't stopping. "W-wait! I wish to speak with you!"

The disciple at the steering wheel looked at Lucia. "Chosen Lucia. What do I do?"

"Just keep going," Lucia said. "If they really wanted to talk, they'd get on the boat somehow." She yawned and smacked her lips a few times. Then she took a mattress out of her interspacial ring and placed it in a patch of sunlight on the deck. Like a log, she flopped onto the plush surface and was snoring within seconds. Lucia is … a terrible, terrible cultivator. But she's a genius with talent that maybe one person per generation will ever have. Despite the impurities she's built up and the constant breaks she takes to eat and sleep, her cultivation is progressing at lightning speeds. I wouldn't be surprised if she reached the sky realm in a decade. Will I still be traveling with her at that time…?

If I want to stay by her side, I have to become stronger. Even Ilya is catching up to me in strength! But I'm not able to plant heart devils as easily as Lucia. And my talent is only so-so. If it weren't for all the immortal pills that my grandfather fed me while I was growing up, I wouldn't even be where I am today. …Maybe I don't deserve to be by Lucia's side. E-even if Lucia grows apart from me, I'll be fine. I was always alone anyway. I, I can go back to living how I was…. No! I have to try harder! Staying by Lucia's side has caused my cultivation to stagnate. I have to stop sleeping and eating and taking breaks to accompany her and her games. If only I could have a miraculous encounter that lets me grow by leaps and bounds…. There are many stories like that. An untalented individual discovers the legacy of a supreme being and suddenly becomes a peerless genius. But wishful thinking won't get me anywhere. At the end of the day, it's hard work that counts.

Well, isn't that also why my grandfather wanted me to join the army? Danger and battle is the best opportunity for growth. Sparring in the sect and meditating inside of a cave can only do so much. I'm nervous and scared though, but I feel a little reassured since Lucia's here. Will I be able to kill someone…? I…, to follow Lucia, I'll do whatever it takes.

"Sister Moonlight, are you alright?" Water Lily, a core disciple, walked next to me. "You're trembling. It must be tiring taking care of Chosen Lucia every day. At least she sleeps a lot."

I shook my head. "It's not tiring at all." I've had the most fun in a long while because of her. "It's quite exciting, really."

Water Lily laughed. "I suppose this is why Sister Moonlight is a chosen and I'm merely a core disciple. Our attitudes are much too different. Thinking of the bounty placed on our heads, I'm more afraid than excited." She smiled at me before gesturing towards the soldiers, who were still running alongside the boat. "Are we really not going to stop? Chosen Lucia rushes as if she's in a hurry, but she acts as if she has all the time in the world. Geniuses sure are different."

"Lu—Chosen Lucia isn't that odd...."

Water Lily raised an eyebrow. "I was referring to Sister Moonlight as well. It's normal for a genius to think of another as an equal."

"You think I'm a genius? I don't think I am...."

Water Lily furrowed her brow. "Sister Moonlight certainly knows how to joke around—I wasn't aware. If Sister Moonlight isn't a genius, then what am I? Trash?"

"N-no. I didn't mean it like that." Before I could explain any further, the group of running soldiers let out a unified shout and leapt into the air, landing directly onto the deck! They really jumped on! Do I wake Lucia? N-no. I can handle something like this. I'm a chosen of the Shadow Devil Sect as well! I cupped my hands towards the soldiers, but I didn't lower my head. "Greetings."

The leader of the group panted twice before lowering the white flag in his hand. "Greetings, Shadow Devil Sect. I'll get straight to the point. Our group was sent by the guard captain to escort you to the imperial barracks."

"Escort us?" The army would never send people out to escort a squad that hasn't even been officially sworn in.

"That's correct. We've received a message that your squad has been causing trouble along the road, and we're here to keep you in check. You can refer to me as Captain Rock. Once you join the army, I will be your superior. Are you the leader of this squad?"

"No." I shook my head and pointed at Lucia. "She is."

"...Her?" The soldiers all stared at Lucia, who was still snoring away in her patch of sunlight. "She won a province exchange and terrorized our patrols?"

"Correct. I wouldn't wake her up," I said as Captain Rock stepped towards Lucia's mattress. "She gets grumpy when she wakes up unnaturally. And horrible, horrible things happen when she's grumpy."

Captain Rock snorted. "Nonsense. Our Kang Country's army has superior discipline. How can I allow my future subordinate to sleep during the day while the sun is overhead?" He took another step towards the mattress, and all the Shadow Devil Sect disciples above deck ran away towards the cabin below. Of course, I followed them. I might not have witnessed what happened, but I could easily tell from the shouts and screams and the familiar wails that accompany men and women as their pants are torn away unwillingly.

***

"Y-you can't do this to me! I'm your captain!"

"Yeah, yeah. Sure. Captain. Okay." Maybe if it was before I had my necklace of intelligence, I would've fallen for his tricks, but too bad for him! There's no way I'll be fooled by some faulty logic. What kind of captain wakes his subordinate while she's taking a nap in the middle of the day while the sun is overhead? That's the perfect time to sleep! "Over you go."

The so-called captain screamed as I tossed him overboard. He was an earth-realm expert, so he'll be fine. I think these saint-realm people will be fine as well. Even if they're naked, bound, and falling down a three-story boat, I'm sure their bodies are tough enough to handle it. "Are the rest of you going to jump down by yourselves, or do I have to toss you over too?"

It might be a waste of rope, but I have a literal interspacial ring full of rope. Rope's such a useful thing—every sect that I robbed had some. The so-called imperial soldiers weren't responding or moving, so I picked them up and tossed them over since they weren't going to do it themselves. Back to sleep? I think it's a good time to go back to sleep. Ah, but first, I should check on Mr. Feathers. Last time, he meowed. Is he fixed now?

"Mr. Feathers?"

Hmm. He was still limp. But he's warm, so he's not dead. It's very hard to kill a phoenix, but apparently, a tribulation can do that. Mr. Feathers is pretty lucky to survive unlike his companion. Ah! I could've just let Ilya cut Mr. Feathers open to retrieve her blood jelly. It's not like he would've died. Darn. Well, this is why Ilya should've given me this necklace of intelligence earlier.

Mr. Feathers opened his eyes and stared at me with a dull expression. His beak creaked open and…. "Woof, woof."

"…Puppers. Did you—"

"I don't speak dog."

What? But you're part dog! "Really?"

"Do you speak squirrel?"

"Well, no." Huh. Puppers has a point. Alright, well, it seems like Mr. Feathers is still broken., so I'll stuff him back into the interspacial pouch. I wonder how that phoenix egg is doing. Should I eat it? I bet it'd taste delicious. Wait…. What if it's uncookable like the phoenix? Yeah, that's definitely the case. Then I guess I'll just have to settle for an aurochs. Mm, but I'm getting tired of aurochs. We should be pretty close to the capital now, right? I want to visit a restaurant! And with my Immortal Poison Body, I have absolutely no need to fear food cooked by others. Life is great. Well, it would be great if Durandal wasn't tiny!

"Stupid Durandal. Give me a sky-realm-ranked sword or I'll rob you of your happiness. Jeez." This is abuse! Right? It totally constitutes as abuse. I'm going to give him a stern talking-to once he wakes up. Hah…, but where am I supposed to find a smith that can make sky-realm-ranked swords? Wait a minute…. I've been going about this all wrong! This is why Ilya should've made me this necklace of intelligence earlier!

Instead of finding a smith and kidnapping his child, I can just beat someone up and take their sword! I can cut out the middleman completely! But how will I find an expert with a sword…. I know! I'll just go over to the steering wheel and … there. All done.

"Lucia?" Softie popped her head out of the cabin that led downstairs. "The boat's flying up?"

Yup. Seems like it. "So it is."

"What happened to the captain of the imperial army?"

"Oh. He was a fake so I threw him overboard." Higher, boat, go higher!

"Why are we flying…? I thought we were riding a carriage." Softie frowned as she walked over to my side.

"Well, see, people don't like it when we fly, right?"

Softie nodded. "Yes. It's against the law."

"And the people who enforce the laws came after us, yes?"

"Okay…."

"Then when I beat them up, stronger people came later, yeah?"

"Right…."

"So if I keep breaking the law and keep beating the people who come after us, eventually, someone with a sky-realm-ranked sword is bound to come out to stop us! Then all I have to do is beat him up and take his sword!"

Softie bit her lower lip. "I think there's something wrong with your plan."

Hmm? "That's impossible. All my plans are foolproof." This was designed after I received a boost to my intelligence. My plans have never failed before, but now they'll definitely not fail! "And once I have a sky-realm-ranked sword, Durandal will come back!"

"Are you sure you can defeat someone who has a sky-realm-ranked sword? And what happens after Durandal comes back? You'll be a wanted criminal for resisting the law so many times, not to mention thievery and aggression."

"Aren't we already criminals?"

"...You're right. But this plan completely hinges on you being strong enough to attract an expert that you can defeat." Softie's forehead wrinkled. "Can't you take it slow? There's no reason not to join the army and slowly build up merits for a reward that you can exchange for what you want."

"No reason? Do you know how long it's been since I've had sex? I'll tell you how long. Too long! There's no time to slowly build up merits. Before you know it, I'll be well past my prime and my chance at having kids will plummet! No reason not to slowly build up merits? I don't have all the time in the world!" That's right. Before I'm too old, I have to have kids! How else will I accomplish my dreams of making a family with Durandal if Durandal's stuck as an orb?

"Wait." Softie held her hand up and used her other hand to massage her forehead. "You partake in, um, activities with Durandal because you want children? Disregarding the fact that cultivators stay fertile for longer, your reason makes no sense because weapon spirits are sterile."

...Say what? "Ste...rile?"

"It means they can't have children."

"I know what it means!" I'm not an idiot! What do you mean Durandal's sterile!? That's impossible! ...It makes a lot of sense, actually, since I'm not pregnant despite how frequently we do it. "Is this true, Puppers?"

"Yes."

"Why didn't you say anything...?"

"Ah. Uh..., I'm pretty sure he already told you...? Actually, ahem. Durandal told me not to. You'll have to ask him."

"Durandal!!! I'm going to stick you into my panties, goddammit! How dare you lie to me!?"

Chapter 16

Lucia's stripping in front of me! Why!? We're out in public on top of a deck; anyone can see if they come upstairs! "W-what are you doing, Lucia?"

"Sticking Durandal into my panties, that's what!" Lucia was practically growling as she retrieved the bright-red orb that held Durandal and kicked aside the pair of pants that was spread out around her feet on the floorboards. She pressed the spirit seed against her pink cotton panties and there was a brilliant flash of red light. When I could see again, Lucia was still holding the spirit seed, and it didn't seem like anything happened. "It didn't work? Then I'll try again!"

The light flashed again with no results. "Um, Lucia. The grade of your spirit seed is too high for the item you're trying to plant it in." Spirit seeds have grades just like items do. Most of the spirit seeds that I've seen are in the mortal realm, but Durandal absorbed a phoenix egg which should've promoted him to the earth realm, or at the very least, the peak of saint realm. I've never seen anyone try to make a spirit out of undergarments, but unless Lucia's underwear is an earth-realm-ranked object, it won't work.

Lucia stopped trying to press Durandal's spirit seed into her underwear. She put the red orb away and slipped into her pants, reaching behind and tying a knot above her tail. Oh, that's how she did it. I always wondered how she managed to fit into pants with a giant tail like hers. Lucia dusted off her hands and nodded at me. "Then what you're saying is I have to upgrade my panties?"

"If that's the conclusion you want to draw…." I'm not sure how Lucia's mind works. Every time I think I figure out how she works, she always does something inexplicable that throws me off. Like her plan to escalate her crimes so she'll have progressively stronger people to rob? That's pure insanity. Should I land the boat? But I don't want to go against Lucia's wishes.... My grandfather did tell me to listen to whatever Lucia told me. Then it can't be helped—I'm following the sect leader's wishes.

Lucia's eyes narrowed as she crossed her arms over her chest. She sat down on her mattress that she hadn't stowed away and harrumphed. "Fine, Durandal. I know you can hear me! You better hope I find a sky-realm-ranked sword before I find a pair of panties that can house you. But I won't forget that you didn't tell me you were sterile!" Lucia sighed and grumbled as she flopped onto her side. "Now I have to find a way to make Durandal virile. I'll ask Ilya!" She sat up and disappeared, presumably into Ilya's room.

Seriously, I'm jealous of Lucia's personality. It must be nice to be as carefree as her. Despite all the trouble she's provoked, she doesn't seem to suffer from any stress or burdens. Breaking the law and assaulting imperial soldiers..., robbing and offending everyone who gets in her way..., completely destroying the Star Phoenix Sect which has a huge backer..., there are just too many crimes to list. I'm surprised the Rainbow Phoenix Sect hasn't sent someone after her yet. But the Rainbow Phoenix Sect isn't the only one she has to worry about. A lot of those sects in Kong County were branch sects—even if they were outcasts or expelled from their main sects—and Lucia basically created enmity with all of them.

Ding, ding.

A message? It must be from my grandfather or grandmother; they're the only ones in my messenger's contacts list except for Lucia.

To Little Moon,

Have you been well? I hope your journey has been proceeding without issue. Unfortunately, I have some bad news involving Junior Lucia. You see…, she's not actually a foxkin. Emperor Yi contacted me and told me she was a squirrelkin. Yes, that's right. A squirrelkin. She's inherited the blood of the mythical sky-realm beasts from the ancient legends that rivaled phoenixes and dragons, the fearsome squirrel. Emperor Yi told me a few powers outside of Kang Country have contacted him about the aura of a squirrel briefly appearing in his lands, which he suspected was the manifestation of Junior Lucia's sin. Tell Junior Lucia to lay low and do her best to not attract any attention. It's possible that even immortals may seek her out. Don't let anyone else know. Junior Lucia must have a reason to keep this a secret from us, but for your safety, you should distance yourself from her as much as possible.
Love,
　Grandpa

　　A squirrelkin…? Lucia? That's … highly possible given her high, natural talent. But squirrels were a monstrous evil purged aeons ago! Lucia … might be a monstrous evil, but her evil isn't malicious. She just happens to do evil things without intending on doing them. I'm not sure which one is worse. Is it possible that the squirrels escaped to a pocket realm during their persecution? That certainly seems to be the case if Lucia is actually a squirrelkin. But, Grandfather, it's already too late to lay low! And I can't distance myself from Lucia now—I promised myself I'd stick by her no matter what happens. E-even if I die while following Lucia, I won't regret it. Wait, actually…, I really would prefer it if I didn't die. I didn't raise any death flags, did I?

　　"Flying is prohibited in this region! Land immediately or face the consequences!"

Trouble has sought us out already. I walked over to the edge of the boat and peered over. We were already a good hundred feet or so off the ground, but I could make out the figures of a group of soldiers standing on top of a building. Did one of them shout that loudly? What were the consequences that we would face if we didn't land? Wouldn't they have to fly up here to stop us? Unless there was a formation in the sky, but I don't think that's the case. The amount of energy required to maintain a formation over a whole county is immense.

"Oh! My plan worked. See?" Lucia suddenly appeared beside me. Then she leaned over and shouted with Emperor Yi's qi-infused screaming technique, "Try and stop me, you army dogs!"

***

When I was back in the Ravenwood army, the worst thing a soldier could be called was an army dog. It's probably the same here. I have to enrage and provoke them more and more until a true expert comes out. And even if that doesn't work, which it will, we're still going to the capital. According to Softie, we're three days away if we continue flying at our current pace. Hmm. But why aren't those soldiers chasing me? "They aren't following?"

"Your roaring technique knocked them out," Softie said. "Do you not know your own strength?"

Hmm. Well, that's that. Next!

And just like that, three days passed by with only fourteen different groups of soldiers trying to stop us. The strongest were some earth-realm experts, but they didn't put up much of a fight after getting hit by a hammer. No one puts up a fight after being hit by a hammer. Fighting's actually gotten really boring. I should hunt some beasts or something. I never thought I'd be bored of living a luxurious life. Well, not really! "Let's go to that fancy-looking restaurant. I bet they sell good stuff." With all these riches I have on me, it'd be wrong not to spend it all. Money is meant to be spent. Mhm.

"Chosen Lucia, won't we be arrested the moment we land?" the disciple on the steering wheel asked. He didn't have a very memorable face or name, so I don't know him too well. I actually can't recognize anyone except for Softie and Ilya. The necklace of intelligence only helps my smartness, not my ability to remember people's faces.

"No, we'll just beat them up if they try."

"But, Chosen Lucia, you have to think of the consequences," the disciple said. "We're wearing the clothes and crests of the Shadow Devil Sect. If we break the law, it will reflect poorly on our sect and possibly cause our sect a lot of grief."

…Hmm. I hadn't thought about that. I've always been alone without any responsibilities for other people. I belong to a sect now; I have to act mature and responsible like the mature and responsible person I am! "Okay. Then we'll wear the clothes and crests of the Bloody Bull Sect. I have lots of robes for everyone but no underwear. You have to supply your own." I picked the Bloody Bull Sect because I'm using their hammer. If I'm going to impersonate someone, I have to impersonate them properly! Why didn't this disciple mention this earlier? Well, the Bloody Bull Sect's robes are grey, so the color is close enough. We've been Bloody Bull Sect members this whole time!

"I-is this morally correct?"

"It's totally fine. If we impersonate people and do bad things, we'll plant heart devils in the people we've impersonated! And planting heart devils is always morally correct." That's what Softie told me. She said something along the lines of planting heart devils is immoral if you don't cultivate the Heart Devil Cultivation Technique, but if you have the technique, you shouldn't feel guilty since cultivation has many paths and only God can judge whether a path is right or wrong. It sounds like some faulty rationalization, but it absolves me of sin, so I like it!

After convincing everyone to change clothes, we finally landed the boat for the first time in a while. Sometimes it gets really stuffy in there. Sure, there's rooms with bathrooms for everyone on board, but it doesn't change the fact it's like staying in a very large cage. A comfortable jail is still a jail after all. And as the disciple on the wheel predicted, we were surrounded by soldiers the instant we landed. I retrieved my trusty hammer and brandished it over my head. "Make way for the Bloody Bull Sect!" Why don't I just stick Durandal into this hammer? I like this hammer a lot. It's much, much more satisfying to hit someone with it: their bones go crunch! But if I hit someone with mini-DalDal, there's no sound or physical feedback. They just scream with their limbs gone. Hmm? Does that make me sadistic? Of course not! It just proves I'm part squirrel. Squirrels crack open nuts; we don't slice them.

"Lay down your weapons and peacefully surrender!"

Softie groaned as she clutched her chest. Everyone groaned as they clutched their chests! What was going on? There was a lot of qi pressing down on us, but it wasn't that unbearable ... for me. Where was it coming from? That man! Is he a sky-realm expert? Mm. My tail is a bit perky, but it's not completely stiff. I can take him!

"Oh-ho? You're still standing?" the person who I suspected to be a sky-realm expert asked. He was bald with a scar cutting horizontally across his face. A large portion of his nose was missing, and his teeth were made of gold. "I am Fierce Fire, guard captain of the imperial army!"

Oh..., so this was the guy who was supposed to give me the earth-realm-ranked sword.... Hm. Hmmm. Hmmmmm. What do I do? If I beat him up now, can I report to him later...? But if I surrender now, then I'll be admitting I'm a criminal. Ah, why are decisions so hard to make? Well, right now, I'm part of the Bloody Bull Sect! All I have to do is beat him up, escape, switch my clothes, and meet him later as part of the Shadow Devil Sect. I'm so glad Ilya gave me this necklace of intelligence or I wouldn't have come to such a clean answer! "Hup! Breaking Madness Hammer Strike!"

The guard captain raised his sword and directly clashed against my hammer. And he wasn't even pushed back! "You think such low-grade techniques with an even lower-grade weapon can compete with my imperial swordsmanship?"

Low-grade techniques? Durandal gave me these! Don't you dare insult Durandal's gifts to me! "Again! Eat my strike!" My hammer roared as it crashed against the guard captain's sword, but he didn't budge again! What the heck!? How does such a tiny body have so much strength? He's only a little bit bigger than me! "Again!"

There's something weird. There's no satisfying hit when my hammer collides with his sword. It feels like I'm punching a pillow. If I had mini-DalDal, I could make my strike even heavier, but I don't! There's only one thing to do: keep on attacking! As long as I have the initiative, he won't be able to do anything. Left! Right! Up! Down! My attacks aren't working, but he can't hit me either. Ah! He's off balance—here's my chance! "Breaking Madness—" …Ah? I dropped my hammer?

"Lucia!" Softie shouted.

Gah! Shit! I didn't drop my hammer; this bastard cut off my arms! How did he do that!? "Puppers! Sneak attack, go!"

Puppers sprang out of my socks with his cloth spear in hand. With a roar, he lunged towards the guard captain and stabbed. I only saw it for a brief moment, but the guard captain's sword flashed and returned to its original position. Puppers' head fell off! But in the time it took the guard captain to dispatch Puppers, my arms regrew. This is scary…. I've never lost my arms in a fight before.

"A body-practitioner! And you've reached the earth realm. Impressive, but you're no match for a sky-realm expert like me." The guard captain smiled as he kicked aside my fallen hammer. That weighed ten tons! No one's been able to kick it aside as if it weighed nothing! "What do you say? Do you surrender?"

What do I do? If I teleport away, I'll be leaving Ilya and Softie behind.... Ah, this is really, really scary! Even my Armor of Slaughter and Impenetrable Shell can't stop his attack. And I can't even see it either. Maybe my Heart Devil Apparition will work? But that'll give away my identity..., unless I shout out a fake name. "Super-Secret Bloody Bull Technique!"

A tiny predator sprang out of my chest and rapidly grew in size until it was as large as the flying boat. It roared and clawed at the guard captain with its sickle-like nails, ripping apart the air. The guard captain raised his sword, but right before it made contact with my heart devil predator's claws, the predator disappeared and reappeared in front of the other soldiers. What are you doing, apparition!? You should be targeting the strongest one!

"Audacious! How dare you resort to sneak attacking my subordinates?" the guard captain glowered at me before whirling around to strike at my apparition.

Now's my chance! While the guard captain's back was completely exposed, I reached into my interspacial ring, pulled out the first thing I touched, and threw it as hard as I could. With a swish, a pair of wet panties struck the back of the guard captain's head with a sickening splat. ...I thought I picked up something solid. Veins bulged on the guard captain's head as the panties slid down, leaving behind a clear liquid residue on his bald scalp. The guard captain whirled around and glared at me with completely bloodshot eyes, his lips bared like a wild animal.

"Uh…, that's not what I meant to do…." Before I could make up any more excuses, the guard captain appeared right in front of my face. There was a familiar piercing pain in my chest…. Fuck! How many times am I going to be hit in the heart!? Ah? Gah! He's twisting his sword! This fucking sadist! Stop it! I grabbed his wrist and squeezed. There was a loud crunching sound followed by a shrill scream. Eh? He stopped? I thought this man was stronger than me…, how come he can't escape from my grip?

"Unhand me!"

"As if I'd do that, moron!" I kept one hand on his wrist and grabbed his elbow with my other hand. There was another crunch! Crunch! Crunch! Crunch! "I'll teach you to stab me in the heart, damnit!" Crunch, crunch, crunch. Grind, grind. Crunch! Ooh. This is pretty fun. It's like tenderizing aurochsen meat. If aurochsen meat screamed, that is.

"Captain Fire! Someone, stop her!"

Screams and more screams filled the air. My apparition was still having fun bullying all the weak people. The Shadow Devil Sect disciples were grouping up and fighting for their lives against the other soldiers. The guard captain was squirming around like a worm as I pinched his bones into powder. This is his retribution for stabbing a woman's breast! How dare he try to mar my beauty? Ooh. This is a fancy-looking interspacial ring; I'll put this in a safe place. I'll take this sword out of my heart too. Ugh. It's such an awful feeling to have metal cut and scrape against my bones and heart. It makes my spine tingle in an unpleasant way. Now I'm mad again! How dare he stab my boob!? Err, heart! How dare he stab my heart!? Crunch, crunch, crunch.

***

"Lucia…? Are your arms really okay?" Ilya pinched Lucia's bare bicep, causing her to twitch and growl. Lucia had

... brutalized the guard captain, stripped him and his subordinates of everything, and left them for dead. Then she entered the restaurant that she wanted to eat in and ordered a private room that could fit a hundred people. The room was already reserved for someone, but the restaurant decided to yield to Lucia after seeing the broken bodies lying outside their front gates. And once all of our sect brothers and sisters entered the room, Lucia had us switch out of the Bloody Bull Sect robes into our Shadow Devil Sect ones. Her plan isn't going to fool anyone..., but she's extremely sure no one will figure it out. I wonder where her baseless confidence comes from. People have the tendency to project themselves on others—maybe Lucia thinks people won't recognize us because she wouldn't if she were exposed to her own plot.

"I can't believe that bastard cut my arms off," Lucia muttered and sniffed her arms, sniffing each one twice. "Only I can cut other people's arms off! They're not allowed to cut off mine! It hurt a lot, damnit."

"Maybe you should consider that and, you know, stop cutting people's arms off?" Ilya asked, raising an eyebrow. I don't agree with Ilya on many topics, but this is one where she has my full support. The fewer arms Lucia removes, the less reputation she'll receive. Immortals may be searching for Lucia because of her lineage. Immortals! They're people who've transcended their lifespans, able to live forever—as long as they're not killed. Immortals can be killed? It rarely happens, but yes, they can. They just won't die of old age. Yes, yes, the name isn't very fitting, but it is what it is.

"Eh...." Lucia's forehead wrinkled. She was about to say something, but a strong aroma of roasted meat permeated the room. The door swung open as a line of waiters entered, each carrying platters filled with dishes on both hands. It didn't take long for the plates to be equally distributed between all of us, and it took equally as long for Lucia to finish her first plate. Then she stole the food off of my plate, but I didn't mind. The less impurities I ingested, the quicker I'd catch up to Lucia. …I shouldn't kid myself; I'll never catch up to her.

"Softie?" Lucia asked. She stared at me with a haunch of meat held by both her hands. Her head was tilted to the side, and a smear of grease covered her lips. "Are you upset I stole your food?"

"No?" Did I look upset? I'm very good at controlling my facial expressions when I'm not nervous or embarrassed. Lucia shouldn't have seen anything wrong with me.

"But the heart devil inside of you is growing," Lucia said. "It's because I stole your food, isn't it?"

"It isn't." A heart devil made of insecurities…. Who would've thought that the chosen of the Shadow Devil Sect would someday be so insecure about her own abilities that she'd develop a heart devil? It's quite ironic, isn't it? Every passing day, I'm sprinting forward in my cultivation with all my might, but Lucia's back keeps getting further and further away. The day where her back disappears completely isn't too far from now, huh? She's part squirrel…, part mythical beast. I'm, I'm just a regular person blessed with a little bit of beauty.

"Oi, oi." Heat spread across my lips as Lucia pressed the haunch against my mouth. "The heart devil's growing larger after you said that. The food tastes great, but it isn't better than anything I can make! You're not missing out on anything even if I steal your food, Softie. But since you're so upset, I'll stop taking yours, okay?"

"It really isn't about the foo—"

Lucia cut me off by shoving the meat into my mouth. I'm glad she cares about me, but all this food will do is increase my impurities and decrease my cultivation speed….

"How is it? Better?" Lucia asked, her face split by her smile. I nodded. My heart always felt fuzzy when she smiled. Lucia exhaled. "Phew. That's good. I thought you were going to cry again."

I-it's true that I cry more often than a normal person, but it's not something that happens every day! "I wasn't going to!"

"Mm. Okay, whatever you say, Softie," Lucia said and nodded before waving at a waiter. "More food!"

"Which audacious person dares to take the reservation of this prince? Come on out!" A male voice drifted into the room as the waiter opened the door. With a grunt, the waiter was pushed aside as a well-dressed man marched into the room. He wore a purple cloak with a golden crest as its clasp, a symbol of the royal family imprinted upon it. "Manager Forest, what is the meaning of this? You gave a third-rate sect the room that I reserved? Are you tired of living?"

"Fourth Prince." The manager, who was cowering in the corner of the room, clasped his hands and deeply bowed his head. "These esteemed guests were the ones who disabled Guard Captain Fire and left those wounded soldiers outside."

The fourth prince stiffened. "Defeated Guard Captain Fire?"

"No, we didn't do it!" Lucia shouted as she shot to her feet. "That's slander! The Bloody Bull Sect were the ones who flew through the air and beat up the people trying to apprehend them. We, the Shadow Devil Sect, have nothing to do with the bodies outside!"

The trembling manager swallowed once before lowering his head, perspiration dripping onto the ground. Heart devil worms were rising and sinking from Lucia's shadow like boats swaying on the surface of an ocean. The prince's gaze shifted from the manager to Lucia, then back to the manager, then back to Lucia, then finally onto me. Onto me…? I resisted the urge to sigh. It's because I'm not wearing my veil, isn't it? Sometimes being born beautiful is a curse. The prince's expression softened as he stepped towards me and extended a hand. "Fair maiden, my—"

"Scram! You're blocking my food's way!" Lucia lifted the prince by the back of his collar and tossed him out the window. The waiter that was stuck behind the prince froze, a dumbfounded expression painted on his face. Lucia's ears perked up as she beamed and sat in her seat before patting the empty space in front of herself on the table. "You can put that right here."

…Maybe Lucia should've continued to wear the Bloody Bull Sect's robes. Defenestrating a prince…, why does it seem like Lucia and royalty just don't mix?

***

Ah, being smart is such a burden sometimes. You think of the strangest things! Like didn't Softie say people ate immortal rice to avoid impurities, especially cultivators? Then why are there restaurants filled with such good food at such expensive prices? Three hundred spirit stones per dish! How is a regular non-cultivator family supposed to afford that? Back home, a single spirit stone was worth tens of gold, and a family could live off of a single gold for a long time! Three hundred spirit stones? That's thirty sets of used underwear! …Huh. Actually, it'd be pretty easy for a family to afford a dish…. If that something succubus sect existed back home, then I wouldn't have had to work a single day in my life. I could've bought my freedom by selling my underwear!

Hmm? Who's tugging on my sleeve? Oh, it's Softie. "Lucia, you, um, threw the prince out the window. I think that's an even worse crime than flying…."

"Prince? What prince?" I tossed someone out the window? Why don't I remember this? Hmm. I was waiting for my food, then there was some shouting and I cleared up a misunderstanding about my identity, then something got in the way of my food getting to me so I removed the obstacle. Was that a person? Nah, it was a bit too tall to be a person.

Softie pointed at the window. It was shattered and had a hole that was in a perfect outline of a person. Huh.... "Did I really throw a prince out a window?" I looked around the room, and everyone nodded at me. Well, in that case.... "What are you all waiting for? Switch back into the Bloody Bull Sect's robes! And you! Witnesses! Swear an oath to the heavens that you won't say anything about our existence!"

As the last disciple finished changing his robes, the door to our room burst open. A fellow with a torn cloak and scrapes on his skin pointed at me. How rude. "Elder Brother! She's the one who threw me out the window!" Another person appeared behind him, wearing the same kind of cloak with the same kind of golden clasp. He was a bit bigger, and there was a nice-looking sword on his waist. Was that a sky-realm-ranked sword?

"Is this true?" the person with the maybe-sky-realm-ranked sword asked. Without warning, he raised his hand and slapped the back of the torn-cloaked person's head. "You idiot! You lost to a woman and came running to me?"

"E-Elder Brother," the torn-cloaked person said with a familiar expression. That's the same kind of expression Ilya gives me when I keep something that she wants away from her! I think I can get along pretty well with this older brother person. Except he's a bit arrogant. What does he mean lost to a woman? It's perfectly natural for me to win any fight I get into! That's just how life works. "She also incapacitated Guard Captain Fire! You can't blame me for losing!"

The older brother person slapped the torn-cloaked person's head even harder. "How dumb are you!? She defeated a sky-realm expert and you want me to fight her!?" The older brother snorted before smiling at me. "Greetings, great expert. I am Second Prince Heavy Sky. I apologize if my younger brother offended you. His eyes are worthless just like the rest of him."

Wow. That's pretty harsh.

"But Elder Brother! You're a sky-realm expert too! You can't lose to her!"

"Moron! You want two sky-realm experts to fight in the capital? Your brain has completely rotted from chasing women all day! Go back to the palace and await your punishment when Father finds out about this." The older brother grabbed the person with the torn cloak by the back of his neck and tossed him out the window. Amazingly, the screaming person passed straight through without breaking anymore glass, fitting perfectly into the hole that was already there. Well, that confirms it. A person, who had the same exact shape as that person, was thrown out the window by someone in this room before. I'm not saying it was me; I'm just saying it happened. Mhm.

The older brother nodded at me. Then he looked at Softie and raised an eyebrow. He grunted. "I roughly understand everything that happened now. Enjoy your meal."

"Wait!" You can't leave yet!

"Was there something else?"

"Is that a sky-realm-ranked sword?" I pointed at the fancy sword hanging from his waist.

"This?" The older brother touched his sword and shook his head. "No, it's a single step below. Of the princes, only my older brother, the crown prince, has a sky-realm-ranked sword."

"Oh. This crown prince person. Where's he at?" I found a lead! Just you wait, Durandal. Don't think I'll let you off easy for lying to me about not being sterile! Thankfully, Ilya said she can create some things to make him virile, but she'd have to do a lot of experimenting since she wasn't sure if it'd work on a weapon spirit.

The older brother, no, younger brother? Hmm. What was his name? Fat Sky? Right. Fat Sky's expression darkened. "He's positioned at the Gates of Hell."

What. "…He's dead?" Then this'll be a piece of cake! Robbing someone's grave is a whole lot easier than robbing someone who's still alive.

"The Gates of Hell is the battlefield I was telling you about," Softie whispered to me. "The continuous one between the two countries, remember?"

Oh, right. That. Hah. I guess the world doesn't want me to have it easy, huh? Why couldn't it just let me rob a grave for a sword?

Fat Sky coughed. "Were you hoping to join his faction?"

"Faction? I just want to steal his sword!" …Did I say that out loud?

"You said that out loud," Ilya said.

Thanks, mind reader. "Ah-ha-ha, I mean, inspect! I just want to inspect his sword!"

Fat Sky's expression lightened as he smiled. "If all you want to do is *inspect* his sword, I can give you a recommendation to join the army under his command. You've defeated Guard Captain Fire; no one will question your qualifications."

"Really? You'll do that?" I guess the world does want to help me after all. Sky-realm-ranked sword, here I come!

Chapter 17

Is this the room? Fat Sky told me to come here to report to the guard captain that I'm going to the Gates of Hell to aid the crown prince.

"…lucky that your injuries are only physical. Your meridians were left intact, and your cultivation was unharmed, but your organs are a mess. Continue taking these pills every day before you go to sleep and refrain from using qi for the next three weeks."

Yup! It sounds like this is the room. The door opened, and a man with a white beard and white robes stepped outside. He frowned at me as his eyebrows slanted, almost touching each other in the center of his head. "The patient is severely injured and needs his rest. Go back and come see him tomorrow."

"Okay." Before, the old Lucia without the necklace of intelligence would ignore the man and barge into the room anyways. But the smarter and improved Lucia isn't as stupid! I love this necklace.

"Aren't you going back?"

"I'm waiting for you to leave first, so I can ignore your advice and see him without you judging me." That's right! I'm considerate now. This necklace is telling me that life's easier with less enemies. And to make less enemies, you have to be considerate. Mhm. So hurry up and scram, old man! I'm a busy person.

"Well, I'm just a doctor," the old man said and shook his head. "Your captain will punish you appropriately." He reached over to the side and retrieved a white bag which he slung over his shoulder before closing the door. As he made his way down the hall, he called out, "Remember, Captain

Fire, refrain from using your qi for three weeks if you want a full recovery."

Once the old man rounded a corner, I kicked open the door and hopped inside. "Lucia Fluffytail of the Shadow Devil Sect reporting for duty!" Inside the room, there was a bed with something that looked like a mummy on top of it. It was completely wrapped in bandages, but there was a tiny gap for two black eyes to see out of. Once the eyes saw me, they rolled up and turned white as the mummy twitched and spasmed. And, somewhere, a heart devil grew. Hmm. "Guard Captain Fiercey? Is that you? I'm here to report for duty!"

There still wasn't any response, so I went over to the side of the bed and reached out to gently shake the mummy awake. He screamed when I touched him. "Have you come to finish me off!?"

Eh.... Don't tell me he's seen through my disguise! "What are you talking about, Fiercey?" Fat Sky told me the guard captain's name was Fierce Fire, but Fiercey sounds so much better, no? "This is the first time we've met."

"W-what do you want from me!?" Tears poured out of Fiercey's eyes, soaking the bandages on his cheeks. "Haven't you taken enough!? Kill me! Just kill me! Is that what you want? To see me die!?"

"Whoa, whoa, whoa. Captain Fiercey, you're overreacting." It doesn't seem like my plan is working.... Where did I go wrong? I'm wearing my pink and black robe instead of the Bloody Bull Sect's grey robes. Neither Ilya nor Softie are here with me just in case he recognizes people as extremely conspicuous as them. And my hammer's not ... oh. I forgot to put my hammer away. Ahem, let me just store that in my interspacial ring and ... done! "Ah, that hammer was, uh, I picked it up off the ground! It was just lying there, so I took it. You know, finders, keepers. I'm Lucia Fluffytail of the Shadow Devil Sect, and I'm in no way, shape, or form related to that crazy Bloody Bull Sect person who beat you up. Look!

Here's my royal crest that I got from winning the King Province Exchange. See? See?"

Fiercey stared at me, but he didn't say anything. Though, a yellow patch did start spreading throughout the bandages on the lower part of his body.

"Anyways…, I'm here for my earth-realm-ranked sword! And the second prince, Fat Sky, told me to come here to tell you that my squad's been assigned to the Gates of Hell under the crown prince's command." I looked around his room, but there weren't any signs of any swords. There's a bookshelf with some books in the corner of the room. There's a desk with a pretty, shiny rock on top of it. Ahem. Shiny rock? There wasn't a shiny rock on the desk. There's just a desk. There's a wardrobe that I rifled through but didn't find a sword inside of. And there's a chest at the base of the mummy's bed that was filled with clothes. I took the underwear. "So, where's my sword?" I already looked through his interspacial ring back at the restaurant, but there weren't any swords inside of it. I did take the sword he stabbed through my heart, but that was *his* sword, not the sword reserved for me.

"G-go to the armory…," Fiercey said.

Hmm? The armory? I guess an army should have one of those, huh? I should've gone there first, what was I thinking? "Okay! Which way is that?"

"When you leave, take a left. It'll be the second building on your right."

Mm. Got it! With this bone of focus and necklace of intelligence, memorizing directions like these is completely a piece of cake! Take a right when I leave, and it'll be the second building on my left. Easy! I can't count the number of times I was beaten in the army for failing to follow instructions correctly, but now I won't have to worry about that anymore—not like I had to after getting Durandal, but still. "And I'll say you sent me, right, Fiercey?"

"Please, refer to me as Guard Captain Fire…."

Oh? How dare he not like the name I gave him after spending so much time and effort thinking it up?

"F-Fiercey's fine too," Fiercey wailed. "Please, hurry up and leave! I, I never want to see you again!"

There we go. Durandal's handy-dandy staring trick works everywhere! It's time to rob a treasury with the owner's permission. Hmm, hmm, happy days. I never get permission to take everything; I knew being considerate was the way to go.

***

Lucia was filled with smiles when she walked out of the infirmary. Just seeing her so happy made my chest warm up. I took an empty jade slip out of my interspacial ring and recorded my memory into it so I'd have her smile with me wherever I went. After tucking the slip away into a safe place, I walked up to Lucia. "How was it? Did you get the sword? Did he recognize you?"

"For a second, I thought he did!" Lucia said before exhaling while patting her chest. "But thankfully, due to my quick thinking and intelligence, he was completely fooled! He even gave me directions to the armory and told me to take whatever and however much I wanted."

"Are you sure about that?" Ilya asked. I nodded. The guard captain didn't seem like the type of person to be so easily fooled. Lucia didn't do anything inappropriate to him inside there, did she? I didn't hear any screaming, so there probably wasn't any violence…. "I still think I should've gone with you."

Lucia snorted. "You have purple skin," she said while placing her hands on her hips. "He'd recognize you in an instant! And Softie's too beautiful to forget, so she couldn't come either."

"But somehow your ears and tail are completely fine?" Ilya asked, raising an eyebrow. I hate when she uses such a condescending and sarcastic tone to address Lucia. Lucia's too slow to understand she's being made fun of! I'll stand up for her.

"There are millions of foxkin, but you're the only person with purple skin around. Lucia's right."

Lucia's head bobbed up and down. "See? I'm not conspicuous at all."

Ilya glared at me. "Don't forget there's millions of women just as beautiful as you—or even prettier. If your looks are one in a billion, then there's ten people like you in Kong County alone. Don't think you're so special."

Why did this become a personal attack on me? Ilya's so hateful! I can never win against her in a battle of words. I'm going to sneak a heart devil worm into her bath when she's not looking. That'll make me feel a lot better. There might be millions of women as beautiful as me, but only one of those women will slip a worm into your bath! I stuck my tongue out at Ilya before smiling at Lucia. "Are we going to the armory now? The guard captain said you could take any amount you wanted?" Does that mean I could get to pick out a sword too?

"Yup, he did," Lucia said as she hummed to herself and turned towards the right. "It's the second building on the left! I'm going to take everything inside! Wait, no. I'll take the whole building too! I'm a genius."

"The second building on the left?" Lucia strode with confidence, but no matter how I look at it, that building's a bathhouse…. Was Lucia lied to? But before I could say anything, Lucia had already appeared in front of the wooden doors and dug her fingers into the ground. With a sickening crack, followed by the sounds of shouts and screams, the building rose off of the ground before disappearing, supposedly, into one of Lucia's interspacial rings. And tens of dozens of naked men and women were left behind in the empty space, some of them still cleaning the shampoo from their hair despite the sudden disappearance of a water source.

Lucia stared at the naked people before turning towards me. Through the slits in between my fingers, I could still clearly see everything even though I was covering my face with my hands. I'm a pure maiden! I always looked away when Lucia stripped her victims, and I did my best to focus on that earth-realm bandit's face when I cut off his … thing. Lucia scratched her head and let out a dry laugh. "Strange armory, huh? Looks like it had some special water inside that cleansed impurities!"

No, I'm pretty sure it was just a bathhouse.

Lucia looked down as if she were rummaging through an interspacial ring. "Ah! An earth-realm-ranked sword. Nice, there's a lot of them. It really was an armory with special water."

"That's my sword!" a naked man shouted, but Lucia acted as if she hadn't heard him. Or maybe she really didn't hear him because she was so preoccupied with inspecting everyone's property. It's quite unfortunate for the army to have rules against stowing one's main weapon inside of their interspacial rings—unfortunate for the army members, that is. An army member's sword represents one's rank and one's oath to fight for the emperor and should be proudly worn on one's waist. "Give it back!"

The man ran towards Lucia, but her tail swished and swatted him away without any effort. She didn't even raise her head. "Alright!" Lucia beamed at me. "Let's gather everyone and set off to the Gates of Hell! I'll distribute these to everyone on the way. My squad can't be lacking!"

What…? Lucia's willing to share her spoils? She never does that! Was she feeling alright? Maybe she had something bad for dinner…. No, that's impossible; her Immortal Poison Body prevents food poisoning. "Lucia? Did you say you were going to distribute those earth-realm-ranked swords amongst us?"

"Of course! I can't use them all. I could sell them for spirit stones, but what's the point? It'll be better to use them to keep you guys alive. Mhm." Lucia wrapped her arms around Ilya's and my shoulders. "The last time I wanted to save resources because I was greedy, Durandal turned into a ball!" Her hand squeezed, and a piercing pain rushed through my arm. Did she fracture a bone? "Smart people learn lessons! Resources are meant to be used, not hoarded. If you guys died because of my greed, wouldn't that be a bummer?"

Ilya's eyes widened to the size of saucers as they met mine. L-Lucia was undergoing character development!

"W-wait! At least return our underwear!"

Lucia turned her head around and growled at the approaching naked people who were attempting to cover themselves with their hands. "What? I can sell those for ten spirit stones each! Scram!"

…Undergoing *some* character development.

***

And once again, we're back on the flying boat. Ilya, Softie, and the ninety-eight other disciples were standing before me on the deck. All the disciples were looking at me with awe in their eyes! And some terror. Well, everyone knows awe is mostly composed of fear, so it can't be helped that they're a little scared of me too. "Alright! I bet you're all wondering why I gathered you." I didn't tell them why; I just ordered them up here. Surprises are fun!

None of the disciples said anything. They were all looking at me, but it felt like part of their gazes were directed towards Softie. Too bad for them, I already told Softie not to ruin the surprise. And Ilya likes watching people as they wait in dread, so there's no chance she'd ruin it either. Wait a minute….

Why are the disciples waiting in dread!? This is supposed to be a fun surprise! I'm giving them swords, not killing their pets! "Stop looking so glum, damnit! You're ruining my good mood." I pointed at the terrified woman standing next to Softie. "You there, laugh!"

"Eh-he-ha-ha-hee...."

...The fuck kind of laugh was that? Alright. My good mood is officially ruined. I knew everything was going too well: My perfect plan to attract attention worked. My perfect plan to pose as the Bloody Bull Sect leader worked. My perfect plan to take everything in the armory worked. My perfect plan to steal the crown prince's sword is going to work. But the people around me can't see that. Look at how terrified they are of going to the Gates of Hell! Ah, the woes of being a genius with no peer, no one can understand me. Except Ilya.

"Why did you call us, Chosen Lucia?"

Ah! One person was brave enough to speak up! He's the fellow that normally drives the boat, yes? I think he is. Wait, if he's standing there now, then who's driving!? Oh, there's an auto-pilot mode for flying in straight lines. I almost made a fool of myself. "Here, catch."

A sword flew through the air, and its pommel perfectly hit the brave disciple's forehead. He fell over with a thud, unconscious. ...I have a feeling that these people stand no chance in a real war. Didn't they rack up a lot of experience while pillaging Kong County? These were the strongest hundred determined by a tournament that Softie's grandpa insisted on holding! I only threw the sword lightly. The woman standing next to the unconscious driver shook him awake. "Where am I?" he asked in a groggy voice. He grabbed the sword that was lying on his chest. "What's this?"

"It's an earth-realm-ranked sword! It's yours now."

The driver's mouth fell open as the murkiness in his eyes instantly cleared. "An e-earth-realm-ranked sword? F-for me!?"

"That's right!"

The driver scrambled onto his knees and knocked his forehead against the floorboards nine times in quick succession. "Thank you, Chosen Lucia! I swear to follow you for the rest of my life! Even if you ask me to swim through a sea of flames or climb a mountain of swords naked, I will do it without hesitation!"

Whoa. Isn't that a bit of an overreaction? His forehead's bleeding from his kowtowing. It was just a sword....

"Seriously?"

"I'm serious! Chosen Lucia can order me, Passionate Cloud, to do anything and I will comply without hesitation!"

He said it twice; he must be serious. Should I test it? "Alright. Then here's my first order." I pointed towards the side of the boat. "Jump off." We're over a hundred feet in the air! I wouldn't get hurt from falling from this high, but these people are a lot more brittle than me. They had to fly down on their swords to prevent injuries back when we were invading other sects.

"For Chosen Lucia!" Passionate Cloud ran towards the side of the boat and leapt with his arms spread out to the side. He really did it! There was no hesitation either! Is an earth-realm-ranked sword really that valuable...?

"S-shouldn't you catch him?" Softie asked.

Ah! I forgot!

"It's too late," Ilya said. "We're only a hundred feet in the air. It'll take him roughly three seconds to hit the ground, and Lucia was standing around in a daze for two seconds. And it took you one second to ask that question. The question you should've asked was, is he still alive? And the answer to that is, most likely because we're flying over a body of water."

Has Ilya fallen from a hundred feet in the air before? How does she know how long it takes? …It's a mystery. Alright, I'll teleport down there and save Passionate Cloud real … quick. Never mind. "Hey, Softie, go fly down there and bring him back."

"Is something wrong?" Softie asked, but she took out her flying sword anyway.

"Uh-huh. I can't do it, but you can. Hurry up and save him before he drowns." I can't swim. And he's slowly sinking into a large body of water, so someone else has to save him. One day, I'll conquer my fear of water. Maybe in like … never. Yeah. That sounds good. Water is an unnecessary force of evil in this world. Right. I should get rid of all the water instead of learning how to swim. That makes much more sense! Whew, I'm glad I have this necklace of intelligence.

While Softie went down to pick up Passionate Cloud, I distributed the rest of the earth-realm-ranked swords. I had enough for everyone and more! I bet Durandal would've liked me to save all of them for him to eat, but he's an asshole who lied to me about being virile. This serves him right! Eh? I'm distributing these swords out of generosity, not out of pettiness! Sheesh. Do one good deed and everyone questions your integrity.

"Thank you for the sword, Lucia." Softie smiled at me and hugged the sword that I gave her to her chest. "Our Shadow Devil Sect only has three earth-realm-ranked swords, but with these, we'll definitely be the strongest sect in King Province."

I thought the Shadow Devil Sect was really rich, but they only had three earth-realm-ranked swords? "How much is an earth-realm-ranked sword worth, just wondering?"

"Close to a hundred billion spirit stones," Softie said.

"A hundred billion…." How much is that in thousands?

"You'd have to take the underwear of every person in ten thousand sects to buy a single sword," Ilya said and paused, "assuming each person only had one set of unwashed underwear."

Thanks, Ilya. Ten thousand is … four zeros? That's…, fuck! That's a lot! That many people for one sword!? I-it's not too late to take all these swords back, is it? But they all pledged their undying loyalty to me…. Alright, fine! I'll be sure to get my hundred billion spirit stone's worth of use out of each and every one of them!

Chapter 18

For a place called the Gates of Hell, this place looks a lot like heaven! The buildings are bright and shining. The sun's overhead and lighting up the brilliant green grass. People are lying about and cultivating out in the open. It's so … picturesque. That's a word, right? The necklace of intelligence is warming up, so it's definitely agreeing that it's a word. Wait a minute…, didn't Ilya say the necklace heated up when I was under the attack of an illusion? "Who's attacking me with illusions!?"

"Oh? Newcomers?"

"They look like province-exchange winners. They only sent one earth-realm expert?"

"Well, we were running out of fodder anyway."

"Hey, Softie. They're looking down on you." I poked Softie, who was trembling while staring at the grassy meadow. "Softie?"

"Ah?" Softie stopped shivering and looked at me when I grabbed her shoulder. "Lucia? Was that an illusion? I, I really thought we were in hell…."

So there was an illusion! I need to reward Ilya some more. She's so useful. "What did you see?"

"It was very similar to the great massacre you performed at the cultural exchange a year ago back at the sect. Lots of blood and screaming and death." Softie shook her head and bit her lower lip. "At least it was just an illusion."

"It might've been an illusion, young lady, but that's just a glimpse of the true battlefield." Someone appeared on the deck! He was slim and feminine and completely not imposing at all. Maybe he was a woman? His black hair was even longer than mine, going past his butt and down to his knees! When he sits, does he sit on his hair? Doesn't it get dirty really fast? "Oh? It seems like someone recognizes me." The long-haired man smiled at me. "And which sect might you ladies be from?"

"Do you recognize him, Lucia?" Softie whispered.

"Nope. The only transvestite I know is Snow."

"Kuack! T-transvestite?" The long-haired man made a very strange coughing sound as if he choked on a roasted duck while laughing. "W-which part of me looks like a transvestite?"

"Your hair."

"Just his hair?" Ilya asked. "Don't you mean his dress? He's wearing a dress."

Well, it's easier for a man to wear a dress than it is for a man to grow out his hair for years. "No, I'm pretty sure it's the hair. Cause a man in a suit with long hair like his can still be mistaken for a woman, but a short-haired man will only be mistaken for a woman while wearing a dress."

Ilya paused. "That placebo's working really well…."

Placebo? What placebo? Is that a type of fish? Ilya mutters the strangest things sometimes. No wonder why she mutters them; people will think she's crazy if she says them out loud. "Anyways! We're from the Shadow Devil Sect. Where's the crown prince?"

The transvestite looked like he wanted to cry. I know this expression! He's about to develop a heart devil. I wonder why. Maybe he didn't intend to look like a woman? But why would he dress that way if that wasn't the case? Mm. People are strange. The transvestite sighed. "There are many crown princes at the Gates of Hell, but I assume you're looking for the crown prince of Kang Country, right, young lady?"

"Yup." I'm here to steal his sword, but Fat Sky gave me a legitimate reason to approach the crown prince. "He's supposed to be my direct superior."

"Your direct superior?" The depressed expression on the transvestite's face disappeared as his eyes widened. He looked around before leaning towards me. "You might not want to say that out loud," he whispered and gestured around with his eyes. Dozens of people had awoken from their cultivation and were staring at me. "There are many people here who wished to be the prince's subordinates but were rejected. If they find out someone like you is a subordinate of the prince, there will be no end to your troubles."

"Eh? No end to my troubles? But my troubles always stop when I hit them." Except for when I have to find a stupid sword for stupid Durandal because he's so picky! Gah. It's a shame I can't hit him into existence. I can only hit things out of existence. Woe is me.

"The people that the prince rejects are all strong. They're always earth-realm experts. People in the saint realm don't even dare to approach him. It's better for you to lay low since you're new. I'm only telling you this out of goodwill." The transvestite paused. "Though I'm not sure why I'm doing that. You've hurt my dignity quite a bit. But putting that aside, you should do your best to be humble or those slighted people will pick fights with you."

"Why would I have to be afraid of a bunch of rejects? They were rejected because they were weak, right? If they try to do something funny, I'll beat them up and take their underwear! I'm not afraid of losers." Hmm? Why's Softie tugging so frantically at my sleeve?

"L-Lucia! They're all coming this way!" Softie yelled in a whisper. How does one yell in a whisper? I'm not sure, but Softie did it. All the cultivators who were sitting around in the grass were flying towards us to pay their respects. Right? I mean, I'm someone who wasn't rejected; it's clear they'd respect me.

One person with gray hair—how come so many people have gray or white hair?—slipped ahead of the pack with his sword drawn. Is that a sky-realm-ranked sword? I don't think it is. "It's easy for you to call others a loser when you've never been here before, but I cannot accept your arrogance, Junior. Today, I'll teach you a lesson in humility!"

Was he talking to me? What arrogance? I'm not arrogant; I'm confident! There's a big difference. One means I believe I'm better than everyone. And the other means I know I'm better than everyone. Hmm. Is there a word for both confident and arrogant? I believe *and* know I'm better than everyone. Mm. As a humble person, of course, I won't say that out loud! But I'm not going to not beat this person up and steal his sword! Who does he think he's picking a fight with? I'll teach him not to be overconfident for the cheap price of one earth-realm-ranked sword!

***

Lucia has this special aura about her that … attracts trouble. It's part of why she's so suitable for cultivating the Heart Devil Cultivation Technique. I've only known her for a little more than over a year, but I've experienced more world-changing events with her than I have in my whole life. When she first arrived, she started a great massacre at a cultural exchange. Then she started a reign of terror, pillaging and uprooting sect after sect until finally eradicating the Star Phoenix Sect completely. She was just as unruly at the King Province Exchange, murdering all the delegates of the Righteous Buddha Sect. And now she's crippling officer after officer in Kang Country's army. If these beatings weren't taking place at the arena of grudges, Lucia would be executed for treason. I wish she wouldn't rob her opponents' swords though….

"Who's next?" Lucia asked. She was standing on the bloody stage, leaning against her hammer's hilt. The head of the hammer was resting on the ground, bits of flesh and bone coating its metal surface. Lucia's tail swished against the stage, her fur turning red, and she swept her gaze over the officers and soldiers who had come to watch. "No one?"

The arena of grudges was silent as people shifted their eyes away. A dull thudding sound echoed through the air. Was someone clapping? I turned my head towards the sound. A man, who resembled Heavy Sky, was applauding at a deliberate pace while walking towards the stage. "You must be Lucia Fluffytail from the Shadow Devil Sect. My brother told me he found a talent worthy of serving under me. It seems like he wasn't wrong." Instead of wearing a purple cloak with a clasp like his brothers, the crown prince had on a dark-green military uniform. It was loose without wrinkles, a little like a robe, but at the same time, it portrayed a sense of dignity. The belt on his waist had four blue stripes on it, signaling his rank as a general. My grandfather made me study the norms of the army after Lucia won the King Province Exchange for our sect.

Speaking of Lucia…, she looked tense. Her tail was puffed out like a hedgehog, and her shoulders were slightly hunched as if she were staring at a puddle of water. She's very suspicious of water. "Right," Lucia said as her feet slid back by an inch. "Fat Sky sent me here to be your subordinate. You're the crown prince?"

"Fat Sky?" the crown prince asked and raised an eyebrow. He mumbled, "Heavy, fat, I suppose they're almost similar in meaning." The prince coughed. "Yes, I'm the crown prince, Single Sky."

"Your name is Single?" Lucia asked. She was still steadily inching backwards. I probably wouldn't have noticed if I wasn't staring at her feet. Every other part of her body was stiff. Why was I staring at her feet? B-because…, just because, alright? "Wait, no, that's not important. You have a sky-realm-ranked sword, right?"

The crown prince gestured towards the sword hanging from the belt on his waist. "I do. Why? Did you want to try to take my sword as well?"

The people that Lucia had stripped and robbed flinched at the crown prince's words. Lucia was definitely going to try. After all, this is what she came here for. She grabbed her hammer's hilt and raised it into the air. Then it disappeared. Huh? It disappeared? Why? Lucia coughed and shook her head. "Of course not! What kind of person do you think I am? I don't take people's swords unless they do something to deserve it. Mhm." She coughed again. "But if you happen to have a spare sky-realm-ranked sword, I wouldn't mind if you gave it to me."

Lucia … was giving up? No way! She's fought against plenty of sky-realm experts without backing down. Maybe there's a special reason that Lucia's taking into consideration. But Lucia never thinks before she acts…. No, that's not true. She makes plans all the time, but she looks like she acts without thinking to fool her enemies. I always thought she was a simple person, but looking back, everything she's done really has worked out in her favor. If she's not a genius pretending to be a fool, then doesn't that mean I, the person who's achieved nothing, am more useless than a fool? Lucia's plotting something right now and taking away the crown prince's sword goes against her designs. That must be it.

The crown prince chuckled. "I do happen to have a spare sky-realm-ranked sword, but I can't just hand it over to you. Everyone here is striving for it after all. But with enough merits, you can earn it, or you can even hire Kang Country's sky-realm smith to personally forge a weapon for you."

"Hmm?" Lucia tilted her head. "How do I get merits? Can I take them from people?"

A faint smile appeared on the crown prince's lips. "You're quite the interesting woman. It's possible to take merits from other people in a sense, but it's easier to earn them yourself.

You receive merits for every enemy head you bring back. You can take the heads from your allies, or you can kill the enemy yourself. If you want to hire our sky-realm smith, you'll need to bring back the heads of ten sky-realm experts or ten thousand earth-realm experts'. If you just want the sword without any personalization, it costs five sky-realm experts' heads or five thousand earth-realm experts'."

"Five?" Lucia asked. "That doesn't seem like a lot. I can count that high on one hand! That actually sounds pretty easy."

"Fang Country only has twenty sky-realm experts deployed at the moment," the crown prince said. "And they don't move often; they're the final line of defense. You'll have to create a great ruckus to draw them out, but they're a bunch of cowards; all of them will come out to suppress you if you do."

That makes sense. The longer someone is alive, the more attached to life they become. There's no reason for them to risk their lives in a battle. I imagine our side's experts have the same thought process. Neither side wants to make the first move—that's the nature of this perpetual battlefield. The weaker people fight under the supervision of the strong.

Lucia stared at the crown prince's sword. Then she squinted at his face before sighing. "How strong are they compared to you?"

"Most of them are weaker, but three of them are on par, and one of them is barely stronger."

Lucia scratched her head. "Then what about panties?"

"...Excuse me?"

Lucia bobbed her head up and down. "How many heads do I need to exchange for sky-realm-ranked panties?"

I don't think the army supplies underwear.

The crown prince shook his head. "We only have saint-realm-ranked boxers."

...Why does the army supply underwear?

Lucia clicked her tongue. "Darn."

***

This crown prince is way too strong! Even after he left, my tail didn't settle down until after I ate a meal. Stealing a sky-realm-ranked sword is easier said than done, huh? And the only other option is to collect people's heads! I'm not a murderer; that's something I can't do. Why couldn't the prince have demanded penises instead? Cutting those off isn't murder. Hah. Well, just because I refuse to kill people doesn't mean I can't collect any heads for merits. All I have to do is rob our allies! The crown prince said that was allowed. I'm not sure why though; doesn't that make absolutely no sense at all? Why would he want infighting in his army? Well, I'm not going to question it!

But it probably is easier to collect heads myself.... Do I go against all my principles and commit murder for Durandal's sake? I'm a good, moral, upright person! I can't do that. Oh! What if I beat the enemies to near death and then have my minions harvest their heads? That way, I won't be responsible for killing them. At most, I'd be an accessory to murder, and that's totally morally okay. And since I gave all my minions earth-realm-ranked swords, they all pledged to do whatever I say. There shouldn't be any issues at all. It's settled then! My genius shines through once again.

Wait a minute.... I could get even more merits if I did both! I'll beat up enemies *and* rob my allies! Wow, I knew I was a genius, but this necklace of intelligence makes me a super-duper even smarter genius with better ideas! Collecting five thousand earth-realm experts' heads will be a cinch. Hmm? Five sky-realm experts' heads? Not happening! If four people as scary as the crown prince are going to show up along with the rest of the sky-realm experts, then I'll die. And I don't want to die, so I won't do anything to provoke them.

Durandal might call me a coward for picking on those weaker than me, but he's not here to judge me, so it doesn't matter. Besides, I'm doing this for him. If he complains about the method I used to stick him in a sky-realm-ranked sword, I'm sincerely going to go on a quest to find sky-realm-ranked panties.

Alright, first things first, we have to settle down in the barracks that were assigned to us. The army camp is nothing like the one back when I was a punching bag for the Ravenwood army. Instead of a dreary place with rotted wooden planks and straw roofs, this training ground is a lot more natural. And, by that, I mean our barracks is a hole in the ground. ...Again. What's with cultivators and their obsession with living like moles!? It's a good thing I stole so many buildings from those sects. Sheesh. These caves don't even keep rainwater from soaking into the ground and creeping up on their inhabitants' butts when they meditate. How are cultivators going to be immortal if they catch a cold?

Anyways, we have a week of rest before we're required to join the battlefield. I don't know why the crown prince thinks we're tired, but he ordered us to standby at the base, and no matter what, we shouldn't approach the warzone until a week is up. But I don't want to wait a week before I can acquire merits! That's why I'm going to place this mansion down by the entrance to the camp, right by this watchtower. As soon as the watchtower signals someone is coming, I'll go outside and rob them! The crown prince said we're not allowed to fight in the camp unless it's at the arena of grudges, so I have to leave the camp first. I'm following the rules like an obedient soldier! Military discipline is very important, mhm. If a soldier doesn't obey orders, then the whole structure will collapse and the soldier will be whipped a hundred times with barbed leather. At least, that's how it was back in the Ravenwood army. I don't care if this army's structure collapses, but I don't want to be whipped again!

"She's not listening."

Who's not listening? Wait, who said that? Ilya?

"...When did she stop listening?" Softie asked. They were both following me around as I set down my furniture in the mansion. I don't have much, just a bed and lots of pillows. But the pillows have to be arranged in a certain way under the blanket to make it seem like Durandal's waiting for me.

"She never stopped listening," Ilya said. "After all, you can't stop what you never started."

"Lucia? Hello?" Softie's fingers crept close to tug on my sleeve. She does that a lot to get my attention. I'm not sure why.

"Hmm? What's up?"

Softie lowered her head and looked up at me through her eyelashes. She's so frail and soft-looking! I'm jealous. Even her voice sounded like a helpless maiden that you just wanted to protect from everything. If I swapped vocal cords with her, would I have her voice? Hmm. "What do you think about what I said earlier? About the formation we should employ."

"The what we should what?" Employ a who? I'm not hiring anyone. "Explain from the top."

Softie nodded. If she were like Ilya, she would've sighed and hung her head, but Softie's a lot more patient. "The battlefield is going to be hectic, with thousands of people on the field at the same time. We—"

"Halt! Who goes there?"

Softie's brow wrinkled. "Maybe we should relocate the mansion to some place less noisy. How about—"

And once again, she was cut off by the shouts coming from outside the open window. "This is Captain Smoke. We've finished the patrol. Requesting permission to enter."

That's my signal!

"L-Lucia!? Where are you—"

I didn't get to hear the rest of Softie's question because the wind rushing past my ears drowned out her voice. She should really learn how to speak louder. Anyways, there's this giant defensive formation surrounding the camp that kind of looks like a fence made of light. Softie told me people could leave the camp without an issue, but they'd be attacked by the formation if they tried to enter without permission. Before this formation goes down, I have to seize Captain Smoke's merits! They're much more useful in my hands; thus, it's totally okay for me to take them from him. But first, I have to make sure I can take him on in a fight! ...My tail's nice and springy, perfect. And since I shouldn't hurt my allies, I'll use my non-lethal technique! "Heart Devil Apparition!"

This defensive formation tickles! It makes me want to scratch my ears when I pass through. Mm. Anyways, there's a big group of people waiting outside standing in neat rows. And my heart devil predator, who I named Fluffles, grew in size and swallowed them all in one bite. A few chewing sounds accompanied by screams later, Fluffles disappeared and left behind a bunch of shivering and sobbing men. They didn't even notice me when I took their stuff, and ... there's no heads. Why aren't there any heads in any of the rings? "Hey, Captain Smokey?"

"Gah!!!"

...Mm. Well, at least I planted a few heart devils. And I got some underwear! I wonder if that succubus sect will pay more if they're soiled. "Lucia Fluffytail, requesting permission to enter the camp!"

***

I wanted to discuss squad formations with Lucia, but she jumped out the window and ran off somewhere.... Did I say something wrong? "Ilya? What was that about?"

"She probably smelled something nice and wanted to eat it," Ilya said and shrugged as she sat on Lucia's bed. I want to defend Lucia, but ... there's a high chance Ilya's right.

"Anyway, you won't get anywhere discussing battle formations with Lucia. She does her own thing, and I wouldn't trust her to be a competent commander. Imagine she runs off in the middle of a battle because someone shot her in the heart again. Then what do we do?" Ilya snorted and rolled her eyes. Then she held out her hand towards me as if she were expecting me to hand something over. "Let me see what you've come up with."

My grandfather gave me these formations before we left, saying they were the special formations of our Shadow Devil Sect that would allow us to defend ourselves from an earth-realm expert with a group of a hundred saint-realm disciples. But the gulf between the earth realm and the saint realm is really too vast to fill up with only a hundred saint-realm experts. The formations only exist to buy time for Lucia to save us. There's also a formation that allows us to share qi amongst each other through heart devil worms. Ilya doesn't cultivate like a normal person though…. I suppose it couldn't hurt to let her take a look at the formations; after all, she is my grandmother's personal disciple.

Ilya took the jade slip out of my hand and squinted at it. A moment later, she nodded and passed it back to me. That was quick! I put the slip away and hesitated. It took me a day to digest everything inside that slip. Maybe Ilya didn't understand? "You … absorbed all the information? Already?"

Ilya raised an eyebrow. "Hmm? What do you mean? There were only ninety-nine formations, right? And most of them shared the same principles behind them. You could probably merge around thirty of them with each other to reduce the number while increasing the effectiveness."

…The difference between Lucia and Ilya is too great. Lucia suffers from a tremendous headache when she absorbs even the tiniest bit of information. Ilya can absorb a tremendous amount of information in an instant—no wonder why Lucia keeps Ilya by her side. As for me, I'm … just average. But forget my lack of ability for now! What did Ilya mean by these formations could be merged? "Our ancestors came up with these formations, and they've worked perfectly as they are. I don't think we should merge them."

Ilya rolled her eyes. "I mean no disrespect to your ancestors, but just because something's working perfectly fine doesn't mean it can't be improved. A lot of people like to say, if it's not broken, don't fix it. But that's a problem. Where's the need for innovation if everyone becomes complacent, content with what they have?"

"But our ancestors were wise!"

"So what, does that mean you're dumb?" Ilya snorted. "You can't improve on the works of someone who's long dead? This is why you've been living in a literal hole in the ground for the majority of your life. Yeah, my ancestors had bows and arrows and those worked perfectly for capturing prey to eat and survive. But that doesn't mean bows and arrows can't be improved. Nowadays, we've taken those bows and arrows and infused them with magic. We can destroy a country with them by shooting lightning bolts from over a mile away."

That's...

"And all of you are like this. Every single person in this Immortal Continent thinks like you do. Why? I've overheard so many conversations between disciples where they're hoping to discover the tomb of a long-dead super-strong expert so they can become exactly like them. I mean, really? Hello? The expert died without becoming an immortal and you want to follow his footsteps on the road to immortality? Isn't that like asking a cow to teach you how to play the harp? What would a dead person know about living forever?"

But...

"I haven't seen a single person here try to innovate for themselves. The alchemists in the sect follow recipes from ancient times that were so damn long ago that some of the ingredients have gone extinct! I looked through those martial techniques in the skill pavilion, and the person at the front desk told me the most popular technique originated ten thousand years ago from a sky-realm expert. Ten thousand years! Have only idiots been born in that time? How do you not improve a technique after ten thousand years? Hell, in the eighty years after the Godking's death, magic's advanced by huge leaps and bounds."

Ilya's so … forceful.

"Wait. Are you crying?" Ilya's face froze. "I don't think I said anything that'd make you cry…. Certainly, I didn't say anything that I need to apologize for."

"I-it's not what you said. It, it's the way you said it." I thought I toughened up a bit after being with Lucia for so long, but I still get really nervous when I'm yelled at and the tears just come out by themselves. I can't help it! I know Ilya wasn't yelling at me, and she was just ranting, but … it's scary.

Ilya sighed and took out a jade slip. She pressed it against her head before holding it towards me. "Here. I did some quick mental math and merged the formations. These formations should be around three times better than the previous ones, whether in power or efficiency. Take the squad and compare these formations to the previous ones, alright?"

That's not something normal people can do in their heads! Mental math is like adding two and two, not creating new formations while calculating their efficiency! Ilya's just as ridiculous as Lucia…. I wonder if she realizes it. But why would Ilya help me? I thought she hated me. "A-are you sure you want to give this to me?"

Ilya pressed the slip into my hands. "You think you're the only one stuck in this battlefield? I'm going to do everything I can to improve my chances of survival and having allies with a better formation should help a lot. Ideally, I wouldn't even have come here at all, but I have to follow Lucia since she's my ticket home. So, look, I don't care if you like Lucia in the way a woman likes a man or whatever. Just stop trying to get rid of me because I'm not going to leave. And if things ever escalate between you and Lucia, I'll be sure to step out of the room and give you your privacy."

W-what is she saying!? M-me and Lucia? Engaging in the activities of a woman and a man? "W-who's the man!?" Wait! That's not what I should be asking!

Ilya didn't react to the obvious blush on my face. I think I could cook an egg if I pressed it against my cheek. "Wouldn't it be Lucia? She's not girly at all."

"Who's not girly at all!?" Lucia's head poked in through the window. How, how long was she there? "Stay right there, Ilya!"

Ilya's face paled and she tried to run away. I say tried because she wasn't successful. "W-wait! Lucia! Stop! I just fixed my hair!"

***

A week passed by pretty quickly. I decided to cultivate the Heart Devil Cultivation Technique since I hadn't done it in a while and I was bored. Because of that, I received a lot of compliments and words of praise from people inside of the army camp. When I cultivate, the skies turn black from all my heart devil wormies! I think I figured out why people lived in caves without doors. It's for them to show off their techniques when they cultivate! Instead of these people surrounding the mansion and peeking through the window, if I cultivated in a cave with a large entrance, they would've been able to see me more clearly. I can't believe all cultivators are so vain, gosh. Immortals should be more modest, like me.

Other than cultivating on the roof of the mansion, I robbed every single person that requested entry back into the camp. Sadly, I only found two earth-realm experts' heads even though there were over hundreds of people. It turns out robbery is extremely rampant on both sides, and the people who were making their way back had had their merits plundered already. Ilya said it made sense since every cultivator was a greedy selfish bastard that didn't care about their countries. Softie said that wasn't the case, but Ilya shut her down through some arguments that I didn't bother to remember. Besides, it doesn't matter why people are being robbed; the only thing that matters is the fact that people are robbing my prey before I can!

But now, I'll finally be able to rob them first! We've received our first mission: Retake eastern outpost number 33421. I don't know where that is, but it doesn't matter. The mission doesn't have a time limit. I'm going straight to the heart of the battlefield to beat people up so my minions can harvest their heads! Wow, that sounds pretty brutal. But I'm not the one doing the killing, so my hands are clean. Mhm. Then, once I have all the heads required for a sky-realm-ranked sword, I'll go capture that outpost and report back. I'll redeem the heads, get my sword, plant Durandal in it, and then desert the army! Hmm. Should I desert the army? It's punishable by death…, but at the same time, I don't want to stay in the army forever. Eh? What was that, necklace of intelligence? I can just apply to leave? Genius! That works too. I'll just quit when the time comes.

And now we're traveling along the road, riding our carriage which is totally not a flying boat that's on the ground. Flying isn't allowed here, sincerely, sincerely not allowed. I tried going up because most rules don't apply to me, but my tail stiffened and I had a really bad feeling that something terrible would happen if I flew a little higher. Some rules are meant to be followed, especially when they concern my well-being! All the other ones can usually be disregarded with enough strength. Mm. I love this Immortal Continent. As long as you're strong, you can do anything you want. It also means people who are stronger than me can do anything they want to me, but I know how to avoid bullies like them.

"This isn't the way to eastern outpost number 33421," someone said from beside me. I'm cultivating on deck so people can see me more clearly to heap praises on me, but sometimes there are people like this person wearing green robes that try to talk to me instead of flattering me. Jeez, get with the program, Mr. Green Robe! Wait. Green robe?

"Uh, who are you?" The Shadow Devil Sect only wears black except for me; I wear pink and black. No one wears green! Our carriage has been infiltrated already? Or I'm in an illusion. Mm, nope. The necklace didn't heat up or break. Maybe the illusion fools me into thinking I'm not in an illusion by not breaking the necklace? ...I need a backup necklace to disillusion the illusion cast on my counter-illusion necklace. I'll have Ilya make that one give me intelligence too. Then I'll be doubly smart! Why didn't I think of this earlier? Ooh, I could be triply smart! Or, or..., uh, fourtimely? I think it's fourtimely. I'll be fourtimely smart!

"I thought I introduced myself to you, Heart Devil Lucia. I'm the navigator that the crown prince sent to acquaint you with the battlefield."

Mm? The crown prince put a chaperone on me? That's..., does he not trust me? I'm totally trustworthy! I haven't even done anything that'd make me suspicious yet! Why did he preemptively try to prevent me from straying off course? Hmm.... He must be a very cautious or paranoid person. That must be it. "Well. How do you know this isn't the way to eastern outpost number 33412?"

"Eastern outpost 33421," the person in green robes said while lowering his head. Was he trying to flatter me? He should've done this from the start instead of talking. Then I wouldn't have to figure out an excuse to explain why we're going the wrong way. "The direction is in the outpost's name. We're currently heading west."

"No, we're not. We're heading east." When in doubt, deny everything!

"The sun rises from the east and it is currently behind us. It would be ahead of us if we were traveling east."

Hmm? Is that how you can tell directions? That would've been nice to know a lot earlier. I'll keep that trick in mind, but for now, I'll still deny everything! "The sun rises from the west."

"...Then let's head to western outpost 33421."

"What? Why? We were given orders to go east. I'm not changing routes now!" This person is sneakier than I thought! Instead of trying to prove that the sun rose from the east, he decided to forfeit logic instead!

"I made a mistake. The orders were to go to western outpost 33421." The green-robed person bowed at me. "I apologize for the miscommunication."

...What am I supposed to deny now? I guess I can refuse his apology? "Mm, well, if you made a mistake once, then you'll make a mistake again. We're continuing the course!"

The green-robed person's brow wrinkled, but it smoothed out in an instant. "Heart Devil Lucia, did you know that you're a bit unreasonable?"

"She can turn a sky-realm expert into a boneless flesh jelly by pinching him. She's allowed to be unreasonable." Ilya appeared from the cabin door leading up to the deck. Hey. I'm a very reasonable person! Sheesh, I always have reasons for the things I do—like because I want to. That reason's my favorite.

***

I've never participated in a war before. The Godking brought peace to the three factions, and though they threatened and postured at one another, a real battle never broke out. As the daughter of a duke, I've read a lot about wars and their effects on the economy, the people living in my territory, and the overall state of the world. So while my only experience with wars is through books and I'm no expert at warfare, I have a feeling—just a tiny one—that this is not how wars are meant to be fought.

"You two are making strange faces," Lucia said. "What's the paper say?"

Right. Lucia received an instruction manual on how to participate in the war from the navigator, and Lucia being Lucia passed it onto Softie and I to interpret it for her. And according to this manual, battles are conducted as one-on-one duels between two willing participants of the opposite sides. Not only that, but each soldier may only engage in one duel per day. How many years will it take Lucia to claim ten thousand earth-realm experts' heads if she follows these inane practices? I crumpled up the sheet of paper and burned it with a fireball. "It's a load of bullshit. Forget about it."

"Eh?" Lucia glared at the crown prince's navigator. "What are you wasting my time for?"

Softie lifted her hand to tug on Lucia's sleeve, but I stopped her. If Softie told Lucia about these rules, there was a chance—no matter how small—that Lucia might actually listen to them, and then I'd be an old woman by the time I returned home.

"I'm not wasting your time," the navigator said. "These are the rules of engagement between our two countries. Heart Devil Lucia, you didn't even read the paper; please, don't dismiss my words as nonsense."

"Well, I can't read!" Lucia smacked the navigator's head, and his knees buckled as his face turned as pale as a sheet. His eyes rolled up into his head and turned white. Lucia snorted and grabbed his collar and threw, no, she stripped him at the same time that she threw him overboard. Lucia's gotten really good at the most absurd techniques. How did she even manage to take his underwear too in that single motion? "Ah, finally.

Some peace and quiet. That person really nagged a lot; I'm glad he finally gave me an excuse to throw him overboard."

An excuse? "What excuse was that?" How is she going to justify her violence this time?

"He lied to me. That's mutiny!" Lucia's hair fluttered as she nodded and placed her hands on her hips. "Wait. Is it mutiny if he's not a part of my crew? Hmm. Anyways, he shouldn't have given me a paper filled with bullshit. Mhm."

So it's my fault. If I see that navigator again, I'll have to apologize. But some sacrifices are necessary for the greater good. And my goal of going home is the greatest good in the world. …I'm starting to sound like Lucia; it's all because she's around me almost all the time! I haven't even had time to myself to increase my circles properly. I'm stuck in the twelfth circle, which makes sense, I suppose. There's the proverbial wall that exists between the twelfth and thirteenth. The only thing I can do is continuously and methodically circulate my mana until I break through. I think the fact Lucia forced me to attune to all the elements while traveling from the third circle to the fourth back in the desolate mountains was a lot of help in setting up my foundation. Most magicians focus on one element, and that leaves the unused parts of their bodies weaker than the rest. But it's just a theory, and I'm the only sample; there's always the chance that I'm an outlier.

"Oh! Ilya, I just remembered." Lucia finished storing the poor navigator's items before smiling at me. "What did you do to my arms? You know, the ones that the mean bully cut off a while ago."

…She actually remembered something? I shouldn't have given her that stupid necklace! It doesn't even do anything except block illusions. I can't tell her what I did with her arms because then she'd—

"Ilya. I want to see. Now."

Well. "I, uh, turned them into jelly, you know, like Quick Shot's arm."

Lucia's eyes narrowed into slits. "You didn't eat them, right!?"

"Of course not!" That's sincerely cannibalism and completely wrong! "Look!" I took the two pink jellies out of my interspacial ring. I'm not sure why I made them into jelly if I knew I wasn't going to eat them. I could've used her bones and blood for something else, but when I actually started to refine them, I went on auto-pilot and turned them into jelly before I knew it.

Lucia frowned. "Why did you make them into jelly? Why not a stew? I would've tasted much better as a stew."

Is it still cannibalism if someone eats herself? Wait. She's having problems with the wrong thing! "I wasn't planning on eating you when I made this!"

"Nonsense! If you weren't planning on eating me, then why'd you turn me into food!?" Lucia took a step towards me, and a red blur flew out of the pouch by her waist.

"Moo! Mooo!"

And the jellies in my hands disappeared, replaced by a phoenix that had its beak stuffed to the brink with pink goo, its throat bulging from trying to swallow a mass that was larger than its head.

"This goddamn phoenix!" It keeps eating my finished products! "I'm going to cut it open!" I pulled out my knife, but the phoenix swatted at me with one wing. My vision filled with red and feathers before a spike of pain stabbed into my forehead. Then I lost consciousness.

When I woke up, I was lying on my bed. Next to me, on a chair, Softie was reading a book, a jar of medicine on the table by her side. Her eyes lit up as she closed the book and placed it down. "Are you alright?"

"I could be better." I circulated my mana to cast a simple healing spell on myself to remove my headache. Right, a simple twelfth-circle healing spell should work. ...But why does it feel like I can circulate my mana one more time for thirteen?

"You're very brave for trying to stab an earth-realm beast while still in the saint realm." Softie nodded. Was she being sarcastic? "If a phoenix was sitting on my arm, I'd be too terrified to do anything."

Thirteen circles! That stupid phoenix made me break through somehow! Alright, it's forgiven for eating the Lucia jelly. Now I have to figure out how that breakthrough logically worked so I can replicate it. If it happened, there must be a reason. I'll figure it out no matter what it takes! …Was Softie saying something? My lord, I'm becoming more like Lucia with every passing day.

***

Mr. Feathers ran away. He smacked Ilya over the head and teleported somewhere before I could catch him. I thought the egg was enough to keep him hostage! Err, I mean, compliant! Right. Mr. Feathers and I have a great relationship! I hold onto his egg as a set of emergency rations, and he stays as my stuffed animal that I hug to sleep sometimes. Mhm. But it was all ruined because Ilya fed him bits of me. Me! She turned my blood, bones, and beautiful skin into jelly! Not just one serving of jelly, two servings! Can you believe that? I'm so disappointed I didn't even get a taste. Humph. If I'm going to be eaten, it might as well be by myself, right? Well, actually, Ilya's cooking tends to suck a lot. Maybe it's better that I didn't get a taste. Hmm. Ah, whatever. If I ever need a soft and fluffy pet to cuddle with, I'll just force Softie to stop cultivating and have her sleep with me instead. She's softer than Mr. Feathers even though she doesn't have any downy fluff. I still haven't figured out why, but one day, I will.

But today's going to be an exciting day! We're finally approaching the real battlefield! I can't wait to see it. I bet there's going to be so much chaos that no one will even notice if I rob our allies. What happens if I bring back the heads of our allies...? Mm, the crown prince doesn't look that stupid, so he'll probably notice. It seems like I'll have to stick with only harvesting the heads of my enemies. But this is what I trained for for the majority of my life! I was in the Ravenwood army for so long, being beaten up and forced to do all the menial chores while lugging around the equipment for the actual soldiers to use. With this experience, I know everything there is to know about wars! I might not have been in one before, but I'm smart enough to not need experience. A smart person will learn from their experiences. A wise person will learn from others' experiences! That's me!

Let's see. The soldiers always boasted about what they'd do to the enemy while they were eating: They'd cut off the elves' ears and make necklaces out of them. They'd make stew out of beastkins' tails and force their prisoners to eat it. They'd string demons up naked, brand them, and parade them around the capital before ransoming them back. ...But what would they do to humans? I've only met human cultivators. Human ears aren't as long as elven ears, but I guess I can still make a necklace out of them. Mn. And humans don't have tails..., but they have penises...? I mean, if you squint really hard at the right angle, you can pretend that it's a type of tail. And I can always parade them around naked, but ransoming them back wouldn't really work since their heads will be gone. Ah, maybe the other side would want their corpses to make jellies out of? I'll try to ransom them back anyway.

"I'm sensing a lot of killing intent coming from that direction!"

"We must be approaching the battlefield. With this earth-realm-ranked sword that Chosen Lucia has bestowed upon me, I swear I'll bring back the heads of a thousand enemies!"

"But don't you think that killing intent is really dense? Will we be alright? Look, my knees won't stop trembling."

"You're an idiot! That killing intent is oozing out of Chosen Lucia! She'll lead us to victory at the cost of our opponents' gruesome deaths! We'll rip their hearts out of their chests and tear apart their stomachs as they beg us for mercy! We'll gouge out their eyes and drink bloody wine using their skulls as our goblets! Ah-ha-ha-ha-ha! Glory to the Shadow Devil Sect! Glory to Chosen Lucia!"

"…Has anyone else noticed that Brother Claw is a bit psychopathic? Or is it just me? It can't just be me, right? Someone else has to have noticed too. I'm a bit uncomfortable following his lead. Why did Sister Moonlight make him fourth-in-command?"

"Fourth-in-command? I thought Brother Claw was third."

"No, that's Sister Ilya. She's the one who gave us the revised and improved battle formations."

"Wait. Why are all of you speaking as if me being the fourth-in-command is a terrible thing?"

"It's not a terrible thing. It's just not … pleasant, Brother Claw."

"But Chosen Lucia is even more sadistic, psychopathic, and bloodthirsty than me, and she's the one in charge, but none of you feel uncomfortable following her."

"Chosen Lucia gave us earth-realm-ranked swords. Besides, I don't think Chosen Lucia will have us do something as gruesome as ripping their hearts out or tearing apart their stomachs. At most, she'll make us take underwear and interspacial rings off of corpses."

These minions of mine sure love gossiping. They're usually cooped up in their rooms, cultivating in isolation. They probably see another person once a week or less. It makes sense for them to gossip when everyone's outside and readying themselves for battle. But what kind of person did Softie place in charge? He sounds like a total psycho! And he's a liar. I'm not sadistic, psychopathic, or bloodthirsty! It's not like I beat people up and chop off their limbs because it's fun. A girl's gotta do what a girl's gotta do. It's a harsh world out there, and the only one watching my back is myself! Durandal watches my back too, but that's only because he wants to stab it when he sees me slacking off. …Why am I trying to find him a body again? Oh, right. Because I want children. Hah…, I wonder if my children will ever appreciate what I had to go through to give birth to them.

"We're entering a clearing!"

Oh? Are we here? There's a huge commotion beyond these trees! Faster, boat-carriage, faster! The sooner I get that sky-realm-ranked sword, the sooner I'll have kids! I'm on a timer, you know? I only have a decade or two before I become old and wrinkly—I have to have as many children as possible before that happens!

Chapter 19

We're here! …Right? What the heck is this? A tea party? "Uh…."

"Chosen Lucia, is this the right place?"

I think this person's name was Brother Claw. Should I call him Clawy? But then his nickname will be longer than his actual name…. Mm, I guess I'll just call him Claw. "I'm not sure. Where's that navigator?"

"He was stripped and thrown overboard," Claw said. He looks especially serious with that long scar running across his face. Where did he get that from? It looks like someone wanted to gouge out both his eyes but only had one knife, so he compromised and cut a diagonal line between them. Wait. Our navigator was stripped and thrown overboard? These minions are crazy! Why would they do such a thing!? What if we get lost, like now? Who was it? I'll teach them a lesson!

"Who threw him over?"

"You did," Claw said. His expression didn't change, which was nice because I feel silly now. Did I really throw our navigator overboard? "He gave you a paper filled with lies, so you decided to dispose of him."

Oh…, the navigator was that guy…. It's his own fault for lying to me! He should've said something, jeez. Then I wouldn't have gotten rid of him. Mm. Well, Ilya's close enough to a navigator. She's good at everything. "Where's Ilya? Is she awake yet?"

"I believe she is still resting. Sister Moonlight is watching over her as well," Claw said. "Sister Moonlight made me fourth-in-command. If you need someone to consult with, please, use me as you see fit."

"Alright, Claw, is this the right place?" Wait a minute.... Wasn't this guy the one asking me if it was the right place in the first place? Why am I asking him? Have I been bamboozled?

"We should pull over and ask that group of people," Claw said, pointing at the group ahead. It was a massive, massive group. Even if I had a hundred hands, I doubt I'd be able to count them all on my fingers. They were sitting in neat rows and columns, making a giant human square on the ground, and all of them had teacups in front of them, resting on pillows. They were wearing the green robes, or military uniform, that the crown prince was wearing. They seemed like allies. Should I rob them before or after I interrogate them?

"Alright, I'll go down and check it out." Why are these people sitting around drinking tea in the middle of a battlefield? I didn't get so lost that we went somewhere with civilians, right?

"Wait, Chosen Lucia, I'll come with you," Claw said. "Sister Moonlight said that none of us should let you proceed diplomatically with any party without supervision."

Oi. What the hell, Softie? Am I a child that needs to be chaperoned? She's the childish one. I'm older than her! When I get back, I'll teach her how bad children are punished—with a spanking! Alright, I'll grab Claw and teleport on over to..., I can't teleport? Odd. Well, one good jump will bring me there.

"Who are you!?"

Oops. I landed on someone. I underestimated my strength a little. "Hi. I'm Lucia Fluffytail from the Shadow Devil Sect. I just wanted to know, is this the battlefield for the Gates of Hell?"

"Get off of me!"

There's no space! I landed right in the middle of everyone, sheesh. If I get off of this person, I'll have to step on a different one. Mm. If I hit him over the head and knock him out, he won't complain anymore.

Thwack.

"Ahem. Like I was saying. Are you guys part of the army?"

"Commander! She killed the commander!"

…Hey. He's still alive, you know? This is so frustrating. Why does everyone keep on ignoring my questions? "He's not dead! I just made him sleep for a bit! Dammit, just answer my question or I'll cut his head off!"

"How dare you attack our commander. Taste my Flaming—"

"Stop it, you fool! She has the commander hostage!" One person stopped another from attacking. Then he cupped his hands at me. "This is certainly the battleground of the Gates of Hell. We were performing our morning ritual before entering into battle. May I know what squad you are a part of? I've never heard of the Shadow Devil Sect."

"Never heard of the Shadow Devil Sect?" Weren't we famous? I thought we were famous. How come these people haven't heard about us? Though, it's true that I don't know which sect he belongs to either. Hmm, I guess it's fair.

"The Shadow Devil Sect hasn't won the King Province Exchange for over hundreds of years. We're relatively unknown. Though we were the biggest in Kong County, we're nothing but a mere morsel on a very large dish."

Mere morsel on a very large dish. I like this Claw person's analogies! They make so much more sense than a frog stuck in a well. I mean, a frog stuck in a well's basically dead. But the saying means something else—so weird, huh? And what squad are we a part of…? I think the crown prince assigned us to one, but I wasn't really paying attention. Hmm. Softie should know! "I'm not sure what squad we're in. Ask someone else. But we're the direct subordinate of the crown prince."

"Which crown prince?"

It's a good thing the crown prince's name is so easy to remember because it's so absurd. "The single one."

"Single Sky?"

"Right. That's the fellow. Anyways, where's the battlefield? Where's the fighting? How come you guys have time to sit around and brew tea for this many people?" I don't get it. War is supposed to be chaotic and bloody and fun! Err, not fun. Serious. Right. War's serious!

"It must be your first time here. I don't know how wars are conducted in other places, but you should throw away all your preconceived notions of what war should be. In fact, a navigator should've given you the rules of warfare at the Gates of Hell."

It's the navigator once again. Why does that person always insist on foiling my plans? "Mm. Sure. So, how's the war conducted then? We don't charge at each other and hack away with our weapons?"

"No. Battles take place in the form of duels. After all, how can any victory be honorable if both sides aren't completely equal?"

War's not about honor....

"Even a sky-realm expert will fall if a thousand earth-realm experts attack him at once. To prevent needless deaths, both sides agreed to the conditions that you should've seen on the instruction manual."

"Wait." Wasn't I supposed to harvest heads? How does that work if there's no bloody battle? "How do I get merits then?"

"You cut off your opponent's head during the duel. Though, most of the time, people agree to surrender and pay a tribute instead if they lose."

Is this even a war anymore? "...What about cutting off people's ears and stringing them into a necklace? What about chopping off people's penises and making a stew out of them?

What about capturing prisoners and branding them with a hot iron before ransoming them back to their families?"

"We..., we don't do that around these parts.... That's ... not normal."

"And these rules were given on that instruction sheet?"

"That's correct. Everyone participates in one duel a day."

...No wonder why Ilya said it was full of bullshit. At the rate of one head per day, it'll take me five thousand days to get five thousand heads! That's like ... so many years! I can't wait that long! Hasn't anyone heard the saying, all is fair in love and war!? Cutting off penises and turning them into stew should be the norm! It'll strike fear into the hearts of my opponents! The victors of the war get to decide what's moral and immoral! What's wrong with the Immortal Continent? Honor? Duels? They're too civilized! Mm. It's clear that there's something wrong with this place. And when something is wrong, it's up to someone to fix it. I guess I'll be that selfless person who'll sacrifice herself for the greater good. With my abundant experience in warfare, I'll teach these people how a war should be conducted!

***

We were given a paper on the rules of engagement, but Lucia didn't read it. When I tried to tell her about it, Ilya stopped me for some reason. And now we're about to enter the battlefield, but I'm the only one who has any idea of what's supposed to happen! The battlefield is one giant arena with a thousand platforms for duels between individuals. It's nothing like what we were expecting. Battle formations are useless, and the risk of death is a lot lower, which is nice. I suppose this is the only way for the perpetual battle to have lasted so long. What other single conflict has persisted for over hundreds of years?

I'm starting to think the war between Kang Country and Fang Country is just a ploy, a distraction of sorts. Maybe other countries will think we're less threatening if all of our supposed resources were being spent on fighting each other. I don't claim to know anything about politics, but I can only view this war as senseless, and there's absolutely no reason to prolong it as much as it has been. But that's just my opinion, and I've lived for a far significantly less amount of time than the people who actually make decisions. There could be something that I'm not seeing, but it's not up to me to do anything about it. My goal is to bring the Shadow Devil Sect into prosperity by doing well on the battlefield. But we have to follow the rules to do that!

"It's right ahead," the naked person who was tied up behind Lucia said. He belonged to the Flaming Sparrow Sect. While I was watching over Ilya, Lucia defeated a squad of people through, what Brother Claw tells me, the ingenious use of hostages, threats, and blackmail along with lots of oaths to the heavens. Brother Claw's the strongest disciple other than Lucia and me; I thought having him in charge would somehow keep Lucia in check, but I realize now that nothing can keep Lucia in check except for Durandal. The only time I've seen Lucia act against her whims was when Durandal threatened her with a lack of … s-sex. I, I wonder if Lucia's the man in her relationship with Durandal too…. Does she prefer being on top? W-wait! What am I thinking!? T-this is all Ilya's fault for saying such embarrassing things to me before!

"Really…?" Lucia asked. "Where?" Her head swiveled back and forth like an owl's without pause. "I don't see a battlefield."

"It's hidden behind a formation," the man said. "Do you see that statue over there, between those three ash trees? Once you touch its head, everyone in the clearing will be transported inside."

"Mm, some more reality-bending nonsense." Lucia nodded. "Okay, got it. You're free to go now. Thanks for the help." Lucia placed her hands onto the railing of the boat before leaping over without hesitation. "Everyone off! It's time to harvest five thousand heads!"

…That sounds pretty gruesome. And did she just tell this poor man that he was free to go but left him tied up? Without warning, the boat disappeared, and I almost didn't react in time to pull out my flying sword. Only the tied-up man hit the ground; it seems like everyone else was already prepared for that. Why was Lucia in such a hurry? Speaking of Lucia, she was standing right next to the statue. For some reason, it looked different from just a few seconds ago as if—its head was on the ground!? S-she broke part of the formation!

"Hmm…." Lucia stared at the headless statue. Then she glared at the whimpering prisoner, whose leg was bending in a way it shouldn't have been bending. "Did you lie to me?"

"N-no! I swear—"

Screams filled the air. A shiver ran down my spine as the sky was torn apart in front of my very eyes. Shattered, hazy images of blood-soaked people shouting and exploding flickered in and out of existence as black lightning rained down from the clear blue sky. And just as quickly as the nightmarish scene appeared, it disappeared again, as if I had hallucinated all of it. I wasn't quite sure if that actually happened, or if I fell for another illusion like I had when we first entered the army camp.

"Oh," Lucia said. "That was weird. The statue's head's back too."

The statue's head? The statue had returned to pristine condition after those images appeared. Perhaps the formation that the battlefield resided in was destabilized for a moment by Lucia, and once the people inside stabilized it, the statue repaired itself too. But if we really saw inside the formation a moment ago…, I swear people were exploding, and I'm sure that's not natural! Don't tell me people died because Lucia destroyed part of the formation.

"It's working!" Lucia said, her tail flicking back and forth. Her hand was pressed against the statue's head, and white light crawled along the ground, filling in a circular formation that surrounded the clearing we were in. "You guys better be ready! No one's allowed to die! If any of you die in there, I'll kill you, got it?"

"Yes, Chosen Lucia!"

It's always hard for me to tell if Lucia is joking or not. When I think she's telling a joke, she's dead serious. When I think she's being serious, she tells me she's joking. It's very confusing. Ilya doesn't seem to have this problem; I wonder if she'll teach me if I ask her. I think our relationship has gotten better since she was smacked over the head by the phoenix. I do wonder what that phoenix was thinking when it fled. It left behind its egg. If Lucia and I had a child and Lucia died, there's no way I'd abandoned our child under any circumstance. ...Wait. There's something wrong with that sentence. What—

"Since no one here wants to accept my challenge, then I'll challenge those newcomers! You! The lady with the fox tail, get on the stage! I love eating fox meat!"

The scenery's changed; this place looks almost exactly like our Shadow Devil Sect's cultural exchange location—there's just a lot more platforms in the center. And someone on one of the platforms just issued a challenge to the newcomers, us, specifically Lucia. I feel sorry for him.

"Is that fatty challenging me?" Lucia asked and tilted her head. "Mm, I could use a quick warmup before I get serious. Alright!"

But, Lucia, you're only allowed to fight one person a day…. Please, follow the rules! There's at least ten million people here, and half of them are not on our side! They don't even have to use any techniques to kill us all; if all of them spat once, we'd drown in a lake of spit! I, I guess it won't be too late to tell Lucia about the rules after she's done with her fight since she's already on the platform….

***

"Who's that woman? It seems like it's her first time here."

"She can only blame her bad luck for being chosen by Butcher. Maybe he'll spare her if she begs."

What are these people saying? Spare me? Is this Butcher person scary? My tail is completely relaxed! There's no way this guy can be scary. Maybe if I was a cookie, I'd be scared of him. He's kind of pudgy, and it's clear he snacks a lot. I thought cultivators didn't eat because they were masochists or something. How did he get fat?

"At least she's not a beauty. It would've been truly unfortunate if that young miss who was beside her was chosen instead."

Oi. Which fucker called me ugly just now? It was that guy with the blue robes and…, why does he look so generic!? There are so many people who look exactly like him! There's no way I'm going to remember him to teach him a lesson! Mm. Fine. Every person in those blue robes and white bandana is going to be stripped and thrown into a dungeon once I get the chance.

"Nervous? Look around all you want, little fox. No one's going to help you," the fat man in front of me said. He was wearing a white robe, but it was covered in bloodstains, so it was red and brown and black. And he was using meat cleavers as weapons. "People call me Butcher! I'm an earth-realm expert who's killed over twenty earth-realm experts and over thousands of saint-realm fodders in the ten years I've been here! What's wrong? So scared that you can't even speak!?"

Mm. I'm having a hard time deciding whether I should use a hammer or an earth-realm-ranked sword. It'll be so much more satisfying to hit him with the hammer, but then he'd go flying and it'd be a pain in the ass to drag him back so my minions can harvest his head. But if I use a sword, I could cut off his limbs and I wouldn't have to go through that hassle. But it'll be so much less satisfying without the crunching sounds. Hah.... Why do I have to make such tough decisions? Being too good at so many things is so hard sometimes. Sword.... Hammer.... Sword...? Hammer.... Sword.... Fine, sword it is.

"Lucia! Watch out!"

Eh? He's running at me. Did the battle start? I wasn't ready! Why didn't anyone tell me it started!? This stupid cheater is trying to sneak attack me! "Madness Strike!" ...And there goes his legs. He didn't even try to block or dodge! I think he said he was an earth-realm expert? Great! Please, deity watching over my life, let every earth-realm expert be as weak as him! Struggle to grow strong? Fuck that! I'm not handicapping myself to artificially increase the difficulty like Durandal wanted me to. If I had a choice to fight a tiger or a baby duck, I'd pick the baby duck every time!

"Gah! My legs! My legs!"

Mm, I have a lot of fights to do today. If I didn't have this necklace of intelligence, I might've done something stupid like Madness Strike a defenseless target! That's such a waste of qi. I'll conserve my strength and remove his arms with my bare hands instead. I'll grab his bicep right here ... and place my foot on his chest like so ... and pull!

"Ah!!! Ah!!! My arm! She's insane! Somebody, help me!"

And I have to remove his other arm too. Can't be too careful. Mhm. What if he pulls something out of his interspacial ring? Just because someone only has one arm doesn't mean they can't be dangerous! I can't stop praising this necklace of intelligence. I'm so glad Ilya made it for me. It must've saved me at least three hours of trouble with the extra brain power it gave me.

Pop!

Okay! He's completely disarmed! Literally. It should be pretty safe to drag him back now. Hmm. Why's everyone so quiet? Ah! It's because I made my debut, isn't it? They're awestruck by how powerful I am. Hmph, hmph. Let's see these people call me ugly now! I dare them.

"L-Lucia. Why did you bring him over here…? You're supposed to take a tribute or take his head…."

"Yeah, I want to take his head, but I don't want to kill him, you know?" Killing is wrong. Well, no, not all killing is wrong. Murder is wrong. Mm, killing to eat is completely fine. "I don't want my reputation to be that of a murderer. That's why, one of you should do it."

"I'll do it!" Claw shot to his feet and cupped his hands at me. "I'm cultivating my family's secret technique that allows me to take the qi of the people I kill. Please, allow me, Chosen Lucia!"

What!? Stealing the qi from the people he kills? How vicious! That's the technique of an immoral murderer! "Can you give me that technique too?"

Softie tugged on my sleeve. "It's a secret family technique. It's impolite to ask that."

"That's not a problem, Chosen Lucia. I already swore to accompany you even through the depths of the underworld," Claw said and bowed. "But this technique can only be cultivated by a man; otherwise, you'll explode. Do you still want it?"

…What is this sexist cultivation technique? "Err, no. I'll pass." Exploding is the last thing I want to do. Actually, no, I don't want to explode at all.

Claw nodded at me before crouching next to the unconscious Butcher. He raised the sword I gave him into the air and chopped down with a grin on his face. …There's something wrong with Claw. He's not normal. Definitely not normal. Who smiles when he kills someone? Claw grunted and grabbed Butcher's head. "Here you go."

Well…, at least someone's willing to harvest heads for me! I'd feel bad if I made someone unwillingly become a murderer, like Softie. But since Claw doesn't seem to have any qualms about killing people, it all works out. I'll just stuff this head into my interspacial ring and wait for the next duel.

"I, Beast Tamer Forest, challenge any earth-realm expert or below!"

"Dibs! I call dibs!" There's a lot of people named Forest for some reason. I swear he's the third or fourth Forest person I've met so far. Or I could just be remembering things wrongly again. Mm. Well, it doesn't matter. It's my turn to fight again!

"You can only fight once a day, Lucia!" Softie grabbed my sleeve before I could run up there.

"Eh…." Right. That prisoner did say those were the rules, and there's an awful lot of people here. If I don't follow the rules, then they could all attack me at once! Teach these people warfare? Harvest everyone's heads with reckless abandon? Fuck that! I'll die if this many people gang up on me! I'll follow those rules, but I'm not going to slow down! With this necklace of intelligence, I've easily come up with a loophole! Err, ingenious idea! It's not a loophole. Nope. "How do you read this?"

"This nameplate?" Softie asked. "Flaming Sparrow Sect's core disciple, Fiery Rain."

"Okay! I'll just wear this nameplate like so…, and now I'm no longer Lucia Fluffytail. I'm Flaming Rain!"

"Fiery Rain."

"Fiery Rain!" There's no way my foolproof plan can fail! "I, Fiery Rain, accept your challenge, Beast Tamer Forest!"

***

There's no way Lucia's plan will work. She didn't even change clothes after putting on that nameplate. Wait, no, that's not the problem with her plan! She's the only fox—err, squirrelkin here! Her pretending to be someone else is going to end in a disaster. At most, she'll be prevented from fighting again, right? The penalty for disobeying the rules was a hundred lashes for everyone in the disobedient person's squad. I've never been lashed before.

"Stop! You're not allowed to fight more than once a day!" And someone's trying to stop Lucia already. Please, succeed.

"Eh? But this is my first time fighting!" Lucia completely disregarded our ally and hopped onto the stage where Beast Tamer Forest was waiting. "See, look! This nametag says Fiery Rain. The last person who was up here was Lucia Fluffytail. We look a lot alike because we're both foxkin, but we're not actually the same person. Mhm."

"That's right!" Brother Claw shouted. I nearly jumped from how loud he was. "Lucia Fluffytail is a chosen of our Shadow Devil Sect. That person, Fiery Rain, has nothing to do with our sect! She belongs to the Flaming Sparrow Sect."

There has to be someone who's in charge of this, right? If someone broke the rules, someone has to act as the judge. And with this many people gathered in one place, it'd be terrible if the rules were broken and a conflict erupted between the two sides. The mediator should show him or herself soon to prevent Lucia from disregarding rules that have persisted for hundreds of years.

"Hold it right there, little fox. Do you think we're idiots?"

There! That person who's flying in the sky. Flying's prohibited, but since he's up there, he has to be strong enough to disregard that rule. His nameplate says he's from the Ascending Phoenix Sect, but I've never heard of them before. They must either be weak, which is unlikely given that they have a sky-realm expert, or they're from Fang Country.

"Of course not!" Lucia shook her head back and forth. "I don't think you guys are idiots. I just know that I'm smarter than all of you. There's a difference!"

"...Are you trying to make me mad?"

"Me? Make you mad? I'm the one who should be angry here!" Lucia stomped her foot against the arena platform. "How dare you question my identity? This nameplate is clear for everyone to see! I belong to the Flaming Sparrow Sect, not the Shadow Devil Sect. My name is Fiery Rain, not Lucia Fluffytail!"

The sky-realm expert's expression darkened. "I don't recall Lucia Fluffytail ever introducing herself earlier when she faced Butcher. How do you know her name?"

"Err..., that's...." Lucia scratched her head and glanced around. I think she was looking for Ilya. When she couldn't find her, Lucia coughed. "That's simple. Heart Devil Lucia is famous; everyone knows her. Yup. That's it. She's famous and totally well-known! I can't believe you didn't recognize her, and I can't believe you'd mistake someone like me for her." Lucia's ear twitched, and she turned her head. "Hey! Where do you think you're running to, Beast Tamer Forest?"

"I-I'm not going to fight someone who's breaking the rules!" The poor frightened man turned to run, but Lucia was one step quicker. She drew her sword and brought it down with a flash, drawing a scream out of her opponent as his limbs separated from his torso. Lucia's so domineering! That's a really attractive trait for a man I'm interested in to have. ...Wait, Lucia's not a man. Nor am I interested in her! Lucia waved at me. My face is on fire! Will she notice? I, I—

"Claw! Come harvest this head for me!"

Maybe she wasn't waving at me.... I'm not disappointed!

"Yes, Chos—Lady Fiery Rain!" Brother Claw nearly ruined Lucia's disguise as he ran up to the stage and beheaded Beast Tamer Forest without hesitation. If I had volunteered to harvest Butcher's head, it'd be me up there on that stage with

Lucia right now.... She'd be depending on me instead of Brother Claw. I shouldn't have promoted him to fourth-in-command! Wait, no. I wouldn't murder people just to gain Lucia's favor. I'm not that kind of person!

"Audacious! You dare to break the rules and kill another one of my Fang Country's men? Descending Phoenix Claw!" The sky-realm expert shot down like a bolt of lightning, colliding into Lucia. She yelped as her robes were burnt away, but she didn't seem injured.

"Bastard! What the fuck are you doing!?" Lucia shouted as she grabbed onto the sky-realm expert's wrist. "Breaking Madness Fist Strike!" With a crack, Lucia's free hand struck the sky-realm expert's nose, causing his face to crumple inwards like dented metal. "I just fought a duel! We're only allowed to duel one person a day! You're the one forcing me to break these rules by attacking me! Stupid pervert, how dare you burn my clothes off!?" In a flash, Lucia pulled robes out of her interspacial ring and donned them in one motion. Then she removed the sky-realm expert's robes while taking his ring off of his finger. Is, is he dead?

"Hey, Claw," Lucia said. "Cut his head off for me."

Brother Claw was standing in a daze, but he flinched at Lucia's voice. "Yes, Lady Fiery Rain!" With a short cry and a leap, he swung his sword down. ...If the sky-realm expert wasn't killed by Lucia's punch, then he's certainly dead now. Unless he's a body cultivator, but that doesn't seem to be the case. But how did Lucia defeat him in a single strike? Was he already weakened?

"Lu—Fiery Rain!" Ilya shouted while cupping her hands around her mouth. "Bring me his body so I can make stuff out of it!"

...I really wish Ilya would stop using body parts in alchemy. People will associate our sect with a bunch of murderers! Though they might respect us as long as we're strong, the instant we show any hints of weakness, a lot of people will point fingers at us and try to tear us apart! …With Lucia's blatant disregard for the rules, Brother Claw's kill-happy demeanor, and Ilya's insistence on experimenting with dead bodies, our sect's reputation is already in the gutter. This isn't the type of prestige I wanted our sect to have!

***

Whew, that's three earth-realm experts' heads already and I've only been here for five minutes! At this rate, it shouldn't take very long to gather all five thousand! …Right? The math's too difficult to do, but my optimism will make it true!

"Thank you, Cho—Lady Fiery Rain! With this sky-realm expert's death, I've broken through to the low-high-ranked saint realm!" Claw cupped his bloody hands at me and bowed. Wait. Did he say sky-realm expert?

"This guy was a sky-realm expert?" I mean, he *was* flying in the sky in a no-fly zone.… Then doesn't that mean I only need four more heads!? This was a whole lot easier than I thought! And that crown prince made this out to be difficult, jeez. What did he say? If I caused a big commotion, then every sky-realm expert would … come … after me.… This counts as a small commotion, right? Right!? "Hey, uh, Claw, what's this guy's name?"

"His nameplate says Sun Fire."

"I, Fiery Rain of the Flaming Sparrow Sect, have slain the sky-realm expert, Sun Fire! You all heard that properly, right? Fiery Rain of the Flaming Sparrow Sect, that's me!" Mm, Ilya said I need to hear things three times to actually hear it for the first time, so I'll repeat my scapegoat's name one more time for good measure. "That's right, I, Fiery Rain of the Flaming Sparrow Sect, a mere earth-realm expert, killed a sky-realm expert from Fang Country! But all of you can call me Lady Fiery Rain or Chosen of the Flaming Sparrow Sect or Fiery Rain the Fang-Country-sky-realm-expert-slaying expert!"

With this, all I have to do is never use any Flaming Sparrow Sect member's nameplate again. The sky-realm experts will chase after them instead of me, and the Shadow Devil Sect will be left completely untouched! Mm, but just in case, it feels like I should leave this place before something bad happens. No one's saying anything, and all the other fights on the other platforms have stopped. This is so unnerving; it's like everyone's staring at me and judging me! "Ahem. Right, it's time for me to reunite with my fellow Flaming Sparrow Sect members who're waiting for me outside. Bye!" And no one's saying anything still. Did they all freeze? Am I in an illusion? Well, I'll just make my way back to the Shadow Devil Sect..., and still no reaction. "Psst, Softie. Ilya. Let's go."

So, in total silence, I left the battlefield with my minions by going back to where we entered from and touching the statue's head. Before my vision completely disappeared during the transportation process, I thought I heard someone say, "Immortal." What was that supposed to mean? Was I mistaken for an immortal? Are they praising me now that I'm gone!? I'm going back inside to check!

"Lady Fiery Rain is definitely an immortal!"

"She killed a mid-ranked sky-realm expert in a single strike!"

"Sun Fire's Descending Phoenix Claw exterminated a whole sect once; I saw it myself! But Lady Fiery Rain was completely unharmed!"

"I, I insulted Lady Fiery Rain's appearance. Do you think she heard!?"

"I'm sorry, Sect Brother. I'll burn paper money for you in the future."

"I wonder if Lady Fiery Rain has a cultivation partner."

"You stand no chance. If you want a cultivation partner, you should search some place filled with people befitting of you—like a pasture."

They were dead silent a moment ago, but the instant I'm gone, they start lavishing praise on me? Why couldn't they do that earlier? I like praise! It makes me feel all warm and fuzzy inside like my stomach is filled with bubbles.

"Wait! Lady Fiery Rain's back!"

...And just like that, the whole battlefield fell silent again. A few people dropped to their knees and cupped their hands towards me though. Hmm. Even the people from Fang Country are worshipping me. What the heck is this? I can't harvest the heads of people who worship me! That's totally immoral; if I take their heads, then the number of worshippers I have will decrease! It seems like I'll have to move on to a new battlefield. There should be more than one, right? This is just the west side: there should be a westernmost side, an easternmost side, and everything in between. Ah, but I really, really want to leave my real name behind so people will know who they're actually worshipping.... But I can't! I can't let my vanity be my downfall! Ah, I'm such a tragic hero. Alas, I'm so amazing, yet no one will truly know who I actually am.... All my glory will be reaped by Fiery Rain of the Flaming Sparrow Sect, but I'm okay with that! Stay strong, Lucia, you're better than this! Stay strong.... Maybe I could tell just one person? No! I'll leave before I fall to the temptation.

Phew. Alright, all the temptation is gone. But I still want to hear some praise! "Ilya, Softie, Claw! Tell me I'm amazing!"

"You're amazing, Chosen Lucia!"

"Lucia, you're really amazing."

Mm. That's right! But one person's missing. "...Ilya? Praise."

"You're *so* amazing, Lucia. Wow."

Did Ilya just roll her eyes? She did, didn't she!? "Give me back that sky-realm person's body if you think you're amazing enough to get one yourself!"

"W-wait! Lucia! Stop! You're amazing! You're really amazing! Don't squeeze it! You're forcing the blood out! You're wasting the blood!"

Hmph. It's not a waste! I obtained the body, so it's mine to use however I please. And if I want to squeeze its blood out, then I can. "Anyways, hurry up and board the boat. We're moving to a new place before those sky-realm experts figure out something's wrong." Ah, I should ask Softie why I was mistaken for an immortal. "And why did those people think I was an immortal?"

"A sky-realm expert is a nearly unkillable existence," Softie said as she stepped onto a flying sword. "To kill an unkillable existence in a single strike, wouldn't that person have to be an immortal? Though, I don't think you're quite as strong as an immortal. Do you remember how you broke the statue earlier? The formation was most likely destabilized, and that sky-realm expert must have expended a great amount of energy to stabilize it. When he appeared to fight you, I don't think he had enough qi to defend himself properly."

Hmm. So I weakened my enemy greatly before even facing him? That's what geniuses do! ...But normally, those kinds of actions are planned. Mm. I have to keep up my amazing appearance. "Aha! Just like I planned!"

"Chosen Lucia's foresight is truly amazing!" Claw said. "If wisdom were a drink, Chosen Lucia would be like hot chocolate!"

Like hot chocolate? That's a compliment, right? Everyone knows hot chocolate is one of the greatest drinks to ever exist, with acorn stew being a close second. And my wisdom is comparable to the greatest drink! I really, really like this Claw person's analogies! "Claw! Here's a reward for being such a good minion."

"...Used panties?"

"You can sell it for ten spirit stones!" That's right. This necklace of intelligence is telling me to reward my followers so they stay extra loyal! And who doesn't want used panties? They're not mine, of course.

"I'm jealous…. I want her panties too…."

Which pervert said that? Was that Softie…? Mm, nah, it can't be. Softie's a girl and she's rich; there's no way she'd want my panties.

Chapter 20

Just like I thought, people were way ahead of me when it came to robbery! When I plundered those people at the entrance to the camp, I only found a couple of heads that weren't worth anything because they had already been robbed before reaching the camp. But now, I get to do the robbing before those people are robbed before reaching the camp! Battlefield? Fighting honorable duels? Screw that! I've already gathered over three hundred earth-realm experts' heads and we haven't even made it to the second battlefield yet. There were even more saint-realm people's heads, but they're worthless since they can't be exchanged for what I want, so I gave them to Ilya to do whatever she does with body parts.

How many people did I have to rob to get that many earth-realm heads? There were too many to count, but we encountered seventy-four different sects! There are so many people on the Immortal Continent; it's great! There are so many people to rob and bully and plant heart devils in. This is paradise. I'm not quite sure I want to go back home anymore, but I have to drop Ilya off at least. She has a dad, so I guess she wants to see him. Mm. I wouldn't know. The only family I have is my husband, Durandal! We're not married yet, but that doesn't matter. Once I stick him in a sky-realm-ranked sword, I'm going to have Ilya experiment on him until he becomes virile, then I'll trap him with kids!

Ahem. Anyways, there's only three thousand seven hundred heads to go! Unless I get lucky and get another sky-realm expert's head from the next battlefield. It turns out that every sect is assigned a navigator by the crown prince. Since I lost mine somewhere along the way, I borrowed the other sects' navigators. They tried to run at first, but after keeping them tied up in the deepest levels of the boat where Ilya does her alchemy stuff, they changed their tunes pretty quick. They're at least eighty-percent cooperative! And when they're not cooperative, I throw them overboard. Because of that, I only have fifty navigators left out of the original seventy-some.

Mm. And I'm supposed to be cultivating right now. But for some reason, Fluffles is outside of my body even though I didn't use Heart Devil Apparition, and he's eating every single heart devil wormy that's flying my way! How am I supposed to cultivate if this stupid technique stops me from cultivating!? "Fluffles, damnit! Go eat something else!"

Fluffles is a terrible squirrel: He doesn't eat acorns. He doesn't drink acorn stew. And he doesn't even look at my hot chocolate! Mm. I guess he isn't really a squirrel, huh? He's made of heart devil wormies. And he's eating heart devil wormies…. Cannibal? First Ilya, now Fluffles? Why am I surrounded by such weird people? Well, anyways, it doesn't seem like I'll make much progress if I keep channeling this Heart Devil Cultivation Technique, might as well take a break to eat!

"Grr."

"Hmm? What, Fluffles?" Is he upset I stopped? He already ate a whole skyful of worms! "If you want food, go get it yourself. Stop eating my cultivation."

"Rr…." Fluffles stood on his hindlegs and sniffed the air. Then he leapt over the edge of the boat. Like black lightning, he disappeared in a flash, leaving behind a trail of afterimages that disappeared when I blinked. Was he really going to hunt his own food? If he eats heart devil worms, doesn't that mean he's going to plant some first? Then that means I'll have planted them as well since Fluffles is part of my technique…. This is amazing! I can traumatize people without even lifting a finger! Wait a minute…. What if I use Heart Devil Apparition again? "Heart Devil Apparition!" …And another squirrel popped out! This isn't Fluffles, right? Hmm. Nope. His ears are slightly different. And his tail is less plump. Great! "Alright, Fluff Two, if you want to eat, you're going to have to hunt your own food. Got it?"

Fluff Two nodded and jumped over the side of the boat, running in a different direction from Fluffles. This…, this technique is the greatest thing ever! "Fluff Three, come on out!"

"Fluff Four!"

"Five!"

"Six!"

…

"Seven Hundred Thirty-Three!"

"Seven Hundred Thirty—"

"Lucia? What are you doing?"

"—Four." Ah, it's Softie. Fluff Seven Hundred Thirty-Four sprang out of my shadow and sniffed Softie. Before she could grab him, Fluff Seven Hundred Thirty-Four leapt into the air and spread his limbs … and flew. Hmm. He was a flying squirrel, huh? Interesting.

"Was that an apparition? Even Grandfather's apparition isn't as solid." Softie's forehead wrinkled. "But what did you mean by Seven Hundred Thirty-Four?"

"That's Fluff Seven Hundred Thirty-Four." I thought it was pretty self-explanatory. "Heart Devil Apparition! And here's Fluff Seven Hundred Thirty-Five."

Softie's already pale face turned even paler. "You've released close to a thousand apparitions? What are they doing?"

Fluff Seven Hundred Thirty-Five jumped overboard and dug into the ground. Was he a mole or a squirrel? Mm, well, I guess there aren't many directions left for them to go. The more areas they cover, the better it is for me! "They're planting heart devils in people for me."

"Wait...," Softie said and placed her hand on her forehead. "Each apparition needs a hundred thousand heart devil worms to act as its base. And you summoned over seven hundred of them. Right. You *do* have that many heart devil worms to spare. I forgot how slow your cultivation was compared to a normal person's because of your impurities."

I'm not impure! I'm very chaste and moral and cute! If I were a horrible person, my apparitions wouldn't look so darn adorable. Something this cute can't come out of an impure person!

"But, Lucia, is it a good idea? Doesn't this count as causing a big commotion?"

"Eh, I've only summoned less than a thousand squirrels, no big deal. At most, they'll only terrorize one sect each. Probably. But there's a lot of sects, right? A thousand sects is like the last drop of acorn stew in your bowl—almost unnoticeable."

"...Did you say squirrels?"

Ah! "Ahem. Foxes. I said foxes. There are less than a thousand foxes."

Softie's eyes widened to the size of saucers. "Call them back! Call all the squirrels back!"

"Uh, can't do that." Mm. I don't know how. And if I don't know, then it's not possible.

"Squirrels are being actively hunted by immortals! If they notice, you'll be hunted down by immortals, Lucia! Immortals!"

What. I was never told this! The crown prince is scary enough as a sky-realm expert, and people scarier than him are going to hunt me down!? I have to call them all back! "Fluffs, assemble!"

...

...

...

It didn't work. Mm, in any case, I can always deny being a squirrel. I'm a foxkin!

***

Surprisingly, I'm not as uncomfortable with dead bodies as I thought I would be. It probably has something to do with my upbringing, seeing my father going in and out of his torture room and all that. Maybe he brought me inside when I was a baby to watch over me while carrying out his duties.... Nah, that shouldn't be the case. He's a duke. There's no need for him to watch over me personally when there are so many servants around. But what if he was just that worried about me? Father, even if you were worried about me, that doesn't mean you should torture people with your baby in the room! ...And here I am, accusing him of things that he may or may not have even done. My thoughts are running a bit fast; maybe it's because I want to distract myself as I dissect this sky-realm expert's corpse.

I've browsed through a lot of cultivation techniques, at least tens of thousands. And all of them have the same basic foundation when it comes to building up qi: harness the qi around you, attempt to contain it within your body, unblock your meridians by circulating it once you make it yours, and eventually, reinforce every part of yourself with it. That's it for the so-called mortal-realm. Once someone's body has been baptized by qi, they enter the saint realm. That's when things start diverging into all kinds of weird techniques. But there are still similarities! And I'm trying to figure out what made this sky-realm expert a sky-realm expert and not an earth-realm or saint-realm expert. But I'm not having any luck. It's also possible whatever made him a sky-realm expert disappeared upon his death.

Knock, knock.

"Ilya, are you there?"

"Yeah, come in, Softie." Even though her voice was muffled and hard to discern, I knew it was Softie because the only other person who would visit me is Lucia, and she'd never knock. And just like I thought, it was Softie. "What's up?"

"I-Ilya!?" Softie let out a weird shriek and covered her mouth with her hands. Her eyes were wide like a frightened deer's, and she took a step back. She trembled as she raised her arm and pointed. "W-what's that?"

Huh? "What's what? That's the sky-realm expert, you know, Sun Fire?"

"I, I see." Softie swallowed. "Um, can I talk to you about Lucia?"

Of course Softie wants to talk to me about Lucia. Lucia's the only topic she'll talk about with me. I wonder if she's having trouble trying to woo her. No matter how I look at it, Softie doesn't have a chance because of Durandal. It's unfortunate because Softie would be a good influence on Lucia, unlike that stupid, sadistic sword spirit. "Alright, come on in."

"Um, can I talk to you outside of your room? The, the body's really creepy. It's unsettling."

All I did was skin him to peel back his flesh to reveal his bones and organs.... Is it that creepy? It's exactly like preparing a divine beast for Lucia to cook. Oh, that's probably why I wasn't uncomfortable with dead bodies. I almost forgot that experience in the desolate mountains with Lucia. Almost. Damn. I really wanted to forget my past trauma! Oh? What's this? A black squirrel?

"Don't touch it!" Softie shouted. But it was too late. The squirrel expanded to a ridiculous size and opened its jaws. Looking into the depths of its mouth, there was only darkness. Wriggling darkness. Why was it wriggling!? And I assume the squirrel ate me because my vision, sense of hearing, and sense of touch disappeared. I could still smell things. And taste things. ...I'm going to vomit. This smell is what one would experience after leaving a prisoner to fester in horse manure for a year but ten times worse. I can tell my eyes are watering even though I can't feel the tears running down my cheeks. And the smell is so thick that I can taste it. It's sour and rancid and sticky like a giant glob of fat, if fat was made of wriggling maggots. There's a rock in my throat and ... no, that's just vomit. I'm pretty sure I vomited; though, it's hard to tell without my other senses.

"Ilya! Are you alright!?"

"...What just happened?" That was absolutely disgusting! I never want to experience something like that again! And this squirrel is just staring at me while eating the heart devil worms coming out of my chest! Wait. Isn't this Lucia's Heart Devil Apparition technique...? "Lucia! Damnit, why are you attacking me!?" There's literally billions or even trillions of other people on this Immortal Continent, but she has to plant heart devils in me!? Is there going to be a tribute system? Am I going to have to offer up a thousand people to save myself? Is that how this is going to work from now on? Fine! Fine! I'll offer up a thousand sacrifices in my place, you damned squirrel!

Phew. Calm down, Ilya. Lucia didn't do this on purpose. She's just an idiot. Lucia has no malice. She's just an idiot. Lucia would never intentionally harm me unless I insult her first. She's just an idiot. So why did Lucia's apparition attack me? Because Lucia's an idiot. Why did it attack me and not Softie? Probably because I was the one who touched it, but also because Lucia's an idiot. Why did Lucia even summon her apparition in the first place? Because she's an idiot. Alright. I'm calm now.

"That's what I wanted to talk to you about," Softie said. "Lucia summoned almost a thousand of her apparitions and set them free to plant heart devils for her. But her apparitions take on the form of the evilest creature known to cultivators, the squirrel! Immortals will hunt her down if they find one of her apparitions and realize it's a squirrel. You have to create an artifact to hide her appearance because I don't think she's smart enough to learn a disguising technique on her own."

What am I, Fix-it-all Ilya!? Though, it's true I can create an artifact to disguise her appearance. It's really not that hard. I just need the appropriate materials. Like, say, a sky-realm expert's bones and blood. How convenient. But why am I helping Lucia after she just traumatized me again? I wonder if I could trade Lucia in to the immortals and have them open my way home for me…. It sounds like a great idea on paper, but Lucia ruins all common sense. I have a feeling those immortals will get screwed over by her if they do chase her. And once she's done dealing with them, the person who sold her out would be next. …I guess I'll get started on that disguising artifact.

***

It's only been a day since I released all those apparitions, but I've already planted several thousand heart devils without lifting a finger. Life's great. And Fluffles isn't around to eat all my heart devil wormies when I cultivate! That means I'm steadily growing stronger with every passing second. Soon, I'll be able to beat the crown prince in a fight to steal his sword! But I'll probably get enough heads before I have to do that. I'm not saying that I won't steal the crown prince's sword later even if I already plant Durandal into a different sword; I'm just saying I'll do it when I'm strong enough. If an earth-realm-ranked sword is so valuable already, then won't a sky-realm-ranked sword sell for enough to feed me for the rest of my life and more?

"Stop right there, Shadow Devil Sect!"

Hmm? What's this? Is, is that a walking fish!? Those fiendish creatures that'll eat me if I fall into any body of water are able to walk on land!? "Ilya! Softie! Claw! Help!" What if they're not walking on water, but transporting invisible water around them? I'll drown! There's so many of them! And these people are riding on top of them! Are they mermaids? Mm, they'd be mermen since they're male. But that's not right. I'm pretty sure those are walking fish! They look exactly like fish and have four legs like a lizard instead of fins.

"Lucia?" Softie was the first to answer my call! I knew I could count on her! "Are we being pursued?"

"We're being pursued by walking fish!"

"Aren't those fish running?" Ilya asked. Mm? Where did she come from? She just appeared out of nowhere! Wait, that's Ilya, but she looks like a generic cultivator! Her skin isn't purple anymore! Is it really Ilya? She sounded like Ilya. ...I should dissect her to check. If her brain is larger than a normal person's, then she must be Ilya. "But of course, Lucia would be scared of fish. Don't you eat them though? You enjoyed them at that one restaurant with the peacocks."

Oh, yeah, that's Ilya. Only she'll talk to me with that sarcastic tone. I thought I noogied it out of her, but she's very stubborn. Mm, she's in her rebellious phase right now, but I'm sure that'll go away once I find her a hot guy—hormones and all that, you know? Right, taking care of my minions' mental health is very important! "I like eating fish, but only as a form of revenge!"

The cabin door leading to the deck flew open. Claw drew his sword and dashed to my side. "Chosen Lucia was eaten by fish before?"

"No! It's taking preemptive revenge! If I ever fall into water, I'm sure all the fish will try to eat me. That's why I have to eat them first!"

"Chosen Lucia is wise! Junior Brother Claw will keep Chosen Lucia's advice in mind. Kill those who want to kill you before you do anything that will cause them to want to kill you. I understand." Claw's head bobbed up and down. He's such a good listener! He's my best minion yet. I'll reward him with another pair of used panties! I'm not showing favoritism because he complimented my wisdom; I'm being completely impartial! Geniuses are always impartial.

"I said stop! How dare you rob my sect brothers and sisters while I was away!? You even stripped them and placed heart devils in every single one of them! The elders had their limbs removed and taken away! Cultivation paths like yours that rely on bringing down other people have no place on the Immortal Continent. Surrender everything you own and maybe our Great Axolotl Sect will forgive your crimes!"

Axo-what-ul? Mm. It's probably the walking fish they're riding on. Why didn't I see them before if I robbed this person's sect? Wait a minute..., I probably did rob these people, but I definitely didn't take their limbs! "Don't slander me! I only cut limbs off! I don't take them with me."

Ilya coughed. Mm. She must be feeling sick. She smells a bit like vomit too. Is she still not feeling too well from getting smacked in the head by Mr. Feathers? He was supposed to be pretty strong compared to normal people.... But I thought she was all better. Ah, it doesn't matter. If she's sick, she'll magic her ailments away. Maybe it's a side effect of turning into a generic-looking person.

"It seems like you won't repent! Don't blame me for being too harsh!"

Whoa. Is this guy a sky-realm expert? My tail's telling me he's way stronger than earth-realm experts, but he's not strong enough to be a real threat. I'll take his head, unless.... "Hey, are you part of Kang Country or Fang Country?"

"Kang Country!"

Darn. That sucks. I won't get anything from this encounter! Unless.... "Hey, is that a sky-realm-ranked sword?"

"It's the peak of earth realm!"

"...Are you wearing sky-realm-ranked boxers?"

"I'll kill you!"

Guess not. ...Does this person have anything worth taking? Mm, well, I guess I'll just take his ring. Sky-realm experts tend to have a lot of stuff. They're like hoarders because they've lived for a seriously long amount of time. "Ilya, burn away any invisible water on the ground." I don't believe those fish are actually walking! This is a trap to lure me into my weakest terrain! But I'm too smart to fall for it.

"It'll be hard to boil away water," Ilya said. "Can I just freeze it instead?"

"There's no water...," Softie said. Ah, this is why this necklace of intelligence is so great. Only Ilya and I are actually able to perceive the trap. Maybe Ilya should make one of these for Softie. It's hard for geniuses to associate with people way below their intellect sometimes—such a tough life we live. I'm sure Ilya knows exactly what I'm talking about.

Ilya leaned over the side of the boat and pointed her palm at the running fish cavalry. "Ice, halt my enemies. Frost Nova!"

And just like that, every single one of those walking fish stopped moving as waist-high ice appeared around them, completely covering their legs and lower belly. I knew there was water there! The riders were thrown off from the sudden stop, and that's when I leapt down to deal with them. How dare these people attack us and stake a claim on our stuff? It's immoral to try and rob beautiful women like me and Softie! Mm. I'll take their walking fish too. Into the pouch they go!

"Chosen Lucia, may I harvest their heads? This sky-realm expert is bound to seek revenge on you. Perhaps he isn't strong enough, but there's no telling whether or not his uncle is strong enough. Or his father. Or his grandfather. Or any members of his extended family who've gone off to make a name for themselves and will conveniently return to seek vengeance on someone who's wronged their family while they were away. If we get rid of these troubles now, no one will know it was us."

"Eh? But then how will we rob the rest of his family if they don't seek us out?"

"Chosen Lucia raises a good point." Claw lowered his head. "It's a bit regretful for me to let such a great chance to improve my strength slip away. How about we harvest all but the weakest person's head? That way, I'll be able to grow in strength to serve you better, and the rest of their families will find out."

"Mm…. That's a good idea…." But murder is wrong. And these people are our allies. The crown prince said internal conflict was completely okay as long as it was outside of the camp, but I, as an upright person, do not approve of wanton killing. There's—ah! Claw cut the person's head off while I was thinking! "What are you doing!? You didn't let me finish my sentence!"

Claw blinked and wiped away the blood that had spurted onto his cheek. "But you said it was a good idea?"

"I wasn't done speaking yet!"

"I apologize, Chosen Lucia." Claw lowered his head. "Punish me as you see fit."

What am I supposed to do? Cut off his head in retaliation? That'd be a waste of my favorite subordinate! "Ah, fine, whatever. You shouldn't cry over spilt acorn stew. You should lap it up instead because you should never waste acorn stew!"

Claw raised his head. "That means I should give the body to Sister Ilya, right? Waste not, want not?"

And this is why Claw's my favorite minion. He understands my food analogies! Ah, but I should still be mad at him for killing someone like that! Killing is wrong. Bad, Claw, bad. "Give me back those panties as a punishment."

"We should make these people swear oaths to the heavens to not speak about what happened here today," Ilya said. "You don't want our allies hating us too. If anything, we can have them say they were ambushed by an enemy party that broke the rules of engagement. And before you say anything about robbing them, they already told us their name, the Great Axolotl Sect. Just go over there and rob them when you want. It's not like sects are very portable."

Well, if Ilya says we should do something, then we should do it because she's most likely right. "You heard that, Claw. Have them swear oaths to the heavens." I'll check our surroundings just in case someone's spying on us. Oh? That's a statue that looks like a formation entrance! That means we're at the second battlefield! Mm, first things first. I'll break the statue to weaken my future opponent!

***

Lucia went off to break the entrance to the battlefield's formation, leaving Brother Claw, Ilya, and me behind to make these people swear their oaths. But I have a feeling that the Great Axolotl Sect members won't comply that easily since Brother Claw murdered their leader. They look extremely angry. If Lucia didn't shatter their elbows, wrists, and knees out of habit, I'm certain they'd try to kill us. Their leader died, their mounts were stolen, and all their belongings were taken away. I'd be angry too if I were in their position.

Brother Claw pointed his sword at the nearest Great Axolotl Sect member. "Swear an oath to the heavens. You'll never communicate to anyone the events that've occurred today."

"I refuse!" the man shouted. "You'll have to kill me before I leave the young master's death unavenged!"

Brother Claw shrugged, raised his sword, and chopped down in one swift motion. The man's head flew into the air, eyes and mouth still wide open. Blood spurted out of his neck, splashing onto Brother Claw's shoes. How could he just kill them like that!? Lucia told him not to! …But she's too busy breaking the statue over and over again to notice or care about what's going on here. Then it's up to me to say something!

"Brother Claw! Lucia said she doesn't like pointless killing. Isn't this why we're having them swear oaths to the heavens? So we don't have to kill them?"

"Chosen Lucia gave me orders to make them swear oaths. She never specified how I should do it, or how many should survive. The greatest way to spur people on is to threaten their lives." Brother Claw pointed his sword at another Great Axolotl Sect member. "Swear an oath to the heavens."

"I will never communicate to anyone the events that've occurred to me today. Let the heavens be my witness." The man's head was lowered, and tears dropped from his eyes. His chest flashed once with white light, and the sky lit up for a brief moment. The oath had taken effect.

Brother Claw grunted and pushed the man over to the side. Then he looked at me. "See?" Before I could respond, he had already approached another person. There were at least a hundred people who had come to challenge Lucia. It's a wonder how she disabled them all so quickly. Well, not really. She's done it millions of times back in Kong County. I don't think I'll ever find anyone who can break joints as efficiently as Lucia.

"I won't swear an oath. I won't! The young master didn't deserve to die! I can't swallow this injustice!"

Brother Claw exhaled through his nostrils and lifted his sword. I can't just watch him cut down a crying woman who can't even resist! My grandfather always told me cultivation could never be wrong. Planting heart devils in people to advance in strength was perfectly alright even though it lowered the other person's chances at immortality. But a technique that required another's death to advance in strength? Surely, that can't be right. Though, who am I to judge? The road to immortality is paved with bones and blood. But this woman is a mortal-realm disciple! Brother Claw will gain nothing from killing her!

"Why are you stopping me, Sister Moonlight?" Brother Claw turned his head towards me. My whip was coiled around his arm, holding back the sword that was less than an inch away from the poor disciple's neck. "I am merely following Chosen Lucia's orders." Brother Claw's eyes held no anger, no curiosity. No respect. Just indifference, as if he were staring at an ant. Why was he looking at me with a gaze like that? I'm not insignificant!

"There are other ways to follow Lucia's orders! As the second-in-command, I will not let you indiscriminately kill people!" Lives are precious. If someone dies, the impact will affect everyone around them. People shouldn't be treated like nothing just because they're weak. ...That's a bit hypocritical coming from me since I follow Lucia, huh? She's the greatest abuser of power, but she tries not to kill people! I think. I really want to believe Lucia kills people out of ignorance. She's not a bad person; she's just an idiot sometimes.

"Right, Sister Moonlight is second-in-command and can order me around. Then I'd like to challenge you for your position. After I beheaded Sun Fire, I surpassed your cultivation level, Sister Moonlight. Shouldn't I replace you as chosen?" My whip uncoiled as qi exploded out from Brother Claw's arm, freeing his limb.

"Hmm? Is this infighting? Were we allowed to challenge people to claim their spots?" Ilya finished putting away a corpse and looked up. "No one told me I could do that. How about you give me the title of second-in-command and both of you can fight for third?"

...Why would Ilya want to join in on this fight too? "You're not satisfied with where you are? Everyone respects you and no one orders you around."

"Yeah, that's true," Ilya said with a nod. "But I just don't like being someone else's subordinate, even if it's in title only. Call it a result of my upbringing."

"Hey! Aren't you guys done yet?" Lucia shouted from her spot by the statue. "I've been waiting for you to get over here already!"

"We shouldn't keep Chosen Lucia waiting," Brother Claw said. "I'll kill them all to speed things up. Our fight will have to wait."

"If you're going to kill me, then I'll take you with me!" one of the Great Axolotl Sect members said as white light poured out of him. *He's going to self-detonate! An earth-realm expert's self-detonation isn't something I can block!*

"Hey, stop right there," Ilya said. As if her words were a prayer answered by a god, the light around the expert's body dimmed. Just above his groin, there was a bloody icicle that pierced through his front to his back. Ilya had stabbed his dantian, releasing all the pressure built up by the gathering qi and crippling the expert at the same time. She clicked her tongue and muttered, "The last time someone exploded on me when I was interrogating him, I nearly died. You think I'd let someone explode on me again? Unlike Lucia, I learn from experiences."

"Guys? What are you doing? I'm going to start without you!" Lucia shouted and kicked the statue that had repaired itself for the hundredth time or so, breaking it again.

"If you wish to live, swear an oath to the heavens, or my Junior Brother Claw will really kill you all." *Maybe Brother Claw was right. The best way to persuade someone was by threatening to kill them. And I have to take the fastest method to keep Lucia from waiting.* "Please, swear the oaths. I don't want to see you all die for nothing."

"Oh! She's like an angel! How could we refuse the young lady crying for us? She cares about our lives."

I'm not crying! My eyes are naturally this watery!

"Don't cry, young miss. We'll swear the oaths."

Brother Claw tilted his head and sheathed his sword. "How come you listen to her, but not to me?"

"Because you're ugly."

"She's beautiful. She must be an angel. An angel wouldn't lie to us."

"Yes, that's right. Young miss, please, exchange messenger signatures with me."

...I'm starting to think I was born in the wrong sect. Wouldn't the Seducing Succubus Sect have been a much better fit for me? Lucia did exchange some used underwear for their techniques.... If I learned them, maybe I could seduce Lucia as well? A-as practice! I'd try to seduce Lucia as practice!

***

Whew, I must've broken this stupid thing over a thousand times, but it keeps fixing itself! The sky cracks apart occasionally like before, and there's some screams, but it's not as vivid as the first battlefield. I don't think I'm weakening the sky-realm expert inside at all! I guess the only thing I can do is keep breaking it. Mm, if this necklace of intelligence was just a bit stronger, then I bet I'd instinctively know when to stop. Ah, I forgot to tell Ilya to make me more necklaces to become fourtimely smarter. Speaking of Ilya, aren't those three done yet? It shouldn't be that hard to make people swear oaths! You just have to grind their bones a few times and hit them to wake them up when they fall unconscious.

Oh? The statue's eyes turned red. Is something happening? A circle appeared on the ground next to me, and a person appeared out of nowhere! They must've come from inside the formation. I'll do a quick check with my tail, and ... he's about as strong as that running-fish rider. So, a sky-realm expert? I thought the crown prince said it'd be hard to obtain sky-realm experts' heads. It turns out you can't really trust anyone except for yourself! And Ilya.

"You're still breaking the formation even after I show myself!?"

Ah. After breaking the statue over a thousand times, I hit it again out of habit when it repaired itself. "Oops. That was an accident."

"Oops? Accident? You think you can get away with what you've done by saying oops!? Which country do you belong to? I'll have them reimburse me for all my wasted medicinal pills. I suffered multiple internal injuries because of your actions! If you're part of my Fang Country, I'll have your whole sect exterminated!"

"Oh? You're part of Fang Country? And you're a sky-realm expert, right?"

"Are you afraid now? It's too late!" The sky-realm expert stretched his hand towards me, but before I could grab him, a white light appeared in between us and another person appeared. She was a sky-realm expert too! The crown prince was right; these people travel in packs!

The woman that appeared glared at the man. "You went outside, but the formation was destroyed again! No wonder why your Fang Country is suffering from internal strife. Your sky-realm experts are completely incompetent!"

"Shut up! This foxkin ignored me and broke the statue under my watch."

"And you didn't stop her? Incompetent!"

…Maybe these two people are enemies? Mm. If Fang Country has a sky-realm expert, then our side needs to have one too! Even without the necklace of intelligence, I can do basic math. For the two sides to be equal in power, the number of sky-realm experts have to be the same. Therefore, this woman has to be on my side!

"And you, foxkin! Do you know how annoying it is to repair a formation repeatedly? I'll skin you alive and turn you into a rug."

Or not...? Mm. Alright. Clearly, there's only one answer: Violence! "Breaking Madness Fist Strike!" Direct—! ...Hit? I was aiming for the woman, but she suddenly switched places with the man! And now the man's crumpled up on the ground with froth coming out of his mouth. Is he dead? Hmm, I think this is what people call on the verge of death. I can't let him die because of my punch! "Claw! Come cut this sky-realm expert's head off before he dies!"

"Yes, right away, Lady Fiery Rain!" Claw shouted. In an instant, he appeared next to me with his sword drawn.

And just like that, I obtained another sky-realm expert's head! Just three more to go! If this woman's head will count, then it'll be two heads left! "Hey, old lady, are you part of Fang Country or Kang Country?"

"K-Kang Country." The lady was holding onto her necklace. If she squeezed it a little more, it'd probably break. It must be a life-saving treasure of some sort, like an instant-teleportation button. It's weird how the sky-realm experts that I've already beaten up haven't had any of those. They just probably didn't have the time to react to my quick thinking! That must be it. When I accomplish great things, it's because I'm amazing. There's no other explanations for the sky-realm experts' failures.

"Mm. I guess there's no point in killing you if your head can't be traded in. How about you leave behind your interspacial ring and underwear and I'll let you go?"

"You're not going to take her clothes too?" Claw asked.

"Well, it's just a white robe. Look at how plain it is. I bet I couldn't sell it for more than a single spirit stone." There's not even a nametag. Why would I bother taking something so useless? Oh, I guess it'd plant a heart devil, but I already planted one in her when the man died to Claw just now.

"No, it's a special robe made of volcanic chameleon skin that can change its appearance at will." Claw shook his head. "It's worth at least ten earth-realm-ranked swords."

"Robes. Give. Now. Or death." Ten earth-realm-ranked swords! That's worth an uncountable number of used panties! Only an idiot would let a chance like this go! I have my Unrelenting Path of Slaughter ready to activate at any moment. I'll drown her with my Tides of Blood if she refuses!

"T-that's a lot of bloodlust you're giving out," the woman said. "H-here. Take it." She stripped and handed me her robes and her ring. She didn't give me any underwear…, but she was completely naked. A pervert?

"Underwear?"

The woman's face flushed bright red. "I usually don't wear any…."

Yup, she's a pervert. I want nothing to do with her. "Okay. Get out of here."

"Yes. Goodbye, Fiery Rain of the Flaming Sparrow Sect." The woman rose into the air and flew away at a lightning fast speed. Ah! She was still wearing her life-saving treasure necklace thing! I was completely distracted by her lack of underwear that I forgot! But why did she call me Fiery Rain? Oh, I'm still wearing the nametag. I forgot to put that away too! Why am I forgetting so many things? Maybe the necklace of intelligence is wearing off. Mm. I'll ask Ilya to recharge its effects.

***

Pledging my undying loyalty to Chosen Lucia was the greatest decision of my life. I grew up without any parents, taken care of by only my elder sister. My parents were mercilessly slaughtered by a group of people because of my family's so-called evil cultivation technique. I was too little to remember who the killers were, and my sister never told me their identity before she died, but she did leave behind a necklace with a message that she made me promise not to read until after I became an earth-realm expert. My sister's life was spared because women couldn't cultivate my family's technique, but they destroyed any chance for her to have children in the future. And I was spared because my mother had fed me to a snake which my sister killed and retrieved me from after the killers left. When I turned twelve, my sister imparted my family's technique to me, but learning such a bloody technique didn't come without a cost. The life of a family member was required to start it. After my twelfth birthday, I no longer had a family.

A few years passed, and I reached the peak of the mortal-realm. A lot of people died by my hands, but I didn't keep track of how many. It's hard to remember. Everyone makes the same face when they die. They make the same sounds: the dying gasps, the whimpers, the last exhalation before they fall still. Everyone's the same when faced with death. Perhaps I killed ten people. Perhaps I killed a thousand. In the end, it doesn't matter.

I attracted the attention of many sects, but the Shadow Devil Sect kept their eyes on me for a different reason than most. They liked me, liked my potential. And I became a core disciple under the terms that I wouldn't kill a fellow sect member. I kept to those terms, and my growth stagnated. If Chosen Lucia hadn't made her appearance when she did, I might've done something that would've gotten me expelled from the sect. She didn't seem special at first, running away from our greeting when she met us for the first time. But not even a day later, she attended our cultural exchange and started the great massacre. My stagnating cultivation grew by leaps and bounds that day, and when Chosen Lucia recruited people to subjugate some sects in Kong County, I was the first to sign up. When we got back to the Shadow Devil Sect after a year, I claimed the spot of number one core disciple.

Now, I'm part of the squad fighting at the Gates of Hell. The first battlefield we went to, Chosen Lucia let me kill two earth-realm experts and a sky-realm expert. Then, I killed another sky-realm expert when he tried to rob us. Sister Moonlight stopped me from killing more, but I had already surpassed her in strength. The next time she tries to stop me, I'll claim her spot as the chosen of the sect. Before we entered the second battlefield, another sky-realm expert came out who Chosen Lucia, once again, gave me the honor of killing. The way she's able to disable people so perfectly is a form of art. I'm just a lowly member of the saint realm, but after Chosen Lucia's done with her victims, they can't resist me even if they're able to kill me with a single glance when they're in their best conditions.

And we entered the second battlefield despite Sister Moonlight's protests. She thought we should flee before anyone discovered the sky-realm experts' deaths. But Sister Ilya gave Chosen Lucia a bracelet that changed her appearance. Combined with the volcanic chameleon robe, Chosen Lucia's appearance changed to a completely different person's. She doesn't even have a tail right now, and her ears are hidden behind her hair. She switched her nameplate to that of the Golden Bush Sect too. They were one of our allies that Chosen Lucia robbed blind on our way here.

"I, Long Mistletoe, challenge any earth or sky-realm expert!"

Right now, Chosen Lucia is pretending to be Long Mistletoe. Before that, she was pretending to be Rough Stone. And before that, she was pretending to be Icy Wind. Every time she wins a fight, she drags her opponent over and has me behead them. Then she changes her appearance, her clothes, and her nametag before running up onto one of the arena platforms again. So far, she's had me kill over two hundred earth-realm experts, but I think people are starting to catch on.

"How could so many of our earth-realm experts lose in a single strike? It doesn't make any sense! Since when has Kang Country acquired that many experts? They must be at the peak of earth realm. But none of them were famous beforehand. Where is Sir Fang? He went outside to fix the formation, but he hasn't shown himself again."

"You're right. There's something strange going on, but there's no proof."

"Whoa! Look at that! Long Mistletoe of the Golden Bush Sect defeated her opponent in a single strike! She's dragging him away to be beheaded like those previous experts!"

"Hey, aren't all of our earth-realm experts being taken towards the same place every time they lose?"

…Yes. People have indeed caught on. But I've been changing my appearance after every kill as well thanks to Sister Ilya's bracelet. Though Chosen Lucia may be abnormally strong, I don't think she can win against a crowd of over a million people. Everyone here is an elite who belongs to a sect that won a province exchange. And there's another problem with having me kill all these earth-realm experts. If I don't stabilize my foundation, I'll explode from all the excess qi. In a few hours, I've advanced to the peak of saint realm, skipping many levels in the process. This rate of growth is completely abnormal.

"Alright, Claw. This one too." Chosen Lucia dumped the limp person onto the ground in front of me. I raised the sword that Chosen Lucia had gifted to me and brought it down without hesitation. There was no resistance, as expected of an earth-realm-ranked sword. Warmth flooded my dantian as the fallen expert's soul entered my body, sucked in by my cultivation technique. I could hear his soul screaming as it was ground to bits before merging with my qi.

"Lady Long Mistletoe, I need to take a break. I can sense my earth-realm tribulation approaching."

"Earth-realm tribulation!?" Sister Moonlight stiffened, her action so quick that it seemed like she had jumped. "I thought Brother Claw was weaker than me just a week ago! C-congratulations."

"Mm. Alright. Anyone else want to harvest heads?" Chosen Lucia asked, sweeping her gaze over our fellow sect members. None of them had a technique like mine, so none of them volunteered. "No one? Oh! I'll just have Puppers do it. I almost forgot he existed." Chosen Lucia bent over and grabbed her socks. Then she lifted her arm and pulled out a wolfkin by the scruff of his neck. "Go do your tribulation stuff, Claw. I'm not going to stop even though you're on break! I still have"—she counted off her fingers, but when she reached the last one, she wrinkled her forehead—"a lot of heads to harvest! Mn!"

Like my technique required a sacrifice to learn, Chosen Lucia's abnormal strength extracts an equally dreadful toll. It's a shame, but her strength is inversely proportional to her intelligence. I fear she'll be no smarter than a vegetable if she ever becomes an immortal.

Chapter 21

Ah..., it's been a long time since I worked so hard for something. But it's finally done! Three thousand earth-realm experts' heads have been harvested! It only took three straight days of nonstop duels at the second battlefield to get this many. I haven't eaten, slept, or cultivated in that whole time. This is the power of the giantest bone of focus in the world! But now that my goal is finally accomplished, I deserve to take a break. A nice meal followed by a nap. Then when I wake up, we'll be back at the camp, and I'll be able to turn in these heads for a sky-realm-ranked sword that I can stick Durandal into. Then I'll have sex with him for a whole month straight! I have to make up all that lost time! Ah, but Ilya should make Durandal virile before that. Mm. I hope she doesn't take too long. Eh, she's a genius. I bet she'll fix him up in an hour or two at most!

"Good work, everybody! Let's go back to the camp now!"

Claw did an especially good job. He easily passed through his tribulation with the help of everyone at the battlefield, and then he became a mid-high-ranked earth-realm expert from harvesting those couple thousand heads. Mm? Is his cultivation higher than mine? I have no clue! I just practice the Heart Devil Cultivation Technique because it gives me tingles; I don't keep track of my cultivation! The only thing I need to keep track of is the number of heads I have, and I don't have to count those anymore. Well, I wasn't the one keeping count in the first place. Ilya and Softie did that for me. Both of them were counting because they had to take turns staying awake.

"Wasn't our mission to capture one of the eastern outposts?" Softie asked. "Don't we have to do that before we can return?"

"Eh..., we'll just say we did it. If we all agree, then the crown prince will have to believe us! And if someone goes to check, then we can just say it was taken back after we left. Mhm." This is called using one's brains to accomplish tasks! Why work when you can lie? I already did so much! I don't want to take a stupid outpost.

"But what if the crown prince tells us to make oaths to the heavens?" Softie asked.

"...Fluff Seven Hundred Seventy-Six, come out!" I made sure to hide my chest from any onlookers before releasing an apparition. "Alright, Fluff Seven Seven Six, your mission is to take over the eastern outpost I was supposed to take over, got it?"

Fluff Seven Seven Six shook his head.

...You were supposed to understand! What part don't you understand!? Mm. Maybe my orders weren't specific enough? "You want me to tell you the specific location?"

Fluff Seven Seven Six bobbed his head up and down.

"Well, I don't know! If I knew, I would've told you earlier. Alright, how about this? I'll summon another thousand apparitions, and you lead them to take over every outpost east of here. If the outpost's unknown, then you'll have to take them all over just in case."

"Lucia!" Softie shouted at me in her whispering voice. I still don't know how she does that. "That's a terrible, terrible idea! Did you forget what I said about your apparitions' appearances?"

Mm.... I can't remember anything. I think that's a side effect of sleep deprivation. Or it's a lack of food that's making my brain weak. Or both! Yeah, I think it's both. So tired. And hungry.... Appearances? Ah! There must be something wrong with Fluff Seven Seven Six's appearance. I'll just use my Heart Devil Apparition to whip something up … and done!

"Lucia! What are you doing!?"

"I made Fluff Seven Seven Six a hat and bowtie." He's presentable now! There's nothing wrong with his appearance anymore. He's very adorable if I may say so myself. If I were full squirrel, I'd definitely fall for him. But I'm only part squirrel, so I won't! Right! I have to fix Durandal! "Okay. All loose ends are tied up! To the camp!"

"Is Lucia alright?" Softie whispered to Ilya. "I think something's wrong with her."

"Well, yeah, something's wrong. There's literally nothing right about her," Ilya whispered back.

It seems like Ilya's head has an itch that can only be scratched by my knuckles. I'll do her a favor.

"W-wait! Stop! How is your hearing so good!?"

Eh? Why's Fluff Seven Seven Six tugging on my sleeve? I thought he was Softie for a second. Oh! I forgot to summon the other thousand apparitions. Is there a fast way to do this? Mm. "Come out a thousand apparitions!" …It worked? It worked!? Why did I summon all the apparitions before Fluff Seven Seven Six one at a time!? Well, you learn something new every day even if you're a genius, huh?

Before I could even touch the statue's head to leave the battlefield, my apparitions bit and clawed at the air until holes appeared out of nowhere. Then they leapt through and vanished, the holes in the air fixing themselves. Softie cleared her throat. "Um, Lucia? Did your apparitions eat the boundaries of the formation just now?"

How was I supposed to know? The only thing I know about formations is … nothing! They're like magic. I'll never understand how they work. All I know is breaking them weakens the person maintaining them. Hmm? If my apparitions broke part of the formation just now, then shouldn't someone be suffering right now? Who's maintaining it? Ah, I guess that doesn't matter. It's not my problem! I have bigger things to worry about! Like the color of the sword I'm going to pick. Hmm, hmm. And the first step is to leave the battlefield!

…What's with this ominous feeling? Why are there so many people standing in the sky?

"They're the Shadow Devil Sect, not the people we're looking for."

One of the flying people landed in front of me, and my tail stiffened. Even though my disguise prevented other people from seeing it, I could still feel my tail! This person's dangerous!

"Have you seen the Flaming Sparrow Sect?"

Crap. These people are looking for me, aren't they? Did I really create that big of a commotion as Fiery Rain!? All their sky-realm experts came out! "Ah…. Yes. Yes, I did. Those bastards robbed us of our merits. Their leader, Fiery Rain, was especially coldhearted! She took my underwear!"

The man's eyes glinted. "Where and when did you see them?"

"Uh, a few days ago near the battlefield in that direction." That's when I robbed them! I'm not lying. I really did meet the Flaming Sparrow Sect there.

"Young Master!" one of the old men flying above said. The man in front of me raised his head. "I'm sensing Sun Fire's aura coming off of this woman's bracelet! It's almost as if his essence was converted into an artifact."

My bracelet? The thing disguising me? Ilya made it out of a person!? What the fuck is wrong with her!? I don't want to wear dead people! That's so gross and … actually, I wore bones all the time back at home during my hunting sprees. Mm. It's not that bad, I guess. Wait, no! This is a disaster! Couldn't she have made the bracelet out of someone less important!?

"Where did you get that bracelet?" the man asked. His hand was on his sword's hilt, his fingers draped across it. He seemed relaxed, but my tail was stiffening so much that my fur was poking into my back.

"I, uh, found it. On the ground. Mhm." He's not saying anything. Did he believe me?

The man smiled and took a step back. He fell for it!? "She's highly suspicious. Capture her."

Well, shit.

***

"Wait!"

The slightly less than twenty sky-realm experts paused in their tracks. Wow, they actually listened? I wasn't expecting them to stop. Now, what can I say that'll get us out of this pinch? Lucia, Softie, and Claw have all frozen up from the overwhelming pressure. I'm not sure why I'm the only one not affected, but that means I'm the one who has to get us out of this mess.

"A saint-realm junior is able to resist us? Interesting. What did you want to say?" the man closest to Lucia turned towards me and smiled. I'm guessing Lucia wasn't being aggressive because she knew she wouldn't be a match for all of them. She's a lot like an animal in that regard. She'll only pick fights she can win.

"This goes against the contract between our two countries." That's right! These sky-realm experts' actions are violating the rules of engagement that the crown prince had given us through the navigator. I read it all and thought it was bullshit, but that doesn't mean I forgot them right away. "Aggression will not be tolerated between the two countries unless the acts of aggression take place on the battlefield in the form of a one-on-one duel."

The smiling man turned to the older one hovering above him. "Is this true?"

"Yes, those were the terms we agreed upon."

"If we capture them all now, will anyone find out?"

"That is highly unlikely, Young Master."

"Then capture them all and don't let anyone find out."

This lawless bastard! He's just like Lucia! "Stop! We're direct subordinates of Crown Prince Single Sky. If you capture us, our crown prince won't be very pleased."

The smiling man blinked and turned towards the old man again. "Will that be a problem?"

"Yes. Since Sun Fire died, we're down a sky-realm expert. The crown prince of Kang Country holds a lot of sway. If he truly is angered by our actions, he'll gather their experts to face us."

The smiling man's eyes lit up. "So you're telling me there's a chance he won't get mad at us?"

Why is he exactly like Lucia!? Hah…. I think the better question to ask is why are all the strong people so irresponsible? Alright, if this man is like Lucia, then he must have a vice. "Have you ever heard of hot chocolate before?"

"Are you addressing me?" the smiling man asked and raised an eyebrow. "No. What is this hot chocolate?"

"It's a very tasty drink fit for immortals." Alright, that may not be true right now, but once Lucia becomes an immortal, it'll be the perfect line of advertisement. "Would you like to try some?"

"Fit for immortals? A saint-realm junior has something like that? Very well, serve me a plate of this … hot chocolate."

"It's a drink. Here's a cup of it." They weren't wary of me at all when I went up to the smiling man, who I assume is their leader. They probably didn't think I could do anything to them, and that was true. I didn't even bother poisoning the cup. I just pray that this man is as stupid as Lucia. If he likes the chocolate, I'll offer him the recipe in exchange for our freedom.

"Peculiar smell," the leader said and swirled the hot chocolate with small motions of his wrist. He brought the cup to his lips and took a sip. His brow wrinkled, and he spat the hot chocolate onto the ground. "This is filled with impurities. Disgusting. No immortal would drink something like this. No, no *cultivator* would drink something like this! Their cultivation would slow by hundreds, no, thousands of times. You realized poisons wouldn't work against me, so you tried to sabotage my future?"

…Well, this plan horribly backfired. "W-wait. But how was the taste?"

"Huh? The taste? It tasted like impurities."

Alright. I tried. I mean, there's another vice I can try. I pointed at Softie. "Will you let us go if I offer her to you as a wife?"

"I-Ilya!?"

"Oh? She's certainly very beautiful, but my cultivation partner would murder me," the leader said and shrugged. "If this is all you had to say, then I'll proceed with capturing you now."

"Stop right there!!!"

I think my ears exploded. I can't hear anything. Yeah, there's blood pouring out of my ears. And it wasn't just me; everyone here has blood flowing out of their ears, eyes, and nostrils. What the hell is going on? Someone shouted and this happened? I'll heal my group first. Light, answer my call, Restore!

"—yaaaaa! Oh? I can hear again." Lucia swiveled her head around before blinking at me. "Good job blowing out their eardrums, but I still don't think we'll win if we fight them."

"No, I wasn't the one who did that." Did Lucia really think I could wound this many sky-realm experts at once? Just what does she see me as…? Her demands for me are definitely going to be impossible to fulfill in the future.

"If it wasn't you, then who was it?" Lucia tilted her head. The sky-realm experts, who had retreated and were standing away from us, seemed to have fixed their injuries as well by consuming pills.

"What was that?" their leader asked. "Was that an immortal?"

The old man hesitated before nodding. "I think so, Young Master. But why would an immortal come to a battlefield like this?"

"You fucking squirrel! You think you can get away after stealing my food!? Let this devil teach you the true meaning of fear! That's right. Run, run! See if you can escape from my ultimate technique!"

From between a cluster of trees that were blocking our view, a gigantic squirrel made of heart devil worms jumped out, running straight towards Lucia while making loud clicking sounds. Lucia's eyes nearly bulged out of her head. "Fuck! Are you serious!? Don't fucking run over here! Run towards *them*!" Lucia whirled around and grabbed me and Softie while sprinting as far away from the squirrel as she could. The other sect members were stunned for a bit, but they quickly ran after us as well. The squirrel, however, ran in the opposite direction towards the group of sky-realm experts. It leapt straight at their leader and dove into his chest, shrinking down to fit inside his heart.

"Beastly Corruption of the Seven Virtues, God-Slaying Beam!"

I saw it clearly since I was slung over Lucia's shoulder like a sack of potatoes with my head being tickled by her invisible tail. A massive pillar of black light engulfed the sky-realm experts and everything around them, and just as quickly as it came, the pillar disappeared. I wasn't sure if I blinked or not because it was over in an instant. The sky-realm experts slowly fell forward onto their faces, unmoving.

Loud laughter boomed overhead as a dark figure appeared above the corpses. He was dressed in pitch-black clothes, but his skin was extremely pale, sickly even. His eyes were red, and he had two horns protruding out of his forehead just above his eyebrows. "Eat that, you stinking tree-rat! I don't care if you're a squirrel or a buddha. No one touches this immortal's meal!" His head turned to the side, and his eyes met mine. The next second, he was right in front of my face. If it weren't for all the times Lucia popped up in front of me for no reason, I really would've screamed. "Hey. Got any snacks?"

Lucia stiffened and stopped running. The front of my robe was wet from the sweat that was profusely leaking out of her back. I swallowed the lump in my throat. "Y-yeah." Even I can't stop myself from stuttering when confronted by an immortal! I slipped out of Lucia's stiff grasp and reached into my interspacial ring, pulling out the first food product I put my hands on: a barrel of hot chocolate. "H-here."

"Oh! This is hot chocolate!" The immortal's eyes lit up as he popped off the top of the barrel. "I haven't seen this stuff for over ten thousand years. Sweet. As thanks, you can have all that crap." He put the lid back onto the barrel and gestured at the sky-realm experts lying on the ground. "Watch out for squirrels, yeah? They love tormenting smart people like you."

Before I could respond, the immortal vanished. Squirrels love tormenting people like me? Well, that's true; just look at Lucia. But did this really happen? We were about to be captured by a group of sky-realm experts, but an apparition that Lucia released on one of her crazy whims stole the food of an immortal and brought that angry immortal over to us, and the angry immortal smote it along with all the sky-realm experts who were trying to capture us. That's a bit … bullshit-like? If anything, I thought we would be saved by the crown prince or a group of sky-realm experts. Life's weird sometimes. Like a poorly written story.

"Um, Lucia?"

"What's up, Softie?"

"I, I think I soiled my panties."

"...I didn't need to know that."

"B-but I..., I thought you'd want them...."

...People are weird too.

***

Rest in peace, Fluffles, you were a good boy—except when you were eating my heart devil wormies. Ah, poor Fluffles, he was eradicated by that freak. Right. That freak. I've never been so scared for my life! It felt like I could've died if he sneezed. Ilya's really brave for being able to talk to him. Mm, well, I'm very grateful to him since he saved our asses, but he's in a whole 'nother realm. One day, I'll become as strong as him! Maybe. As long as the road there doesn't take too much effort and isn't painful. But today, my eyes have been opened. There are some really fucking scary individuals out there. I should just go back to the little pocket realm and hide for the rest of my life. Mn. That sounds like a good goal. I'll have a lot of children with Durandal—after Ilya fixes him—and live out the rest of my days drinking hot chocolate while minding my own business. Right. Squirrels are hated by the Immortal Continent; I have no reason to stick around! Softie said people as scary as that immortal were going to chase after me if they found out I was summoning squirrels with my Heart Devil Apparition technique. Speaking of Softie, "I don't want your panties, damnit!" ...It feels weird to take the panties of someone I know. She should just hand me the ten spirit stones I could've sold her panties for instead; I have no qualms with borrowing and never returning my friends' money! Though, for a while, Ilya was my only friend. I'm sure she didn't mind either.

"Lucia? The immortal's gone now, …I think. Do you want to loot those corpses?" Ilya grabbed my sleeve, separating me from Softie. Her fingers were trembling. "I'd check it out myself, but … yeah."

You think you're the only terrified one here, Ilya!? "Ahem. Passionate Cloud, you're up! Go bring those bodies over here while we hide in this hole that I'm going to dig as a precaution."

I figured out another reason why cultivators live in holes. It makes them feel safe. There's just something about a burrow that's comforting. Like, if you're hiding in a burrow, there's no chance an owlkin is going to swoop down and eat you in the middle of the night. Mm, owlkin's don't eat beastkin, but you know what I mean. Ah, my train of thought keeps running away! Did my giantest bone of focus wear off already? Well, that's no biggie! If those corpses aren't a huge trap left behind by that immortal, then I'll have so many sky-realm experts' heads! Wait a minute…, I'm sure their leader had a sky-realm-ranked sword! I'm sure of it!

"Chosen Lucia, I brought the corpses over. Can you move the boulder blocking the entrance?"

I know boulders won't do much to stop that freak if he wants to hurt me, but it's comforting to have out there blocking me from view! It's like covering your head with a blanket even though ghosts can pass through cotton. Right, if you're being chased by monsters, hiding under your blanket will make you feel better, but they'll eat your face anyway and you'll die. But at least you'll die in comfort! …Maybe I should find another bone to carve a focus rune into. "Alright, bring them in." I moved the boulder aside, and Passionate Cloud scrambled inside. Then I moved the boulder back into place.

"Here. I didn't miss anything," Passionate Cloud said. He handed me a pouch of rings before pulling corpses out of his interspacial ring. "I swear an oath to the heavens that I didn't keep any of their items for myself." His chest lit up for a brief moment, signaling the oath was made. My subordinates are so loyal. The disloyal ones are treated by Ilya. Mm, I make it sound like there was more than one, but there wasn't. After the first time, no one tried to lay their hands on the things I wanted.

"Alright, like I thought, this guy had a sky-realm-ranked sword! Right? This is a sky-realm-ranked sword, right, Softie?" It's a rapier! It's … kind of thin. If I stick Durandal into this, will his spirit body reflect this shape…? I…, I waited so long for an appropriate sword, but … if Durandal's penis ends up shrinking because of this…. I can't! Alright, I have twenty sky-realm experts' heads. I'll just have the crown prince get the smith to make a sword that looks exactly like Durandal's previous weapon body!

"I don't think she heard you," Ilya said.

"Lucia? Hello?" Softie waved her hand in front of my face. "Yes, that's a sky-realm-ranked sword. But it doesn't look like the hilt is thick enough to embed Durandal's spirit seed."

Like I thought! This sword isn't thick enough! Yup, that reaffirms my decision to hire that smith! "Mm. Alright." I'll just hold onto it for now. Oh! I'll motivate my minions. "I'll give this to the first person who reaches the sky realm." And if that's me, I'll give it to myself! But they don't know that. It'll be a while before any of them reaches the sky realm anyways. I'll be sipping hot chocolate with my kids fanning me with giant palm leaves back in the pocket realm by then!

"I still can't believe we met an immortal." Claw shook his head. "I think he left us alone because we're like ants to him. It didn't matter whether he killed us or not." Claw sighed and clenched his fists. "One day, I'll surpass him."

That's the spirit, Claw! The stronger my minions are, the easier the life I'll have in the future. Mm, anyways, there was only one sky-realm-ranked sword. Even sky-realm experts are dirt poor, huh? Alright, let's move this boulder out of the way and board our ship and get the heck out of here! My army of apparitions should've accomplished their mission of destroying the outposts by now. I really hope they weren't hunted down by that immortal. …I didn't just jinx myself, right? …Hmm. Oh wells, what's done is done!

"Aroooo! Ruff! Ruff!"

Mn? It's Mr. Feathers! He came back! And he brought back a … kid? "Mr. Feathers, the heck is this?"

"Ruff!" Mr. Feathers barked before flying towards my waist and crawling back into the pouch. I guess it's a good thing I didn't eat that egg yet. And I hope Mr. Feathers will get along with those running fish that are still in there. I should probably eat them soon. If you keep fish out of water for too long, they'll start to smell. Mm. I haven't eaten in a while! It's been three whole days! I nearly forgot. How sad would it be if I died of starvation right before accomplishing my goal?

The kid that Mr. Feathers brought back jumped up and down while shouting. He was naked, and he was covered in bubbles. Was he taking a bath before Mr. Feathers snatched him? No, why the hell did Mr. Feathers snatch a kid!? "My father won't let you get away with this! He's a sky-realm smith! How dare you kidnap the son of a smith!? My father's friends with immortals! They'll come find me and make you regret this!"

"Lucia…? It seems like your first plan worked…." Softie bit her lower lip before taking a cloak out of her interspacial ring. She draped it over the kid and hugged him. "It's alright. We saved you from that dreadful phoenix. You don't have to be scared, okay? We'll take you back to your father right away."

The kid screeched and whirled around. Then he saw Softie's face and promptly shut up with his mouth still hanging open. "P-pretty…." His cheeks turned bright red, and he lowered his head, his eyes flitting up and down to look at Softie's face without trying to be obvious about it but totally failing to. Hmm. Maybe I should give Softie those manuals the succubus sect gave me. I think it suits her much more than planting heart devils. Softie's too nice to traumatize people. Wait, if I captured the child of a smith, then doesn't that mean all my work at this battlefield has been for nothing!? I demand a refund on my time!

***

"Your face is really red right now, you know that?"

I know! It's not my fault the contents of these manuals are so embarrassing! Ilya doesn't have to rub it in…. Why is she even in my room? "Did you need something, Sister Ilya?"

"No. I wanted to see your reaction to those manuals since I already know their contents," Ilya said and shrugged. "And, as I thought, it was very refreshing. I can only spend so long turning corpses into jelly every day. Ugh, it's practically soul-sucking work."

"Why are you turning the sky-realm experts into jellies again…?" I don't understand why she makes people into food products even though she's not going to eat them. Maybe if she were a cannibal, I'd think of it as a little more acceptable, but … wait, no, it should never be acceptable to turn dead people into gelatin.

"I can't figure out how else to refine their bodies." Ilya sighed. "If the temperature is too low, nothing happens. I can't even break their bones with a twelfth-circle spell. I have to superheat them first before I can attempt to manipulate them, but then they always end up breaking down into this goopy, fatty substance. And when it cools, I'm left with jelly."

"But didn't you make a bracelet for Lucia?"

"It's filled with jelly."

I can't give her any advice since I'm not too familiar with alchemy. But it didn't seem like she came here for advice; she wanted to see my reaction to the Seducing Succubus Sect's core techniques. I thought they'd be perfect for me, and they are…, but they're so embarrassing! This passage especially! The more servile cultivators of this technique take on the role of an impurity cleanser. Through the exchange of saliva with someone of higher cultivation, the servile cultivator can increase in strength by absorbing the impurities within that person's body, ultimately converting it into one's own qi. It is quite common for newer disciples to become servile to elders within the sect. For more effective cultivation practices, it is recommended to receive the saliva of many different people.

The Seducing Succubus Sect is filled with degenerates! Their techniques are so vulgar! This is how they use other people's underwear: If one wishes to increase their cultivation speed, it is recommended to fill one's immortal cave with used underwear, preferably of the opposite gender's. The pheromones released by the fabric will heighten one's senses and increase the qi flow within one's body. For more effective cultivation practices, it is recommended to wear soiled underwear directly on one's face.

"Your face turned even redder. I bet I could melt sky-realm experts' bones with the heat your cheeks are giving off." Ilya nodded and yawned before leaning back in her chair. She smirked at me. "Which part are you on? The swapping spit? The wearing underwear? Or are you on the kinky bondag—"

"Don't say it!" R-right. The Seducing Succubus Sect's core technique ramps up in vulgarity at an exponential pace. The depraved acts that saint-realm experts and earth-realm experts have to do are too…, too…, I can't say it. For now, I'll focus on cultivating the first part of the Seducing Succubus Sect's core technique! L-Lucia has a lot of impurities. If I become servile to her, there's no doubt my cultivation will increase by leaps and bounds. B-but we'd have to k-kiss each other!

"Hum, whatever. But should you really be switching techniques like that? What kind of immortal is wishy-washy about their cultivation?" Ilya shook her head. "I'm really curious about that immortal now. Just who was he? Do you know?"

"I don't." I've only heard about immortals in stories. I've never actually met one in person until two days ago. The pressure coming off of him was enough to make me pee myself; it was really embarrassing. I appreciate the fact he helped us out when all hope was lost, but I wish he could've done it in a friendlier way.

Ilya shrugged. "Well, thanks for amusing me. I'm going back to finish refining those sky-realm experts. Oh, Lucia's in a deep sleep since she didn't rest for three days while harvesting those heads." She smiled, but why did her smile seem more evil than nice? "It's the perfect chance for you to practice your newfound technique."

Perfect chance to ... kiss Lucia!? I shouldn't let this go to waste! "I'm going right now!" T-this is practice for the cultivation technique! I'm practicing with someone I'm comfortable with before moving on to the real thing. After all, Lucia and I are both women. Kissing each other doesn't count for anything! It's not a taboo like kissing a man out of wedlock. A girl can't get married if that happens, so it only makes sense for me to test this technique on Lucia first. "Thanks, Ilya!"

Ilya scratched her head as I ran past her. "Huh. You're a lot less flustered than I thought you'd be."

Lucia's room is right next to mine. She's the one who wanted it that way so she could sneak into my room to interrupt my cultivation whenever she's bored. I knocked as softly as I could on the door to prevent Lucia from waking up as etiquette dictates, and I slipped inside without a sound after a few seconds passed. The door didn't make any noise as it closed, but there was one problem!

"Oh, good afternoon, Soft Moonlight. Lucia's sleeping right now. You probably shouldn't disturb her."

This stupid wolfkin is watching over her! "Um, Gae Bulg, can you step outside of the room for a moment?"

Gae Bulg shook his head and crossed his arms over his chest. His cloth spear lay across his lap. "I can't do that. Though Lucia's a terrible master to me, it is my duty to keep her safe while she sleeps."

"I, I wanted to help Lucia by performing a technique that would transfer some of her impurities to me. And the method is a bit ... embarrassing."

"Wet eyes and crying will not sway me. A weapon spirit has no emotions." Gae Bulg narrowed his eyes. "And have you forgotten what happened when Lucia touched the impurity-cleansing pool? You want to try to take some of her impurities?"

"Wait. You saw that?" We were in the impurity-cleansing pool alone with each other.... Did this spirit watch me bathe!? I, I still had my clothes on because Lucia threw me in, but still! My purity....

Gae Bulg nodded, crushing my heart. "Naturally. I am always watching over Lucia."

"...Always?"

"Yes. Even when Lucia drags you into bed and cuddles you to fall asleep while her fingers roam about inappropriately, I am watching."

T-this perverted spirit! "You shouldn't sound so proud of that!"

"Ah? Softie? Mm. Are we at the camp already? I wanted to sleep some more." Lucia yawned and rubbed her eyes. My shouting woke her up.... This stupid, stupid wolfkin! I'll...,

I'll..., I'll tie him up and practice the third level of the Seducing Succubus Sect's technique on him in front of Lucia!

***

We're almost at the camp! I'm one step closer to accomplishing my goal! Once I hand over these heads, I'll order up the best sword ever for Durandal to inhabit. Then, once he's all solid and manly and not a spirit seed anymore, I'll flee back to the pocket realm! This necklace of intelligence let me realize something while I was daydreaming. Only a sky-realm expert or above could open the path back home. I might not be a sky-realm expert, but there are so many that I can kidnap and threaten that it doesn't matter! Just look at all these heads I harvested. As long as the sky-realm expert isn't as abnormally strong as that crown prince or that person who got obliterated instantly by the immortal, then I'm super-duper confident that I'll be able to browbeat them into my whims!

And this time, I have no intentions of letting Durandal bully me as he pleases! I'm not going to fall for his threats of refusing me sex any longer! Ilya already made me a spirit-restraining rope out of sky-realm experts' hair. There's absolutely no way for Durandal to escape my bed! So, even if Durandal wants me to cultivate longer, become stronger, or work harder, I'm not going to listen to him. Hmph, hmph. Let's see how he'll threaten me now. I still haven't forgiven him for dragging me into this Immortal Continent against my will! Mm, actually, I'm a little less angry about that since this place turned out to be like a paradise filled with fat sheep, but that encounter with the immortal nearly made me crap my pants. My principles won't allow me to forgive Durandal for forcing me into such a dangerous place! What was that lunatic thinking anyway? How could a weapon spirit be so cruel as to force his cute and defenseless master into such a conniving, bloodthirsty, and perverted world! If it weren't for my quick wits and sharp thinking, I'd definitely have gotten the short end of the stick somewhere. Mm, that saying doesn't really make any sense. Isn't a stick just one giant end? How do you get the shorter end of a single end? Ah, whatever. As a genius, I shouldn't criticize other people's lack of common sense; it'll make me look arrogant, which I'm not.

"Captain of the Shadow Devil Sect Squad, Lucia Fluffytail, requesting permission to enter!" We made it to the camp! Mm, Softie said there was a giant defensive formation around it. I wonder what I'd have to break to weaken the person controlling that formation. The battlefield formations had statues, but I don't see any statues around here. Hm. Maybe I could summon an apparition to eat its boundaries. But why would I do that? This formation's helpful! It let me rob many people in the past. I didn't get much out of it, but that doesn't matter because robbing people is fun. Err, good practice! Robbing people is good practice. I rob people completely out of necessity! Only a sadist would rob others for enjoyment.

"Dismount from your boat first before entering the camp."

Oh, right. I forgot about that. But this is a carriage! Eh, carriages aren't allowed inside either, so that excuse wouldn't work. Hah. I guess I'll have to walk like a peasant. Wait a minute. I have a mount! Where are they...? Mr. Feathers didn't eat them all, right? Ah, caught one! "Alright, running fish. If you don't want to be eaten, you're going to obediently be my mount, got it?"

"Can I have one too?" Ilya appeared out of nowhere! Well, everyone appeared out of nowhere since I stowed the boat into my ring.

"Ah, yeah, sure." I pulled out a second running fish for Ilya. It was bigger than the first one, so I hopped onto it and gave the first one to Ilya. The leader of the group has to have the best things; otherwise, she'll lose all respect! This applies to everything, including mounts—even if the mounts are fish with legs.

"I want an axolotl mount too! Give me one!"

Ah. It's the spoiled brat that Mr. Feathers kidnapped. Wait, no, I shouldn't be thinking of him as a spoiled brat! Let me try that again. Ah. It's my ticket to a sky-realm-ranked sword that Mr. Feathers picked up off the ground. Mm, sky-realm-ranked sword tickets should be treated with respect too. I'll give him a mount as well. I have at least ten running fish stowed away in my pouch; letting him use one won't hurt.

"Are those the mounts of the Great Axolotl Sect? They came back the other day without their leader. They wouldn't say anything to save face, but it was obvious their leader had died and their mounts were taken from them. Why are those axolotls with you?"

Oi. Is this guy a doorman or a detective? Just do your job and let us in, dammit! "That's none of your business. Are you going to let us in or not? I have something super important to report to the crown prince!"

"…Please proceed, the defensive formation has been deactivated."

That's more like it. Durandal's already been gone for so many weeks. I don't have the patience to answer some random side character's questions! If it weren't for the fact that Durandal might change appearance if I stick him into the sky-realm-ranked rapier, I would've already planted him inside of it. "Alright, fishy, to the crown prince!" My running fish mount didn't move. "Mm. You probably don't know where he is either, huh?" That's okay! I'll use that roaring technique that Quick Shot taught me. "Crown Prince! Crown Prince Single! Single Sky! Eternal Bachelor Sky! Mr. Bachelor! Mr. Eternal Bachelor Crown Prince Single—"

"Who's shouting this late at night!? I was about to break through a bottleneck in my cultivation!"

Ah? I thought cultivators didn't sleep. Why would it matter if I shouted at night or not? Mm, but I smell a lot of blood for some reason. Don't tell me they all coughed some out because of my shouting. Cultivators get internally injured by the strangest things.

"Captain Fluffytail."

It's the crown prince! "Hey! I have these twenty sky-realm experts' heads! I want to select my reward; hire that smith for me!"

The crown prince stiffened. He looked angry before—for some unknown reason—but now he looks shocked. That's right, be amazed! I might not have done any work to get these heads and leeched off an immortal, but the merits belong to me! The crown prince swallowed and stretched his hand out to touch one of the heads. It was the Fang Country's experts' leader's. "This, this is Crown Prince Fang. You claimed his head?"

"Yup! These guys cornered me, but I called on the help of my immortal buddy and he wiped them out instantly! Then he gave me the heads. Turn them into sky-realm-ranked swords from a smith, please! They have to look like this!" I gave the crown prince the blueprint that Ilya had created based on Durandal's previous appearance.

The crown prince took a step back. "You're friends with an immortal…?"

"Are you going to fulfill your end of the bargain or not? You said ten heads for one sword. I want two! They have to look exactly the same and be made of the same materials." The second sword is for Durandal himself. Weapon spirits are supposed to use weapons similar to their weapon bodies, but Durandal couldn't because his sword was lost or something. I bugged him about it, but he wouldn't tell me where his sword went, so I stopped asking.

"Right…. I'll contact our smith right away, but it may take a while because his son was kidnapped."

"This guy?" I grabbed the spoiled brat, err, free ticket, wait, no, smith's son, and held him up in front of the crown prince. "I saved him from a phoenix. Mm. Definitely. He said he's the son of a sky-realm smith."

The crown prince's eyes nearly fell out of his face. "You, you are quite the capable woman, Captain Fluffytail. Th—"

Wait! "Hold on! Ilya! Are you listening?"

"What is it?"

Okay, she's listening. I nodded at the crown prince. "Repeat what you just said."

"You're quite the capable woman, Captain Fluffytail?"

"Did you hear that, Ilya!? I'm capable! And you said no one would unironically call me that."

"You heard me when I said that…? And this doesn't count." Ilya flinched when I showed her my fist. "I mean, it counts, alright!? It counts! You're very capable."

Just like I thought. Hmph, hmph.

Chapter 22

"Thank you for saving my son."

This person is the smith? He's damn huge! He's at least ten times my height! How the heck is his kid so short!? "Are you a giant?"

The smith laughed with his mouth wide open, revealing a lot of missing teeth, and the ground shook from the tremors. Jeez. Softie said really good smiths were hard to find, but I could've spotted this guy from miles away. "I get that a lot, but no. I just have the blood of a titanic metal-eating bear running through my veins. You're the captain who claimed twenty sky-realm experts' heads and returned my son to me. I'll create three weapons for you, free of charge."

Mm. The crown prince sent a message to this smith letting him know about me. And it only took about twenty minutes for him to arrive. Thankfully, I got a meal in during that time. I'm still eating through my supply of aurochsen that never seems to run out. Anyways, I get three free weapons! "I want two swords that look like this!" I gave the giant smith the blueprint that Ilya made. It was about the size of his fingernail. Could he even make a weapon fit for someone like me with such large hands? "And, and, uh, I wasn't expecting a third weapon, but I want something that I can sell for a lot of money!"

Ilya hit her forehead with her hand. Sheesh, for an alchemist who has to be very precise with her hands, she sure is clumsy sometimes.

"You're quite the honest foxkin," the smith said with a smile. "Aren't you afraid of offending me?"

"Uh...." Did I say something he'd be offended by? I don't think I did.... Is it because I asked if he was a giant? "I don't care what other people say; you're very not large at all and it's totally every doorframes' faults for not being large enough to accommodate you."

The smith stared at me. Then he turned his head to the crown prince, who looked like he was sobbing in the corner. "Is she ... alright? You know, up there."

Hey! I try to be nice and he calls me an idiot!? This bastard. If he wasn't the one making my weapons, I'd have beaten him up and stolen every ... single ... thing.... Wait a minute. A smith who can make sky-realm weapons must be filthy fucking rich! If I rob him now, I'll literally be set for life! But the spoiled brat did say his father knew immortals.... Darn. I can't let my greed override my sense of self-preservation! I guess I'll let this man be rude to me. For now. I'll remember his face to beat him up later when I become an immortal. Mn.

"Sorry, she has a defect that prevents her from hearing things."

"Who'd you call defective, Ilya!?"

"Why did you hear that sentence but not the sentences before that one!?" Ilya tried to run, but I didn't let her escape.

"Excuse me, foxkin," the giant smith said. "You wanted two of these swords and a third weapon, correct?"

"That's right. Oh! Make the third one a hammer. It has to be big; the head has to be at least as wide and as tall as you! And the handle should be as tall as me, but it has to be thin enough for me to wrap my whole hand around it. And it can't be big by being hollow! It has to be completely solid and filled with the best metals you have so I can thwack things properly with it!"

The smith scratched his head, and the spoiled brat stared at me as if I had three boobs. "You know you won't be able to sell a weapon that big, right?"

"It's not for sale! It's for gently thwacking misbehaving people."

Ilya shivered. Jeez, if she's cold, she should pull out a jacket.

The smith frowned. "A gentle smack will kill someone. A weapon that big will weigh a little over a hundred tons."

"That's it?" A hundred tons? That's not heavy at all! Durandal's previous maximum weight could go up to five hundred tons. And I could use something that heavy just fine when I was a saint-realm expert. Hmm. How much can I lift as an earth-realm expert? "Can you make it ten times heavier? Wait, no, twenty times! No. Thirty? Mm. Why is math so hard? Ilya, help!"

Ilya sighed and rubbed her slightly swollen head before giving me a pebble. "Here. I'll put a block of mana in front of you. By calculating how fast the pebble moves through the mana, I'll be able to—"

"Stop! You lost me at calculating. Just tell me what I have to do." Ilya always insists on speaking with big words to show off her intelligence. That's the only bad part about her.

"Throw this pebble as hard as you can through this blue light," Ilya said. A blue box appeared in front of me. Wouldn't it have been easier for her to say that the first time? Alright. Throw this pebble as hard as I can. Does that include with qi? Hmm.

"Unrelenting Path of Slaughter: Breaking Madness Pebble-Throwing Strike!"

"...What are you doing?" the smith asked. "Are we still designing your weapon or not?"

"I'm not sure, but Ilya knows!"

Softie's face paled as the pebble disappeared off into the distance. "If that hits someone, they'll die...."

Mm, would they? Nah. It's just a pebble. A pebble never killed anybody. ...Did someone scream just now? Hmm, it was probably my imagination. Anyways, blue symbols made of mana flashed in front of Ilya's face, and she nodded. "Alright. The maximum weight you can swing is around four thousand tons. You'll want your weapon to weigh about three thousand five hundred tons to use it comfortably."

"Mm. You got that, Mr. Smith? The hammer should be three thousand five hundred tons."

The smith furrowed his brow. "Does that have to be its base weight, or can I install a formation that can manipulate its weight freely?"

"Formation!" I'm starting to love formations. They can do anything! Just like magic. Maybe I can learn how to create formations? I might not have any mana, but formations are powered by qi! I can totally learn how to create them. ...But learning makes my head hurt, so I'll have to take it really slow. I should just delegate the learning to one of my minions. That's right! I don't have to learn how to create formations myself. I can make someone else learn it for me! Like Ilya. She already knows how to create formations. But if she already knows, then hasn't my goal already been accomplished...? I'm a genius! I achieved a goal before even starting! I bet Durandal would be proud.

"Yeah, she'd like that formation on the two swords as well," Ilya said. "Sorry for troubling you. She daydreams a lot."

"I do not!" I just don't listen!

"Alright, then shall I get started?" the smith asked. "These are the final plans, right? You can't change them once I start."

"Right, go ahead!" I've been waiting for this day for so long! My bed's just not the same without Durandal. I can kidnap Softie to replace his cuddles, but she doesn't have a penis. But if she had a penis, I wouldn't have sex with her because I'm loyal to Durandal! Probably. Well, it's not like she'd grow one, so this train of thought is stupid. Durandal's getting a body again!

The smith reached into his mouth and ... pulled out a tooth!? He rubbed the blood off against his shirt and nodded. Then he squeezed it with his hand! What was he doing? Is this smithing? Maybe it's a good-luck ritual. When the smith opened his hand, there was a sword! It looked exactly like Durandal's previous weapon body! "One sword done."

"...The heck?"

The crown prince cleared his throat. "Yes, this is the power of our Kang Country's sky-realm smith. Thanks to his titanic metal-eating bear bloodline, his teeth can transform into sky-realm-ranked weapons. Of course, he has a limited number of teeth, and they take quite a while to grow back."

"Two swords and a hammer, just as you requested." The smith held out his palm, and there were two mini-DalDals and one giant hammer—well, the hammer was on the ground since he couldn't hold it in his palm. This smith is amazing! ...Couldn't I have stolen all of his kid's teeth? Mm, it's too late now. If I had known, I'd have had Mr. Feathers collect those too. Ah, what's done is done. I have a sky-realm-ranked sword for Durandal now!

"Durandal! Come on out!" I retrieved Durandal's spirit seed from my secret spot and grabbed one of the swords. Phew. Let's do this. Careful, careful. Place the seed into the hilt..., and there's the flash! ...Eh? Durandal didn't go inside? "Why didn't it work?"

The smith leaned over and squinted at Durandal's spirit seed and the sky-realm-ranked sword. "It seems like the grade of your spirit seed is too low. You'd have to put it in an earth-realm-ranked sword."

...

...

...

"Durandal!!! I'll fucking fuck you to death, you fucker!"

***

"L-little foxkin, please, calm down," the smith said, his hands waving uselessly in front of Lucia. "There are ways to improve the grade of a spirit seed."

"Calm down!? Do you know how long ago I've had an earth-realm-ranked sword!? But I resisted the urge to stick this bastard inside of it because he insisted on a sky-realm-ranked sword! And you're telling me he couldn't fit in one in the first place!?" Lucia's tail was thumping against the ground, breaking it while causing miniature earthquakes. I feel bad for the people living inside the burrows of the camp. I already counted thirty that caved in. I think I'll go hide somewhere for now until Lucia's anger blows over....

"Ilya!"

Why me!? Is it because I wanted to hide!? No, it's probably because I showed fear. Lucia can smell fear. She's like a predator—the hunting kind, not the giant squirrel. Well, she's like that too, but ... ah, you know what I mean. "Yes, Lucia?"

"Give me a sky-realm expert's body!"

...What would she want one of those for? Well, I'm not going to deny her demands when she's in this state. Do I still have any intact corpses? I knew I should've started with the earth-realm corpses first. Let's see..., found one. "Here."

Lucia raised her new sword and diced apart the poor corpse. Then she dug out its sternum and carved a rune on its surface. She exhaled and squeezed the sternum with her free hand and it disappeared along with all the ribs. "Okay. I'm focused now!"

...Did she just absorb a sky-realm expert's bones? I know she didn't make stew out of it and eat it, but somehow, it feels like she cannibalized it. Has she ever absorbed a person's bones before? ...Maybe.

Lucia inhaled then exhaled and glared at the smith. "What was that bit about improving the grade of the spirit seed?"

"You can improve a spirit seed's grade at the Cave of Wonders. You can also increase the grade of a weapon but improving a spirit seed is significantly easier." The smith licked the bloody hole left behind from when he had pulled out his teeth and nodded. "You just need a sky-realm-ranked object—even this hammer will do. Under special circumstances—the right material or location or timing—spirit seeds can absorb the energy within an item. The Cave of Wonders bypasses those circumstances and allows you to fuse the spirit seed."

A little like how Durandal's spirit seed fused with a phoenix egg, huh?

Lucia furrowed her brow. Did she understand? "And it'll still be the same spirit inside?"

She did! Amazing. ...I should stop thinking such mean thoughts about her. They'll slip out when I'm not on guard and I'll be gently smacked to death by her eight-million-pound hammer.

"As long as the sky-realm-ranked object you're fusing it with doesn't have sentience. If it does, there's a conflict between the two. The winning sentience absorbs the losing one and becomes the main spirit inside." The smith pulled something out of his interspacial ring and offered it to Lucia. "The Cave of Wonders can only be accessed by sky-realm-ranked smiths or those they let inside. With this token, no one will stop you from entering. Once you're inside, there'll be an altar that you place the spirit seed and sky-realm-ranked object on. Oh, I forgot. You'll also need a million spirit stones. You feed a million spirit stones into the altar's mouth, and the spirit seed and object will proceed with their fusion. It's easy, no?"

"Hmm? Why does it sound like you're not coming with me?" Lucia tilted her head. "What if I mess up? I can't remember such a complicated task!"

The smith sighed and scratched the back of his neck while lowering his head. "I'd go with you if I could, but ... I'm too large to fit inside the cave."

Lucia's shoulders slumped. "Seriously...? Can't you widen it or something? How do you even know it does what it's supposed to do?"

"The cave is composed of immortal bricks. It's actually a small portion of a much larger necropolis built by immortals. For mere mortals like us, it's impossible to even leave a scratch on the ground, much less widen a whole cave. The rest of the necropolis is a dangerous place, and only the Cave of Wonders is overseen by the Royal Smithing Sect that I belong to. You'll have to be careful." The smith sighed. "I'll write down the instructions for you, so even if I'm not there, you'll be able to figure everything out."

"Mm. Alright, I guess I'll have to bring Ilya along."

Of course. Bring the person who's still in the saint-realm to a place that even a sky-realm smith thinks is dangerous. Nothing could possibly go wrong with that. ...Can't Lucia just let me go home!? She could kidnap a weak sky-realm expert and force him to open the way back for me! Literally anyone else can read the instructions for her! She's the only idiot that can't read! Well, Puppers and Durandal can't read the Immortal Continent's characters either. Why doesn't she have an intelligent spirit following her? ...It's because she has me, isn't it? Gah, she even calls me her encyclopedia sometimes!

"Anyways, where is this cave and how long does it take to get there?"

"It's in Dragonhead Country."

Lucia and the smith stared at each other. Lucia tilted her head to the side. "And how far away is that?"

"It'd take you ten years by flying boat, but.... Foxkin? Hello? Did she stop listening again?"

"No, I just decided it wasn't worth it," Lucia said and pulled out her earth-realm-ranked sword. "In you go,

Durandal!" She pressed Durandal's spirit seed against the sword's hilt. There was a bright red flash..., and nothing happened. "Why!? What is it now!?"

A voice that I hadn't heard in a long time came out from the spirit seed. How come Durandal always speaks at the most convenient times for himself? I swear he's awake. "I said a sky-realm-ranked sword, Lucia."

"Fuck you! Go in!" Lucia made strange chattering noises as she growled while pressing Durandal's spirit seed against her sword's hilt. There wasn't even a flash of light this time. "You stupid unreasonable bastard! Go in!"

"Uh..., foxkin," the smith said in a tiny voice that didn't suit his large frame. "If you take a transfer gate, it'll only take three hours to arrive at the Cave of Wonders...."

Lucia froze. "Hmm? Three hours? ...Fine." She sighed and stuffed Durandal's spirit seed into her panties before stowing away her weapons. Did she always keep his spirit seed down there...? Well, it's not my problem. "Let's go! To the Cave of Wonders!"

***

Just like I thought, formations are magical. The place that was supposed to be ten years away became only three hours away because of this gate. I should get one of these for my mansion back home. I'll set up a gate to Ilya's dad's house; that way, I could bother Ilya whenever I'm bored! Mm, it was a bit expensive to use the gate though. It took a hundred thousand spirit stones! ...That's a lot, right? I think it is. But it doesn't matter. I almost have infinite money because of all those sky-realm experts from Fang Country! I tried counting all my spirit stones on the boat ride to the necropolis from the gate, but my head started hurting so I gave up. Anyways, we're here!

"Remember, stay close to me," the smith said. Only he and Ilya came to the necropolis place with me. According to Ilya, a necropolis is a gravesite! Why do I sound so excited about that? Because bones! This is a necropolis made for dead immortals! I'm not sure how immortals die, but surely, they'd leave their bones behind! That giantest bone of focus was amazing. I'm consuming sky-realm experts' bones right now, but they run out pretty quick. "We are heading straight to the Cave of Wonders. Don't wander off. Though long dead, these immortals left behind many formations to protect their corpses and items."

...Those selfish bastards. If they're dead, they should relinquish their stuff without a struggle! Why would a dead person need treasure? Hah, I guess I won't be getting any immortal bones.

"Halt! Who goes—oh, it's you, Brother Bear."

Where did this person appear from? She's huge too! Are all smiths big chewy-metal bears? Hmm. She's not missing any of her teeth. Maybe not?

"Good Evening, Sister Bull," the smith said. Now that I think about it, I don't think I ever found out the smith's name. Mm. He might've told me, but I wasn't listening or something. Well, I can always address him as hey, or you, or Mr. Smith. "This is Lucia Fluffytail of the Shadow Devil Sect from Kang Country. I'm taking her to the Cave of Wonders."

"The Cave of Wonders, huh?" the lady smith mumbled. What was that supposed to mean? "She might have to wait a few years. The Tablet of Madness roamed over and planted itself at the entrance. Sister Mochi almost lost her life earlier this month."

"Eh!? Is she alright?" The smith's eyes widened. "Of all the places to show up, why would that cursed tablet appear in front of the Cave of Wonders?"

...So I can't upgrade Durandal? I'm confused. If this tablet is what I think it is, then I'll just eat it and be done with it! It won't be the first time I've eaten a tablet!

The lady smith shrugged. "Sister Mochi will be fine. If the cave's all you came here for, then you wasted your time."

The smith sighed and lowered his head to look at me. "I'm sorry, little foxkin. It seems like the Cave of Wonders can't be operated right now."

"Why?" This tablet sounds like a non-living object. Why are they so scared of it? "What's this Tablet of Craziness?"

"Madness," the lady smith said. "It's exactly what it sounds like. Those who view the tablet lose their minds. Legend has it, an immortal recorded the secrets of the universe upon the tablet. Mortal minds aren't meant to understand the universe. Even if you're an immortal, the knowledge will consume you and drive you mad."

Hmm? "...Can't I just close my eyes and enter the Cave of Wonders?"

"If it was a normal tablet, then you certainly could do that," the lady smith said and shook her head. "However, the Tablet of Madness speaks."

"Then I'll plug my ears...?" I'm not seeing the problem here. And if I'm not seeing it, that means there is no problem! This stupid Tablet of Madness isn't going to stop me from bringing Durandal back!

"The Tablet of Madness speaks directly into your mind," the lady smith said. She sounded a bit annoyed. "What could you possibly have to do in the Cave of Wonders that you're willing to risk your life?"

"Rebuild Durandal's penis!"

Ilya made a choking sound. Was she drinking something without me? How dare she!? Oh, no, she probably choked on her spit or something. Like I said, she really did get a lot clumsier after becoming an alchemist. Eh? Both smiths choked too! There must be something in the air. It's a good thing my body's immune to illnesses! Ilya said idiots never get sick. …Wait a minute.

"I must've misheard you," the lady smith said. "But I understand that you wish to repair an item, but is that item worth your life? The Tablet of Madness has existed for over thousands of years. No one has been able to do anything about it."

"I'm not going to lose to an inanimate object! I don't care about the stupid tablet; take me to the Cave of Wonders." If my tail stiffens in front of the cave, then I'll run. It's that simple. But I don't believe I'll be defeated by a piece of rock!

"…I'll bring you there," the smith said.

"Brother Bear!"

"Sister Bull, Lady Fluffytail has clearly made up her mind. According to Crown Prince Single Sky, she's friends with an immortal. Perhaps she has methods to deal with the Tablet of Madness."

"Hey, uh, Lucia. This is probably a really bad idea," Ilya said and tugged on my sleeve. Ah! She called me an idiot earlier! "W-what are you doing!? I'm being serious! Stop! That hurts! I'll go, I'll go!"

Hmm. That only made me feel a little better. Hmph. Why does she always say such mean things about me when she knows I'm going to hurt her? Maybe she likes…. She's a masochist, isn't she? That explains everything! I have to find a new way to punish her instead. Tickling? No, she'll still enjoy that. Hmm. Hmmmm. Hmmmmmmm. Eh, well, I'll figure something out later. There are more important things to do! Tablet of Madness, Tablet of Madness, get in my way and I'll eat you! Unless you're strong, then I'll run away. There's no shame in running, but there's plenty of shame in losing to a rock!

***

If I die to this Tablet of Madness, I hope Lucia survives so I can haunt her. How can she be so unreasonable? I'm only in the saint realm! Lucia should've brought Claw or Softie along instead.... I know Softie's also a saint-realm expert, but I'd rather her die than me. Not that I want her to die or anything; I'm just saying I want to live.

"We are close," the smith said and swallowed as he turned a corner. "The Cave of Wonders is straight ahead."

Oh? Juniors! How can you traverse upon the path of immortality when death is inevitable?

What was that? Was that the Tablet of Madness? It spoke right inside of my head, exactly like the other smith said it would.

"Mm? It's been so long since I've eaten something that I'm starting to hear things," Lucia said and pulled out a pre-cooked aurochs' leg. She munched on it while the smith stared at her with a pale face.

"C-Captain Fluffytail, this is the furthest I'll accompany you," the smith said and nodded before stepping backwards. "The voice you heard just now came from the Tablet of Madness. Be careful!"

Can I go with him? Please?

Lucia finished eating her snack and blinked. "Hmm? Where'd the smith go? Don't tell me the Tablet of Madness ate him!"

And she wasn't listening. As usual. "No, he left. That voice just now was the Tablet of Madness. You heard it too, right? It said something like death is inevitable."

That's right. Immortality is impossible to achieve. All roads lead to death.

"Oh...." Lucia nodded. "Does this mean the tablet's alive? Like it has a spirit inside of it kind of like Durandal and Puppers?"

"I wouldn't know." Lucia always thinks I know everything. But I'm younger than her and, in theory, should have less life experience! "But you're hearing the same thing as I am, right?"

"Yup." Lucia bobbed her head up and down. "This tablet is such a pessimist. All roads lead to death? Nonsense! The road to immortality leads to immortality. That's why it's called the road to immortality. Sheesh, just like Puppers, this spirit inside the tablet isn't the brightest, huh?"

Lucia's socks fluttered. "...Did you really have to take a jab at me, Lucia? You can't read either."

Lucia stomped her foot and placed her hands on her hips. "At least I can beat things up. You can't even do that! So you're dumb and useless, hmph."

For some reason, Softie has been putting Puppers down in front of Lucia, and Lucia, being Lucia, was easily influenced by her words. I feel bad for Puppers sometimes. But I'm a little glad he gets abused too. Misery loves company, after all. If I was the only one suffering under Lucia, then I'm sure it'd be a lot more unbearable. Partners in misery.... I want to go home.

...Even the road to immortality leads to death. Everything you've ever accomplished will cease to exist. Your legacy shall disappear in the passages of time. When the sun and stars stop burning, the universe will come to an end. The heavens shall collapse and the underworld will implode. Once again, everything shall become nothing. Even immortals will not be spared.

"Hmm...." Lucia scratched her ear before looking at me. "Is this tablet stupid? It thinks the sun will go out like a bonfire or something. Now I know why it's called the Tablet of Madness—because it's not right in the head. Let's ignore it and hurry up and fix Durandal!"

I don't think you're one to talk about being not right in the head, Lucia....

Do you think the sun is eternal? Like everything else, it shall eventually run out of energy. When that happens, everything dependent on it shall die. Immortals will not be spared either when the heavens fall apart.

Lucia sighed and shook her head. "Some people just can't be helped. The sun's never going to run out of energy. It's not possible! Sheesh, this is why I hate arguing with idiots." Lucia grabbed my arm and pulled me forward down the alley. A cave entrance came into view along with a glowing purple slab of stone.

If you don't believe me, then I shall show you.

My vision disappeared for a brief moment. When it came back, I was surrounded by darkness. Below me, there was a massive green disc with jagged edges. I could barely see the darkness past the disc because it was so large, but I managed to make out some floating chunks of rock circling it. Encasing the disc, and me, there was a translucent dome. I couldn't tell how far away it was, but the dome was dotted with lights with one light being especially prominent—the sun. Then, the sun winked out of existence. Darkness fell over the disc, and the green surface became brown, then black. Like brittle scorched bones, the disc disintegrated into tiny specks starting from its edges, merging into the abyss underneath. A few insect-like lights surged up, gathering together above the crumbling disc. A small beam of light shone out of them, lighting up a portion of the land beneath. The illuminated portion regained its color, flourishing with green once again as the rest of the disc disappeared, but the insect-like lights vanished in the next moment, and the flourishing portion crumbled apart as well. The translucent dome dimmed as more and more lights winked out of existence, and soon, I was left in complete darkness, unable to even see my own hands that I was sure I was holding in front of my face.

Do you understand now? The universe was born from nothing, and to nothing it shall return. In the face of the inevitable end, even immortals are like insects ground mercilessly underneath the feet of time.

"Ilya!" Lucia's voice brought all the color back. I was standing in front of the Cave of Wonders again. The next thing I felt was a sharp pain on my head. Why was Lucia grinding her knuckles against me!? What did I do this time!? "You said this necklace prevented illusions! Of course, I'm too smart to believe what I saw, but it was still unpleasant to see!"

...No. That may have been an illusion, but it was a vision of the future. What you saw will come to pass.

Lucia snorted. "Like I'd believe a talking rock! You don't even have a penis!"

What does a penis have to do with anything...?

What does a penis have to do with anything...?

My lord, my thoughts are in sync with this tablet. But if everything the tablet says is true....

I cannot lie. Continue on with that train of thought. Wouldn't it mean everything you've ever done was pointless? Your struggle for immortality is futile.

Lucia hummed and pulled me along into the Cave of Wonders. Wasn't she going to argue with the tablet some more?

I ceased communications with her. I conversed with a broken blade of grass once. It was more reasonable than that woman.

Well, can you stop talking to me too? I feel like I'm not your target audience. See, immortals might despair at what you showed me, but I haven't invested anything in the path towards immortality. Quite frankly, I didn't even believe in it in the first place. I've lived the majority of my life under the pretense of every living thing dies. This isn't some amazing new discovery, and I'm pretty sure anyone from my pocket realm will agree with me.

You don't feel despair at the pointlessness of your life? Not even a tiny bit of existential dread? You and everyone you know will disappear. There will come a time when no one will remember your existence. Anything you've left for the future generations will be lost, eroded away by the passage of time.

Eh.... If I really ended up living forever, chances are I'd be stuck with Lucia for that whole time. I think I'd rather be able to eventually die, you know? So, I don't feel any dread; maybe I feel some relief? That doesn't mean I want to die though! Please don't kill me.

...I understand. My master told me to pass on his techniques to someone who's strong enough to traverse the necropolis and able to comprehend the end without turning insane. You've passed.

"...Ilya? Ilya!? Why is the tablet chasing us!?" Wind cut my face as Lucia sprinted forward, pulling me along. From behind, the Tablet of Madness was flying towards us, glowing with an ominous purple light.

Stop running, please. This won't hurt.

Somehow, I don't believe that. Maybe it's because there's a giant spike made of purple light jutting out of it that's cutting the supposedly impossible-to-cut cave walls.

This transfer needle is necessary to impart my master's technique.

"Holy shit! That spike is massive! What did you do to provoke it, Ilya!?" Lucia ran even faster, her tail fur stabbing into my face. She turned a corner and abruptly slammed into a dead end. And since I was pulled along by her, I slammed into it too. That hurt! Lucia grabbed me and hugged me to her chest as the tablet rounded the corner, surging towards us. "P-Puppers! Human-Shield Technique!"

Puppers flew out of Lucia's sock and collided head on with the flying tablet, stopping it in its tracks. ...Did he die? It wouldn't be the first time he died to defend Lucia, and it probably wouldn't be the last. I really do feel bad for him sometimes.

***

Why is this tablet suddenly attacking us!? It shut up once I proved it wrong, but it must've still been talking to Ilya! Just how strong is this inanimate thing? Wait. Is it still an inanimate thing if it can move, communicate, and attack? Wouldn't it be an animate thing? But it's not living! Right? Hmm, what are the characteristics of living things? How can I tell if something's alive? If it breathes, it's alive. But this tablet doesn't breathe! I think. If it poops, it's alive. But Softie doesn't poop. Is she still alive? Hmm. This is very difficult. Gah! Focus! The tablet's slaughtering Puppers, and he can't even fight back because it tore off his limbs! "Ilya! You're a genius! Figure something out!"

"Instant-teleportation button!" Ilya pulled out a button and crushed it with her hand. Nothing happened. "Uh…. One-week shield!" She threw a talisman towards Puppers. A barrier of yellow light appeared over him. The tablet stopped poking Puppers and turned to face us. Did it work?

Pop.

The shield broke! It burst like a bubble! We're so fucked; this is all Durandal's fault! "Heart Devil Apparition! Eat the tablet, Replacement Fluffles!"

The black squirrel made of heart devil wormies leapt forward, its jaws expanding until—it died!? The tablet instantly skewered poor Replacement Fluffles! He's been turned into a kebab…. Even Fluffles didn't die such a vicious death.

"W-wait!" Ilya shouted as the tablet drifted forward. Why is it moving so slowly now? Is it taking its time because it knew it had us trapped!? Who designed such a sadistic tablet? If I live, I'm going to beat that person up and shove his head up his ass! "You said you wanted to impart your master's technique to me, right? I don't cultivate! I don't have any qi. I'm completely positive I won't be able to learn it."

The tablet stopped. Eh? It listened? I knew Ilya was communicating with it! This is all her fault. Right, let's separate myself from her and try to bring as much distance between us as I can…. Like a dog smelling cheese, the tablet pointed its sharp spike at Ilya, turning its back completely to me. Phew. Alright. Now that its guard is down, I'll pull out that massive hammer the smith made for me and, huh, it fits in the cave? I thought the smith said he wasn't coming because he was too large to, wait! Focus! Focus…. And … swing! "Unrelenting Path of Slaughter: Maximum-Weight Breaking Hammer Madness Strike!"

…Did I get it? There was a really loud cracking sound. Why's the cave so small? I can't see what's behind my hammer. I'll put it away for now and, gah! It didn't work! "Eh-he-he. I, I was just testing to see how hard you were, Mr. Tablet! Y-you can discuss things with Ilya now, okay?" The tablet stared at me. It didn't have any eyes, but I knew it was staring at me! And that's because the massive purple spike was pointed directly at my forehead.

If she cannot use qi, then you will have to do. After seeing the end, you did not lose your mind. Though you did not quite comprehend it, I believe that is good enough to fulfill my master's qualifications. That strike you performed was impressive. I may have misjudged you.

…Is it complimenting me? I thought it was upset at me for soundly beating it down with logic. Why is it acting all buddy-buddy now? No, why is the spike moving closer to my face!? Dive to the side! "I'll die if you stab me!"

Nonsense. This transfer needle is perfectly harmless and painless.

"You tore apart Puppers with that perfectly harmless needle!" Gah! I shouldn't be shouting right now. It's taking all my focus to dodge this giant spike! Mm, this tablet's like a bee. They both have sharp pointy ends that, ah! I almost lost focus just now! Dodge, Lucia, dodge! No matter what, don't think of acorns!

You're mistaken. I tore apart that spirit with my edges. My needle didn't touch him. And what exactly is an acorn?

"Eh? It's the most delicious food in the world." Phew. I barely managed to dodge it again. And with my perfect planning, I managed to position myself with my back facing the exit! All I have to do now is turn and run. I'm sure Ilya will be fine since this tablet's focused on me.

The most delicious thing in the world? Is that it, on the ground over there?

Hmm? The tablet pointed its needle at my feet. "No? There's no ac—"

Gah! Fuck! It tricked me! It fucking tricked me! I was tricked by a rock! …Eh? I'm pretty sure the needle's stabbed into my forehead right now, but it doesn't hurt?

I told you. The transfer needle is painless.

Oh…. Maybe this tablet isn't such a bad person after all?

I am starting the technique transfer process. Rest assured, this will be painless as well … unless you're an idiot. On second thought, this is going to be very painful. Brace yourself.

"W-wait! Ow! Stop!" It, it hurts! I'm going to die! It feels like someone stabbed my head with a giant fucking purple needle to mush up my brain! I hate learning! Why is learning so painful!? This technique sucks! Stop, stop, stop, you stupid tablet! Gah! This really, really hurts! I'm going to die. Here lies Lucia Fluffytail; she was murdered by a rock. That's what Ilya will inscribe on my tombstone. And Claw and all my other minions will kowtow in front of it over and over until their heads are bleeding. And Softie's going to cry a whole bunch before burning her panties as an offering for me in the afterlife. And I'll never get to see or fuck Durandal again. And Puppers will be so devastated that he'll never search for another master right up to the day he disappears. And poor

Mrs. Wuffletush is going to eat Reena out of the hunger that comes with depression. And—

You know the process is over, right? Now that my master's final wish has been fulfilled, I can finally rest. I wish you luck, airheaded squirrelkin.

—Mirta, ah? It doesn't hurt anymore? Whew! I thought I was a goner. What did I end up learning anyways? "The Despairing Blade…." Wow. Just like the tablet, the name of this technique is super depressing. I don't think I'm going to use it. Ah! This mind-reading tablet's going to hate me for thinking that!

…Tablet? Hello? Mm? It's not moving or glowing anymore. "Is it dead?" Hmm. Did it say something about leaving? I think it did….

"Weren't you listening?" Ilya asked. "It said it can finally rest since it fulfilled its master's final wish. And, uh, thanks. I thought you were going to leave me behind to die but was pleasantly surprised you only used me as bait instead."

…Is she sincerely thanking me or is that sarcasm? I can never tell with Ilya. I'll ignore it. Mm, the best way to win is to not play! "So, you think I can use this tablet to upgrade Durandal at the altar? We're at the altar, right?" There's writing on the wall, and we're at the very end of the Cave of Wonders, so I'm assuming this is the right place.

"Probably. The tablet wasn't damaged by your sky-realm-ranked hammer. It must be made of something of equal or higher rank."

Great! "Then I'll use this tablet! How's the altar work?"

Ilya stared at me. "Just a few moments ago, you were nearly crapping your pants from fear. How does your mood change so fast, and how can I become like that too? My knees are still shaking!"

Mm? Did my mood change really fast? I didn't notice. It must be because I'm a fearless genius!

Ilya sighed. "Right. Ignorance is bliss. The ignorant are always happy."

...I'll noogie her after she tells me how to work this altar.

Chapter 23

I made a mistake. I thought I could merge with a sky-realm-ranked sword after facing my tribulation, but it turns out I was wrong. I wouldn't have minded being placed in an earth-realm-ranked sword at that point, but the smith offered Lucia an alternative to increase my grade. So, when Lucia tried to place me into an earth-realm-ranked sword, I refused and told her that I said a sky-realm-ranked one.

That's right. I've been conscious this whole time. Normally, a spirit is dormant if it isn't housed in a weapon. But for some reason, after defeating that featherless bird, which I now know was an unborn phoenix, I've kept my consciousness despite living outside a weapon. I do feel a little bad for ignoring Lucia, but ... I need my space. Every time I tried cultivating before my tribulation, Lucia would always interrupt me. I'd never get a good session in because she'd drag me off to bed without caring for my cultivation. Besides, Lucia has Softie now to take care of some of her needs. And my absence drove Lucia to greater heights. Taking a break has been beneficial to both of us. The only thing I have an issue with is..., sometimes, I wish Lucia would keep me in a more ... normal ... place. I know Lucia knows about my dislike for interspacial dimensions, but really? She stores me down there instead?

Anyway, it seems like I'm about to be upgraded at this altar in the Cave of Wonders. Lucia plans on fusing me with the tablet she just obtained a few moments prior. There was a spirit inside it, but according to Ilya, it should be gone now. ...It should be gone. What if it isn't? That spirit overpowered Lucia in a body that didn't even have arms or legs. If it's still there, this'll be quite the ordeal. But no one ever grew stronger without taking risks. I'll face this spirit and consume it to fuel my growth.

Lucia placed my spirit seed atop the altar and laid the tablet down beside me. Then she dumped a tremendous amount of spirit stones on top of me, blocking my view. "Is that it?"

"It should be," Ilya said. "The spirit seed, the item, the spirit stones, yeah. Everything's in place. Now you have to start the altar by kicking it."

"Kicking it…?"

That doesn't sound very reassuring. But the altar must've been designed by an immortal seeing as it's in a necropolis for immortals. It should be sturdy enough to withstand one of Lucia's kicks. There was a thudding sound and a slight tremor. My vision, which was black, turned golden as the spirit stones smothering me lit up. The light grew brighter and brighter until all I could see was white. Then a stone tablet with a small cactus growing out of its face came into view. Was that the Tablet of Madness?

"What's this? That stupid girl used me as a fusion material?" The cactus spoke! Its body split apart as it talked, forming a crude mouth. "Right after I exerted so much energy too…. This is going to be annoying."

I seem to be fighting the strangest things to grow stronger. First, it was a featherless bird. Now, it's a talking cactus. I'll slice it apart with…. I don't have a sword. No, I don't have anything. I'm completely naked right now, and I can't circulate any qi. Am I being suppressed?

"Are you mute? You have a mouth; use it."

"Greetings." I've never spoken to a cactus before. What am I supposed to say? "Nice weather we're having, huh?"

A pair of eyes sprouted out the top of the cactus like ant antennae. Was it looking at me with disdain? "You're a mere earth-realm bug. Defeating you will lower my worth. Get out of my sight."

But there's no place to go? "How strong are you?"

"Can't you tell? I'm an immortal. Behold my qi!" The cactus stiffened before wiggling. Was something else supposed to happen? "...My qi? Why can't I use it? Hmph. It doesn't matter. Bow before me, puny mortal spirit." The cactus grew in size as a pair of arms and legs sprouted out of it. They were green and bristling with yellow spikes. The cactus stopped growing when it was as tall as me, the tablet that it was attached to left behind as the cactus stood up and walked towards me.

Is everything equal in this altar? If neither of us can use qi, then all I have to do is fight a cactus with my bare hands. While naked. …This might be a bit more difficult than I thought. Let's retreat a bit and think of a few ways to defeat this monstrosity. There's nothing around to use as a weapon. The ground is white and endless. There are no walls, and the sky is also white and endless. I'm naked and unable to strengthen myself with qi, and there's a thorny cactus stomping towards me. The only thing I can do is grit my teeth and bear the pain…. Unless I pick up the tablet and use it as a weapon? Can I do that? I'll try it first before I wrestle this thing.

As I approached the tablet, the cactus' eyes narrowed. "Aiming for my tablet body? I won't let you."

"Wait a moment. If you have a tablet body, how come my sword body isn't here with me?" Everything's equal? Nonsense! Where's my sword?

The cactus snorted. "You're a spirit seed, what sword body? Besides, you seem more human than weapon."

Right. My sword body broke during the tribulation. In that case, I'll have to grapple with a cactus! I'll subdue it and break its tablet body to solidify my victory. Why did Lucia have to use this tablet as a strengthening material? Couldn't she have used the hammer or the rapier at least? Those didn't have spirits inside of them! When I get out of here, I'm going to make Lucia wrestle a cactus under the guise of training. "Let's see if you can withstand my armbar, cactus!"

Ah, damn, this hurts a lot.

***

I hope this works. No, this better work. If this doesn't work, someone's going to have a bad day! I followed Ilya's directions perfectly, so there's no way this can fail. Right? Please don't fail. If this doesn't work, I'm going to cry. Stupid Durandal! Why couldn't you just accept your fate as an earth-realm-ranked sword? Mm, once he's no longer a spirit seed, I'm going to punish him under the guise of training. Right. Okay. Phew.

The spirit stones are glowing gold and melting. The altar's like a giant mouth, drinking all of it down. It didn't swallow Durandal, right? I want to take the spirit stones off to check, but what if that ruins the process midway? Gah! This is so frustrating! I wonder if this is what giving birth is going to feel like. Hmm. It's probably a bit similar? Minus the pain, of course. But the anxiousness! Anxiety? The anxiety! Gah!

"Lucia," Ilya said. "Take some deep breaths and stop pacing in a circle, please. Every time you turn around, your tail smacks my face."

Ah, so that's what that feeling was. I thought my tail was a little stiff because of my nerves, but it turns out it was just hitting Ilya. Hah…, I wish Softie were here. Then I'd have a way to vent all my stress! She's like a giant squeeze toy with how soft and pliable she is. I guess I'll have to squeeze Ilya for now…. "Why are you so hard?"

"What the heck are you saying?" Ilya wriggled around, but I didn't let her escape. Nothing can escape from my grasp!

Except Durandal. Gah! This stupid, stupid, stupid spirit! "Did I do something wrong? Why are you doing this to me?"

"To relieve some stress." Ooh, the pile of spirit stones is half gone. It's almost over. Should I be excited or should I be nervous? I don't know! How about both? Can I be both? There should be a word for that. "What's the word for both excited and nervous at the same time?"

"Aflutter."

"I'm aflutter?" ...That doesn't sound right. "You're trying to make me look stupid, aren't you?"

"I'm not! It's in the dictionary. If you could read, you could look it up."

Yup, she's trying to make me sound stupid! Geez, Ilya's always bullying me. Why can't she be more like Softie? But if she didn't bully me, I wouldn't have any excuses to punish her, and that'd make my life less interesting. Mm. "I like you just the way you are, Ilya. Never change, alright?"

Ilya stopped struggling. "...Other than imparting that technique, did the Tablet of Madness destroy bits of your brain? The needle was stabbed pretty deep in your head. You weren't replaced by anything, right?"

Why do I even bother being nice to people? They always mistake my niceness for insanity. Ah! The spirit stones are almost all gone! I released Ilya and ran up to the altar. A layer of gold liquid covered an ... egg? Where did this egg come from? The tablet and Durandal's spirit seed are gone! No way! Durandal had sex with the tablet and laid an egg! He, he cheated on me! How dare he create offspring with a rock!? I'm going to smash this egg. Where's my hammer? Here it is. Alright, Breaking Madness Hammer Stri—ah? The egg's hatching. If I smash the egg now while it's in the process of hatching, is that murder or is it still abortion? Hmm. Hmmmm. Hmmmmmm. Ah, too late. It hatched. And out came a ... spirit seed? It looks like Durandal's spirit seed! Well, all spirit seeds kind of look the same, but still. "Durandal?"

"Yes, it's me. Place me into the sky-realm-ranked sword now."

Can I stick him into the hammer instead? The hammer's much more fun to use. But then he might become fat if I do that. Or a certain part of him will be too thick! Hmm. That doesn't sound too bad, actually. Should I? But then those two swords will go to waste if I do.... Alright. Fine. Into the sword he goes. I put away my hammer and took out one of the swords. Now I have to embed the seed into the hilt and ... it's done! There was a bright flash of light, and the seed finally disappeared! He really went in! He's back in a weapon! "Durandal! Come out!"

Out of the sword, Durandal appeared! He looks exactly the same! But his face ... looks a bit angry? Mm. Maybe that's his new resting face? Why!? The new mini-DalDal looks exactly the same; Durandal's appearance shouldn't have changed! Then that means he's angry. At me? I'm the one who should be angry here! What do I say? I hate you for making me do so much work? I really missed you? You're finally back? Welcome home? Let's fuck?

And do I hit him? Or do I hug him? Or do I take his clothes off and throw Ilya out of the cave? Wait, no, I should throw Ilya out of the cave before I take his clothes off. Gah! I don't know what to do!

"Lucia."

"Durandal!"

"Good job. I'm proud of you." Durandal walked up to me and hugged me. His right hand snaked towards my ears and rubbed them. Ah..., I missed this so much! I can't be angry at him right now. Once he's done, I'll start getting mad. Right. Once he's done. Mm. Ah, I'm getting sleepy and tired. So relaxing.... Durandal's touch. Durandal's heat! Durandal's ... smell? Why does Durandal smell like a plant?

"Durandal? You smell like vegetables."

Durandal sighed and took a step back. "The spirit inside of that tablet was a cactus. I had to wrestle it while completely naked. Do you know how painful that was? Why'd you fuse me with that tablet and not something else?"

Eh? "But Ilya said the tablet was dead?"

"I'm pretty sure I said probably," Ilya said and coughed. "Which means if I'm wrong, you can't blame me."

"Well, whatever! You upgraded and entered a sky-realm-ranked sword! It doesn't matter, right?" That's right. It doesn't matter! Durandal beat up the tablet spirit and leveled up. Does that mean he's a sky-realm expert now? …Is he stronger than me? There's no way…, right? Eep! My tail's stiffening! Who's letting out this bloodlust!? "D-Durandal?"

"Doesn't matter? Do you know how sharp a cactus' spines are!? They tore apart my ballsa—ahem! No, never mind." Durandal glared at me and crossed his arms over his chest. Why is he letting out so much qi!? He's much more intimidating than the crown prince! He's almost like that freaky immortal! "Hmm? Lucia? Are you…?" A smile blossomed on Durandal's face as his glare disappeared. "Since you used an immortal-ranked item to upgrade me, is it possible that I'm stronger than you right now?"

T-that sadistic smile! He's thinking of terrible, terrible things to torture me with! The last time he smiled this broadly, he made me hold a horse stance and stuck a wooden spike underneath my ass! I-I can't show weakness! "N-no! I'm definitely, definitely, much, much, much stronger than you!"

Durandal's eyes gleamed. "It's been a while since we've last dueled each other, hasn't it?"

He's a sadist! A fucking sadist! "Ah-ha-ha, look at the time. Those smiths must be super worried about us. Can't keep them waiting!" Flee! I've made a horrible mistake!

"Why are you running from me, Lucia? I thought you missed me." Durandal's voice appeared right by my ear. He's next to me!? How is he so fast!?

"Lucia! Durandal! Goddammit! Wait for me!"
Ah, I forgot about Ilya.

***

I thought I'd never surpass Lucia again after she became stronger than me. I'm pleasantly surprised to find out I was wrong. There is no better feeling in the world than bullying someone under the guise of training. People can accuse me of being a terrible person, but I'm sincerely helping Lucia become stronger! If some people view me as a sadistic monster, that's a sacrifice I'm willing to bear for Lucia's sake. "Are you tired already, Lucia? Raise your sword."

"We've been sparring for three days! Let me sleep, dammit! Gah! You evil un-needing-of-sleep bastard!"

It's only been three days. Lucia's been defeating me in duels for the past couple years. I still have many, many days of revenge, err, guidance that I'd like her to experience. Am I a spiteful person? Of course not. Weapon spirits don't have emotions. I'd never feel something like satisfaction when I pay someone back for unjust treatment—catharsis is reserved for the angry. Maybe I should let Lucia rest a little; it's not like I've been denying her food, but simple people like her can't concentrate for too long without building up a lot of mental fatigue. "Alright. We'll pause our sparring for a few hours. You should get some sleep while you can."

"Evil...," someone muttered. It was Softie, who was sitting off to the side of the boat's deck. We were flying back from the battlefield to the Shadow Devil Sect since Lucia accomplished her goal and the Gates of Hell temporarily ground to a halt because Fang Country lost all their sky-realm experts.

But evil? Me? What was this girl accusing me of? She's the one who uses a technique that emotionally scars others to advance in strength. "Did you say something?"

"N-no!" Softie shook her head back and forth before walking over to Lucia, who was already sleeping on a mattress, resting on her stomach with her face buried in a pillow. She didn't even ask me to go to bed with her. I think I figured out a way to save my dignity. All I have to do is wring out her pent-up energy through spars. Then, when nighttime comes, she'll be too tired to do anything other than sleep. Yes, this is perfect, a win-win situation for both of us. Lucia will become stronger, and I'll be able to cultivate in peace as she sleeps. ...But why is Softie crawling into bed with Lucia?

Anyway, after entering a sky-realm-ranked sword, all other swords have become unpalatable. Even earth-realm-ranked swords taste bitter, and Lucia won't let me eat that sky-realm-ranked rapier. Nothing's stopping me from eating it, but I feel like I should respect at least some of her wishes. Now that I've become this strong, how do I become stronger? Before, I had to eat swords to advance. Don't tell me I have to find immortal-ranked swords to eat? Doesn't this mean I'll be stuck at this strength until Lucia becomes stronger than me again? For my pride and dignity, I can't let that happen! There's only one thing to do in this situation: find Ilya.

Why Ilya? Because Lucia's right. Ilya does have the answer to everything. If Ilya could create a necklace that even made Lucia smarter, then I'm sure Ilya can come up with a method for me to increase my strength. Now that I'm a sky-realm expert, I can teleport freely. No wonder why Lucia enjoys teleporting so much. This saves quite a bit of time.

Ilya sighed. Her back was facing me, and she was holding a glass vial filled with red liquid over a cauldron, slowly pouring the contents inside while using her other hand to stir the cauldron with a metal rod. "Lucia. How many times do I have to ask you to not teleport into my room like this? If I spill something because you startle me, I could start a fire or something could explode."

"I'm not Lucia."

Ilya stiffened and dropped the vial into the cauldron. "Shit!" She dove towards the side and covered herself with a layer of ice, taking on the shape of a turtle. Then the cauldron exploded, but I smacked away the pieces that were flying towards me with my sleeve. Being a sky-realm expert is nice. I can infuse my qi into anything to turn it into an unparalleled weapon. The layer of ice covering Ilya disappeared as she sat up. "Dammit, Durandal. You scared the crap out of me."

"Sorry. Since Lucia did it so often, I thought you'd be used to it by now."

Ilya sighed and dusted off her robes. "What do you want? I'm a very busy person, you know?" She swept her arm over the shattered cauldron pieces, causing them to disappear into her interspacial ring.

"I was hoping you could help me out."

"Oh. Is this about Lucia's request to make you virile? Here, for now, wear this necklace," Ilya said and retrieved a necklace from her interspacial ring. It looked suspiciously like Lucia's necklace of intelligence. Well, Ilya's an alchemist, not a fashion designer. I can't blame her for being unoriginal. But that's not what I came here for.

"Thanks." I took the necklace and clasped it around my neck. "But that's not all that I'm here for. You see, I used to get stronger by eating swords, but that doesn't seem to work anymore; at least, it's very inefficient. Do you have a way for me to cultivate?"

"Huh? Oh, yeah, I do." Ilya nodded. Wait, she did? Ilya really does have the answer to everything.... Maybe I should treat her with a little more respect. Sure, we started off on bad terms and all, but I think we can get along now. "But I'm only going to give them to you under one condition: bring me home."

"Bring you home? You mean back to the pocket realm?" I suppose Ilya was dragged here against her will.... I didn't mean to bring her with me while transporting Lucia, but Lucia wanted Ilya to suffer, err, experience a new world too. "Alright. I can do that." As a sky-realm expert, I feel like I can do anything. Opening a path to a pocket realm will be as easy as snapping my fingers.

Ilya exhaled. "Great. That's good. That's really, really good." She nodded twice before handing me a scroll made of some kind of leather. "This is a cultivation technique for weapon spirits. It belonged to one of Fang Country's sky-realm experts, but as usual, Lucia passed anything she couldn't comprehend to me."

Great. With this technique, I'll be able to stay ahead of Lucia. There's just one problem. "…Can you read it out loud for me?"

"…You're the perfect fit for Lucia."

***

Gah! Damned Durandal! That stupid, stupid idiot! He forced me to spar with him for three days straight! Well, he let me eat in between rounds, but still. Three days! Then he didn't even have sex with me before I went to sleep! What was the point of bringing him back!? I, I'm going to…, gah! I can't even do anything to him because he's too strong! This is frustrating. Very, very frustrating.

"L-Lucia. Y-you're being rougher than usual."

Ah. Woops. I forgot I was squeezing Softie as stress relief. Wait, why is she in my bed? Did I bring her here? I can't remember. Hmm. I was dueling Durandal…, then I fell asleep. Maybe I did? Eh, it doesn't matter. This is all Durandal's fault! This…, this can't be allowed to continue. At this rate, I'll be dragged along by every one of Durandal's crazy whims. "Softie."

"L-Lucia?"

"I … want to take a bath in the impurity-cleansing pool." People kept telling me I'd grow stronger without impurities, but I always ignored them because I was strong enough. I can't do that anymore!

Softie's eyes widened to the size of saucers. "Really!?" She covered her mouth with her hands and blinked twice before exhaling. "All this time I tried to convince you to lose impurities.... It hasn't been wasted."

Well, it wasn't really Softie's convincing that made me make up my mind. It's the fact that I'll do anything to become stronger than Durandal at this point—even face my greatest fear of water. The world isn't right when I'm not stronger than Durandal. He's not even teaching me anything anymore! He's sparring me to vent his frustrations. I know because I do it to Puppers all the time. Hmph.

"W-wait. I have another method to remove some of your impurities," Softie said and placed her hands on my shoulders. We were still lying down on the mattress with a blanket covering our lower halves. Hmm? I'm pretty sure I didn't fall asleep with a blanket on. Mm. Oh wells. "D-do you trust me?"

Softie looks ... off.... What's she planning on doing to me? "Is it going to hurt?" It better not hurt! And it better not be throwing me into a lake. Eh? Her face is getting awfully close. What's she...? Is she...? Oi! Softie! "If you get any closer, we'll—!"

...

...

...

"L-Lucia?" Softie whispered. Her face was super red. Her neck was super red too. And the bit of skin that showed underneath her robes was the same shade. She.... Did she just—!? "T-t-t-that was the impurity-cleansing technique of the Seducing Succubus Sect! P-please don't misunderstand!"

"But you put your tongue inside!" Surely the technique's not that deviant, right!? If I had known Softie was going to learn something like this, I wouldn't have given her the technique in the first place! This..., this..., is it cheating? Does it count as cheating if I kissed Softie?

"T-the technique requires a thorough swapping of saliva." Softie's face was even redder than before. She withdrew her hand and clutched her chest. Beads of sweat formed on her forehead. "T-there's a lot of impurities inside you. I have to circulate the technique properly." She sat up and crossed her legs before placing her hands on her lap, one over the other with her thumbs touching. Her robes were turning transparent because of how much she was sweating. Maybe I do have a lot of impurities....

But Softie's suffering so much because of me! She wanted to help me remove my impurities, so she took some for herself.... This isn't cheating! I can't believe I thought Softie would have impure thoughts about me. I'm sorry for doubting you, Softie! ...But I'm a little hungry after that nap. If I ate now, wouldn't all the impurities that Softie removed be replaced? She's such a great friend! By taking away some of my impurities, she's allowing me to eat without feeling any guilt! Not that I feel guilt normally, but still. Now I'll feel even less guilt. What's for breakfast...? Aurochs. Of course.

"Eating again, Lucia?"

Durandal? Gah! He's back! I mean, yay! He's back...? Do I really mean that? Why do I feel so conflicted about seeing Durandal again? It's because he's a dirty selfish bastard, isn't it? Mm. That must be it. And what the heck does he mean by eating again? "What are you trying to say?" That I'm fat? I'm not fat! These meals turn straight into qi and energy! It takes a lot of energy for my brain to work so smartly. I don't get fat!

"Hmm. Nothing?" Durandal smiled and raised an eyebrow. "I was just making an observation."

"Don't insinuate my fatness!"

"No, no, you're not fat at all," Durandal said and shook his head while smiling. "You're just ... well-fed?"

I'm going to kill him. "Unrelenting Path of Slaughter: Tides of Blood! Tides of Blood! Tides of Blood!" Turn into an ocean of blood, dammit! Drown this smiling bastard like a rat! I worked my ass off to bring him back, to fulfill his nonsensical wishes, and this is how he repays me? When I become stronger than him, I'm going to lock him up in a dungeon and strip him of his freedom! "Grah! Breaking Madness Hammer Strike!"

...This isn't fair. Why did I give him that sky-realm-ranked sword!? It cuts through everything: my Tides of Blood, my hammer strikes, my pride and dignity.... Dammit, Durandal! I'll smash you to death! "Stop resisting!"

"An enemy won't go easy on you just because you ask nicely," Durandal said with his sadistic smile plastered all over his fat fucking face. Gah! Don't pretend to be teaching me when you're trying to cut my tail off with your sword! "It seems like I still have a lot to teach you."

...I'm going to cry. He's an inhuman devil! This mean bully! Stupid dummy Durandal! Once he's done with me, the only thing left will be despair. Despair.... Despair? That weird tablet taught me a technique that had despair in it, didn't it? What was it called again? Right, the Despairing Blade.

"Putting your hammer away? Did you give up?" Durandal paused as I took out my sword. "Mm. That's right. I taught you how to fight with the sword, didn't I?"

Grrr. Alright. This Despairing Blade better be impressive! I got it after having a massive spike shoved into my head; if it's not strong..., I'll probably cry. This is so frustrating! "Despairing Blade!" Ah? Did a cloud pass over the sun? Did it become nighttime? It's so dark! But it's still afternoon. Maybe I fainted after using the technique and woke up a few hours later? I don't think so.... Hmm? Is someone sobbing?

Out of nowhere, Durandal appeared in front of me, lit up by some lights underneath his feet. Tears were streaming from his eyes, and his sword was nowhere to be seen. "Lucia...,"

Durandal said and hugged me, burying his face deep into my chest. "I'm sorry. I'm so, so sorry. Please, put your sword away. We can talk it over."

…What the heck is going on?

***

I thought I was going to die. I only absorbed a small portion of Lucia's impurities, but that was enough to force me to the edge of death. But at the same time, the gains were proportionate to the risk. The short time that I spent purifying Lucia's impurities was equivalent to cultivating for two years. I almost lost my sense of self and entered a near-death state, but I think it was worth it. The only problem is … I'm not sure what I woke up to. Why is everyone crying?

Everyone's on the boat's deck, bawling their eyes out. Even Brother Claw, who laughs when he beheads people, has tears streaming down his cheeks. And Ilya too! Ilya never cries despite the unending abuse she suffers at Lucia's hands. Just what happened to make everyone so sad? The only person who isn't crying is Lucia. Did, did something terrible happen? Was our Shadow Devil Sect wiped off the face of the Immortal Continent? I have a feeling Lucia wouldn't shed a tear if that happened. But Durandal is crying too. This makes absolutely no sense whatsoever. "Lucia, why is everyone like this?"

"Softie! You're alright! Quick, help me comfort these people. Their sobs are making my skin crawl," Lucia said and shuddered. But she didn't answer my question…. I suppose I'll help regardless.

The person closest to me is Ilya. It's a smart choice to fix her first because she'd be able to explain the situation much more clearly than Lucia. "Ilya, is everything okay? Why are you crying?"

"W-when I was four, my father took me to the market to, to buy things. And I was little so I was curious, and when, when I looked away for a second, he disappeared! I was so scared! I thought he abandoned me like my mom!"

...How am I supposed to comfort her? "B-but you found him, right?"

"No! I, I tried looking for him, but then I got lost, and no one found me until the next day!" Ilya sniffled and wiped at her eyes with the backs of her hands, but the tears didn't stop flowing. Her mouth opened wide as her wails rang through the air, causing goosebumps to run down my arms.

"Then you haven't seen your father since you were four?" I can relate to that. I don't remember much about my parents.

"No! He, he found me the next day! W-weren't you listening?"

"...Then why are you crying?"

"Because I'm sad, dummy! Idiot! Why are you so inconsiderate!? Y-you can't just ask someone why they're crying!"

...Tournaments to determine rankings in the sect are very common. People strive for higher rankings for a better standing in the sect, which leads to more resources and a better life for their kin. But for one person to improve in ranking, another person has to decrease. Though I haven't personally experienced that struggle, I've seen the losers of the tournaments while walking around the sect. They'd cry and let out their grievances and swear to do better next time, but sometimes, some people were inconsolable like Ilya is now. However, there was always one thing that would stop their crying: cold-water therapy. I'll take this barrel of ice-cold water out of my interspacial ring and hold it over Ilya's head. I'll give her a chance to stop sobbing..., which she's not going to take. Okay. Don't hate me for this, Ilya; this is for your own good.

"Wuah!? Softie! What the hell!?"

"Are you back to normal now?" I wasn't expecting that to be satisfying, yet it was. I hope she's still sad so I can do it again.

Ilya glared at me. "I don't know if soaking wet and shivering is what you'd define as normal. Why did you…? Huh. Alright, what happened? I was down in my room making some pills, but the sunlight suddenly disappeared. The next thing I know, I'm freezing because someone dumped cold water on me. This is Lucia's fault, isn't it? Seeing as she's the only one not crying." Ilya looked around before nodding at me. "Well, you're not crying either, but you're kind of useless and unable to do something like this, so it can't be your fault."

…I think I should be feeling indignant at that, shouldn't I? "At least I'm not the one who cried at a market because I got lost when I was four!"

Ilya's eyes widened. She coughed and cleared her throat, her expression returning back to normal. "That's an oddly specific scenario you picked out. It hasn't happened to me either. What's with the accusing tone?"

"Okay, forget I said anything. Help me wake these people up by pouring cold water on them." I'll move onto someone else, like Brother Claw. What could he possibly be crying about? "Brother Claw, what's wrong?"

"If that immortal didn't interfere, I could've killed twenty sky-realm experts. I could be a sky-realm expert now. What a shame. What a shame. This loss is unbearable. I only killed three thousand earth-realm experts."

I think I'll let Ilya wake Brother Claw up…. Who knows if he'll lash out and kill the person dumping cold water on him? Moving on, who's this? Brother Cloud. "Is everything alright?"

"My Wife Moonlight was violated in front of my very eyes by Chosen Lucia…. But I can't do anything about it! Even today, this morning…, Chosen Lucia and Wife

Moonlight were in bed together, k-kissing. My heart's broken!"

I finally found the culprit who keeps calling me Wife Moonlight. I ... want to throw him overboard. No one will know, right? W-what am I thinking!? Those are thoughts Lucia would have! Her impurities haven't corrupted my mind, have they? No, that's impossible. I'll wake Brother Cloud up before anything can happen.

"Hah!? Wi-Sister Moonlight!"

"Help comfort people by dumping cold water on them."

"Yes, Sister Moonlight! I won't fail you."

It's odd how he didn't even question his circumstances, but I suppose that doesn't matter. The next closest person is Durandal, who's crying into Lucia's chest. Get away from there! "Lucia. If you dump cold water on Durandal, he'll turn back to normal."

"Huh? Cold water? What are you doing with that bucket, Softie!? Get away!" Lucia practically disappeared as she scrambled backwards at a breakneck speed, dragging Durandal with her. "Don't you dare pour cold water on Durandal!"

"But this is the easiest way to wake him up...." Am I wrong for suggesting such a thing? No, I don't believe I am. Why didn't Lucia—

"If you turn him back to normal, I'll go through hell again! I'm keeping him like this because he can't resist." Lucia's eyes lit up. "Right! He can't resist! And it's nighttime! You wake these people up while I go do stuff with Durandal!"

...And Lucia vanished. By stuff, did she mean...? But isn't it immoral if one party is crying during the act...?

Chapter 24

I finally got to vent all my built-up frustrations! It would've been a lot more pleasant if Durandal wasn't crying, but he fainted after the thirtieth time or so. Turning into a sky-realm expert really boosted his stamina! And he once told me weapon spirits couldn't sleep. Psh, look at him now! He's like a dead fish that occasionally whimpers. Anyways! Now I can.... Uh, do I have a goal now? I thought I needed to get stronger to force Durandal to submit, but I can just abuse the Despairing Blade. Hmm. Right! Ilya has to make Durandal virile! Let's store Durandal inside of new-mini-DalDal, and back to the deck I go. I hope Softie managed to comfort everyone. Their crying made me feel so awkward.

"Lucia, w-welcome back," Softie said the instant I appeared on deck through teleportation. Her face was bright red. Was she still thinking about that kiss? I hope not. That kiss wasn't a one-time thing, right? I have to kiss her after every meal to reduce my impurities to get stronger faster to subdue Durandal.... Eh, I guess I don't need to do that anymore, huh?

"Where's everyone else?" Oh! We're back in the Shadow Devil Sect. How much time has passed? Mm. Well, that doesn't matter! In the Shadow Devil Sect, I can finally do whatever the heck I want and be praised for doing it! I can eat aurochsen or running fish and everyone watching will think I'm amazing! Being a chosen is great. I don't get why Softie didn't abuse her status more often, sheesh. She can live such a good life, but she lives in a cave.

"They went to report to the sect first," Softie said. "I also had them tell my grandfather that you were looking to bathe in the impurity-cleansing pool. He's setting up certain measures to prevent the pool from being contaminated again."

Right.... In my fit of madness, I did tell Softie I wanted to bathe in the impurity-cleansing pool.... But I don't need to do that now! Honestly, there's absolutely no reason for me to work hard or get stronger at all. If anyone as scary as the crown prince tries to kill me, I'll have Durandal beat them up! And if Durandal tries to bully me, I'll make him despair. Hmm? What will I do if an immortal tries to kill me? Hah! That won't happen because I'll be spending my days in luxury without provoking anyone!

"Junior Lucia! Welcome back." Ooh, that's a familiar voice. Like I thought, it's Softie's grandfather. "I've set up the perfect system to cleanse you of impurities. You'll sit atop a mountain, and we'll pour the impurity-cleansing liquid over you. The impurities will be flushed away, and the impurity-cleansing pool will remain unsullied. How does that sound?"

Even though he calls it impurity-cleansing liquid, I know it's actually fish pee. But if it washes away my impurities, wouldn't it count as clean fish pee? Hmm. Eh, it doesn't matter, I guess.... And this method sounds acceptable. There's no reason for me not to accept even though I don't need to grow stronger. But there's just one thing.... "You'll pour it over me slowly, right? Like one bucket at a time?" If they poured the whole pool on top of me at once, then it'll be the same thing as drowning me!

"Yes, of course," Softie's grandfather said and nodded. He stroked his beard. "I've taken your strange phobia of water into consideration."

It's not a phobia! It's a justified fear! Phobias are exaggerated and irrational fears. But fearing water is completely rational! If you drink too much of it, you can die. If you drink too little of it, you can die. You can drown in it. You can choke on it. Heck, you can slip on it and crack your head open and boop! You're dead. Right. It's not a phobia.

"Okay. When do we start? Now? Yeah, let's start now." I need a bath after all that strenuous activity with Durandal.

"We can get started right away. Follow me," Softie's grandfather said and floated into the air with the assistance of a flying sword.

Why didn't he just command the boat? Mm. Well, I can do that. I went to the steering wheel and had the boat take off after Softie's grandfather. A few minutes later, we ended up at a mountaintop ... that was occupied by a ton of people. These people aren't all here to watch me bathe, right? At least they're all women, so I guess it's not too bad. It's still weird though! "Why are there so many people?"

Softie's grandfather cleared his throat as he stopped and landed on the ground. "They're here to make sure nothing happens. Don't pay them any mind."

That's easy for you to say! You're not the one stripping in front of all of them! Ah, I guess I can wear a towel. Mm, right. That'll work. "You're not thinking of watching, are you?"

Softie's grandfather stiffened and took a step back. Good, Durandal's glare worked. "Of course not," Softie's grandfather said and took another step back. "You've certainly gotten a lot stronger since the last time we've met." He cleared his throat. "Enjoy your cleansing; I'll be making sure no one comes to interfere." Then he flew up into the sky and disappeared somewhere to the east. At least, I think that's the east. Softie said the sun rose from the north, right?

"Chosen Fluffytail, please, change into these robes before we begin. They're made of impurity-cleansing fish scales. The effects of the impurity-cleansing water will be greatly amplified while wearing these."

A sect member handed me some transparent robes. Why were they transparent? Were they even robes? I can feel something in my hands..., but I can't see it clearly. It makes sense since those fishies were invisible too. I stripped off my clothes and put on the robes. At least, I think I put them on correctly. "Alright. Now what?"

"Stand over here, so the impurities will flow down in that direction."

The sect member guided me to the edge of the mountain. It was really an edge because the mountain was actually like half a mountain. Like someone had taken a normal mountain and cut it in half, leaving a giant vertical cliff on one side. At the bottom of the cliff, there was an empty basin for the liquid to flow into. They really were pre—pared!? "Gah! You should've told me you were going to start!" I didn't get to take my socks off! There we go. Mm, I'll leave them to the side since I shouldn't store Puppers in an interspacial space.

But the fish pee is cold, dammit! I mean, I guess it's better than it being warm. If the liquid was warm, then that'd mean it came fresh out of the fish! Wait. Is it better to bathe in fresh fish pee or stale fish pee? I should really stop thinking of it as fish pee because I think I got some in my mouth. It tastes kind of salty. Blech.

***

"Sister Moonlight. There's only twenty more buckets of impurity-cleansing water left. Should I retrieve some more?"

"Yes, please do." Lucia's cleansing started over thirty minutes ago. Around seven hundred buckets of impurity-cleansing water have been dumped on top of her, yet her impurities show no sign of ending. All the sect members kept their distance from her because none of us wanted to gain or lose any limbs. I called out to Lucia from where I was standing. "Lucia, how do you feel?"

"I feel like I'm melting! But in a good way." Lucia was lying on her back with her eyes closed. Her arms and legs were splayed to the side, and a patch of sunlight lit up her skin. She was smiling as a sect member, who was standing over her, poured a bucket of impurity-cleansing water onto Lucia as if she were a plant that needed watering. When the clear liquid made contact with Lucia, it rolled down her body, turning black like ink before falling off her tail which was hanging over the edge of the cliffside. Lucia exhaled as the bucket emptied and the sect member backed away. "This is really relaxing. I should've done this a long time ago."

I went over to the side of the mountain and peered down the cliff. The basin at the base was almost half full, and strange fumes were rising out of it. *I hope the nearby vegetation and creatures aren't disturbed. Was that movement?* A frog hopped along the edges of the basin. Without warning, it stiffened and tilted over to the side before rolling towards the black pool. It bounced off the slope once and landed in the water with a splash. *Did, did I just jinx a poor frog?* I shielded my eyes from the sun and squinted at the pool, but there were no signs of the frog resurfacing, not even any bubbles or ripples. *I … think it melted on contact. I voluntarily took those impurities inside of me…? It, it's a good thing we're flushing out Lucia's impurities now. It'll be a lot safer to kiss her in the future.*

"It's hard to believe Chosen Fluffytail accumulated so many impurities, isn't it, Sister Moonlight?" A sect member walked past me, holding a bucket of impurity-cleansing water. She laughed. "We keep pouring and pouring, but it never stops coming out. An ordinary person wouldn't make it past the first layer of the mortal realm if they had even a fraction of the impurities Chosen Lucia does." She tilted the bucket and let a steady stream flow onto Lucia, causing her ears and tail to twitch as she sighed. *Lucia really did look very comfortable. Maybe cleansing felt more soothing depending on the amount of impurities someone had.*

Boom!

What was that!? The ground's shaking! Lucia leapt to her feet and reached to the side, grabbing onto her sword.

"Explosion?" she asked and tilted her head. Her ears perked up as low rumbles echoed through the valley and mountaintop. "Mm. Well, it doesn't seem like someone's tribulation. Maybe—" Lucia's tail stiffened as her words cut off. Her head swiveled from side to side before she sliced at the earth with her sword, digging out a burrow that she disappeared into in an instant. Like magic, a pile of dirt replaced the entrance to the burrow in a flash, almost as if the burrow was never created.

"Ribbit!!!" A sound like thunder boomed through the area, causing fissures to appear in the earth and forcing trees to bend as a shockwave rammed into them. Black clouds gathered in the sky, swirling like a massive vortex as red thunder crackled. What was happening!? That's the largest tribulation cloud I've ever seen! Did Lucia enter the sky realm after her impurities were washed away?

Someone tugged on my arm and shouted, "Sister Moonlight! We should retreat to the center of the sect! Even looking at this tribulation is causing my cultivation base to tremble!"

But what about Lucia? I can't leave her here! "Wait! We have to get Lucia out of here!"

Peals of thunder rumbled louder and louder as the surroundings turned red, lit up by the monstrous lightning bolts that were thicker than trees. They snaked through the clouds, crashing into each other, growing larger with every collision. Within seconds, a massive red ball of lightning that resembled the sun took shape in the center of the vortex of clouds. With an ear-shattering bang it ... disappeared? A massive black pillar blocked the ball of lightning from view. Then, the pillar shrank downwards, dragging the lightning down past the peak of the mountain. The tribulation clouds froze in place, almost as if the heavens themselves were stunned. Rays of sunlight broke through the clouds, dispersing them as if everything had been a dream. I swallowed even though my mouth was dry and approached the edge of the mountain. I knelt down and peered over the edge with as much caution as possible. A black frog was sitting by the edge of the pool of impurities, chewing on something. Bolts of red lightning shot out of its rear with every passing second. …Wasn't that the frog that fell into the pool of impurities?

The black frog blinked and raised its head, making eye contact with me. It smacked its lips together one more time and swallowed, its abdomen letting out a red glow. If it shot its tongue out at me, I wouldn't be able to dodge. I wanted to hide, but something told me the frog would attack if I moved, so I held my breath and prayed. The frog's mouth ballooned a few times, letting out some croaks before it turned around, one step at a time. Then it hopped once, shooting into the sky and disappearing from view. That … was terrifying. It was almost like meeting the immortal back at the Gates of Hell. After regaining my calm, I crawled backwards to—the earth shifted beneath my knees!

"Wah!" Lucia's head popped out of the ground like a sprout. "The danger's gone. Sheesh, what the heck was that anyway? I thought I was going to suffocate. Next time, I'll leave a hole for some air."

I almost fell over the side of the cliff because of her sudden appearance, but thankfully, Lucia caught my ankle with one hand. "L-Lucia. Thanks."

"Phew. Caught you. Let's hurry up and remove the rest of my impurities before whatever that was comes back!"

***

Though there was a slight interruption, I had all my impurities washed away without any serious problems. I feel great! It took a few hours, and there was an issue with the basin down below overflowing, and there was another issue with the impurity-cleansing pool running out of impurity-cleansing water, but somehow, the sect managed to pull through. It's like I had a whole-body exfoliation; I'm like a new person! My skin is glowing, and my skin is so smooth and silky and soft. Oh! That's it! This is how Softie's so soft! She has no impurities; the mystery's finally been unraveled. I'm much prettier too! Not that I was ugly before, but I went from a beautiful woman to a peerlessly beautiful woman. Mm. That's right.

Softie exhaled and wiped away the sweat on her brow with the back of her sleeve. "It's finally over. How is it, Lucia? Do you notice any difference?"

"Yup! It's great!" But a few hours have passed.... I'm hungry now. "Time for my pre-dinner meal!"

"W-wait," Softie said. "You just removed all your impurities. If you eat now, it'll ruin everything. At least channel your Heart Devil Cultivation Technique first."

Hmm.... But I'm hungry! But at the same time, it couldn't hurt to cultivate to stir up my appetite. Alright, it's settled. I'll cross my legs and close my eyes and place my hands on my knees and channel that technique. I wonder how many more heart devils my apparitions planted while clearing out those outposts. Huh. I forgot to get them once I came back from the Cave of Wonders. Are they still out there planting heart devils in people? ...Nah. The war's over! I bet everybody already went home. Mm. No doubt, my fluffs are running back to me at this very moment.

"Wow...."

"Chosen Fluffytail is amazing!"

"If I had even half of Chosen Fluffytail's talent, my family could live well."

Mm? I know I'm amazing, but what am I being praised for now? All I'm doing is cultivating. The heart devil wormies haven't even entered me yet. What's taking them so long? Is Fluffles eating them again!? Wait, no, he died to the immortal. Then...? I opened my eyes and looked around. Is it nighttime?

Already? No way, I couldn't have lost track of time that easily even if I'm not using a focus bone. Then, oh…. The black sky is wriggling. Those are all heart devil wormies, flying straight at me. That's a lot! How many people did my fluffs terrorize!?

One, two, three, four, five…, yeah. That's way too many to count. They're disappearing inside of me faster than I can calculate. Mm. Well, the amount doesn't matter; I'll keep cultivating! If I become stronger than Durandal, then I won't even have to subdue him with the Despairing Blade. It's a little awkward when he cries; it makes me feel like a sadist.

Pop.

Pop, pop.

Pop!

Hmm? It feels like things inside of me are breaking. Like invisible weights that I didn't know I had were being shattered. Each heart devil wormy is giving me so much qi! Easily hundreds of times more than before! Is this the power of having a completely pure body? Why didn't Softie convince me to do this earlier? I'm overflowing with qi! The qi's so thick and dense that I'm not even hungry anymore—it's filling my stomach! It's, it's filling everything. Wow!

Pop. Pop. Pop. Pop!

More shackles have been lifted! I bet I could beat up Durandal right now!

Pop. Pop. Pop. Pop!

Mn. My muscles are melting and regrowing. My tail and ears are shedding and refurring. Is that a word? I'm sure it is. If it isn't, it is now because I used it properly. My bones are breaking and solidifying. And my skin is falling off, revealing new skin underneath! At least, I hope there's new skin underneath. I'd look pretty freaky if it was just flesh. I'll open my eyes to check. Mm, yup. There's new skin. It feels like I turned in my old body for a new one! The sky's still filled with heart devil wormies. I advanced so far, and I didn't even absorb them all yet! Time to cultivate some more. I'm really motivated since I can feel my progress in real time. Most of the time, I don't like doing things that Durandal says will help me in the future because there are no immediate gains. But this is different; the gains are amazing and immediate!

"Did Chosen Fluffytail break through to the sky realm?"

"I felt it too!"

"Wait, doesn't that mean she has a tribulation to overcome?"

"We, we should run while we still can!"

Wait, sky realm? I became a sky-realm expert!? It was that easy!?

"All disciples, retreat back to the sect." Oh, it's Softie's grandfather. "You too, Little Moon. I'll watch over Junior Lucia. Though, I don't think I'll be of much help. The very least I can do is prevent her tribulation from damaging our sect too greatly."

Everyone's leaving. Should I stop cultivating and prepare for the incoming tribulation? My tail isn't stiff, so it must not be coming yet. Right, I should keep channeling this technique until the tribulation arrives. I have to increase my strength as much as possible before it does! Circulate faster, Heart Devil Cultivation Technique. Fly faster, wormies!

"Junior Lucia, the clouds are gathering. The lightning will fall soon," Softie's grandfather said. "If you don't start preparing now, it might be too late."

Mm, my tail is stiffening a bit. Alright, I'll conquer this tribulation and become a sky-realm expert! And to do that, I'll call out my super-duper-strong trump card, Durandal! It makes sense, right? Durandal's already a sky-realm expert. There's no way he'll lose to a tribulation to become a sky-realm expert, mhm. As I thought, I'm a genius. "Durandal, come on out!"

The lightning was gathering in the sky, and it was already balling up as per usual. It was a lot bigger than an earth-realm tribulation's lightning, but I'm not scared even if my tail is completely frozen like a statue. "Durandal! Destroy my tribulation for me!"

Durandal appeared with his sword raised. He turned to look at me, and the sword fell out of his hand. He collapsed to his knees as fat tear droplets plopped onto the ground followed by his wails. "D-Durandal!?" He's still despairing!? Water! I need water! Ah. It's too late. The lightning's coming! I cut apart a dragon; I don't believe I can't cut apart lightning! They're almost the same, right? One's a giant loud lizard, and the other's a giant loud lizard if I squint really hard. "Breaking Madness Blade Strike!"

Bang!

Gah, fuck! I was wrong. I can't cut apart lightning! This stupid necklace of intelligence failed me in my time of need! That really, really hurt! I'm going to die. I can't move my limbs; they're twitching too much! I'll circulate my qi to recover—another ball of lightning already formed!? I'm going to die at this rate! I'm really, really going to die! "Durandal! Help!"

Durandal didn't move. He was still crying, and his face was buried in his hands. I don't think he can even hear me! If I live, I'm never ever going to use the Despairing Blade on him again! For now, I'll take some buildings out of my interspacial ring and take shelter under them. These buildings belonged to the Bloody Bull Sect; they're sturdier than most! They should stop at least one lightning ball; there's a hundred buildings stacked together!

Crash!

Shit! I was wrong again! I think my tail's on fire. My newly refurred tail! It's already ruined! But that's not the biggest issue. I can't hear anything other than this constant ringing in my head. And my vision is blurring in and out. Ah, is that another ball of lightning? It formed so quickly.... How is anyone supposed to survive a tribulation!? This is horseshit! If my Breaking Madness Blade Strike didn't work, then I'll pull out my strongest technique. "See my might and despair, you dumb tribulation! Despairing Blade!"

Durandal sobbed harder.

Boom!

Fuck! It was useless! Ah, I can't feel my limbs. I can't even pull anything out of my interspacial ring. I'm tired.... Is this it? Am I dying? I think I'm going to die. I can see my life flash before my very eyes: I didn't even know how to crawl when my grandfather tried to drown me in a barrel. I didn't even know how to talk when my parents sold me to the slave traders. I didn't know how to count when I was sold to a noble. I didn't know how to read when I was sold to the army. ...I still don't know how to read. Why was my life so shitty? I want a redo! Gah! I can't be killed off, not like this! Not to some stupid lightning ball that only has one testicle!

Kaboom!

Ow...? Mm, that one didn't actually hurt. I don't think I can feel pain anymore. Maybe my skin melted off. Hah.... So much for willpower. So much for growing stronger and surpassing my limits in a desperate time. So much for being saved at the last minute by Durandal or some other plot device.... Ah, I feel cold. I can barely even see anymore. It's dark. So, so dark.... My body's so heavy..., comfortable.... Once that last ball of lightning forms and crashes down on me, I really will die...? Are the clouds dispersing? There's, there's no ball of lightning forming!? The tribulation's over!? I, I passed!?

***

I hope Lucia's okay. A sky-realm tribulation isn't supposed to last that long! According to what I've read, a sky-realm expert's tribulation only has one lightning bolt. My grandfather must be shocked as well; four lightning strikes rained down on Lucia! Does this mean the heavens have assessed Lucia's strength as that of four sky-realm experts'? Or perhaps the heavens really wished to exterminate Lucia; after all, four is a horrifically unlucky number....

The first bolt was enough to nearly make my heart stop. When another three strikes rained down on the mountaintop, I, I think I died emotionally. Lucia.... I really hope she survived. T-that settles it. If Lucia makes it back safe and sound, I'll, I'll ask her to be my cultivation companion for life. I don't want to regret anything! Almost losing Lucia made me realize how dear she is to me. I know that she has no redeeming aspects, and she's a bit loony and hyperactive, but I want to stay by her side for as long as possible. Though that might not be very long since she's a sky-realm expert now.... She'll move on to bigger and better pastures.... I'm making myself depressed.

Ow!? Someone slapped my back! "I'm sure Lucia will be fine," Ilya said and tugged on my robe, smoothing out the wrinkle her palm caused. "You should stop looking so worried and down. What would Lucia think if she knew how little faith you had in her?"

"A-are you trying to cheer me up?" Ilya? Supporting me? There's, there's something wrong. Maybe Lucia died!?

"Somehow, that made you panic even more," Ilya said and sighed. "Look. Judging purely by the number of lightning bolts, wasn't Lucia's earth-realm tribulation a lot more arduous? It lasted much longer too; the clouds are already dispersing."

"C-clouds disperse early when the cultivator dies during a tribulation." Lucia's dead. She's really dead. I, I've experienced a lot of loss in my life: my parents, my pet rock, my dignity, and now Lucia.... The Immortal Continent is a cruel place where only the truly strong can survive. Death is a natural occurrence; I understand that. But losing Lucia....

"Softie? What's up? You look glum. And Ilya! My necklace became faulty! I want a new one."

L-Lucia!? "You're alive!" I tackled Lucia and buried my head into her chest. So this is what people mean when they say a sense of relief washes over them. Like a boulder was lifted off my back, all the feelings of negativity and anxiety are gone. "I thought you were dead!"

"H-hey! Don't cry on me!" Lucia wiggled around, but I didn't let her go. This is the technique I learned from her after being trapped in her grasp in bed all the time! It's not perfect because I don't have a tail, but it's good enough for clinging onto someone. But Lucia should be a lot stronger than me since she's a sky-realm expert now. Could it be she's not throwing me off on purpose? She wants me to embrace her like this! "Whew. I'm too exhausted right now to argue, but I'm definitely punishing you later for not letting go!"

...Sometimes Lucia has trouble expressing her true feelings. Since she decided to punish me later, that means she wants me to spend as much time clinging to her now while I still can. Oh, right. "Where's my grandfather? Is he alright?" He stayed behind to shield the sect from the tribulation. I hope nothing happened to him.

"Oh, he's fine. He went down to collect the impurities before they drained into the earth or something," Lucia said. She pulled a mattress out of her interspacial ring and dumped it onto the ground in the center of the sect. Then she wrapped her arms around me and fell forward, completely limp. "I'm so tired. I thought I was going to die. Dumb Durandal...."

"What did Durandal do?" I asked. She didn't answer. "Lucia?" She fell asleep already.... She must've been drained. A tribulation with four times the difficulty as a normal one; it's a miracle she's only tired. Wait, doesn't this mean our Shadow Devil Sect has a sky-realm expert now? Our standing in Kong County is bound to increase. No, we might even become notable in all of King Province. We won the King Province Exchange and obtained a sky-realm expert. We're a first-rate sect now! Lucia's even stronger than our ancestor.

Does that mean she's our new ancestor? But she's a bit too young to be an ancestor; I'm sure she'll get mad at us if we call her that.

"Everyone, I have an announcement to make," my grandfather's voice echoed through the central plaza where everyone had gathered to avoid the tribulation. I looked up. My grandfather was standing on a flying sword, his beard pushed to one side by the wind. "As of this moment, Chosen Fluffytail is no longer a chosen of our sect. The elders and I have come to a unanimous decision: Lucia Fluffytail shall be referred to as Sect Leader Fluffytail from now on! I've heard nothing but good things about Sect Leader Fluffytail's decision-making and leadership skills, and I have no doubt our sect will prosper under her watch!" My grandfather cleared his throat. "And I personally witnessed her surpassing a tribulation with strength beyond my imagination. With one strike of her sword, she destroyed the first lightning bolt! With her quick thinking, she set up a barrier that prevented another strike. Through a mysterious technique, she reduced the damage of the third blow. And after realizing how pitiful the tribulation was, she willingly surrendered all resistance and let the last strike of the tribulation wash over her, baptizing her body, tempering herself to reach further heights! With a sect leader as valiant and heroic as her, our Shadow Devil Sect shall climb to the top of the Immortal Continent!" My grandfather swept his arm to the side, summoning a breeze that brushed past all of us, causing our robes to ripple. "Please, Sect Leader Fluffytail, come up and deliver a speech for us. Let us know the direction in which you want us to head."

Everyone turned to stare at the bed Lucia and I were resting in. My face turned red as a line of drool leaked out of Lucia's mouth, seeping into the robe on my chest. Her not-loud-but-definitely-not-silent snores echoed through the otherwise silent plaza. "She's sleeping, Grandfather."

"...Oh."

Chapter 25

"Sect Leader Fluffytail is awake!"

Hmm? Where am I? All I remember is barely crawling down the mountaintop after surviving my tribulation and … talking to Softie. Did I fall asleep? Mm. I'm on a mattress in the center of the sect. Whew, I hope people didn't see me drool. It's a good thing I don't snore; otherwise, people would stare. But Sect Leader Fluffytail? Who's that? I knew Fluffytail was a completely normal name when Ilya told me it was strange! If even a sect leader has the same last name as me, then it has to be an acceptable one. Mm.

Softie reached towards my face and wiped the crud out of my eyes. "Good morning, Sect Leader Fluffytail."

Me…? "Sect leader?"

"That's right," Softie said and smiled. "Since you became a sky-realm expert, you're the strongest person in our sect. My grandfather made an announcement: from this day forward, you're our leader. Your display of leadership skills, conquering Kong County, winning the King Province Exchange, obtaining many merits at the Gates of Hell, all contributed to his decision."

…When Softie puts it that way, doesn't that mean I'm amazing? With my charisma and charm, I swayed a group of a million people, putting them under my rule! That's a whole million people! That's a thousand thousands! And I always thought I'd amount to nothing while I was growing up, but look at me now.

"I'm glad you're happy about it, Lucia," Softie said. She lowered her head. "I was worried you might not like it. My grandfather didn't ask for your opinion before making you sect leader, but it seems like he made the right choice. The fate of our sect rests on your shoulders; I believe in you, Lucia."

The fate of the sect.... Wait, wait, wait! Isn't this actually a huge responsibility!? I hate responsibilities! One time, I was responsible for watering that noble's plants back when I was little, and I watered it too much so it died! Then I was beaten with a wooden stick. Right, responsibilities aren't good things. But I like the sound of Sect Leader Fluffytail.... I know! I'll make Ilya responsible for everything important, but I'll pretend I'm the one making all the decisions. I'll make Ilya my puppet ruler! ...Or does that make me the puppet? Hmm.

Ah, wait. Ilya wants to go home to the pocket realm; I can't make her my puppet. Can I take the sect with me? Nah, there's not enough space for them. I think. Mm, there definitely isn't. And am I staying in the Immortal Continent to watch over them? I wanted to hide in the pocket realm where immortals wouldn't be looking to slaughter me.... Is the joy of being sect leader more important, or is my life more important...? Hmm. Why is this decision so tough? It's probably because Ilya's necklace of intelligence stopped working.

"Lucia? Hello, Lucia?" Softie waved her hand in front of my face. "Did you hear me? My grandfather wants you to deliver a speech for your inauguration. We decided to hold a banquet for you on the night of the day you woke up, which is tonight. There's still some time before it starts; do you want me to help you come up with something?"

"A speech from me? What am I supposed to say?" I've never prepared a speech in my life! I remember listening to a noble's speech once while walking through the market. I was amazed at how he could speak so much without forgetting his lines! Later, I found out he was just reading off a scroll in his hand. But I can't do that—memorizing a long speech is impossible and reading is even more impossible! "Mm, alright, Softie. Make and deliver the speech for me, thanks. That's my first order as sect leader."

"I can't do that, Lucia. This is your speech! It makes no sense for me to deliver a speech in your stead."

I took off the bracelet that Ilya had given me and wrapped it around Softie's wrist. "This thing lets your appearance change into anything you want. Just turn into me so people think I'm the one delivering the speech; problem solved! Oh, and give it back when you're done." I have more important things to do than preparing a speech. Like fixing Durandal! If it wasn't for his sobbing ass, I wouldn't've suffered so much during my tribulation! Mm, but I have to find a private place to fix him. The chosens' mountain! No one's allowed there except for me and Softie.

"Lucia, wait!" Softie said.

But it was too late. I already teleported away. Good luck with the speech, Softie; I believe in you! Alright. "Durandal, come on out!"

A sobbing spirit appeared in front of me. He cried about his insecurities, but I'm not going to say what they were because they should be kept private! Anyways, what did Softie say the fix was? Cold water? Let's hope it works. I pulled a barrel of cold water out of my interspacial ring and dumped it onto Durandal. He yelled and stiffened while standing up. He whirled around to face me, pulling out his sword at the same time. "Lucia? Weren't we dueling just now? Why am I wet?"

"Because you're turned on?"

"...Did something happen? The aura you're giving off is ... different." Durandal frowned and completely ignored my comment. Rude. He glared at me, and his killing intent washed over me, but my tail didn't stiffen. Hah! Now that I'm a sky-realm expert too, I don't have to be scared of him anymore! Everything is right in the world.

Let's test how much stronger I got! "Breaking Madness Blade Strike!"

"Incredible!" Durandal shouted as he raised his sword to block mine. "I don't know what happened, but you improved, Lucia. Path of the Sword: Ascending Phoenix Slash!" His sword turned red and flames appeared on its blade! Why didn't he teach me something as pretty as that!? Our swords collided. There was a giant bang, and Durandal ... went flying away. He crashed into a cliffside, and the whole cliff collapsed on top of him. Did he die!?

The rubble rustled and a hand poked through the top of the debris. Durandal coughed as he dug himself out, blood pouring from his nose, mouth, ears, and eyes like a fountain. He looked freaking scary! He coughed up a few mouthfuls of blood before shaking his head. "Lucia. That's not enough to defeat ... me...." Then he vanished. I felt him reenter new-mini-DalDal with my qi. I guess he did die.... Ah, the struggles of being a genius. Finding a sparring partner is impossible. But wow, I really did get super strong! I should've cultivated without impurities a lot earlier. Then I could've beaten up that crown prince of Kang Country to take his sky-realm-ranked sword without needing merits. But if I didn't set out to obtain those merits, would I have planted enough heart devils to become this strong? Mm. Well, you know what they say! Good things happen to good people. I deserve this strength!

***

I wonder when Durandal will fulfill his deal with me. Yeah, I gave him a necklace that doesn't actually do anything in exchange for my passage home, but what else was I supposed to do? Lucia expects me to fix Durandal's sterility, but I'm not omniscient! I don't know everything there is to know in the world. I'm not even twenty years old yet. It's not like I haven't thought about how to fix Durandal, but I simply have no idea where to even start. Quite frankly, I have zero experience with sex. How am I supposed to figure out the mechanism to create babies and figure out why Durandal doesn't follow that norm? It's impossible without extensive research, but that's not the kind of research I want to delve into! I'm fine with dissecting bodies and salvaging them for medicinal ingredients, but there's something about genitals that makes me avoid them. I think it has to do with some underlying trauma caused by adventuring with Lucia.

"Ilya!"

Think of the devil and the squirrelkin shall appear. "Yes?" I've given up on telling her to stop teleporting into my room. I don't know how she always manages to find me. This is a cave I've never been to before in the sect—she probably asked someone, huh?

Lucia skipped towards my desk, her eyes lighting up. She dipped her hand into my still boiling cauldron and pulled out a few medicinal pills, throwing them into her mouth as if they were snacks. "We're going home to the pocket realm!" She fanned her mouth with her hands. "Ah, this is hot."

My pills…. Well, I was going to give some of them to her anyway. "When are we going?"

"How about after the banquet celebrating my rise to sect leader?" Lucia nodded as she pulled out a cup of hot chocolate, rinsing her mouth with it. "I've decided; it's more important to hide and stay alive than it is to show off my prowess as sect leader. What if one of my apparitions provokes another immortal? Besides, I can always take Softie and Claw and the people that I really like into the pocket realm too. I won't be missing out on anything!"

I thought saint-realm people and above weren't allowed inside of pocket realms if they weren't born there. That's why only mortal-realm disciples invaded, no? Well, I'm sure Lucia will figure something out once she realizes. Will she? Either way, Durandal promised to open the way back for me. It won't matter even if Lucia changes her mind. "But don't you feel bad for abandoning the Shadow Devil Sect like this? They're going to go through a great ceremony to inaugurate you, yet you're going to leave after they're done."

Lucia tilted her head to the side and blinked at me. "...Is that something I should feel bad about?" Her arm rose into the air, and her hand reached over her shoulder to scratch the back of her neck. "I mean, didn't I abandon my territory back in the pocket realm too? I don't feel bad about that."

"Well...." Right, the question of whether or not Lucia has a conscience is up for debate. I'm sure she has one, but it's broken. Things she should feel sorry for aren't being felt sorry for, and things she shouldn't be worried about are made into a big deal. Saying acorn stew tastes horrible makes someone a blaspheming heretic. Harvesting people's heads is perfectly fine if you're not the one dishing out the final blow.

"Besides, Softie's grandpa ran the sect just fine before I came along," Lucia said and yawned. "He can lead the sect while I'm not around. Then, on the occasions I come back, I'll dish out commands and lead properly. Simple, see?"

Lucia does have a point..., surprisingly. "Makes sense. Did you only come here to tell me that, or was there something else?" I'm on the verge of creating a medicinal pill that'll improve my mana circulation. Sure, I've failed hundreds, maybe even thousands, of times by now, but I'm close this time; I can feel it. I mean, I thought I was close the past couple hundred times, but this time for real!

"I was going to bring you to the banquet. It's starting soon." Lucia grabbed my shoulder, and before I could pack away my things, she teleported us away. Why is she like this? What if a fire starts? Well, I left my cauldron on the lowest setting, so at most, I'll come back to a pot of burnt ingredients. A fire shouldn't break out. "Softie! I brought her."

Huh. The plaza's changed a lot in the short time I was experimenting. How many days has it been? Lucia went to sleep and didn't wake up until now.... Two days, I think? It's easy to lose track of time inside of a cave. No wonder why cultivators like living inside of them. If they could see the sun and moon swapping places while cultivating, they'd literally be watching their lives tick away. The cave removes the pressure of time. Maybe I was wrong about them being unprogressive backwater ancestor-worshippers. They certainly didn't hold back while preparing for this banquet. Well, they say it's a banquet, but all the food is meant for Lucia since no one wants to ingest any impurities. But everyone's drinking something. "What's this?" I pointed at the jars of liquid that peppered the surfaces of the multitudes of tables.

"That's spirit wine," Softie said. "It's an impurity-free wine made from immortal rice. Feel free to try some."

Why haven't I seen it around before? Shouldn't it be a very popular drink, considering it has no impurities? "I've never heard about it."

"That makes sense," Softie said and nodded. "It's only taken out on very special occasions. Drinking it disorients you, so many cultivators avoid it. It used to be more popular, but people figured out they could kill someone higher ranked than them if their target drank enough of it. Offering it to someone outside of your sect is akin to offering someone poison. It's a good thing you haven't seen it outside because you'd be dead if you drank it."

Lucia's eyes lit up and she snatched a jar of it off a nearby table. She sniffed it, and her ears and tail perked up. Before she could bring the jar to her mouth, Softie placed her hand on Lucia's sleeve. "Wait! S-share a jar with me." She grabbed onto the jar and leaned over, placing her mouth on the lip and took a gulp. Then she rotated the jar so that the spot she just drank from was in front of Lucia's mouth. Softie's eyes stared at Lucia with so much expectation; I couldn't help but feel sorry for her.

Lucia blinked and shrugged before drinking from the jar. Is Lucia weak to alcohol? I don't think so; I've never seen her act drunk before. A drunken Lucia would be a disaster. I think I'll distance myself from her just in case....

Wandering around the sect, I noticed a lot of couples. Men and women who were sitting underneath trees, on narrow benches meant for two people, on the shore by bodies of water, under the eaves of some buildings. All of them were sharing jars of spirit wine in the same manner that Softie had Lucia drink in. Once again, I couldn't stop a feeling of pity from rising out of my chest. What horrible crime did Softie commit in her past life to fall in love with Lucia?

"Oh, if it isn't Sister Ilya."

Claw? "Hey, Claw. You're here too, huh?" I didn't expect Claw to show up to the celebration. He's a very serious person focused on getting stronger. "You don't seem like the celebrating type."

Claw nodded at me. "I'm not, but I wanted to spend some time in the sect before I set off to avenge my parents. I don't know if I'll have another chance to experience a day like this."

"Oh. Why don't you ask Lucia to help you avenge your parents? I'm sure she'd be a huge help. And she sees you in a favorable light; I don't think she'd deny your request." Lucia mentioned bringing Claw to the pocket realm; I'm sure she thinks highly of him—even if it's just as an executioner.

Claw shook his head. "This is something I must do by myself. I don't want to drag Chosen Lucia into my troubles. A subordinate is meant to hoist his leader up, not bring her down."

"Hm. Well, if you die or get captured, Lucia will probably be upset and try to avenge you. So don't do either of those, okay?" Lucia already has a lot of bad will aimed at her. I'm surprised the grievances she caused haven't caught up to her yet. There was the extermination of the phoenix sect, the killing of a country's crown prince, the fact that she's a squirrelkin spreading squirrel apparitions in a world where immortals want to kill squirrels. Deciding to hide in the pocket realm is probably the smartest decision Lucia has made since she came here.

***

I … don't remember anything. Where am I? There was supposed to be a banquet for me, celebrating my new position as sect leader…. Hmm. I'll use my brain to puzzle it out! Right now, I'm lying on a bed with my arms tied together by their wrists. My legs are tied at their ankles. And my tail seems to have poked through the bed because I can feel the floor with it. Can I break this rope? Ah, yeah. That snapped pretty easily. How was I tied up in the first place? Anyways, I'll undo the ropes at my legs and pull my tail out of the bed and … I'm free! It looks like I'm in a pavilion, and there's a Shadow Devil Sect crest on the wall, so I wasn't kidnapped by an immortal. I guess I'm safe? Hmm…. Using my brain's too hard. I'll just cheat. "Puppers! What the heck happened!?"

Hmm? Is he ignoring me? "Puppers…?" Ah, it seems like he's dead. Okay. That's not a good sign. Only I'm allowed to kill Puppers! Which bastard did this? "Durandal! Are you there?"

Wait, no. He's dead too. I killed him before the banquet even started. Should I get another spirit just in case something like this happens in the future? Maybe it could learn how to read too…. Well, for now, I'll just leave the pavilion and see what happened. It's very quiet. Normally, the sect is bustling since there's a million people inside of it. And there was a banquet last night; there's no way silence should be the main ambient sound. People should be having fun at afterparties! Eh, cultivators are prudes; they don't even eat snacks. Maybe it's a normal day—let's see. Mm, the sun's out and shining. The sky is clear and blue. The fancy sect buildings are in complete ruins. Hmm. That's not normal. Were we attacked? The pavilion I was in is in horrible shape too! If I stayed in there any longer, it might've collapsed on me.

Where is everyone? "Hello? Anyone out there?" Ah, I shouldn't have used Quick Shot's roaring technique. The pavilion collapsed, and I can hear other buildings crumbling in the distance. Jeez. It's like the world ended or something.... Oh! I can contact Ilya with my messenger. I'm so smart.

I pulled the messenger out of my interspacial ring and navigated through the pictures until I could send Ilya an audio message. "Ilya, what happened? Where are you? Wait, no. Where is everyone?" And now I wait! I'll eat a meal while I'm at it. Hmm? I think thinking of eating triggered a memory.... Gah! I hate not being able to remember things! Eating..., eating, eating, eating.... What is it!? Eating and ... drinking? The spirit wine! I drank a whole lot of impurity-free spirit wine.... And then I forgot everything. Ah, this must be what those army soldiers called blacking out. I always thought they were lying to not be held responsible for their actions while drunk! It turns out alcohol really does cause memory loss. Who knew?

If I'm not mistaken, blacking out causes people to do and say terrible things buried deep within their hearts.... But I'm a good person—there's no way I said or did anything inappropriate! Isn't that right, Mr. Fluff?

...Wait. Why's there a squirrel apparition in the sect? Ah, I see. It must've returned from the Gates of Hell. Yes, that must be it. Oh, look! There's another one and another and another ... and another. Oh, jeez. There's a lot of them. But I don't recognize any of them. I might not be so good at remembering people or their names, but when it comes to my heart devil apparitions, I can differentiate all of them by their fur patterns alone! And none of these apparitions were present at the Gates of Hell.

Ding, ding!

Ilya responded! I opened the messenger and pressed the audio button. Ilya's voice drifted out. She sounded a bit, okay, very annoyed. "Are you finally sober? Right now, I'm underground in the main shelter with Softie and a few other people. It's in the basement of the pavilion that you should've woken up in. Everyone else fled from the sect because you went on an apparition-summoning spree. Wait where you are; we'll come outside."

Huh. Just because I summoned one or two apparitions doesn't mean everyone had to run away! Mm, apparently, I was an unruly drunk. Puppers probably died trying to tie me up. I wonder how they managed to tie me, a sky-realm expert, up with normal ropes. Well, I vaguely recall Softie saying something about the spirit wine being like a poison that allowed lower-ranked people to kill higher-ranked ones.

"Lucia!" Softie's voice appeared from behind me, and when I turned around, Softie was already flying through the air in a leaping tackle! I caught her, but I staggered back by two steps! What the heck?

"Did you get heavier?" How did she push me back? Why do I feel like I'm not a sky-realm expert anymore? First, I wake up with my arms and legs tied by ordinary ropes. Now, even Softie's able to push me around!

"W-what are you saying?" Softie leaned back and glared at me, but her arms were still wrapped around my back. "The only thing that changed about me is my advancement to the earth realm!"

"Yup," Ilya said. "She advanced with the Seducing Succubus Sect's technique. You should've seen the ropeplay she performed on you while you were sleepi—"

"Ilya!" Softie shouted as she teleported away from me. She reappeared in front of Ilya and covered her mouth. Ilya struggled while letting out muffled cries, but Softie didn't let go until Ilya's face turned blue from exertion—or lack of air. One or the other. Softie glared at Ilya, who had collapsed, before smiling at me. "I bound your arms and legs after you passed out to prevent you from hurting yourself in your sleep. Don't listen to anything strange coming out of Ilya's mouth."

…What kind of excuse is that? Have I ever hurt myself in my sleep before? Hmm. Even if I did, I wouldn't know because my wounds recover in a flash. "Okay…. Then what's rope pla—"

"Sect Leader Fluffytail!" Softie's grandpa appeared out of nowhere. "You were planning on returning to your pocket realm, correct? Junior Ilya told me. With the thousands of apparitions you let loose in Kong County, there's no doubt immortals will catch wind of you now. For your own safety, you have to return quickly. A special seal prevents anyone higher than a saint-realm expert from entering the realm; immortals won't be able to get you there."

"Huh. What—"

"There is no time for anything else!" Softie's grandpa pulled out a boat that was much smaller than the flying boat that I had. "This is a flying boat built solely for speed. With this, you'll reach the pocket realm in three hours."

"…Can't I just teleport?"

"No. You'll get lost because you're directionally challenged."

Oi. I thought sect leaders were supposed to be respected.

"Little Moon will fly you and Junior Ilya back. I'm sorry we had to part ways like this. Cultivate hard until you can defeat an immortal. It doesn't matter how many years it takes; the Shadow Devil Sect shall await your glorious return."

***

"We're here," Softie said. She stopped the boat at the destroyed temple-like area where we had entered the Immortal Continent from. It seems like no one repaired it after the tribulation that occurred on my and Lucia's arrival. The boat alighted to the ground, and Softie stowed it away inside of her interspacial ring. "If you channel your qi on the center of the altar, the pathway to the sky and earth plane will open." Her lips trembled as her eyes glistened with tears. "I, I'm going to miss you. Thank you, Lucia, for being my first friend." She paused. "Um, and you too, Ilya, I guess."

So I'm an afterthought.

"Hmm? Why does it seem like you aren't coming with us?" Lucia asked and tilted her head. "You're not thinking of ditching your commander, me, right? That's deserting! And deserters are executed in the army."

"D-didn't you hear what my grandfather said? Anyone in the saint realm or above is barred entry from the pocket realm unless they're a native. It was a seal put in place by the people who created the realm," Softie said. "A-and we're not in the army right now. This isn't deserting…."

"Hmm." Lucia scratched her head while grumbling. "There's no way to take you in? Can't I stuff you into this pouch or something? Ah! Doesn't that mean I have to leave Mr. Feathers and these running fish behind?"

"There's no way," Softie said and shook her head. "Mr. Feathers managed to kidnap a sky-realm smith's son; I think he'll be fine if you let him do as he pleases. As for the axolotl's, they're peak saint-realm beasts. They won't be able to go in either."

Lucia hung her head. "But … my tasty portable snack mounts…." She sighed and untied the pouch on her waist before tying it around Softie's. "Alright. You take care of them. If you eat any without me, I'll beat you up, got it?"

"Neigh!" A red chicken-like head popped out of the pouch. "Neigh, neigh!"

Lucia patted the phoenix's head. "Alright, Mr. Feathers. Take care of Softie, you hear? She's a weak crybaby, so don't bully her too much."

"Lucia! I am not!" Softie said and stamped her feet while sniffling. A tear leaked out of her eye and rolled down her cheek, and she wiped it away before pulling something out of her interspacial ring. It looked like a lantern, but instead of an orange flame, it was burning with a white light. Softie bit her lower lip and grabbed Lucia's hand, depositing the lantern's handle into her palm. "This is my soul lantern. As long as I'm alive, it'll burn. And if you hold it up, this mark over here will always rotate and point in the direction I'm in. You can use this to find me once you become an immortal and return.... I'll miss you, Lucia. I promise I'll cultivate hard by ingesting and purifying the impurities you left behind. When you come back, I won't be a crybaby anymore, and I'll at least be a sky-realm expert!"

An odd expression appeared on Lucia's face. "...You're going to drink my bathwater?"

"Don't say it like that!" Softie's face flushed bright red. She took in a deep breath and stepped forward, pecking Lucia on the lips like a sparrow. She lowered her head and looked to the side. "W-we shouldn't part like this. This isn't goodbye. You're coming back; there's no need for me to be so emotional." Softie raised her head, tears dropping from both of her eyes. "Promise me you'll come back, Lucia."

Lucia scratched her nose. "Eh.... But won't it be dangerous for me?"

Rest in peace, Softie. Lucia's too dense to understand your feelings.

Softie glared at Lucia, but she didn't look intimidating at all because of her tears. "I'll be waiting, so you better come back!" Then she turned around and took out the slim boat. She hopped inside as it rose off the ground before Lucia could react. The boat charged forward, and Softie looked back once, her body getting smaller and smaller as the boat got further and further away. "You better come back!" And then, just like that, she was gone, the boat disappearing over the horizon.

Lucia sighed and looked at me. "You know, sometimes, I think Softie's in love with me."

That's right. She is.

"But then I think about it a little, and the necklace of intelligence tells me I'm wrong." Lucia nodded. "There's no way Softie has any feelings for me other than that of admiration and awe."

Maybe it's time to give Lucia a new necklace. "Right. Of course."

"Oh wells, let's go!" Lucia looped her hand around my waist and lifted me like a bale of hay. She skipped towards the center of the temple and dropped me onto the ground. "I just put my qi inside? Like this?"

The temple trembled as a blue gash formed in front of us. It opened up like a mouth, and the inside of it was black, speckled with white lights. Lucia stared at it and rubbed her chin before grabbing her tail. She patted it a couple of times, checking its springiness. She nodded. "Mm. Doesn't seem dangerous."

I have a theory about Lucia's tail. I think all her qi and excess energy is stored inside of it. She eats a tremendous amount of food, but none of it goes to her waist or thighs. But, clearly, it has to be going somewhere—why not her tail? Her tail almost has a mind of its own, telling her when there's danger or—not!?

"Testing!" Lucia said in an upbeat manner. And she threw me into the portal! Why am I always being treated like this!?

Passing through the portal was like passing through a layer of ice-cold water. I had to pat my robes to make sure I wasn't wet—I wasn't. Where am I? This looks like … an unexplored area. Great. Well, I guess I'll wait for Lucia to show up first. I'll prepare a teleportation spell while I'm at it. I might not be an earth-realm expert who can teleport instantly, but it's not like it's impossible for me to create a spell with a similar effect.

I didn't have to wait long for Lucia to appear. She landed right on top of me.

"Oh! Ilya, you made it across safely. Great!" Lucia stood up and dusted herself off. "Where are we?"

"I'm not sure, but I'm setting up a teleportation sp—"

"Then I'll figure it out!" Lucia grabbed me before I could even finish my sentence, and then the ground disappeared. She had teleported into the sky. And she's still standing in the sky. Can she fly after becoming a sky-realm expert? "Hmm. Hmmmm. Hmmmmmmm. There! I see my palace. But why does it look so green?"

***

"I wonder if I've been forgotten. Probably, right? Ever since Lucia disappeared, no one's even acknowledged my existence other than you guys." And that's only because I feed you. I'm so lonely. Why was I hired to take care of the predators? Actually…, I wasn't even hired! Lucia kidnapped me and forced me to become their caretakers under the threat of being eaten! She told me to find food for them or else I'd become their food! "And these plant people just keep spreading and spreading. Look, they've even taken over Lucia's palace since she's gone. …You're not listening to me, are you, Mrs. Wuffletush?"

Mrs. Wuffletush smacked my head with her tail.

…If my life were a story, I'm sure I'd be a side character that's mentioned once or twice before being discarded and forgotten about. The poor Reena Flopsy, she went on an adventure to make a name for herself at the Godking's Brawl. She was never heard from again. The end. Yes, that'd be the perfect autobiography. Hah…, at least I'm still alive; I suppose that's something. Right, a year after Lucia disappeared, a lot of people have been dying. And it's all due to that giant plant monster taking root inside Lucia's palace.

"What do you want for dinner today, Mrs. Wuffletush? Roasted boar belly?"

Mrs. Wuffletush shook her head and pointed at the palace. We were on a nearby mountaintop since we were forced out by the plant people. For some reason, the predators didn't attack the plant people. Knowing them, it's probably because they hate their vegetables and the plant people taste too similar.

"You want something that can be found in the palace?"

Mrs. Wuffletush nodded. My life would be a lot easier if the predators could speak. But if they could speak, they'd give me hundreds of impossible orders to complete. It'd be like living with five Lucias.

"Um, let's not go to the palace, okay? Those plant people will stick a seed up my nose, and I won't be able to feed you anymore. How about roasted bird? Or roasted fish?" I can only roast food with a campfire. Well, I could boil it too, but it'd take too long to cook enough for the predators to eat. It's much easier to cook a whole boar over a large fire than it is to cut it apart and boil bits of it at a time in a small pot.

Mrs. Wuffletush shook her head and pointed at the palace again.

Why? Why are squirrels so unreasonable? "If you want something, how about you go get it … yourself.…"

Mrs. Wuffletush glared at me. She raised her front leg and pointed at me. Then she pointed at the palace. Her tail slapped the ground a few times as her eyes narrowed into slits.

"…Alright. What do you want?" I might not be the best fighter, but I'm very good at hiding and sneaking around. "The only thing inside the palace that can't be obtained outside is acorn stew and hot chocolate. Do you want acorn stew?"

Mrs. Wuffletush shook her head.

"Then it's hot chocolate."

Mrs. Wuffletush nodded.

I can't believe I'm risking my life by sneaking into a danger zone for the sake of a luxury drink. Lucia pampered these predators too much! "Are you going to come with me?"

Mrs. Wuffletush shook her head.

This predator! One day, I'll be free from it. When Lucia comes back, I'm going to hand in my application to quit. This isn't the kind of life I imagined for myself. I was supposed to accomplish great things, live out my dreams, not become an animal caretaker.... Okay. Well, this isn't the first time I've snuck into the palace, and it's not even the second time. But every time I enter the palace, the security keeps growing tighter and tighter, and the plant that took root keeps growing larger and larger. I hope it didn't drink all the acorn stew and hot chocolate. If only Lucia had left behind a larger interspacial ring for me. Sure, I can take out ten barrels at a time, but the predators drink that much in one meal!

"Ugh, fine. I'll be back soon."

Mrs. Wuffletush snorted and dropped onto the ground, resting her chin on her front paws. This lazy predator! Just looking at it infuriates me! If it couldn't kill me with a single swipe, I'd definitely hit its snout!

The walk to the palace doesn't take that long. But that's because I'm pretty fast. I've broken through to the realm of divine warrior after Lucia left. I'm the second divine warrior in the whole world after Lucia! ...But I'm stuck taking care of animals. Yeah, yeah.

The security seems pretty lax this time around. That doesn't make any sense. Is this a trap? But even if it is a trap, I have no choice but to enter. If I don't get Mrs. Wuffletush her hot chocolate, she'll go on a rampage and kill everyone in sight. I can't be the one responsible for the deaths of hundreds of people. Only a monster would let that many people die in front of them!

Let's see. I left behind a burrow the last time I came. I actually left behind many burrows just in case. This time, I'll make a new burrow since I have a bad feeling. Ugh, I really want to leave, but I can't. Alright, Reena, start digging. You're really good at digging. If my sense of direction is correct, which it usually is, then the basement of the palace is that way. Yeah, when Lucia returns, I'm definitely quitting. I don't even get paid in money. I'm paid in acorn stew and hot chocolate. But so is everyone else; I suppose that makes those two liquids a currency. You could even call them liquid assets. ...I'm no good at telling jokes.

I should be approaching the basement by now. Just a few more meters and ... what is this!? A-are these roots!? How the hell am I supposed to dig into the basement with this giant wall of roots in the way? If I cut it, then that plant will definitely notice.... Then I'll dig deeper? Just how far down do these roots extend? Okay, I'll dig down some more since I don't have any other options. I should switch to a better shovel since the rocks are harder the further down I go, but the only higher quality metal I have is my sword.... Alright, I'll soften up the ground with my sword first, then I'll dig out the dirt with my shovel. Here we go.

Ah, crap. I just cut a root, didn't I? The ground shook, but since I was inside the ground, everything was shaking. Am I going to die now? If the burrow collapses..., I'm screwed. The roots squirmed and wriggled and surged ... upwards? They're ... gone? Sunlight shone into my eyes, and I nearly went blind from the sudden exposure. Why is there sunlight underground!?

"Whoa! Ilya, look at this giant plant! It's as large as a mountain! A single one of its roots is thicker than a tree! But why was it growing on my palace? Reena probably planted it to feed my predators, didn't she? But she's kind of dumb, don't you think? Everyone knows predators don't eat vegetables."

Oh, Lucia's back. I'm supposed to feel relieved and glad that Lucia's here to clear up the plant problem. I'm supposed to feel happy, ecstatic. ...So why am I angry instead?

***

"T-this is impossible! Unhand me!"

"Ilya...? Did this plant just speak?" Right. Ilya and I are the only people standing in the sky. There's no one in the plant that I'm holding. And I'm pretty sure the voice just now wasn't Ilya unless she turned into an old man while I wasn't looking. Mm, her personality is like an old man's though, so I wouldn't be too surprised if she did, I guess. Ah, but what the heck was Reena thinking when she planted this thing? "It's so ugly, and I'd bet it'd taste disgusting. Maybe rabbits like eating it. Mm, that'd explain this abomination."

"Who are you calling an abomination!? How, how did you uproot me!? Y-you're the true abomination!"

Yup. It's a talking plant. Is it immoral to cook and eat it? Is a plant a person...? Maybe a person is just a talking plant.... I'm not sure what to make of this thing; it's unnatural. Alright, that settles it. I'll burn this thing to ashes and pretend it never existed. As the only sky-realm expert inside of this pocket realm, I have to do my best to maintain the logical rules of the world. No talking plants allowed!

"Ah! Ah! What are you doing!? Such a small flame won't even burn me!"

My trusty firestarter.... It never failed me before. Like I thought, this plant is a horrible rule-breaking existence that can't be allowed to exist! "Ilya. Burn this thing."

Ilya raised an eyebrow. "Are you sure? It sounds like a person."

"No, no. It's a plant. Even some really rare monkeys we encountered on our travels could speak and I killed them without guilt, remember? It's the same thing now! Just because something can speak and hold a conversation with you doesn't mean you can't kill them as long as they're different enough. Besides, the plant said so itself; it told us to use a bigger flame to burn it."

"I did not! Give up! Only the flames of a legend will have any effec—I'm on fire!?" The plant wriggled like a worm pulled out of the ground by a bird. But all the wriggling did was make the fire on its leaves spread faster. There we go; fix the wrongs of the world, flame!

"Hey, Lucia," Ilya said. "Do you think this plant has anything to do with the thing that killed Snow?"

"Ah?" The thing that killed Snow? Wasn't that me? He died because I pulled a plant out of his ear, right? This giant plant is related to me!? ...Is it a different type of squirrel that I've never heard about? Ilya does know obscure things....

Ilya rolled her eyes before I could respond. "Right, I forgot you don't think. Why'd I even ask?"

Oi. I knew it; Ilya really does enjoy getting her head massaged by my knuckles. "I think! I think about a lot of things a lot, sometimes! In fact, I think so much and hard that I lose track of things I'm not thinking about, got it?"

"G-got it! I got it! S-stop grinding my head! Lucia, it hurts!"

Hmph. "Oh, the plant's finally burnt up, huh?" Ilya's flames are way too strong! Normally, when you set a tree on fire—not like I have; like seriously, who'd be clumsy enough to set a tree on fire, right? Ha-ha. Anyways, normally, when you set a tree on fire, it takes a while to burn and the whole thing doesn't even turn to ash. It turns into this black charcoal that's still solid. But Ilya's flames completely incinerated this plant; there weren't even ashes left! "Alright. Let's go say hi to everyone in the palace!" I missed my cute predators! Reena better have given them all the belly rubs they asked for. Ah! It's Reena's head! Don't tell me someone planted her into the ground! "Reena?"

"Welcome home, Lucia," Reena said. She crawled out of a tunnel in the ground that looked like it had been left behind by the giant plant's roots. Was she fertilizing it? "You're amazing. The instant you came back, you solved the apocalypse."

"The apocalypse?"

Ilya snorted. "It means the end of the world."

"I know what it means, Ilya!" Gah! Why does this girl like pain so much? I can't grind her head anymore! It's exactly what she wants. I shouldn't encourage bad behavior. Then what do I do? Hmm. I guess I'll just hold her upside down by her ankles for now....

"Lucia!?"

"Anyways, what were you saying about the apocalypse?"

Reena stared at Ilya, but she cleared her throat and faced me again. "The plant you just killed. It was the source of all the seeds possessing people. Remember the people with plants growing out of their ears? They were being controlled by this thing. Duke Pentorn theorized that destroying this plant would free everyone with a plant inside of them."

"My father did?" Ilya asked. She flailed her arms a few times, but I didn't let her up. "How is he? Is he alright?"

"Your father's the leader of the resistance," Reena said. "Without him, the whole world would've ended a long time ago. I'm sure he's doing fine, and he'll be here to investigate once he figures out the main plant is gone."

...This conversation is hard to follow. Let's change the subject! "Where's Mrs. Wuffletush?"

Reena's face darkened. Did something happen to Mrs. Wuffletush!? "When the plant people invaded..., Mrs. Wuffletush and the other predators escaped to the mountains instead of helping us. They're doing just fine."

Phew. What the heck, Reena? Why would she say such non-ominous things with such an ominous expression? I almost panicked. "Hmm, alright. Well, if you need me, I'll be in my palace!"

"W-wait," Reena said and chased after me. "You're not going to ask some more questions? Don't you want to know what happened in the time that you were gone?"

"Uh, you can talk to Ilya about that stuff. She turned pretty strong too." I released Ilya and nodded. I have more important things to do! Ilya can take care of all the little things with her saint-realm strength; I'm not even needed. …I like feeling needed though, but for the sake of my dreams, I'm willing to give up a little praise! Durandal and I have a lot of babies to make! Ilya said she fixed him with a necklace, so there shouldn't be any issues now. Unless I'm infertile, but that can't be, right? I have so much strength and liveliness, there's no way that's true!

***

My father's theory was right. The giant plant that had infested Lucia's home was the leader of all the plants. Once I destroyed it, all the people who were possessed regained their sanity. Removing the plant that had sprouted in their heads was a bit harder, but it was a simple process once I figured out the trick. All I had to do was put them under a sleep spell, crack their heads open, and burn away the roots while maintaining a healing spell so they didn't die during the surgery. My father thought my cure was barbaric, but I didn't think he was one to speak considering the fact he's very good at torturing people.

Anyway, since I became a thirteenth-circle magician, I realized how small our pocket realm actually is. I could fly from the southern pass to the desolate mountains in a day. And I also saw the edges of the world. Our pocket realm is flat. To the north, there's a humongous glacier that's nearly impossible to traverse. To the east and west, there are mountain ranges made of marble and obsidian respectively. And to the south, there's just a really steep cliff. I flew up to see what was over all of them, and it was the same sight for each: an endless sky. I had a feeling I'd fall to my death if I tried flying over them to see what was underneath the world, so I didn't try.

It feels weird being the second-strongest person in the world. According to Reena, Cain disappeared around the time Lucia dragged me into the Immortal Continent, and no one has broken through to the legendary, err, saint realm in the time that we were gone. Using my newfound strength, I bullied the emperor and forced him to step down, elevating my father's status to ruler of the empire. ...Just kidding. I actually failed the surgery on the emperor to remove the plant in his head and he died. It was an accident, I swear. After the first successful surgery, the royal family implored me to fix the emperor. I warned them I needed more time to perfect it, but they insisted, so ... yeah. It was quite unfortunate, really. I'm crying and feeling a lot of remorse right now, okay? I didn't do it on purpose.

"Hey, Ilya! You look cheerful today. What's up? Did you figure out how to cure Durandal's sterility?"

...Okay. The botched surgery happened over a year ago, alright? You can't expect me to grieve forever. The survivors have to move on instead of living in the past. Speaking of surviving, if I don't answer this loaded question carefully, I might be the next person to lose her life. "You're not pregnant?"

"Nope! You've given so many cures to Durandal too. What if he's actually not sterile anymore, but there's a problem with me!?" Lucia's eyes widened as she gripped my shoulders. Her pupils shrank as she ground her teeth together. I didn't think it was possible for a sky-realm expert to look as if she hadn't gotten enough sleep.... I only need to sleep once a week or so ever since I reached the saint realm. "Right, right. The next time you give Durandal a cure, give one to me too!"

"You know..., there's a way to test who's the sterile one amongst you two...."

"Really!?" Lucia's eyes gleamed as her tail rose into the air and swished around. "What is it? Tell me, tell me!"

"You can mate with, uh, other people."

Lucia's grip tightened, and I'm pretty sure both my shoulders shattered. Luckily, I had obtained a technique from a sect—that I refuse to name because it's embarrassing—that converts pain into a sense of pleasure, but I pretended to be hurt anyway and yelped. Lucia shook me back and forth. "Are you crazy!? Absolutely not!"

"Okay, okay! You can stop shaking me now." For the past year, I've been giving Lucia placebo after placebo, but all that does is delay the inevitable. I've been working on finding a real cure, but it's difficult. Really, really difficult. In fact, I've forcefully recruited every professor, teacher, and self-proclaimed genius to tackle this problem, and we've gotten nowhere. Well, I suppose we figured out a few things that don't work.

Lucia snorted and glared at me before placing me back into my chair like a doll. She dusted off my shoulders and stared me in the eyes. "Alright, Ilya, be honest. Can you fix Durandal or not?"

"If I devote the next eighty years of my life to solving this problem, I'm sure I can." Well, I think I can figure it out in fifty years or so but giving myself a buffer is nice.

"Eighty years is too long! Shorten it!"

"Alright, how about seventy years?" Wow, the buffer came in handy already. No wonder why everyone calls me a genius. ...My lord, I sound like Lucia. I'm not an idiot, I swear.

Lucia's tail twitched. She exhaled and lowered her head, staring at my feet. "Alright, you can stop then. If I try really hard and cultivate nonstop, I can become an immortal in one or two years. Then, I'll go back to the Immortal Continent and find a cure there. There has to be a cure there, right? There are billions of old fogeys who're over hundreds of years old! It'd be weird if none of them had issues with their penises, right? There's definitely a cure out there. Mm. Alright. Work hard, Lucia. You can do this."

Lucia teleported away, leaving me behind. ...She's gone baby crazy. I know she wasn't right in the head before this, but at least she was somewhat predictable. But now...? There's no doubt she's going to kill someone if they get in the way of her goal, so I think I'll leave her alone for now. While she isolates herself in cultivation, I'll be the strongest person in the pocket realm.... I think I could get used to this. And the next time Lucia leaves for the Immortal Continent, I'm definitely not going with her. Definitely, definitely not. Now that I don't have to worry about Durandal's sterility problem, I can finally do what I want! I'm finally free! Yeah, it'd be nice if life could continue like this: no worries, no responsibilities, and no one stronger than me to threaten my lifestyle. Yeah, that'd be real nice. ...I really do sound like Lucia now, don't I?

Afterword

Thanks to Simon T Andreasen, Sharda Hartly, Travis Cox, Kyoma, David C., A Big Axolotl, Tyler Loeffler, Moth, Hadrian Battlefury, and Zachary Smith, Moth, William N., Taylor T., Roman V., Magnanix, and Donald Fuqua for supporting me on Patreon.

If you liked the story, feel free to check out my website at www.virlyce.com.

There will be a sequel to this book.

Thank you for reading!

Other books by Virlyce available on Amazon:

The Blue Mage Raised by Dragons

The Kingdom Razed by Dragons

A Demon and a Dragon

The Godking's Legacy (Prequel to *The Immortal Continent*.)